Praise for Julia Glass's

A House Among the Trees

"*A House Among the Trees* shows [Glass] at her tender, compassionate, thoughtful best, thinking about art, about life, and the way they intertwine so beautifully to make us, finally, fully human."
—*The New Orleans Advocate*

"Gripping and evocative. Glass is a formidable storyteller."
—*The Washington Book Review*

"Enthralling. . . . Glass is a master at withholding information until just the right moment." —*The National Book Review*

"Glass is a pro." —*The Washington Post*

"A fascinating look at a world in which a creative artist becomes a hot property to be both honored and exploited. . . . A compelling story with fully realized characters." —*Booklist* (starred review)

"Radiant. . . . Warmhearted. . . . Grippingly readable. . . . [Glass's] conclusion finds room for compromise and mutual fulfillment among her full-bodied, compassionately rendered characters."
—*Kirkus Reviews* (starred review)

"Excellent. . . . [Glass] excels at bringing her many characters to life and at imagining vivid scenes from the rarified world of art and entertainment." —*Library Journal*

Julia Glass
A House Among the Trees

Julia Glass is the author of five previous books of fiction, including the bestselling *Three Junes*, winner of the National Book Award, and *I See You Everywhere*, winner of the Binghamton University John Gardner Fiction Book Award. Other published works include the Kindle Single *Chairs in the Rafters* and essays in several anthologies. A recipient of fellowships from the National Endowment for the Arts, the New York Foundation for the Arts, and the Radcliffe Institute for Advanced Study, Glass is a Distinguished Writer-in-Residence at Emerson College. She lives with her family in Marblehead, Massachusetts.

Also by Julia Glass

And the Dark Sacred Night

The Widower's Tale

I See You Everywhere

The Whole World Over

Three Junes

A House Among the Trees

A House Among the Trees

Julia Glass

ANCHOR BOOKS
A Division of Penguin Random House LLC
New York

FIRST ANCHOR BOOKS EDITION, MAY 2018

This is a work of fiction. Names, characters, places, and incidents either are the
product of the author's imagination or are used fictitiously. Any resemblance to
actual persons, living or dead, events, or locales is entirely coincidental.

The Library of Congress has cataloged the Pantheon edition as follows:
Names: Glass, Julia, [date] author.
Title: A house among the trees / Julia Glass.
Description: First edition. New York : Pantheon Books, 2017.
Identifiers: LCCN 2016043794 (print). LCCN 2016055002 (ebook).
Subjects: LCSH: Inheritance and succession—Fiction.
Self-realization—Fiction. Artists—Fiction.
Classification: LCC PS3607.L37 H68 2016 (print). LCC PS3607.L37 (ebook).
DDC 813/.6—dc23
LC record available at https://lccn.loc.gov/2016043794

Anchor Books Trade Paperback ISBN: 978-1-101-87359-5
eBook ISBN: 978-1-101-87037-2

Book design by M. Kristen Bearse

www.anchorbooks.com

Printed in the United States of America
10 9 8 7 6 5 4 3

To the high school teachers whose voices still resonate:

Mr. McFarland
Miss Mendenhall
Mr. Perkins
Mrs. Shannon
Mr. Shohet

In the theatre, the tendency for centuries has been to put the actor at a remote distance, on a platform, framed, decorated, lit, painted, in high shoes—so as to help to persuade the ignorant that he is holy, that his art is sacred. Did this express reverence? Or was there behind it a fear that something would be exposed if the light were too bright, the meeting too near?

—Peter Brook, *The Empty Space*

Love art in yourself and not yourself in art.

—Constantin Stanislavski, *Building a Character*

A House Among the Trees

One

Today, the actor arrives.

Awake too early, too nervous for breakfast (coffee alone makes her more nervous still), fretful over what to wear (then irritated at caring so much), Tommy patrols the house that is now hers, shockingly and entirely hers—not just her bedroom and all it contains but everything she can see from its two windows: seven acres of gardens and grass and quickening fruit trees, fieldstone walls and stacks of wood, shed and garage and hibernating pool. The sky above: does she own that, too? Owning the sky would be easy. The sky would be a gift. The sky weighs nothing. The sky is unconditional.

She roams and circles through rooms she knows by heart: living room, dining room, kitchen, den, mudroom, pantry, porch. She cannot enter a room these days without beginning a mental inventory: What to keep? What to give away? (Worse, far worse, how much of it will she sell?) She goes to and from the studio, back and forth between this world and that—in that one, he simply *must* be alive—so many times that her skirt is now damp from brushing against the tight-fisted buds of the peonies flanking the path.

Will she have to change again?

The birds are in prime song, the sun beyond a promise, the day upon them all. Five hours to fill, and Tommy has no idea how.

She still finds it hard to believe that Morty agreed to this. But he did. He spoke to the actor more than willingly—to Tommy's embarrassed ears, unctuously—only a few days before his fall. His eager remarks punctuated by a forced, nasal laughter, he said that he looked forward to welcoming the actor to his home and studio, showing him "everything—well, almost everything!"

Unlike many women around the civilized world, Tommy does not yearn to meet or spend time with or even catch sight of Nicholas Greene. That she will be alone with him—if he complies with her conditions, and he must (Yes, Morty, you are not the only one with conditions!)—is even more unsettling, but one thing she knows is that she will not allow a wolf pack of movie people to poke around the premises. It was bad enough letting the art director visit last month. "Just a walkabout to soak up the spirits," he claimed. He arrived with a photographer and two assistants, who managed to trample flat a swath of crocuses emerging from the lawn. Morty behaved like a puppy, tagging along rather than leading them through, setting no limits to their invasion.

She has seen Nicholas Greene's face on the racks at the CVS checkout (though a year ago, Americans hadn't a clue who he was), and she did share Morty's excitement when they watched the Academy Awards and saw the actor hoist his trophy aloft, thank his costars, his director, his agent, and (tearfully) his "courageous, unforgettable mum." Even then, barely three months ago, Tommy was confident that this proposed "biopic" of Morty would, like countless other movie projects, wither on the vine. (How many books of Morty's had been optioned yet never come close to the screen?) She has to wonder if Nicholas Greene's Oscar galvanized the project, to which the actor had already been "attached"—as if he were a garage adjoining a house or a file appended to an e-mail.

There is something shamefully alluring to Americans about a British accent, whether it's cockney or sterling-silver Oxbridge. Even Tommy is not immune. Given the choice, who wouldn't rather listen for hours to Alec Guinness or Hugh Grant, over Johnny Depp or even a velvety vintage Warren Beatty? But why in the world, with all the platoons of hungry, gifted, handsome actors out there (Morty *was* handsome in his youth), would anyone sensible pick an Englishman to play a guy who grew up in Arizona and working-class Brooklyn? Maybe that's why Morty was so enthralled. Maybe he couldn't resist the flattery of seeing his life story told through the medium of a boyishly sexy, upper-crusty-sounding younger man who had been nurtured, almost literally, on Shakespeare and Dickens. Morty had a passion for Dickens. (She will certainly show the actor the glass-front cases containing Morty's book collection; no harm there.)

Once Morty learned that Nicholas Greene had signed on, he asked Tommy to do a little research. As he leaned toward the computer over her shoulder, taking in the googled stills of the actor playing Ariel at the Globe, Sir Gawain in a defunct but cultishly admired TV series, and of course the doomed son in the film that just won him a slew of prizes, Morty's face shed years in expressing his naked delight. It was a face he might have drawn for five-year-olds, a face to be duplicated millions of times, seen by children who spoke and sang and shared their secrets in two or three dozen languages.

Maybe it's because Tommy lived with Morty for twenty-five years and knew him better than anyone else possibly could (even Soren) that she cannot actually see why he would be chosen as the subject of a feature film; not a documentary, which made sense—there were two of those already, one for children, one for adults—but the kind of movie you watch in order to be swept away by crisis or intrigue or menace or laughter or the conquering power of love. Maybe she's too close to Morty's everyday life—"the monotony of quiet creativity, imagination fueled by routine and isolation," he mused aloud in the PBS series—to see it as a source of entertainment. At the same time, she is dead sure that Morty would not want certain details of his life offered up as fodder for strangers' titillation or tears. God forbid they should delve into the mercifully obscured months of his clubbing binge, for instance, the breakdown that led to Soren. Maybe that's why she can't stop rushing about, as if she's taken some kind of mania-inducing drug, fretfully scanning shelves of mementos and knickknacks, walls crowded with framed photos and cartoons and letters, searching for anything that might expose unnecessary personal matters to a curious stranger passing through.

Morty's lawyer, Franklin, has passed through several times, as well as Morty's agent, Angelica, who is still in shock over the will. Franklin has always treated Tommy as an equal and seems to like her—or at least he's done a convincing job of pretending. What upsets her (though logically, why should it?) is that Franklin knew about Morty's latest will for weeks. He assures her that Morty meant to sit down with her and explain the reasons for the seismic shift in his intentions. He was simply waiting for the right time—because time, he had good reason to assume, was something of which he still had plenty.

Tommy never doubted that Morty would be generous to her, but she had no idea he would leave her the house and the surrounding property outright; even less than no idea that he would name her his literary executor, assigning her a series of detailed responsibilities as variously remote from her experience as foraging for mushrooms or Olympic diving. And some of them will be deeply unpleasant: first and foremost, telling the people at the museum in New York that no, he will not be leaving them the bulk of his artwork and letters and collections and idiosyncratic belongings, as Tommy knows he led them to believe he would do. Now, she must somehow repossess the drawings, manuscripts, and annotated book proofs that have been on loan with the general understanding that the loan was a prelude to a gift . . . a very large gift. Tommy has yet to answer the e-mails and phone messages from the distressed director. Even though Franklin is confident that the museum has no legal grounds for challenging the will, Tommy herself is the one who will have to face up to those messages. She can only hope she won't have to tell the woman why Morty turned sour on them. She doesn't like remembering how easily his ego was bruised these past few years.

She wishes that somewhere among all the legal surprises, Morty had also left directions to cease cooperation with the movie people. But up through the very last night of his life, he was beyond delighted; he was as close to rapturous as Tommy ever saw him. Silly of her not to have realized that as he aged, his ego was as readily inflated as it was bruised.

As usual, he spent that afternoon working and napping in the studio, then joined Tommy in the kitchen at six. And, as had become his habit in the few days since his second transatlantic conversation with Nicholas Greene, he wanted to talk not about the story or drawings in which he was immersed (how deeply Tommy already misses seeing new images, listening to Morty read out loud new constellations of words—to her before anyone else) but about what it would mean, what it would feel like, to be the subject of a "real-deal movie." Morty never cared much for drink, but that night he went to the back fridge, the extra one they had installed in the early years of Soren (the party years), and rooted out a bottle of true champagne, then stood on a stool to reach a pair of dusty flutes. Tenderly, he soaped and rinsed and polished the glasses, insisting that he and Tommy share a "properly classy toast."

After Tommy returned to sautéing garlic for the linguini with clam sauce that neither of them knew would constitute Morty's last supper, he sat at the table, refilled his glass, and rambled on in earnest wonder about the prospect of being played ("Like an instrument!" he exclaimed, miming a violinist) by an actor who had won both an Oscar and whatever the British equivalent was. "Tommy," Morty said—uttering her name with such gravity that she turned away from the stove—"just think: you'll be on my arm at the premiere . . . or I suppose, considering my infirmities, I'll be on yours, my dear." He raised a second toast, to her.

"What infirmities?" she said.

"You know how long these projects take. I'll be eighty by then."

Tommy still saw Morty as essentially youthful, but she had become aware that his agility and sense of balance were diminishing, that he should hire younger men to climb tall ladders or scrunch down into a crawl space. He did not agree. (Last fall she caught him on the phone, trying to cancel the handyman she had hired to clean the gutters.) And so, the next morning, while Tommy was off at the UPS Store, copying and shipping a batch of color sketches for Angelica,

Morty climbed out an upstairs window onto the steeply pitched roof above the screened porch, intent on removing a limb that had fallen from the granddaddy maple, his favorite of all the fine old trees for which he had bought this property—a tree whose likeness he had rendered in his books again and again. Tommy knows he waited until her car was out of sight.

Far too often now, she must force her mind to detour sharply away from the predictable ambush of her suffocating sorrow (not guilt, because she was away doing her job, and he was being foolish) whenever she imagines Morty lying on the flagstones for God knows how long before she reached the end of the driveway and saw him there, out cold—the bough having tumbled down after, landing across his legs. He was already dead, she would learn, but for the time she sat beside him on the damp frigid stone, wishing she could just hold his head in her lap, and for the time the EMTs tried to bring him to consciousness, she had a wish that generally only a wife or a parent would have: Take me instead.

When had she crossed that line, from being the big sister of his favorite model, the boy whose doppelgänger put him on the literary map, and then his indispensable helper, his fifth limb (maid, cook, driver, party escort, website warden, proxy on difficult phone calls, repository of names), to finding herself so inescapably devoted to the man, the porcupine as well as the genius, the hermit as well as— something surprisingly new, perhaps even to him—the starstruck fan?

Breakfast. Please let this mean breakfast, he thinks as he wakes to the ringing telephone on the side table in the unfamiliar wash of radiance across the unfamiliar ceiling above the unfamiliar bed. Another hotel room, that much is certain. The needle of his inner compass spins, quivers. . . . Right, yes: New York again.

He rolls over and grapples the receiver to his ear.

"Nick, your cell phone's off."

He yawns and clears his throat. "The object is not to be reached. Even by you, Silas. Especially by you."

"That's not an option, I'm afraid."

"Si, please. No lists or lectures."

"I know: don't be a mum. But listen. We're to be picked up in an hour."

"We?"

"We have to allow three hours to get there."

"There is no 'we' today, Silas. She said no people."

"Last I heard, Nick, you are still a people."

"Hilarious, Si. You know what I mean. No entourage. Just me. That's what her note says. You get a day off. Go shopping. Drinking. Or sleep! You're always moaning you never sleep. And blaming it on me."

The note from Lear's assistant, delivered by Silas, lies beside the telephone, barely ajar from its single, stalwart fold, embodying the cautiousness, the protectiveness, of its scribe. Her handwriting is equally guarded, each line straight, each eminently legible character discrete from its neighbors: no lazy loopings or punctured margins. If Nick is good at what he does, it's not because he's a born mimic or a chameleon or a practiced show-off but because he reads other people well. (Or so he believes; it is, in the dizzying moment of all this attention, sometimes hard to know what he believes anymore, especially about himself.) Two months ago, one brief phone conversation with the assistant—through which he gained access to Lear— told him everything he needed to know about what he is dealing with here. Whom he is dealing with. Though he could not have known, back then, how important she would be. This relationship—the one he hopes to have with a woman he has yet to meet in person— matters a great deal more than his manager or the shifting posse of clammy-handed handlers and smartly suited producers understand. They see her as a potentially cantankerous guard dog; Nick sees her as a daughter, mother, gatekeeper, and amanuensis merged into one grief-stricken, probably lonely, possibly frightened woman. She is certainly in mourning, likely still in shock.

"You really want to take time for this visit?" says Silas. "If he were still alive—"

"Yes, I do," says Nick. "This is unfinished business for me.

Research. Besides which, it's only courteous. She mustn't think we've abandoned her." Nick is now seriously hungry. For a proper breakfast; also for time to think.

"She isn't a widow," says Silas.

"I'm not sure you're right about that. Figuratively speaking."

Clear as anything, Nick remembers the man's voice, the gruffness of age tinged with a robust yet honeyed cynicism, the specter of a backstreet childhood irrepressible in his accent (classic Brooklyn, a vernacular Nick will somehow crack). Forget all the piles of honors, awards, black-tied ovations: the man was still the fragile, struggling, striving boy—and, to fall back on current euphemizing, he was still the survivor.

Was. And there's the rub.

Nick oscillates between panic and relief. From the moment Andrew gave him the role, Nick counted on meeting the man he's to become. He looked forward to studying close-hand Lear's gestures, his unwitting tics and the rhythm of his breathing, how often he blinked, how tensely he held his shoulders. Nick counted on hearing about Lear's life as lived from within, directly from the man's lips—in short, to *witnessing* Lear. But then, were he still alive, there would have been the *after*. Among all the critics, schadenfreudians, crackpot bloggers, and bean-counting box-office vultures who must and will descend on Nick's performance once it's been primped and packaged for the world to see, the ultimate judge will not be present. Call him a coward, but Nick couldn't help feeling a burden lifted when he realized that Lear would never see his own personification.

"Silas? Do me a favor," he says. "Could you please ring the kitchen for a pot of very black tea? And two poached eggs over boiled spinach? Toast? I'll be a more reasonable people once I've been fed."

It's not Nick's habit to use his manager as a valet, but he wants Silas off the phone. Silas is a godsend (and charges accordingly), but in preparation for the day ahead, Nick needs a good dose of solitude, dearer to him now that it's so hard to come by. Ten years, thirty-some projects, working (not unhappily—even sometimes gratefully) in the shadows of others . . . and then, just like that, the golden goose. Or golden noose, as his older costar joked after Nick's third statuette in a single season, his second dive-bombing by the red-carpet harpies and rumoristas. Deirdre's had it rough, of course: redundantly but crucially, she is a *she* in this business puppeteered by men. She's been in rehab three times—common knowledge, hats off to the scrappers at the tabloids and dailies—and in divorce court twice. She blames her follies on her conspicuousness, the risky convergence of beauty, talent, and a bloodlust for fame. (She would even put it that way: Deirdre is blunt as a cudgel.)

Nick wouldn't argue—personal demons are just that, not another soul capable of judging—but if he had made similarly imprudent choices (like anyone, he's a fool as often as not), he likes to think that he wouldn't peg them as the wages of celebrity. All celebrity does is arrange and spotlight your foibles as if they were mannequins in a shopwindow, tart them up for all to see. You become a parade unto yourself, but if you are diligent and have a decent sense of direction, you determine the route.

He can hear Deirdre, her sad smoky laugh. *Oh, bear cub, just you wait.* Oddly, he's begun to miss her since all that tiresome campaigning came to an end. He may have told Silas that he doesn't need mothering, but over their weeks of joint interviews, bungee jumping from coast to coast, one continent to the next, Deirdre very nearly became to him in life what she had been to him in *Taormina*: his mum. Except that the movie mother was a cyclone, a tragedy, a rendezvous with death, while the road-companion mother was a mentor, a calmer of jittery nerves, a sorely needed wit in the absurdity of the careful-what-you-wish-for life he found himself leading after the film premiered at Toronto, where one of the many clamoring critics called his performance a cinematic coup de foudre. "Enjoy it," Deirdre said of his jack-in-the-box stardom, "but don't get between the sheets and fuck it. And whatever you do, don't fuck it up."

At the outset, speculative hearsay and even oddsmakers leaned toward their sweeping the big awards, side by side, but while Nick raked them in as predicted, Deirdre was passed over time and again, never more than a nominee, an almost, her steel grin shown repeatedly in close-up as another actress frolicked to the stage and took the prize of the moment. Hollywood might pretend to applaud comebacks, but second acts, Deirdre warned Nick, are secretly panned. "To vain, insecure people—oh, nobody *we* know—a rise from a fall is merely an impolite reminder that from most falls there will be no resurrection. The lesson? Don't fall. It's that simple."

He knows that the next thing he does—the next public thing—is crucial. Everybody (in Deirdre's words, "your newspaperboy and your senile drooling *wet nurse*") is watching.

Nick strips to take a shower, but first he steps into the light from the window to cast a glance at his pricey view, over low industrial buildings and an avenue streaming with those cheerful American taxis, out across the Hudson River. If he isn't careful, this is what he will begin to take for granted: standing above it all. As if the view is limitless, the future as wide and straight and cordoned off from chaos as one of those silly red carpets.

An astonishingly massive cruise ship glides into view as Nick stands in the riverine glow, the gooseflesh rising palpably on his skin. Crikey, how deep can that river be? That ship is the size of a *cathedral*. Distracted by a burst of honking below, he presses his forehead against the plateglass and peers straight down. He can just see a margin of the sooty yet fashionable street ten stories below, but he cannot see the entrance to the hotel. *Not photographers, please not the bloody photographers,* he prays. He tries always to be gracious, but today is not the day. (Yesterday, in the lift, a woman took a Biro from her handbag and asked him to sign her bare arm. And he did. What choice did he have?)

A knock sounds on his door. That's exactly how he found out about his first nomination: a knock one morning on a hotel door. But all he wants from this knock is breakfast. "Hang on!" he calls out, and makes for the closet, the hotel robe.

Nick loves breakfast. He loved it as a small child because it was the slim chink of the day when he had his mother to himself: after his older siblings had gone off to their school, before Mum dropped him off at his and went to work. He loves it now because it's the only meal he seems ever to have alone. Since a certain Sunday night at the end of February, company of any kind requires all the adrenaline he can muster. He recalls the last time he was alone with Deirdre, in the car after their final interview, the day before the Oscars. The studio sent them everywhere in cars the size of tanks, and sometimes, stepping out from a twilight-windowed, climate-controlled leathery interior, for a second Nick would find himself baffled by the temperature— whether arctic or balmy—because he'd dozed off and lost track of whether they were in New York or L.A. or Chicago or London. For a flash, he would scramble to find the proper public face (it was different, just a bit, from one city to the next). How delicious it felt— how brilliant—when, that very last time, in Beverly Hills, as the car peeled away from the curb to join the wave of traffic flowing in the direction of their hotel, Deirdre put a hand on his sleeve and said to Nick, "Guess what? You can stop sparkling now."

Over the past twelve days, Tommy has spent too much time standing in this spot, just behind the swivel stool at Morty's drafting table. She does not sit on the stool—she never has and cannot imagine doing it now—but looks at the drawings and notes, still undisturbed, that he must have been working on the afternoon before their champagne-and-linguini supper (after which they went to the den and watched a documentary about the building of the Brooklyn Bridge, at least until they nodded off). Or did Morty get up the morning after and work for an hour or two before his fatal decision to move that limb?

Two sketches are tacked to the top of the slanted surface: one depicts a pair of galloping horses, the other a tall skinny girl in a pleated dress carrying an absurdly tall stack of books. They are new images, foreign to Tommy. Is it possible that they were Morty's first inklings of what he had been aiming toward for decades: a new, extravagantly illustrated version of *Alice*? This was a project he had talked about (or talked around) for as long as Tommy could remember. He joked that it would be his "final masterwork"—except that she knew he wasn't really joking. Which was why he kept putting it off.

So who is this roughly hewn girl? Are the horses part of her world or something entirely other? A new picture book? Instinctively, Tommy wants to search for Morty, to find out. Is he checking the vegetable garden for early pests? Reading on the porch? Sneaking a piece of leftover cake while she is away from the kitchen? She has to remind herself that there is no Morty to track down.

Both sketches represent the stage of Morty's process that he called "looselining": soft gray pencil on lined paper ripped from a cheap college-ruled notebook. For years, Tommy has bought those notebooks in bulk, first from a school-supply company in Queens, then from a stationery store here in town (before it closed), more recently from Staples. These drawings were often ruthlessly smudged from the passage of Morty's hand across the lines, prone to casual tears and humid puckerings.

Enrico, the paper conservator at the museum, scolded Morty for doing so much of his work on such a cheap, impermanent surface when he could afford better. Morty's answer was "Don't ever want to take myself that seriously. Like who am I here, da Vinci?"

But Tommy knows that's simply the way he started drawing, long before she met him: in the margins of his school notes and composition books. (Or so he described it, since the evidence is long gone, well composted decades ago in some Staten Island landfill.) And, almost proudly, Morty was prone to superstition. Some of his habits verged on fetish: his stationery, the brands of his pastels and paints, the timing of meals. After Soren, he took to dressing in the same jeans (summer) or corduroys (winter), the same shirt or sweater, with little variation. His life, for several years now, had ticked like a metronome.

Just beyond the drafting table, through the window, the branches of the fruit trees have begun to fog over in flowers, masses of blossom that seem to bring the boughs closer to the ground, obscuring the view of the pool. Tommy will have to decide whether to uncover it, whether to call the pool people, ask them to swing by and perform their chemical ministrations. She doesn't use it much, and neither did Morty—but he liked being able to offer that luxury to guests.

Whether she likes it or not, there will continue to be guests. This is something she must discuss with Franklin soon: whom to consult in order to carry out Morty's final wishes.

Against the wall to the right of the window is the desk with Morty's computer. Two days after his death, Tommy put an autoreply on his e-mail account, but Franklin tells her she must start looking through his correspondence, working backward, or hire someone to do it for her. Tommy has always handled the business side, using a separate, more public e-mail address, devoting two hours a day—on her own computer, in the house—to answering queries about book signings, charity events, conferences, commencement speeches, awards juries. . . . Morty said yes less and less often—not because his energies had diminished but because, as he told her a year or so before, the older he got, the more privacy he craved.

So how could he have welcomed this intrusion? She looks at her watch: three hours. Maybe the actor will be hopelessly mired in traffic, decide it's not worth his time to come all this way.

Morty left the crush of the city, decades ago, for a reason. He joked once that the worst thing about being a quasi-somebody in the city is being mistaken for another quasi-somebody—or simply for a not-quite-familiar nobody. Because his apartment building was next to a nursery school, more than once he was mistaken by one loitering parent for another. He enjoyed recounting the story in which a pretty woman saw him on his street from a distance, shouted "Wait! Wait!" and ran toward him. He assumed she was eager to praise him for his work, but when she caught up with him, she said in a breathless rush, "Aren't you Richard's daddy? My Damien is dying for a playdate, but Richard tells him you're always in the country on weekends, so we were thinking, a sleepover maybe? We'd even be happy to keep him over two nights. And I hope you won't be missing the auction. Is it true that maybe you're donating a stay at your beach house? That would be awesome!" Which was how Morty ended up donating a set of autographed books. Turned out, when Morty told her his name, that the mother had actually recognized his face from the author photo on the back of a deluxe new edition of *Colorquake.* "One of my Damien's absolute favorites of all time!" As if the child were holding him up against Faulkner or Dostoevsky.

In their Connecticut town, a hamlet just far enough from the city to discourage commuters, Morty could walk into the grocery store without risking a fuss over who he really was or enduring a case of mistaken identity. He was simply The Famous Author Who Lives Here, no big deal. At the video store, one of the sleepy teens who worked the desk might say, "Hey, Mr. Lear, when's *The Inseparables* going to be a movie? Like I hear that kid from the vampire sitcom might be playing Boris? How cool is that." This predictable sort of exchange he even enjoyed. But what demons had he unleashed by welcoming the notion of a movie based on that profile published nearly fifteen years ago in the *Times*? And now she wonders: Did he give them permission to shoot actual scenes on the property? There's so much she doesn't know, though she's heard—and is relieved—that they have made her, Tommy, a minor character at best.

The magazine profile caused a sensation when it was widely e-mailed by weekend readers of the *New York Times*—and set off a gossipy implosion in the cliquish and envy-ridden yet self-protective world that Morty referred to as Little Reader Land. Tommy found the entire episode embarrassing not because Morty had been so open about a secret source of pain but because it must have looked like a tell-all cliché: the Beguiling Journalist coaxes the Esteemed Celebrity to share the Signature Trauma. Morty spoke almost blithely about details of his childhood that no parents would ever have shared with the Little Readers who bent and scribbled on, even chewed, the pages of his books.

"Was it the reporter?" Tommy asked when Morty told her, over dinner one night, a few days before the article was due to appear. Sheepishly, she remembered making fun of the reporter's odd name: Calum Bonaventura. "Was he so likable that you just . . . decided to hand him your soul?"

Morty was silent for a moment, then laughed. "That's a little cruel, don't you think? Ouch."

"I'm sorry."

"Tommy," he said, "secrets will out. Sometimes it's better to out them before others do, just to make sure that the surprise isn't yours."

"You're not running for office. You don't have media gophers dashing around digging tunnels beneath your public life. Although," she said, to soften what must have sounded like a scolding, "I'll bet Rose said you'll sell a ton more books."

"Rose," he said, "will learn about my indiscretion when everybody else does. When, as they say, it hits the stands. Or percolates up through the pixels. Whatever journalism does these days. If anybody even pays attention."

Tommy felt a pang of mean satisfaction. Rose, the editor who took credit for "discovering" Morty by publishing *Colorquake*—though it was hardly his first book—had been polite to Tommy since Morty hired her, but she made Tommy feel less than essential, as if she had never evolved past the assistant who knew how to change the cartridges in the printer. More than once, in the early days, Tommy had overheard Rose referring to her as "Morty's girl."

"And look," he said. "It's just a magazine. Who bothers with magazines these days? They're here to reassure us, falsely, that grown-ups really do still read. Two months from now, what will my story be? A pair of fleece socks or a roll of politically correct paper towels. Whatever recycled pulp becomes in our clever world of 'Let's just make more stuff!'"

Yet it still bothered Tommy that he told this reporter—perhaps not casually, though that was how the article made it seem—something she hadn't learned about Morty until she had been with him for years, until they went through the divisive trauma of Soren's dying. That was when Tommy learned why Morty tended to avoid any talk of his boyhood in Tucson—why his hazy tales resembled those "looseline" sketches, smudgy pencil on cheap, disposable notebook paper.

The reason Morty's mother had moved them east (Morty's father dead five years already) was that a man who worked at the same hotel where she washed the linens—a man who had worked his way into her trust, possibly even her heart—had charmed Morty into a shed on the outskirts of the property and exerted his sinister persuasions on the boy. It had happened more than once—how often or for how long, Tommy isn't sure and wouldn't ask—but Morty's mother had found out.

In the magazine, Morty discussed the usual things artists are expected to discuss—his early doubts, his sudden success, his reasons for leaving the creative hive of the city to live in the woods—but the heart of the story was his revelation of the abuse.

CB: Let's talk about that hotel—the place where you first knew you wanted to be an artist, right?

ML: I suppose. But you know, I doubt most artists ever remember accurately when they foresaw growing into this kind of life—unless maybe they had parents who were artists. Because it isn't real, this life. It can't be imagined from the outside, not like being a doctor or a bus driver or a banker, the working adults a child sees in the course of an ordinary day. To most children, art is not a grown-up thing; it's an indulgence, an escape.

CB: Which was it for you?

ML: Both, of course.

CB: What were you escaping from? Certainly, your father had died—

ML: I didn't know my father. Or don't remember knowing him. That tragedy was my mother's, almost entirely. It was her loss and her burden. I never saw how much more work she took on. I didn't know she had a "before." I think she married because she was so desperate not to be alone, and then, well, it ended up being worse than alone. But nothing like that would have occurred to me then.

CB: But her burden—by extension, it had to be yours.

ML: Daydreamers are generally pretty oblivious. It would be a mistake to see those children as logically empathic. "Sensitivity"—that old cliché—is not the same as compassion.

CB: It's obvious you're pretty hard on your youngest self.

ML: No. I endured plenty. I had every reason to grow a coat of armor, and after we moved from Tucson, I made a conscious decision to do that. I had to.

CB: Okay. So I know we talked about the gardening shed—the gardener who took advantage of you.

ML: I guess we did say we'd cover that ground.

CB: Just for the record, you told me the story. This man you believed to be a friend. Even a mentor? I was stunned.

ML: I still am. If I let myself think about it. Because, yes, he was a kind of mentor to me—someone who encouraged my art life. My mother neither encouraged nor discouraged me there, simply because she worked so hard. She had so little energy, I realized decades later. . . . So here was this man, who seemed to be, at least from a child's limited perspective . . . a good guy. A smart guy. Friendly. An expert at what he did. He had a family, but they didn't live on the grounds. And this place we shared—the hotel, the fantastical gardens where I was free to roam and dream and draw—was a place of trust. Or it was elegant—"classy" was my mother's word. And protected—literally surrounded by walls. You'd never dream there were dangers.

CB: Like what went on in the shed, once he befriended you. That man.

ML: I've begun to think that my general mistrust of older people, of authority figures, started right there. All my adult life, I've preferred the company of people younger than me. Sometimes a lot younger. Ha. You know, I genuinely enjoy being surrounded by children. Which, believe me, isn't something you can assume about authors who write for children.

CB: But so . . . your mother found out.

ML: She was devastated. She knew she had to get us out of there, and not just a town or two over. It was a huge risk. She didn't know anyone in New York. It just seemed to make sense to her, a place to disappear.

CB: This was in the late 1940s, right? So the economy was in good shape.

ML: She can't have been so coolheaded. She just knew we had to go somewhere earthshakingly different. What happened to me in that shed would never happen again: I knew at least that much when our final train reached the farthest coast. No room for garden sheds in the neighborhood we moved to. That much was certain! What I didn't know was that this did not mean I could leave it behind. But then, at the same time, I learned about worse things.

CB: Worse than—

ML: Than my personal shake-up, my "trauma."

CB: You're not going to dismiss it.

ML: Of course not. It turned my life, and my mother's life, upside down. But our life in Tucson had been strangely isolated . . . insulated. In Brooklyn, solitude took more effort. Which wasn't bad. For a change, I had neighborhood friends. This boy Adam, who lived upstairs, shared my aversion to anything involving teams or physical exertions. The first time I went up to his apartment, this man was there—an uncle, some older relative—and I happened to see him roll up his sleeves for a task in the kitchen. I saw the number. I was smart enough to wait and ask my mother. The camps weren't something people talked about, least of all to children. The entire concept of being a Holocaust survivor wasn't . . . I mean, look, "survivorship" wasn't pinned on people like some societal badge of honor, the way it is now. But my mother, when I asked her about that number, she pulled no punches. For a while, I looked obsessively at all the adults' arms. I looked for those numbers. I decided maybe the cause of my nightmares was of a lower order.

CB: But you had nightmares about it.

ML: Who wouldn't?

CB: Would you call it a driving force behind your stories? Are they redemptions?

ML: I don't analyze my work. That would be to challenge the gods. Nor have I ever let myself be analyzed—not on the couch, at least. I don't tell you this to seem brave or stoic. I'm simply of a certain generation. Younger people presume a choice: Is it better just to suck up the pain and endure—or to share it, assuming somehow that will weaken its hold?

CB: You are sharing it right now, aren't you?

ML: Okay, yes, you have me there.

CB: Why now?

ML: I write for children, which makes me part child if I do it well. Or maybe all child, God knows! People say children's book authors are kids who still haven't figured out what they want to be when they grow up. But it means I act more on instinct than maybe even you—and I'd say you're easily half my age. Something—I call it my inner imp—tells me it's time to bring up this story. You happen to be the receiver, all because you, or your editors, decided it was time for a puff piece on Mort Lear. Not sure you got the puff piece, did you?

CB: Well. No. I would say definitely no puff.

ML: In any case, timing is everything. In love. In war. In telling your history.

He went on to say how lucky he felt to have escaped when he did. He speculated mournfully about children who never get away, whose abuse goes undiscovered or unchallenged.

When the story came out, Morty did seem surprised to see it in the blunt form of a transcribed interview. He had spoken with the magazine's fact-checker, who relayed to him only paraphrased details.

Immediate response from readers was dissonant and loud, the loudest voices those of the child-welfare advocates, the people who felt that any disclosure of such terrifying cruelty could only serve to help others come forward, shed light on evil and strip it of power. And then, as Morty predicted, the tide of attention receded—or came to a full stop for reasons of timing that Morty could not have predicted: the story came out in the summer of 2001.

A few years later, however, Calum Bonaventura called Morty to tell him that a movie director had optioned the story. When Morty came into the kitchen that night and told Tommy about the call, she said, "Andrew Zelinsky? You know who he is, right?"

"Rings a foggy bell," said Morty. "I could have asked for details, but I was writing. Shouldn't even have answered. I told my reporter pal congratulations, but I'm sure he knows the deal—or the no-deal. He gets to buy a car. Used. More likely a couch. Option goes up like a cinder when Zelinsky decides he'd rather make the next big over-larded action movie. No superheroes in my tawdry tale."

"Zelinsky's movies aren't big—or not big budget. He doesn't do superheroes. In fact, they're more sad than heroic. He's not exactly Ron Howard."

"Now there's a thought, Tommy. My story as told by Opie."

They laughed at the absurdity—a life told in two hours or less; really?—and sat down to another meal at the kitchen table, followed by another bout of Scrabble or an early parting, each to read or catch up on e-mail or have a look at the news, always fraught with war and disease, fateful weather, unscrupulous bankers, and yet another TV show concerning zombies or vampires or aliens bent on colonizing our planet.

Years went by before Tommy answered her work phone and found herself speaking to someone in the office of a movie studio on the opposite coast.

Silas hovers, both peevish and deferential, as Nick climbs into the Town Car.

"I could stay in the car while you pay your visit."

"You'd go mad," says Nick. "This is not some charity drive-by. I plan on overstaying my welcome as long as I can. This woman knew him better than anyone else in the world. That's obvious from all the tributes and rehashings."

He practically wrenches the door from Silas's hand in order to pull it shut. Once the car is moving uptown and turns a corner, Nick leans back on the barricade of black leather and sighs, twice, with deliberate volume. The driver, thank God, ignores him.

He brought along the big book, the lap-flattener published five years ago now: *Chiaro Scuro, Childhood Hero: The Art of Mort Lear*. Silly title, forgettably fawning text, but the pictures are sumptuous, and Nick has nearly memorized the annotated chronology at the back. From it he knows that Mort Lear hired Tomasina Daulair to be his assistant in 1982. She was twenty-two and had just finished university; Lear was forty-two, wealthy, revered, and turning out one successful, striking picture book after another. A few years later, with his lorryloads of royalties, he would buy the country house.

That was one of the many things Nick and Lear had e-mailed about, with surprising fluidity and frequency, in the month between their two conversations: how being showered with prizes does and does not change you; how it invigorates and imperils your work; how it leads to privilege yet also to the threat of paralysis; how even the oldest of alliances shift, like boats at the turn of a tide. (*Ah, dear gifted young man, just you wait,* Lear had written—his words and his tone, Nick now sees, echoing Deirdre's.) Of course, they had touched on a great deal else—and it's this, the "else," that Nick can't help wanting, *needing,* to pursue. The only person to whom he can turn is the cryptic Tomasina . . . although, unless the man was flattering Nick with false confessions, even she does not know the extent of the perversity Lear endured as a boy. Nor do the readers of the splashy profile that Andrew optioned, along with the rights to *Colorquake.*

According to the chronology in the book, Tomasina worked for Lear in the city, maintaining his office there until 1989, when she moved out to Lear's Connecticut house to care for the author after surgery for an abdominal infection. *Whether the living arrangement was meant to be temporary or permanent at the time is unclear, but Daulair stayed on and remains Lear's closest professional affiliate to this day.* (Leaving aside that Lear's closest physical affiliate, for nigh on ten years, was one Soren Kelly, the younger lover who died of AIDS—or, correctly, of course, its "complications," as the book duly notes—in 1999.)

The late eighties and early nineties were a time when Lear seemed infallibly productive, hoovering up the awards and becoming a household name—at least in households including a nursery. But sometime in the midnineties, Lear began work on *Diagnosis,* the first book in his trilogy, *The Inseparables,* aimed at a much older audience than the one he usually wrote for. Around the same time his lover's health was failing, it won every conceivable prize for "young people's literature" and was optioned by Disney, although it never rose from the cruel flames of development hell (flames that have scorched Nick himself from time to time). The critical consensus is that helplessly watching the love of his life dwindle and die somehow stoked Lear's creative fires into a conflagration.

The first and last books of the trilogy are dedicated to the doomed and then deceased Kelly. In the first, a blank page bears simply the lover's name, *Soren,* floating in the center like a lone boat on a vast sea. In the third, *Remission,* it reads *To Soren, at peace.* The middle volume, *Metastasis,* is dedicated to the memory of Lear's mother.

Nick has done his homework—or, actually, he's in the midst of it, having given himself a clear two months before the first day of shooting (which will probably be delayed while they decide whether Lear's death necessitates another rewrite, even though the current narrative ends soon after Soren Kelly dies). These biopics of living geniuses are all the rage now, but they're complicated by the very livingness of the geniuses in question—or of people who knew them well. Geniuses may have susceptible egos, debilitating vices, wicked tempers, any number of base afflictions, but they are not pushovers, nor do they suffer fools. Which is why, when Nick heard about Lear's accident, his shock and sadness were followed by a spasm of shameful relief.

Lear was not a scientist or a politician; he was an artist. But you'd have to be daft to believe this made him less complicated than, say, that Nobel-winning fertility doctor who'd been the subject of Amar's last film or Benazir Bhutto or Bill Gates. (And what was the deal with *two* films about the barely departed Steve Jobs?)

Then there's the tricky bit of the backstory, the child actor who has to look enough like the storybook Ivo and enough like the flesh-and-blood Nick *and* be able to do a convincing job of portraying Lear as the boy in that shed. (For the most agonizing scenes, clever Andrew has dreamed up a half-animated sequence, inspired by *Colorquake,* that should bypass the demand for graphic sexuality and might even hold the rating at a palatable PG-13.)

And here is the problem for Nick. Before Lear's unexpected disclosure to him about what really happened in that shed, Nick saw his primary challenge as interpreting the lifelong ripple effect of the trauma as depicted in the script, the one everybody talked about after the interview in the magazine . . . but now—he can't block it out—that trauma has been swapped for another. In fact, if you read the interview closely—which Nick has done countless times—the "darkness in the shed," as he thinks of it, is never described in any detail. Certain conventional assumptions were made about the nature of the violation that turn out not to be true.

It shouldn't matter, but it does. It bothers him. And he has to wonder whether he should complicate matters by telling Andrew the different story—because Nick would, in effect, be asking for a rewrite. The last thing anybody wants is further delay.

Nick was moved by Lear's forthrightness in their correspondence—and doubly glad that they had dismissed any notion of a go-between. The level of trust, without intermediaries, was, by the end, staggering. Lear had asked that Nick delete his e-mails after reading them and, though his cursor finger had paused as the quivering arrow approached the little dustbin, he had done so. Could you honestly portray a man with whom you hadn't been honest?

"You'll learn to be the wily fox soon enough, and you'll have to, baby," Kendra said to him, the day after the Oscars. She lay on their hotel bed, in nothing but her pink lace knickers, reading aloud to him samples of how the papers, tweeters, and blog-floggers had variously praised and mocked the sincerity of his speech, even questioned his tears (which, let the world think otherwise, erupted against his will) as he dedicated the hefty golden chap to single mothers who scrimped and saved for their children to follow their passions (not that Nick's mother would have had to scrimp so much if she'd exercised common sense—though if she'd done that, Nick would not *exist*). At any rate, that remark of Kendra's was the beginning of their end. Kendra's edges are too sharp.

For advising Nick to hold off a marriage proposal till after awards madness waned, Silas deserves every green dollar he earns and then some. Which is why Nick tolerates his American manager's tendency to meddle in bloody everything now that Nick has to worry about encounters with the sort of people who make their living by popping out from behind the shrubs wielding a camera—or, these days, any old anybody whipping out a phone in a tube station (not that his way of making a living is really any less peculiar).

In dense traffic, the car inches north on the motorway skirting the river. The George Washington Bridge looms to the left. Nick heaves the book into his lap and opens it to the introduction, which he could practically recite by heart. It's illustrated with pretentiously sepiaed photos of Lear: as a teenager in a school play, brandishing a wooden sword; as a striving young illustrator bent over a drafting table, his hair long and flaxen; with Soren Kelly and Tomasina Daulair at a posh party in New York sometime in the nineties; as a much older man, leaning against the door of his brick farmhouse. In this final image, only fugitive traces remain of his youthful beauty, but the triumphs of his long career are evident in his cocksure smile and, metaphorically, in the voluminous blooms of a rose trained in an arc around the fanlight over the door.

Flipping deeper into the book, Nick finds himself at the chapter devoted to *Colorquake,* the book that launched Lear like a NASA space shot. It wasn't his first, though most people wouldn't know that now, not even the thousands of women who have named their sons Ivo, after the impish, stout-limbed lad at the center of the story. Quietly, doggedly, over the crucial years many would consider a young man's prime, Lear published a handful of earnest storybooks aimed at children with the usual aversions: to manners, to sleep, to the dark, to vegetables, to the sermonizing of grown-ups. All were quirky and finely drawn, but the young heroes and heroines had a bland, generic appearance a little like the children of Edward Gorey, as if drawn by an adult who had never enjoyed being a child and certainly wouldn't want to raise one. All that changed with the perennially beloved Ivo.

Nick turns a page and starts reflexively at the image that once terrified him (though he would never have admitted it to whichever sibling was reading aloud at the time): Ivo standing in the forest clearing, barefoot, his clothing in tatters, his eyes closed. He stands with his arms stretched out to either side, and from every direction, birds, butterflies, and insects alight on his body as if he were a tree, while squirrels and moles convene at his feet. To young Nick, it wasn't just the squeamish notion of having grasshoppers and crickets perched along his arms that gave him the willies; it was the way the boy's pose reminded him of the crucifix he'd glimpsed on the wall of a playmate's house. His mother had explained the Easter story to him, but not till he left home for school would he come to realize how odd his religious ignorance was.

Nick has always wondered whether *Colorquake* appeals more to the adults who read it aloud than it does to their children. In the forty years since its publication, endless theses have been published on the allegorical power of the story, claiming allusions to the Holocaust, to Saint Francis, to sexual awakening, even to the civil rights movement and the Vietnam War. Lately, there have been murmurings that Lear was even, presciently, writing about the potential disaster of climate change. Good Lord, how could Lear have tolerated all that lily gilding, that cerebral fuss? That is one of the questions Nick would have asked him today.

His mobile hums. Andrew. He cannot ignore Andrew, whose faith in Nick won him the role over far more bankable actors—and, notably, before the awards. Now Andrew buzzes with glee, gloating to the formerly fretful execs that he knew all along; he knew Nick would prove his mettle, would *go fucking platinum*. Andrew could practically have cast a random nutter plucked from the street; that's the clout of three Oscars (one of which he won as a young actor, two as a director). Back in more barbaric times, he would have had a gold-tasseled casting couch, the exclamation point concluding an epic line of women stretching from his sentried gate on Mulholland clear to Venice Beach.

A text: Can Nick fly out for a meeting tomorrow?

Impossible. So sorry. Heading out to Lear's house. Speak tonight?

Tied up tonight.

Tomorrow morning?

I'm up early. 8 ET? Keep your phone on, bro.

Has Silas been telling tales? Nick feels like a truant schoolboy caught at the park. He returns to looking at illustrations from *Colorquake,* which the animators will weave throughout the movie. At times, Nick's acting will be green-screened, stitched into the backdrop of Lear's imagination: a technical frontier he's eager to cross, since every story in which he's acted so far has been set in literally fabricated surroundings.

By now, Nick has committed the book to heart, every picture, every word. It begins, famously, *Ivo's mother kept a perfect house, a house among the trees.* In a lilting paragraph, printed in large white type on black ground—by far the most text on any one page—the perfection of the house is described. *The sofas were serene, the bedrooms were bucolic, the rugs were resplendent. . . .* The final sentence on the page is *Ivo's mother called him her budding artist, her little Cézanne, and she loved him like no one else, but she didn't want his colors to spill on her perfect armchairs, her perfect lamps, or her perfectly framed perfect paintings by artists more famous than Ivo who lived and died a very long time ago.* All this perfection, visually if not verbally, is left to the reader's imagination—and the vocabulary signals to any remotely clever child that there will be no condescension here. In a way, the words are beside the point, as if that daunting passage is nothing but a heavy door to be pushed aside, perhaps like the one that Ivo opens a short while later.

A turn of the page reveals a wide double spread of intoxicating softly penciled color. Balanced on one bare foot, smiling gaily, brandishing a dripping brush, a wee lad stands in the middle of a windowless room whose walls are mostly (but not yet entirely) covered with a tropical fantasia: tall spiky trees and flowers, toucans, parrots, butterflies. On one wall, where he has only begun to paint this jungle, you can see his previous painting: a cityscape, about to be engulfed—or overgrown. The only piece of furniture in the room is a step stool, draped with a color-stained rag.

Barely noticeable, hugging the bottom margin of the two pages, runs the text *So Ivo's mother gave him the cellar, all of it. It was his to decorate however he pleased. Sometimes Ivo stayed there all day long.* Yet suddenly, perhaps deliberately, the words cease to matter so much, because to all but the most heartless reader, Ivo himself is utterly beguiling, from his stubby, paint-stained toenails to the multiple cowlicks that rise in inky tufts from a head as round as a billiards ball. (Every mother who sees him must long to hold him in her lap and comb his unruly hair.)

Until the day of the earthquake.

Ivo is so busy painting in his windowless cellar that he toils on without realizing that the house above him is shaking. In a trio of wordless illustrations, the reader sees him on tiptoe, rendering a passionflower; up on the stool, one leg raised, at work on a butterfly bigger than his head; and, crouching in a corner, frowning with concentration, bringing to visual life a coiled black panther. (In the first image, the lightbulb overhead swings to and fro; in the next, a jar holding Ivo's brushes shatters, scattering them far and wide; take three, the stool tips onto its side.)

The following spread is divided into four scenes:

Ivo finds himself painting a large meaty sandwich.

He stops and frowns. Why hasn't his mother called him to lunch? (Any child can read this thought on Ivo's deftly rendered face.)

He goes upstairs. But the door at the top is stuck fast.

Puzzled, he goes back down and forces open a medieval-looking wooden door that leads to a rising flight of stone stairs and, beyond, a modest garden.

Another spread—this time one wide image, still wordless—shows Ivo from behind, paintbrush at his side, beholding a suburban landscape that is largely undestroyed (a few branches and shutters askew, a chimney leaning) but entirely monochromatic. Ivo himself is black and white.

On the next page, he looks down in alarm and confusion at his own grayness and then at the paint on the end of his brush: now black when, two pages back, it was red.

Ivo sets forth and encounters other children, emerging from their own homes, all equally puzzled by the sudden change in their world: the ashen flowers, the brooding black trees, the sun shining cold paper white. No one speaks; perhaps no one can. Ivo quickly leaves them behind, however, and plunges into a nearby wood. How long he wanders is unclear, but in a few pages he happens upon a panther—to the vigilant eye, exactly like the one seen lurking in the corner of his mural.

What follows, in a swift series of cardlike frames, is a kind of tele-pathic communication—not a conversation—in which Ivo, unafraid of the big cat, discovers that the creature is a man transformed by a curse to spend eternity speechless and colorless, pure jet black, unless he finds a fearless love.

The panther, however, grew impatient and jealous as well as lonely. Despairing, he bargained away his redemption, surrendering his immortality to a fairy in exchange for a cataclysm that would steal color from the rest of the world as well. If he was to live life deprived of color, so would everyone else.

The fairy, long departed, is never seen. For six pages, the boy and the panther seem to dance and tumble and spar with each other as the boy learns the cat's story. Words, in this sequence, are few and far between. It's clear that the story is being "told" through the ongoing tangle of boy with cat. Only on a recent read-through did it occur to Nick that, to a sophisticated adult reader, that tangle suggests Her-cules wrestling with the lion, perhaps even Jacob with the angel. The boy and the panther seem to be fighting as much as playing, their limbs at times intertwined, their faces an emotional spectrum rang-ing from gaiety to grimace. A marvel, the way in which the images seem as sexual as they do purely playful—though how much is Nick projecting Andrew's vision onto Lear's?

At last, the boy and the big cat fall asleep together in a clearing, but when the boy awakens, he is alone.

Ivo was not dreaming, he discovers. The world is still like one of his mother's old photographs: the leaves overhead a cloudy gray, the grass in shadow a mat of blackened bristle. He stands and stretches and closes his eyes, homesick and lonely. He stretches out his arms, from which his shirt hangs in shreds.

The next image is the one that frightened Nick (and surely he wasn't alone in feeling this way). As the flying and creeping creatures land on or brush against Ivo, they regain their color, and as they fly out into the world, their flight paths brush color back into the air, through the trees, across the horizon, just as Ivo's paintbrush colored the walls of his cellar.

Ivo searches for the panther but finds no sign of it. Emerging from the woods, he is greeted by the sight of the happy children of his neighborhood, their cheeks rosy again, their pinafores and pants cheerfully patterned once more. They are out in their gardens and on the pavement, jumping rope and playing marbles; they pay no heed to Ivo in his ragged clothing.

The boy runs toward his house. As it comes in sight, he sees a tall man in a multicolored patchwork greatcoat knocking on the door. The man's head is thick with black hair, and trailing from beneath the hem of the coat is a long, elegant black tail. He enters the house before Ivo reaches it.

The last scene is the door of the house (a red door with a lion's head for a knocker) opening wide. The doorway is filled with a prismlike explosion of color.

The final page is, like the first, black, but the paragraph printed on it is, this time, in a rainbowed font. The page resembles those old-fashioned drawings made by scrubbing a thick layer of black crayon over a field of colored markings, then scratching through the waxy scrim.

Ivo's mother hugged and hugged him. To his amazement, the rooms were as perfect as ever: the sofa, the rug, the lamps, the potted ivy, everything in its place. Only this was different: Ivo's mother was in love, and she was also in love with Ivo's art. On the walls, instead of the perfectly framed perfect paintings by the perfect but long-ago artists, hung Ivo's pictures: birds and butterflies and grasshoppers. Ivo ate a big dinner with his mother and her true love, the man with the black hair and tail, and then he went back to the cellar.

Everything was just as he left it, but . . . wait . . . where was his panther?

And if the reader turns to the endpaper, there stands Ivo, facing the reader directly, a silencing finger raised to his lips, laughter in his eyes, a bright blue butterfly sitting on top of his head.

Single mothers must love this story, Nick thinks, setting the book aside to gaze out the window. The car speeds along now, unimpeded, beneath a blur of trees. Green signs with rusticated borders announce exits leading to towns with an ethnic hotchpotch of names, some American Indian, some Anglo nostalgic, others just plain odd (is Mount Kisco an actual mountain?).

Nick's own single mum had little time to read to him; she was too busy trying to scramble a living to support three children whose two fathers had each, in succession, gone his merry, scoundrely way. When all three of them were old enough to sit still at a table, their grandfather took them to lunch once a month—somewhere posh, with stiff napkins and stiff-backed waiters (and, for Grandfather, stiff drinks). He would lecture them on manners, money, and the importance of attending university (which, somewhat miraculously, all three of them did). He made a show of planting seed money in trusts for each of them, which they were told they would inherit when they were "too old to be as foolish as your mother was." As for helping Mum directly, he did so only through the stingiest of loans, never enough to alleviate her air of suppressed panic, artificial cheer, and almost unrelenting fatigue. Nick wonders if, as the youngest, he was the only one home often enough to overhear the arguments Mum and Grandfather had on the telephone—though of course he had no idea what life had been like when Nigel and Annabelle were small and their father had yet to decamp. Was Grandfather more or less condemning back then?

Children do not try to make sense of their grandparents' actions. Whether they behave endearingly or tyrannically, grandparents, like dinosaurs and Vikings, are outmoded and illogical beings, exempt from the rules of physics or decent modern behavior. Any eccentric or even brutal actions they perpetrate are excused by their being so ancient. (Perhaps in *their* time it was normal to shame your children, just as it was normal in the era of the Norse gods to pillage and burn.) Not until Nick came into his trust, at thirty, did he realize how cruel his grandfather had been not only to his daughter but to her children as well, by refusing to give her enough support to spend more time with them.

Or maybe that was the point. Maybe Grandfather, more than punishing Nick's mother for her impulsive bohemian couplings (no legal strings attached), wanted to ensure that she had scant opportunity to expose the carriers of his genes to her possibly contagious and definitely intemperate romanticism. Poor Mum outlived Grandfather by little more than a year. She died of breast cancer, her unfavorable spot in the chemotherapy queue no doubt abetting its fatal metastasis. Grandfather had expired while snoozing in a leather chair at his club one afternoon. Nick despairs at the injustice, not just at the loss of the years his mother might have had—enough to see him up for an Olivier or cast in that BBC docudrama as Sir Walter Raleigh (she was reading history at Cambridge when her affair with Nigel and Annabelle's father led her astray)—but at the inequitable distribution of the physical pain: all of it, and plenty, suffered by his mother alone.

By the time Mum died, Nick's brother and sister—Nigel now a barrister in Glasgow, Annabelle a wife and mother in Dorset—had established workaday lives of their own, quite separate from Nick's. They were eight and six years older. He invited them to an "intimate reception" (was there such a thing?) that his agency arranged the week after the BAFTA win. By post, each of them declined, their notes congratulatory but brief. Nick's disappointment was overshadowed by guilt; their courteous snubs only served him right. What efforts had he made through his scrabbling, hand-to-mouth years, before the trust kicked in? (He hasn't laid eyes on his niece, Fiona, since her christening. She must be four or five by now.) Their formal regrets arrived on the same day, reminding him how much closer they are to each other than to him. Not only are they full siblings, but they can remember the early rows between Mum and her parents; they can even remember Grandmother, who died the year Nick was born. (Anyone could guess that Grandfather blamed her demise on Mum.)

Well, this is rich. He's managed to work himself into a cavelike funk just as the road signs are beginning to herald the town where Lear lives—or lived: Orne, a curious name that comes out like an utterance forced through a mouthful of cotton wool at the dentist's.

As if to reassure himself that it's all real—these woods, this car, the visit he's been anticipating for months—he lays a hand on the beribboned box beside him. It contains a basket of blood-red pears, fancy chocolates, and—two weeks too late—a slim red volume of tributes written to Charles Dickens by other great writers, some of them modern, others his peers. Silas is to thank. He, too, has done his homework.

Will she give him lunch here, in the kitchen? She made a quiche, has the ingredients for a salad with avocados. Morty never tired of avocados; he ate them nearly every day. As he told Tommy years ago, any man who spins his success from thin air should have a favorite daily indulgence with which to pat himself on the back. But now, she wonders if it would be better to suggest they go out, to the village center, the one decent restaurant that's open for lunch. It's quiet then. The waitresses are efficient matrons who aren't likely to recognize Nicholas Greene—or are they?

No, that's a stupid idea. And rude. Never mind whether he'd draw attention. (Would Tommy secretly like that? Had Morty not gone out on the roof, he would be here to tease her about their visit from a man deemed one of the past year's most eligible or sexy or talented, depending on which magazine was concocting the list.) If they go out, the actor will insist on treating her, and she will owe him something. Better to be the one extending favors. That's what

Morty would say—at least, the Morty of ten and more years ago, who endorsed so many young writers' first efforts, who made Tommy deliver bags of apples and plums from their little orchard to all their neighbors, even the ones who refused to honor civilized hours for construction or mechanized lawn work.

And just like that, here it is: the crunch of tires on gravel, earlier than expected. Unless it's Franklin—but Franklin always telephones first. It's been eerily quiet since the day they spent together making the most important calls: the funeral home, the credit card hotlines, the banks, and the broker. "Call this the eye of the storm," Franklin told her, standing in the driveway before he left. "I'll give you a week off before we tackle the work ahead." Next month, in the city, there will be an obscenely large memorial gathering for "colleagues and friends" in the American Wing at the Met. To keep Morty's agent distracted, Tommy asked her to take on that affair, not just the logistics but the politics. Let Angelica juggle the fragile egos, take the heat for leaving anyone off the list. Apparently, there will also be a public gathering at the Central Park Alice. City booksellers planned that one, and Tommy is hoping for a graceful out.

She should meet Nicholas Greene at his car, but she remains seated at the kitchen table, stilled by the sudden certainty that she should have said no. *I'm so sorry, but everything's changed, and it's simply not a good time. Oh, and I do admire your work, Mr. Greene. We both did.* Morty, you vain old fool, she thinks.

Too quickly, there's a single strident rap of the front-door knocker. Through the dining room, the living room . . . She pauses after catching a glimpse of blue shoulder through one of the sidelights. Followed by a face, shadowed by two hands cupped against the pane.

She rushes to open the door. He mustn't see her hesitating, peering out.

"Ms. Daulair?" His hand, his blue sleeve. He wears a velour jacket with crisp narrow jeans and a white button-down shirt. Draped around his long neck is an orange scarf, bright as a burst of song.

"Yes," she says. "Me."

Me, she thinks, meet Him.

Because it *is* Him, the man from the magazines and movies, yet it isn't. Nothing could prepare you for this: how . . . *indelible* he is. Not *sexy* or *dishy* or *hunky* or any of those insufficiently two-dimensional teenybopper adjectives. And he's too thin to be "handsome," strictly speaking. But what he is—like a rose in a color you've never laid eyes on before or a dress in a store window that suddenly you dream of wearing on a wedding day you haven't even planned—is impossible to stop looking at, demanding memorization. Both his hair and his eyes are a blondish brown, his nose long and slightly skewed, his pale skin vivaciously freckled—all these features reminiscent of Morty's looks around the time Tommy met him.

"May I trespass?" His laugh sounds genuinely nervous or shy. (But he's an actor! Who can tell what's "genuine"?) He leans over and picks up a box from the brickwork at his feet (blue Converse sneakers, toes unscuffed). He hands it to her. "A bribe. Please tell me entry does not require a password. I'm hopeless at passwords. Shakespeare monologues, a cinch. Logging in to my e-mail account, a perpetual trial."

Hugging the box to her chest, Tommy stands planted just inside the front door: what is the matter with her? "Yes," she manages. "Please."

He thanks her. "Old," he says, stepping inside. "I love old houses. Houses that have really been *lived* in. Lived in again and again. I have a flat in a crumbling old row house. In London. Where I rarely ever am these days. I miss it!" And this room makes him miss it more acutely still. In the wide, warped floorboards, the faded Oriental rugs and dependably aging sofas, he sees immediate similarities between their outer lives, their tastes. The similarities between their inner lives, those he's seen already.

Realizing how rude he must seem, looking greedily about as if he's an estate agent calculating a value, he turns quickly back to his hostess. She seems every bit as off-balance as he is. Is she shy? Her reticence might be distrust.

"I feel fortunate to be here," he says.

The more the actor speaks, the less Tommy feels capable of responding. There is something suffocating about being in the presence of celebrity, as if the man is literally taking in all the available air.

Christ, should she offer to take his jacket? His expensive scarf?

He winds the scarf deftly around a hand, like a skein of yarn, and pushes it into a pocket. "I really am grateful," he tells her. "I'm eager to see everything you'll show me, but I don't want to intrude. All right, well, that's not entirely true."

Still speechless, she leads him into the kitchen. She sets the box on the table.

They stand on opposite sides, and simultaneously they speak.

She: "May I offer you tea, coffee—a beer? I could make you a lemonade." He: "How boorish of me. I wanted to say, first thing, how sorry I am. I've read all the tributes and the obituaries and . . . it's still so hard to believe. So awful."

In the lull that follows their jumbled words, his outpacing hers, they laugh.

"Well," says Tommy. "Thank you. It has been awful. And I'm sorry for you . . . that you missed meeting him. He was looking forward to . . . that." *To you.*

She repeats her offer, determined to hold the upper hand. She mustn't turn to sand just because the man is famous. Not so long ago, she reminds herself, he wasn't, so maybe he's not yet accustomed to being a Face. And it's not as if hanging out with famous men is something new to her—though famous for looks is different from famous for brains. Not that one precludes the other. . . .

"Tea would be great," says Nick. "And you'll join me?" He longs for the beer she offered, but if he can win her over, he'll have that beer in good time. And tea—tea will make him feel more grounded. A beer would make him giddy. Even dead sober, he's jabbering.

"I have lunch for us. A quiche and salad."

"Thank you. That sounds brilliant. And too good of you."

"Please sit," she says. "And I'll open this."

She recognizes the box, by its trademark magenta, as coming from the gourmet purveyor in Greenwich Village that Morty often uses to send holiday gifts to his editors, agents, and other enablers of his creative life. (*Used* to send, she reminds her mind.) So the pears and chocolates aren't a surprise to Tommy, but the book . . .

She takes it out and sits down. She hasn't put the kettle on, but here she is, paging through this small book, her eyes welling up. This isn't going well. She isn't the slightest bit in control—not of her emotions and definitely not of the situation.

"Now I really *am* sorry," says Nicholas Greene. "I've upset you. I bought the book before your boss had his accident. I read about his passion for—"

She looks up quickly. "I didn't think of Morty as my boss, Mr. Greene." She gets up, setting the book on the table, and goes to the stove to heat water—and to turn her face away. She feels herself growing red, moved yet also irritated by the postmortem gift. How could he not see it, now, as a purely obsequious gesture?

"Nick," he says. "Please call me Nick. And I'd very much like to get to know . . . Mr. Lear as you knew him. Whatever you'll share with me. I liked him so much, based on our early exchanges. I want to do him honor with this film. We all do. I mean, do you know—and I'm hardly the only one among us—I remember so clearly reading—or, I suppose technically, listening to *Colorquake*. My older sister read it to me, sometimes my brother. And the one about the fox and the balloon, the boy who—

"Listen to me. As if you need my ramblings to know what a genius he was." He sounds like a dithering sod.

Deliberately, Tommy keeps moving. As she extracts the toweled bundle of greens from the refrigerator, she says, "No amount of praise was too much for Morty, especially from grown-ups remembering his books from when they were small. He lived to delight small children." (Not primarily, but what does it matter?)

"I'll show you his studio after lunch." *And then I will see you on your way.* But already she's mesmerized, suddenly averse to the thought of his leaving too soon. At thirty-four (which she knows from the profiles she and Morty read), Nicholas Greene is young enough to be her child, so the lure she feels is hardly romantic—but perhaps she understands now what makes a successful actor into a star: a literal radiance, something molecular. And then there's his accent, which, to her gullible American ears, inspires an exasperating degree of knee-jerk reverence.

"Do you like avocado?" she asks.

"Avocado? It's one of the best things about spending time in this country," he says. "I am mad for avocado!"

"It was one of Morty's favorite things. That he could afford to eat it every day. Sometimes he'd have half an avocado with lime juice for breakfast. Maybe with an egg white, scrambled."

"You cooked for him."

She sets the table around him. She likes that he doesn't offer to help, an offer that would only confuse her. "Not always. Though usually dinner," she says. "And there was a time when we entertained a lot. We'd cook together—or hire somebody. There was a local caterer everyone loved back then." Now she is the one who's rambling.

"Back when Mr. Kelly lived here, too?"

"Yes. That was a very social time." She reminds herself that Soren, as a character, will be in the movie. Which brings up yet another source of anxiety. Will the movie show Morty's most private moments, the way he ran wild after his mother's dementia set in? What happened in Tucson—the reason the director is probably making this film in the first place—is worrisome enough.

"I hope you're willing to talk about what it was like then—and before. And since then, too. Not that . . . I don't want to turn this into some sort of interrogation."

"But you're here to ask questions, and I do want to help," says Tommy. And it's beginning to feel as if, despite herself, she does.

"Look, I'm sure part of your job—I mean, a natural part of living with him—was to guard his privacy."

Tommy concentrates on the food for a moment. Nicholas Greene is right, of course, but when she thinks back to those days, the "very social time," she recalls how pathetically powerless she was to "guard" Morty from anything. Against his very nature, Morty pandered to Soren's longing for the limelight. The gatherings of artists and writers in this house were legendary; invitations to the parties—almost always mailed—became objects of envy. The most opulent, a fund-raiser for Act Up held under a tent in the garden by the pool, was the subject of a *Vanity Fair* article. "Of Titans in Tuxes and Tomtens in Trees," it was called. Among the photographs of Morty and his wealthy guests (many of them younger men who would die in the next few years) was an image of one of the hand-colored engravings in the limited-edition book that went to the most lavish donors: Morty's Christmas tribute to Astrid Lindgren, *The Tomten in the Orchard*. Wearing his conical red hat, the bearded elf perched high in a tree whose gnarled branches were laden with apples yet traced in snow. The tomten reached up into the night sky with a long-handled butterfly net, aiming at the brightest star. Tommy saw the tone of the article as subtly mocking, but Morty found it flattering. He invited the reporter to the next party they gave.

The parties stopped after Soren's illness outfoxed the best treatments Morty could buy. That was a terrible time for all of them, but the hardest part for Tommy (harder even than Soren's rage, directed so often at her) was how distant Morty became, how he kept things from her that normally she would have been the first to know. After Morty told her about Soren's diagnosis, it took her a month to find a way to ask Morty about his own health; his reaction was angry, as if this were none of her business. Hadn't it occurred to him that he would be her first concern? Worse still, she had no idea if Soren's being diagnosed so long after he'd moved into the house meant something she couldn't bear thinking: that he had been unfaithful to Morty or that, contrary to everything Tommy assumed, the relationship between the two men had openly admitted others. How naïve she had been to assume that Morty had no life beyond what she could see.

"You've known Mr. Lear in just about every era of his life," says Nicholas Greene. "How astonishing. And, really, what a privilege."

"I don't think about it that way," she says, "though maybe I should."

Tommy sets down the salad bowl, then the plates with their wedges of steaming quiche. The fragrance of tarragon pervades the kitchen. Coins of sunlight, scattered through the leaves of the cherry tree, form a quavering pattern across the table setting.

Nick spreads his napkin over his lap. "You were with him when he lost his mother, then his lover—and the editor he told me he loved so much."

"Rose." Morty cried more after his editor's death than he had after his mother's.

"I'm sure he felt lucky to have you with him, right here, for support. And trust. When you're . . . prosperous"—Tommy notes the care with which he chooses this word over, perhaps, *famous* or *popular*—"it's hard to know whom you can properly trust."

Tommy looks Nicholas Greene in the eye—which isn't easy. "He would have had someone else, if not me. He didn't want a family, he didn't want to live in the city, but he didn't want to live alone."

"But he chose you."

Tommy feels strangely proud to have him say this to her—but he would be saying this to anyone sitting in this chair at this moment in time. Actors live by their scripts. "I suppose he did. And I chose him." She adds quickly, "He used to joke that he'd have chosen a cat instead, except that a cat would refuse to stand in line for stamps."

"He wasn't one for flattery, was he?" The actor deploys his golden smile.

Now it would take an industrial crane to lift her gaze from the plate. Over the past week, she has felt these inklings of dread, each like a subtle draft from an open window. She tells herself it's simply the dread of all she faces in following through on Morty's intentions. Tommy takes little comfort in the security of knowing she is now the "prosperous" one, especially because she is not the famous one, the gifted one, the like-nobody-else-on-earth teller of tales. Morty was anything but her twin, yet it's as if she somehow believed that, like those three children he dreamed up, they were inseparable, mortality itself the source of their alloyed strength.

Tommy can't help hearing her brother's voice, one of the last things Dani said to her last year before she kicked him out of the house: *You're not his "friend." You're just a wife without the sex. Not even a modern, liberated wife. You know that, don't you, Toms?* Another problem she's yet to deal with: Dani. If Dani knows about Morty's death, it would be from the news at large, perhaps that one-two punch in the *Times:* first the sprawling obituary (a color photo above the fold; how Morty would have swanned about the house had he lived to see it) and the subsequent "appreciation" posted on the next day's editorial page, adorned with a tiny engraving of a wreath.

"Am I tasting mint?" says Nicholas Greene, a forkful of salad midair.

"I toss a few herbs with the lettuce."

"Lovely."

They eat a few bites of food, sip their tea. Furtively, she watches him, the way he touches the corner of his wide mouth with his napkin. Impeccable manners, she observes, and she is reminded of the times she and Morty, after a night out at some public affair, would sit at this table and dissect the personalities.

"Can I ask what you'll miss most about him?"

Tommy is startled. "Well. This will sound strange . . . but right now what I miss most is the sound of his breathing at night. Which was loud. My bedroom is—was—separate, of course, but I'm a light sleeper. The last few years, we left our doors open. He was afraid—" Why is she telling him all this? She takes another bite of salad.

"Afraid?"

"Of dying, in the middle of the night, alone, no one to hear if he called for help. And then, in the end, he dies in broad daylight, outdoors—but alone just the same."

Nick, who rarely lets a conversation lapse into silence (of which he isn't a fan; in truth, of which he's afraid—there's *his* fear unmasked), reaches for something polite to say. He wishes the vibration of his phone in his breast pocket would stop interrupting his concentration. (He promised to leave it on; he did not promise to answer.) "Lovely, this salad," he says. (Didn't he say the same thing two minutes ago?) "Very fresh."

"If you were to visit in July or August," says Tommy, "everything would have come from our garden. Except the avocado."

"Yes. Quite!"

She must want him gone. *He'd* want him gone. But he is intent on winning her over. It's not just that she seems guarded. She's so . . . dignified. And she is younger, or seems younger, than he thought she would be. (Kendra told him he had the typically cruel eye of a caddish young man when it came to meeting women over fifty. "Like they might as well pack it up, hurl themselves down the nearest chute to oblivion. I see it in your shifty eyes," she said after that endless carnival of drinks parties in Toronto. If he looked shifty, it was surely an expression caused by digestive mayhem and overimbibing. But Kendra had to drive her point into the ground, informing Nick that if his mother were alive, she would still be wearing heels and dancing. "Except that she bloody isn't," he snapped. Another rung down that ladder.)

Tommy can hear Nicholas Greene's phone calling for attention inside his jacket. Should she be flattered that he ignores it? "I have to confess," she says, unable to tolerate the pause, "we hadn't seen *Taormina* yet. It was out of theaters by the time we heard that you were cast. As Morty."

"'Out of theaters'!" Does his laughter always sound so much like braying? "I wish we still lived in an era when such phrases had meaning. Most people seem to get their entertainment pirated these days. And then they watch it on a laptop while marooned in some airport or up all night in a panic over paying taxes. People watch films on their *phones*." How many calls is he ignoring? Will this person never give up? Probably Si. Nick is going to get hell.

"We didn't exactly see movies in theaters much, either," she says. "There's a monster Cineplex twenty minutes away, and that's about it. You can be in one theater watching a French love story, and if there's a shoot-'em-up thriller showing next door, the gunfire comes right through the walls. I think we keep our local video store in business." Will she continue to do that? She has a miserable vision of herself eating dinners, alone, in front of the flat-screen TV they purchased barely a year ago.

"Not to worry," says Nick. "There are a million things to see out there and not enough time. Films are becoming almost quaint." Should he offer to send her a screener, or would that seem cheeky?

"But people say your performance . . ." She stops, blushing.

"Whatever people say, it's not a film that will change your life, I promise you that, Ms. Daulair."

Tomasina Daulair—who still hasn't asked him to address her with the slightest informality—is rather striking for a woman of fifty-five: slim, with long silver hair worn loose. Around her throat she wears a dark, silken beach stone in which a small pearl has been embedded. Her faintly striped blouse is tailored close, autumnal in color, and her long velvet skirt is more dreamy than prim. A slit along her left calf reveals a glimpse of orange stocking. All right, full disclosure to self: he expected a whiskered, gum-soled spinster, a secular nun. Kendra wasn't entirely wrong.

"Do you want to answer that?" says Tommy, pointing at his hidden breast pocket. "Please go ahead, if you need to."

"I do not need or even want to answer it," he says with a vehemence that takes him by surprise. "What I'd like—and I hope it's not too forward—what I'd *really* like is if you'd show me around a bit."

"You still have time?"

"All the time in the world, Ms. Daulair." To reassure her that she has his full attention, Nick removes his mobile from his pocket and turns it off. Damn whoever this is, pestering him. He will call Silas from the car when he returns to the city. He will sit back and take whatever bollocking he's due.

And though she still does not put him on less formal terms, Ms. Daulair leads the way toward a back door. She takes a man's barn jacket off a nearby hook and shrugs it on before he can offer an assist. It occurs to him that she's taken excellent care of herself as well as Mort Lear, that dependent as she may have been on the prosperity of another, she is also independent as can be.

As she strides ahead of him along a flagstone path through the garden, a flash of orange leg catches the sun. Nick has to jog a bit to keep pace.

"You'd like to see the studio most of all, I'm sure," she says, and he heartily agrees, as he would if she had proposed they tour a potting shed—which only reminds him of the bind he's in, the things he knows that he's beginning to wish he didn't.

He watches her take a key ring from a pocket in the jacket (Lear's?) and unlock two separate locks. "Morty never worried that anyone would steal his work," she says as she pushes open the door, "but he kept some valuable items in here. As you'll see. Even out here in the country, you can't be too careful."

Stepping into the cool interior, Nick sighs. "Wow," he says, sounding as childlike as he feels. All around him—on the walls, on the surfaces of tables, no doubt in the many drawers and cabinets—are hundreds, probably *thousands,* of artifacts defining a life. Not just any life, and not just the life of a famous man, but the next life Nick will wear like a masterfully tailored suit. A bespoke role. A self as captivating and rich in varied destinations as an entire country.

"I know," says Ms. Daulair, "and it's the real thing. Or so we believe."

Only then does he see the Greek vase, in a fixed case, on a shelf above the great man's desk. "Oh, *all* of it," he says, "looks like the real thing to me."

Two

In what circle of hell do apparently spiteful, possibly demented art-ists punish unto eternity the patrons and curators who devoted themselves to polishing the artists' reputations and lavishing expert care on their work . . . only to be spurned, kicked in the proverbial jaw, when the artists finally keel over? Meredith Galarza now knows there is precisely such a place and that, undeservedly in the extreme, she has won a skip-death-do-not-pass-Cerberus ticket, express to that very station.

She takes out the folder of correspondence for what must be the hundredth time in a week. She reads the letter on top, the most recent (unless others went astray and, considering the state of the postal service, why not?) dated three months ago. One of the sev-eral ways in which she and the writer of this letter had bonded, or so she believed, was through their love of handwritten communica-tion. How painfully she remembers the glow she felt whenever her office mail contained a square envelope of the sturdy saffron-yellow stock on which he had written his personal letters for twenty-seven years. And how naïvely she took for granted that she would be the one to sort and archive thousands of missives written on that stock to hundreds of people over those years and possibly many more beyond.

Dear Merry,

As always, what a reliable pleasure to share lunch with you in the sultriest corner of our secret bistro, so outdated that even the canniest critics would pass it witlessly by—and a good thing, as they would sneer at its dowdy-yet-timeless offerings, its blessed blindness to the Next Nouveau. I seem unable to veer from my "usual" sole bonne femme, and I like to flatter myself that Jacques keeps it on the menu just for codgers comme moi. Vive le senescence!

While I won't deny a certain disappointment, I see the wisdom in shooting for what one might call "aesthetic diversity." Stuart's work and mine may not see eye to eye, but they occupy the same planet in relative peace, don't they? And what's in a name, especially the name of a gallery, some pompous engraving on a wall? Puts me in mind of tombstones.

I'm feeling in decent fettle—we won't talk about the heavy cream on that sole—and thus am not overly impatient, either. It's good news that the building is well under way, and how shrewd of you to aim for "carbon-neutral"[sic??]. Green-minded efforts do more than feather one's cap. They pull in the $hekels. In all affairs related to the arts, deep pockets are the only true insurance nowadays.

To have a "wing of my own" (pace Mrs. Woolf) would have been a dream come true, but if Stuart's on board for a "shared" enterprise, so be it. If anything reveals how swiftly times change, it just might be Stuart and his apocalyptic fantasies.

BTW, I am impressed by Enrico's work on the Ivo drawings. What would the slapdash memo-pad artists of the world do without magicians like him? He is our passport to posterity. Please be sure to pass on my gratitude and awe.

A bowl of soup summons; my nostrils detect ginger, that noble cleanser of arteries.

Yours as ever,
Mortadella

She can find no sign of his impending desertion here. He signed off with one of his playful, self-appointed nicknames (others she loved: Mortopoulos, Mortissimo, Mordred the Malcontent). And in the margin, he penned a steaming bowl of soup, above it a nose with flaring nostrils, beneath it a forked gingerroot . . . hinting, now, at a forked tongue . . . from which a long curlicued tendril of ink descends to become a kite string in the hand of a scrawled boy. Merry remembers the relief she felt on reading this letter—her conviction that she was more secure than ever in their partnership, in her future as the guardian of all things Mort Lear. (She feels another stab at the thought of his Wonderland collection, a further loss. Oh, that pair of 1920s evening gloves embroidered with the Mad Hatter on one sleeve, the March Hare on the other; how she had itched to try them on!)

Each time she reads this letter, with its collusive flirty tone (so go ahead and call her a fag hag) and its graphic embellishments, she is baffled all over again. She had even begun to fantasize that the Greek vase in his studio might come to roost at the museum. As recently as two weeks ago, she envisioned creating a partial facsimile of his studio as a foyer through which viewers would enter the gallery devoted to his work—like a literal gateway to the man's imagination. She hadn't had a chance to mention the idea to Mort—would it have made a difference?

How on earth could Mort have put the destiny of all his work and all his collections—including the drawings that Enrico had so masterfully saved from the swift entropy that dooms most works on paper—in the hands of that caretaker woman? How on earth could *she* begin to understand what to do with her boss's brilliant, prolific, and materially fragile legacy? The lawyer Merry had spoken to— Mort's lawyer—said something about his client's wish to establish a foundation that would fund a shelter for runaway boys. Forget the *why;* what, practically speaking, did this mean? That his drawings, manuscripts, and collections would be *sold* to fund this place? (Well, what else could it mean? Unless, even through the recession that had led to her husband's layoff and the loss of the insurance that covered in vitro, Mort was a crack day trader. The sale of his snug estate might bring five or six mil, but that was pocket change when you aimed to endow such a thankless if worthy mission.)

She spent most of that phone call in a sweaty, panicked delirium—

probably a preview of hot flashes, about which she's heard plenty of complaints from friends who don't see them as a minor price to pay for the gift of bearing children. Hot flash or mortification, she ought to have quickly and graciously ended the call, gone off and had a whopper of a drink, a good cry, or both, then lawyered up and called back on speakerphone for details. Such as, was his client in sound mind? (Could you enter dementia that fast? The will had been revised a month after Mort's cozy letter with the charming bowl of soup.)

Photocopies of every letter in the folder before her, along with every e-mail and faxed scribble that ever passed between Mort and members of the museum staff over the past eight years (nearly the same time Merry spent attempting to get pregnant), are now in the hands of the museum's board members and lawyers. She feels like a death row prisoner, waiting for the Supreme Court to grant her a stay of execution. Because without the keystone of Mort's artwork and papers, the new museum, as presented to the donors already on board, is in trouble. For God's sake, the floor intended to contain the Shine/Lear Collection is probably being girdered off this very minute, halfway across the city.

She looks grimly around her small, windowless office in the building she has regarded as a waystation en route to something sleeker, even modestly grand. Long Island City has grown hipper (and more expensive) around them over the past several years, but even a Frank Gehry or a Santiago Calatrava would be hard-pressed to turn this drafty, monolithic sarcophagus—hemmed in on three sides by taller industrial buildings—into anything with a vision, let alone a view. The new site, airier if not trendier, began as nothing more than a weedy, garbage-strewn acre of Gowanus Canal wasteland where a condemned casket factory had crumbled to the ground, its "vintage" bricks hauled away for salvage. Jonas Hecht, the architect they chose, immediately saw the forlorn setting as a favor from the gods. Unlike a building wedged between two skyscrapers at some imperial Midtown address, this structure would be filled with light and watery gleamings—and there was room to spare for a small parking lot. Good Lord, parking!

Privately, Merry has already fantasized about her view of the canal, possibly even a glimpse of the distant harbor.

It's driving her crazy that Mort's gatekeeper won't return her messages and calls. She has only the office contacts now, because of course Mort's cell phone is defunct. Why did she never bother to forge a personal connection with Daulair? *Because, you fuckup,* she tells herself, *you never thought you'd need her, not with your "direct line" to the Great Man himself.* Sometimes Merry fears that the so-called art world is turning her into a knee-jerk snob. It has already turned her, by necessity, into a social climber.

She will wait to hear what the suits have to say, the board members who have ruthless real-world jobs and salaries to match. And then it's likely she'll have to drive all the way to what she's always thought of as Lear's Lair in the mosquitoey wilderness beyond the suburbs. If she has to, she will beg.

Before leaving, she puts in her briefcase a photocopy of that magazine profile on which it is rumored a movie's being based. Well, more than rumored by this point. The actor who signed on to play Lear just won a dozen awards and is now the subject of magazine profiles himself.

How in the world any of this can help her cause, Merry has no idea. But not since her do-or-die last-ditch shot at childbirth-through-chemistry has she felt this desperate or determined. She texts the girl next door to take Linus for an extra loop in the park, since she will be getting home late.

If Linus were a cat, and if she drank Chardonnay and believed in the soul-cleansing powers of yoga, Merry would fulfill every single criteria defining a tiresome urban cliché: the well-educated, well-heeled, well-respected nouvelle spinster. Here she is, thirty-nine years old, her marriage shipwrecked on the shoals of infertility angst, her apartment stripped of rent stabilization (what *is* stable anymore?), careening perilously toward a size twelve, wondering if it's time to stop coloring her hair and whether, if she does, she'll luck into that stately shade of chrome, the one you picture whenever you hear someone—though is it ever a woman?—described as an éminence grise.

She tries, but fails, not to look at the framed sketch on the wall beside her office door, another of Mort's chummy cartoons. In a speeding car shaped like a snail, with a large Superman *S* mounted on the roof, two figures lean forward: in profile, Mort and Merry. Their faces, just a few strokes of ink, are gleeful, giddy with speed. They look like a pair of outlaws, Bonnie and Clyde as book nerds. The caption reads *M&M in their S Car GO!*

Mort had sent it to her after a lunch, two years ago, at which they shared an order of escargots and marveled at how or why people had come to eat these creatures in the first place, let alone regard them as a "delicacy."

Looking at it now, she realizes, feels almost exactly like looking into Benjamin's eyes just before they left that conference room after signing the divorce papers to go their separate ways forever. Benjamin had looked away first, quickly, probably dying to get back to the girlfriend he'd found all too quickly after moving out. Merry had to wonder if there had been, to put it discreetly, some "overlap" there.

But, to put it less discreetly, who could really blame him for growing cold toward a woman he must have heard, countless times, burst into tears behind the bathroom door at the sight of her own blood?

"Step away," she says to herself firmly. "Step away from the self-pity."

The thing to do, and she will, is to call her mother, a woman who embraced her later-life singlehood, years ago, with grace, even a wry sort of cheer. Merry's mother is a model of fortitude. She will know, the minute she hears Merry's voice, that her daughter is distressed. Without prying—though Merry could tell her about almost anything—she will calm Merry down. Calm is essential. Calm and then a plan.

The engine ticks as it cools. She holds the keys in her lap but does not reach to open the door. Through the row of dogwoods between the studio and the garage, the pool's slick cover glares darkly in the sun, as if indignant at being ignored.

Tommy cannot seem to get out. She keeps glancing at, then looking away from, the box on the passenger seat. It sits, unceremoniously, on top of the day's mail (dozens of pastel-colored envelopes: the tide of condolence continues to rise).

She heard little to nothing of what the funeral director said after handing her the mahogany box containing Morty's ashes. She does recall his giving her a plain, unmarked envelope—which she knows contains the receipt for all the charges associated with the "cremains"—and her subsequent refusal of a shopping bag in which to carry the box. ("How eco-smug we are," Morty would say whenever they remembered to shop with their own bags, a collection of colorful totes foisted on them at bookshops and literary festivals.)

Finally she gets out. She goes around the car to retrieve the box, balancing the bundled mail on top. In the house, she sets it on the kitchen table. She hasn't thought about where to put it or even, in the long run, whether she should open it and spread the ashes, bury it, or regard it as a portentous keepsake, a lead box containing a radioactive jewel. Morty left no wishes about what to do with his remains; cremation itself was a guess, based on casual remarks like "Someday, when I'm nothing but a heap of ashes . . ."

The junk mail she always discards at the post office. At home, she separates the true mail into personal and business, then the personal into letters addressed to Morty and those addressed to her. Normally, by far the greater share would be Morty's, and while the flow of generic fan letters has hardly dried up, letters and cards to Tommy have begun to proliferate. Among them, she recognizes Dani's awkward script immediately. She forces herself to open it first.

Dear Toms,

I saw the news. That's sad. Jane and I want you to know we're thinking of you. What a shock. When I was with you and Morty in the fall, he seemed in great shape.

We're all okay if pretty sleep deprived (me and Jane, that is). Joe is growing like a weed. Maybe it's my imagination, but he's looking like Dad. Definitely the eyes.

Call sometime if you like. You know where we are. Jane sends a hug.

Yours,
Dani

So now it's on Tommy to close the rift, isn't it? She can't help feeling annoyed, however unfairly. All his life, Dani has stirred up in Tommy a strange stew of exasperation, concern, and guilt.

Tommy was, typical of eldest children, the obedient one, the good student, the make-no-waves, so-mature-for-her-age daughter of hardworking parents. Dani wasn't exactly the opposite—he did nothing malevolent or hurtful—but he was a boy's boy, restless and prone to inadvertent trouble, a shirker of homework and curfews. Their mother was always telling him—in her liberal-pacifist-we-love-you-no-matter-what tone of voice—how worried she was that he wouldn't find his way in the world if he couldn't take school seriously.

"Or just find your *passion*. God knows even your daydreamy sister is passionate about her books, and I'm sure she'll find a way to make hay of that passion, even if she doesn't make a lot of money. Because life is not about money, and neither is happiness! As your father and I have always tried to show you by example. We are well off because we know how lucky we are to have what we do. Most of all, the two of you."

Dani's teenage resistance took the benign form of turning sullen, resistant to communication. Back-talking, with which their friends could so readily enrage their own parents, only made Mom or Dad sit Dani down for a "centering talk" or some "collective deep breaths." Even when he discovered Pink Floyd and Aerosmith, and tried to deploy their music as a blaring form of disrespect, a pointed push-back to his father's hallowed blowin'-in-the-wind, let's-be-Woody-'n'-Arlo nostalgia, that backfired, too.

"Sit me down, Danilo, and help me get an ear for this music," their father said one evening over dinner. "I want to be enlightened. I mean it!" (Never mind that Dani's music drove *Tommy* nuts.)

At the time, Tommy took it for granted how "all-accepting" her parents were—even after Dani was suspended for spray-painting the back wall of a local school with a group of devil-may-care (but hardly delinquent) friends. It wasn't as if they covered that wall with obscenities; they simply mounted a battle cry for freedom, painting in large, sloppy letters something like RIZE UP 2 REBEL! or YOUTH

REBELZ ROOL! Juvenile, insipid stuff. He had just started his senior year in high school.

Dani's mother, after picking him up from the precinct, told him that she was glad he had the urge to express himself, but he needed to "channel it differently." All this she reported to Tommy over the phone. Tommy had been working for Morty, at his apartment, for two years. She was twenty-four and had just saved enough to rent a studio in the East Village.

Tommy was content to listen to her mother's all-suffering complaints, and then Mom said, "So your dad and I have a proposal." In an effort to separate Dani from his circle of what she called "overly expressive" friends, they came up with the notion of paying part of Tommy's rent in exchange for having Dani live with her during the week so that he could attend a more liberal high school up in Manhattan, perhaps even make a more promising set of friends. On weekends, he would return to Brooklyn.

Ever the obedient daughter, Tommy said yes. Because she spent long days working at Morty's place, often staying till six or seven, Dani met her there after school, instead of going back to her apartment— which was dark as well as cramped. Morty's place occupied the top two floors of a brick town house. The lower level had been sculpted into an open, loftlike space, airy and colorful, strewn haphazardly with large cushions where Dani could curl up with his Walkman and do his homework (or go through the motions). He clearly liked it when they stayed on for dinner.

Tommy enjoyed cooking—like her apartment, her skills were modest but made her feel grown up, the way reading Thomas Hardy had made her feel grown up a decade before—and though he never said so, it was obvious that Dani was just as grateful as Morty to be fed.

It was unsettling, however, to see Morty and Dani together. It forced her back to her childhood, to those afternoons at the playground. As they ate together in the kitchen (Morty sometimes standing by the counter, on the phone), she could tell that Dani had no recall of the connection—but what if a memory was tripped by this renewed proximity? And Morty treated Dani almost *too* kindly. Once he even said, out of the blue, "You know, if you graduate and can't figure out what to do with yourself, I'll find you something, somewhere. I have plenty of friends with interesting jobs. You don't need to worry about moving back in with your parents. That's a fate worse than an IRS audit."

Then it happened; Morty apparently couldn't resist. (And why *should* it be a secret?) The three of them were eating Tommy's cheeseburgers when she noticed that Morty had gone quiet and was staring at Dani. So abruptly that it startled her, Morty looked at Tommy and said, "Did you ever tell him?"

Dani turned to his sister.

"No," she said. "I didn't."

"Finish up," Morty said to Dani. "I want to show you something. But no—don't rush. Slow down, my friend, or you are going to choke." He got up from the table, took his plate to the sink, and told them to join him in the studio after they finished.

"What's he talking about?" said Dani.

"You'll see," said Tommy, but she couldn't meet his eyes.

After he had finished the last of his sister's sweet potatoes as well as his own, they took the spiral staircase to the upper level. Morty's bedroom was at the back; the rest of the floor comprised a glass atrium where he wrote and drew. To Morty, this aerie was ample justification for walking up four steep flights of stairs just to be home.

He was arranging a row of drawings across the wooden table at the center of the room. "Dani," said Morty, "meet Ivo. If you haven't already."

Merry wants a martini—or three—but she's sitting across from Sol, the smartest and least arrogant of the museum's directors, so she orders a glass of Sancerre, vowing to sip it slowly rather than roll up her sleeve and ask the waiter to inject it directly into her arm. (She imagines pulling from her purse one of those blue rubber ties brandished by nurses. "Pump your fist, darling," the fetching gay waiter would purr.)

"Sol," she says, "I'm so grateful you could make it."

"Merry, no one's more shocked than I am. What the hell happened here?"

God, is he blaming this on her? Well, of course he is. Maybe, in fact, it is Merry's fault. Maybe there's a subterranean corollary between the failure of her marriage and Lear's postmortem slap in the face. She tries to channel her mother's fortitude.

Sol orders a martini.

She tells Sol how she's pored over the correspondence and can't see any sign of displeasure—or not enough that he would pull the rug out from under her. (She knows that she needs to stop taking this personally, but since she can never speak face-to-face with Mort again, what difference does it make?)

"The only thing I can think of is that he didn't come clean with me about equal billing with Stu. I should have made it clear that his art was the deal breaker, not Stu's. Maybe I didn't handle that diplomatically enough." Christ, was she being submissive? Enormous mistake.

"Did we ever have it in writing from Lear—his intention that we would have custodianship of the work?"

Merry would love to lie or obfuscate, but she can't. "Apparently not." She has plunged deep into the well of e-mail going back nearly a decade. Nothing. All those conversational assurances—at their lunches, at the museum fund-raisers—are pointless. (Didn't he mention it in a keynote? Do they have that keynote on video?)

"A halfway house for runaway boys? Oy." Sol shakes his head.

"Well, are you up for fighting such a cause?"

"We do have a lot of his work in our possession. That gives us bargaining power. We could salvage something if we negotiate with his executor—Tomasina, right? Please tell me you've done nothing to put her off. Because look, even if we find 'proof' of his promise at the back of some forgotten file, we can't look like the litigious family of the little old lady who leaves her nest egg to the local animal shelter."

The waiter conveys a brimming martini glass to their table with the concentration of an acrobat on a tightrope. The wineglass is, of course, barely half full.

Sol owns several blocks of the Meatpacking District—or what you might now call the Haven't-we-met-on-Twitter? District. Not that he would know Gansevoort from Little West Twelfth. It's all Monopoly to him. But people respect Sol, no one more than Merry. If not for Sol, the Contemporary Book Museum would still be a pop-up shrine in her broom closet (an amenity she can kiss goodbye in whatever future abode her jacked-up rent will force her to choose; or perhaps that abode will have to *be* a broom closet).

"I'm going to be honest, Sol," says Merry, reminding herself to *sip* the wine. "I have always focused on Mort. I feel as if I am perfectly friendly with Tomasina, but we are nowhere near chummy, and I can't remember the last time I saw her in person. I took a lot for granted, I have to confess." Global understatement.

The waiter is hovering. Sol orders oysters for both of them, an elaborate list of two this, four that, six whatever. Which earns them a basket of hot corn bread. Merry decides that the stress she is under justifies corn bread. But no butter.

"Look," she says. "I think I have to go out there and visit her. She's not answering my messages. I suspect that with all she's handling, we are nothing but a headache. I need to reassure her that we are her ally in preserving Mort's legacy."

"Do you suppose," says Sol, "we could find a way to merge the interests of the boys' home and the museum? A joint philanthropic-arts something or other?"

Merry almost coughs her ninth sip of Sancerre onto the shiny blank plate awaiting her oysters. "Like what, bunk the boys in our museum? Offer them internships with Enrico? I can't imagine what you're thinking."

"I'm not thinking anything concrete," says Sol. "I'm just creating portals of thought." He winks and takes a large bite of corn bread.

Portals of thought? Is this really what Sol meant to say? And what was that wink about? She notices that he is looking trimmer than the last time she saw him. He is easily twenty-five years her senior, but he has the boyish luster of a prosperous man with a deservedly well-paid trainer.

"I wish this were a time for humor," says Merry.

He sighs. "The summer gala . . ."

"I know. My thought, before all this, was that Mort would help us announce the rollout." Their annual glad-handing party—extra lavish this year because they plan to introduce the architect to their patrons and show off a model of the museum—is a month away. They have reserved a new party space in Red Hook, overlooking the harbor, and plan to run a shuttle bus for those who want a glimpse of the nascent structure.

"There's Shine. Who is, in some ways, bigger. Sexier."

"That's a stretch, Sol." From a younger perspective than hers, what he's said is true, however, and it's also depressing—though not in a million years would she say so aloud. Shine is the pen name of Stuart Scheinman, a dystopian graphic novelist whose beefy biker body is as littered with eclectically grim tattoos as his speech (among adults) is with raw expletives. There are rumors that he was an Idaho skinhead in his teens, anything to hide that he was an outnumbered Jew. Only midway through his twenties, he's built a vast, amoebalike fan base among urban and wannabe-urban teens of both genders (and the growing demographic of those in between). Progressive educators give him credit for steering the Snapchat generation back toward real, turn-the-pages books, just as J. K. Rowling did for the Nintendo crowd.

The idea of the rollout is to spotlight the children's literature wing of the museum, the obvious media bait in a city now powered by adults for whom bright, accomplished children are the sine qua non of social status. They wax sentimental about the likes of Sandra Boynton, William Steig, Eric Carle, and Suzanne Collins, clever creative types who helped them (or their nannies) steer their children toward Stuyvesant High and the shimmering Gold Coast of the Ivies beyond. If Merry is cynical about the skewed ideals of these adults, she is not cynical about the books their children loved. She reveres those books and, to some extent, their authors—among whom Mort Lear is a god. Now that Merry has also been appointed the first director of the Consortium for Outer Borough Museums, it would be devastating if this snub were to tarnish the launch of the new museum.

She must shed the fantasies she had of making her entrance on opening night with Mort at her side, her manicured hand on his sleeve, radiant in their mutual pride.

Sol wants to talk about plans to draw adequate traffic from the museum district of the Upper East Side and the gallery glut of West Chelsea all the way to nether-Brooklyn. Merry assures him that by the time the museum opens, they will be in a prime cultural location.

"Merry, this is the you I know and have confidence in," says Sol. "Both delphic and positive in your predictions."

"Thanks, Sol." She hopes his patronizing praise is merely a side effect of his second martini. "I'm going to solve the Lear problem, but I think I need a change of subject now."

They wind up debating whether Staten Island is the next Brooklyn, and in the lull between the main course and the cheese plate, Merry dutifully asks about Sol's three fortunate children: one at Harvard Law, one tinkering with fitness apps out in Silicon Valley, one about to deliver twins.

Which leads to Sol's mordant commentary on what it feels like to know he's about to be bumped one generation closer to death.

By dessert (unadorned berries for her, molten chocolate cheesecake for him), Merry is exhausted and wonders why she thought this meeting would produce any useful solutions to the crisis. All it's produced is her reckless promise to solve it herself.

"I'm glad we've figured out what needs to happen," says Sol. "You're good with the artistic egos, the care and maintenance. That's no minor talent." He grins.

Is that her signature talent? Merry contemplates the epitaph: STROKED ARTISTIC EGOS WITH THE BEST OF 'EM. "I don't want to think too hard about that," she says. "What it means."

"What it means, Merry, is that you're astute. Likable. Unspoiled."

Merry lets the conversation rest there. The truth is, she feels as if she has lost her balance. Getting it back is not so simple.

At the coat check, as Sol beckons her into her jacket, he presses a hand lightly against the small of her back, shocking her briefly with the cold touch of the zipper bisecting her dress. "A nightcap?" he says. "I'm staying in the city tonight."

Merry moves toward the door and faces him only when they're on the sidewalk. "Sol." She tries for a tone more reasoning than shocked.

He smiles ruefully. "A man about to be a grandfather needs a little novelty now and then."

Merry lays a hand against his tie and says, "You'd be in big trouble if I were ten years younger."

"I know that." He is already scanning the avenue, over her shoulder, for taxis.

"But believe me, Sol, I'm flattered." Has she offended him? Christ.

"Merry," he says, "let's pretend I never went there. As you said earlier, let's not take too much for granted." He flags down a cab and says, as he opens the door, his smile now pure courtesy, "Here you are."

The cab flies along like a speedboat, bouncing on potholes as if they were waves, passing through one just-green light after another. Merry thinks, *Here I am. Here I am.* Recently, her mother told her to appreciate her young body, to really feel how lucky she is to be where she is—in the prime of life—rather than fretting over all the things she doesn't have (or won't ever have in the future; like, say, grandchildren and the luxurious sense of mortality they bring). "When you are my age," her mother said, "you will look back from the prison of your arthritic joints and your fading eyesight and totally untrustworthy mind and you will wish that you had been thankful for every single minute of your twenties and thirties—even your forties, which you have yet to enjoy!"

But what did Sol mean by repeating her foolish mea culpa, her confession of taking too much for granted? Oh God, here come the tears.

She is glad that she runs into no one as she takes the stairs to her apartment. As always, Linus somehow recognizes her footfall and launches his barking salvo when she is thirty feet from her door.

"Only me, only me," she murmurs as she greets him, leaning over to rub his floppy ears (telling herself to appreciate that her spine and legs allow her to bend so far over without a twinge). She tosses her computer bag and her jacket onto the couch and goes to the kitchen to check the dog's water bowl and give him a tiny biscuit.

She was going to sit down and write a real, heartfelt letter to Tomasina Daulair, but she is too discouraged as well as too tired. In the bedroom, she kicks off her heels and lies on her back on the bed without undressing. Linus jumps up beside her, and she folds him against her left side, into the crook of an elbow. Her dress will be covered with his reddish hairs, but never mind.

"Linus," she says, "please tell me your day was better than mine."

On days when she's lingered in the apartment for hours, to read a good book or make a meal for friends, Merry has noticed how Linus follows a particular swatch of sunlight that migrates across the living room rug and up onto the couch. That patch of warmth, to him, is utterly sublime. For a few years, her marriage to Benjamin felt like that. Being with him at the end of a long workday, or through a lazy weekend, was like following a slice of sun across a soft, richly patterned carpet. Was she selfish to want a child so badly? Benjamin had told her, toward the end, that it didn't matter to him whether or not they became parents.

Did she always want too much? Or was she beating herself up merely for her own perfectly respectable longings?

Merry met Mort ten years ago, when both she and the book museum were ingenues in their world: bright-eyed, yearning, optimistic. She had conceived of a small but gemlike show based on beloved child protagonists from illustrated children's books: a gallery filled with original images, one each, of Eloise, Harold, Homer Price, Fern Arable, Harriet the Spy, and their literary compatriots. No animals (sorry, Frog and Toad, Horton and Lyle) and no adults (ditto, Mrs. Piggle-Wiggle, Miss Poppins, Doctor Dolittle). Some of the illustrators were long dead, but a few contemporary characters were crucial, and Merry had her heart set on Ivo.

Her boss, the museum's original director, was skeptical that Lear would cooperate. He was at the height of his fame and yet, perhaps not so ironically, in retreat from the social limelight. He also seemed to have retreated from picture books. The *Inseparables* trilogy continued to ride a wave of conspicuous favor. To Lear, the director told Merry, Ivo was surely a relic of his past, no matter how immortal that book might become.

A return letter from Lear's assistant, expressing cordial regret, confirmed this speculation—which only deepened Merry's resolve. So she took the train to Orne on the following Saturday, a festive October day of splintered sun and skittering leaves. From the station, she walked the two miles to Lear's house. She felt absurd as she walked along the driveway, carrying a shopping bag containing a gardenia plant—what was she thinking?—and she half expected some alarm to go off. But she reached the house without deterrence or even apparent notice. She was about to follow the walk to the front door when she saw the building out back, clearly an artist's studio. Through the window, she could just see the artist himself, working.

What would he do, shoot her? Call the police? She did not have to summon the courage to knock, because he opened the door.

"A visitor," he said, sounding neither pleased nor disapproving. He glanced at her bag. "Bearing gift, it would appear. Was I expecting you?"

"Not really," she said. "No."

He did not invite her in, but he did not close the door. She noticed, first and foremost, the horizontal smudge of charcoal across the pale blue shirt, bisecting his subtle paunch, a mark left by a table's edge. He wore loose jeans and a pair of ramshackle moccasins.

"I'm Meredith Galarza. I'm from the museum that wants you to lend us a drawing of Ivo. I know you said no, you turned us down, but I thought that maybe, if I could just talk to you, tell you how much it would mean to us, to *me*, then . . ." *Then you might say yes,* she couldn't quite say. Really, how ludicrous.

"Come in," he said. "I happen to be in search of distraction. You'll keep me from eating another candy bar. Would you like a candy bar?" He waved at a bowl of miniature chocolate Hershey's bars.

She took one and thanked him. But then she felt too self-conscious to take off the wrapper. "Go ahead and eat it," he said. "I like that you didn't assume the safe stance of refusal."

Had she been a child and told that she was in Santa's workshop, she wouldn't have been half as enchanted and amazed as she felt stepping into this room, not large, low-ceilinged, but impossibly, exquisitely cluttered and crowded with sketches, constructions, jars of brushes and pencils. . . . There were even sketches taped to the ceiling above a drafting table. Sketches of clouds, washed over in pale blues and pinks.

"Tell me about your show," he said. "After you finish your little chocolate bar. And please eat more. I stole these from the ammo supply for Halloween. I love chocolate. I loathe Halloween."

"Oh, I hate it, too," she said, relieved that she could mean it.

He took her tiny crumpled wrapper and pointed to a rolling stool in the middle of the floor. He asked her what she had in the bag.

"It's a plant. I was brought up to bring something when you go for a visit."

He took the bag and removed the gardenia. He pulled away the tissue, closed his eyes, and inhaled the fragrance of the forced blossoms. "Heavenly." He set the plant on a wide windowsill. Then he settled in a large leather armchair and regarded her, waiting.

She told him about the characters so far featured in her show—as if they were the artists, not the creations. "So I want Ivo," she said, finally. "I want him very badly. I want him as the star."

Mort Lear smiled casually through her gushing, inane soliloquy. After a pause, he stood up and walked past her. Was he going to kick her out, just like that?

He disappeared behind a half wall toward the back of the room. Listening astutely, Merry trembled with anticipation when she heard him opening drawers to a flat file. She knew that precise sound, that soft rolling grumble, from life in a museum. To Merry, a flat file was a treasure chest. She loved the casual privilege she had to slide open such drawers, whenever she liked, to take out and marvel at any of the works they contained.

Lear came back around the wall cradling a broad sheaf of papers, which he set down at the edge of a vast wooden table that was filled, from end to end, with manuscript pages and sketches, along with two stained mugs and a plate peppered with bread crumbs. He cleared a large space in the center and then, as she watched, laid out three of the drawings from *Colorquake.*

"Clever of you, showing up in person," he said. "Also, coming while my assistant is out on errands. I won't ask if you lurked at the foot of the driveway until the coast was clear."

Would one drawing suffice? She could pick from the three that lay before her.

She shot up from her stool to join him at the table. The stool rolled a foot away. Quick, she thought, before the assistant returns.

"This one." On impulse, she chose the largest sheet of paper, the one divided into three cells: Ivo in the basement, so engrossed in his painting that he doesn't notice the earthquake. "Oh, thank you," she added. "Really?" Why oh why, she thought, did she add that caboose of verbal insecurity? What a *girl* she sometimes was.

After a short, awkward silence, he said, "Tell you what, Meredith. I'd like to see your museum. So how about we make a lunch date. I'll bring the drawing with me. You give me a tour. I promise not to change my mind. And lunch is on me."

She wanted to snatch the drawing and bolt. *Thank you! Yes! Contract to follow! Don't want to miss my train!* Not that he could ever have simply let her walk out with it. She reminded herself to breathe. "I suppose you need to consult your agent."

For an instant, the look on his face alarmed her. "I don't actually need to consult anyone, Meredith."

When he beamed at her then, she had a strange dropping sensation in her gut, the kind of inner collapse that signifies falling suddenly and hard, a feeling she knew from Fede, her first grown-up boyfriend, and earlier flames; from, most recently, Benjamin. Lear was twice her age, but when he smiled like that, she could see in his face the roguishly magnetic younger man, the one whose picture was tucked inside all his books published after the first edition of *Colorquake.*

"You have gumption," he said. "I look forward to our date in the city." He asked for her card, which she fumbled from her wallet (which she fumbled from her bag). "I'll call you," he said. "I will."

He saw her out. "No car?" he commented, looking around. "Or did you park out on the street, to be sly?"

"Well, yes," she lied—although what if he insisted on walking her to the road?

He didn't. She hurried, suddenly aware how lucky she had been not to be waylaid by the assistant. (When she said no, had the woman even consulted her boss?) As she turned onto the road, a car turned in behind her, from the opposite direction. Merry quickened her pace, afraid she might be stopped, but she wasn't.

He did call her. He brought the drawing, with paperwork drawn up by the assistant. He took her to lunch, where they drank a bottle of wine (or perhaps he drank a glass and she drank the rest). Lunch lasted nearly the entire afternoon, and when Merry returned to Benjamin's apartment, she was still tipsy. She made love to him that night with a ferocity that pleased yet alarmed him. "If I didn't know any better, I'd say you're falling in love with somebody else," he said, afterward, in the dark.

"Don't be ridiculous," she said, laughing through her innocent lie. Because she had in fact been imagining Lear beneath her, and not the younger, bygone Lear but the fleshy man in the tweedy jacket who had flirted over lunch the way only gay men flirt with women: safely (unless the woman harbors false hope) and dangerously (because he can still, if chastely, break her heart).

Over the next ten years, she had come to see her relationship with Mort like a meta-marriage. Even Benjamin could tell when she was dressing not just for work but for lunch with the Great Man. And once she knew she was losing Benjamin, she had assured herself, however pathetically, that she was secure in the consolation of Mort.

But clearly she wasn't.

Through the window across from the bed, cars, unseen three stories below, cast a pulsing tide of bluish light onto the ceiling as they turn toward Gramercy Park. She shifts her gaze lower and sees the glint of the glass in the frame that protects the drawing she brought home last month, just as a covert loan. Now it taunts her. It's the picture of Ivo in the forest, his outstretched arms adorned with flying creatures, their feathered and gossamer wings filling with color. If she were never to return it to the museum, especially now that the collection must be returned to Orne (or must it?), she wonders if anyone would guess its whereabouts. She would never sell it, of course. She could live out her husbandless, childless years, with Linus and then another dog, and one or two others beyond them if she's lucky, and even if she were to leave the drawing displayed openly in her bedroom—her next bedroom, wherever that will be once she's forced to move—who would ever see it?

She gets up and turns on a lamp. She goes to the framed drawing, takes it from the shelf, and carries it back to her bed, where she holds it in her lap. "Ivo as Saint Francis," some people call this image. But what a beautiful child. So—there—she would have a child after all, wouldn't she?

Three

Tomasina was twelve when she decided she would rather be Tommy. This was the year she became fully conscious of how much she disliked being lumped together with other girls, being seen as typical in any way. Her mother called her an "obstinate nonconformist," making it obvious that her daughter's individuality pleased her. "I'm an *ist,* too," she said. "A leftist optimist activist feminist!" Tommy's father laughed, kissed his wife, and said, "Call me a recidivist hedonist satirist anarchist!" Out came his guitar—he loved any clever exchange that might inspire a song—and he improvised some verbally gymnastic goofball lyrics. The singer-mathematician Tom Lehrer was his idol.

Tommy's parents loved making music, but to "pay the avaricious piper," as Dad put it, they ran a travel agency on Bleecker Street. They worked every weekday till six o'clock and took turns on the weekends. After school, Tommy looked after her brother. He was in kindergarten that year, and it seemed like all he ever wanted to do was run, climb, and leap—often from a sidewalk into the street. Looking after Dani was like being in charge of a raccoon or a cheetah, a wild animal prone to mischief and speed. Dani couldn't stand the confines of their apartment, so Tommy took him as often as she could to the library (her preference) or the playground (his).

So of course she hated that she hated math, because girls were *supposed* to hate math. This was the source of her quiet fuming as she sat on one of the playground benches, watching Dani go up the ladder, down the slide, up the ladder, down the slide, over and over until Tommy began to wonder if she could hypnotize herself simply by watching. But the alternative—dividing fractions—might just kill her.

She had become aware that a man sitting a few feet away from her was sketching her brother—or possibly pretending. She couldn't see the paper. It was well into April, but the day was cloudy and bitter, so there weren't many children or mothers around. Tommy had been drilled by her parents on the necessary suspicion of strangers, no matter how nice they seemed (especially if they seemed *too* nice), and already (if only because the man had a ponytail, a silver bracelet, and wore a girlish paisley jacket she might have liked to own herself) she had assessed this one as a possible pervert. She didn't feel unsafe—the playground was a fishbowl, surrounded by sidewalks and traffic—but she was on alert.

She slumped back and raised her eyes to the branches that crisscrossed overhead. Their tiny budlets had sprung forth just this week; furtively glancing sideways, she saw how the limey glow tinted the man's blond hair ever so slightly green. He had a squarish little beard to match. The word *beatnik* drifted through her mind. She'd heard her father say, to one of his musician friends, that the era of the beatnik was over. He sounded sad.

She nearly slipped off the bench when the bearded man spoke.

"Looks like you're avoiding something." He did not look up from his drawing, but he was speaking unmistakably to her. They were the only people on the bench.

"Excuse me?" she said, because pervs could not be ignored.

"The book in your lap," he said. Now he laid his sketch pad aside, between them, and Tommy could see that the drawing was a good one, even upside down.

"I'll get to it," she said, using her oldest voice.

"I don't mean to be nosy," he said, "but I saw your name. It's the same as the last name of some famous authors. Who wrote a book about Greek myths."

Tommy knew it was time to go. It gave her the willies that he was looking at her name on the cover of her workbook. She would have to drag Dani off the slide and bribe him to go back home or he would protest; they'd hardly been there fifteen minutes. Dani knew how to make a scene like nobody else. She would have to use her allowance to buy them a Sky Bar or a jumbo Tootsie Roll. But because she hated the man's condescension, she answered him. "I have that book. Everybody I know has it. The name is different. It has an apostrophe and an *e* at the end." Decisively, she put her workbook into her book bag.

The man laughed softly. "So it does."

She stood and called out, "Dani, let's go! It's too cold." She pulled down her skirt, conscious of her yellow tights. Her father was always saying her skirts were too short, her mother telling him not to "die on that hill," an expression that Tommy found ominous. It sounded like war talk, like something her social studies teacher would mention when he talked about Vietnam during current events.

Predictably, Dani ignored her, not even pausing in his ascent to the top of the slide. He sat, stretched his arms out wide, and pushed off.

"Your brother?"

Tommy struggled not to answer the man. This did not deter him.

"He's quite nimble. And fearless."

"Dani!" she called. "I'll buy us something chocolate!" She wondered if the man would now offer to buy them both chocolate: the classic lure. If he did, should she go to the package store across the street and ask the man at the counter to call the police?

"People who aren't parents or guardians aren't supposed to be here. There's a sign on the gate," she said. Better to warn him off directly.

"Who says I'm not a parent?"

Maybe he was a perv, but he also had the look of one of her father's artistic friends, the people he jammed with on Saturday nights: from the peace-sign patch sewn onto his jacket to the black high-top sneakers. Were the paint stains on his ragged jeans for real, or were they a ruse?

"Where's your kid then?" She felt her own pulse, hot in her throat.

He smiled steadily at her, but he raised his hands in surrender. She noticed how smudged they were with pencil and ink. "Well, you caught me there, my friend. I come here just to draw. I've seen you and your brother before."

Enough. Tommy walked over to the slide. "Hey. Come on. Really. You can choose the candy." Finally, she had her brother's attention. She was thankful when he took her hand and let her lead him toward the gate.

"But I get two and you get one," he said. "Or I get the big half."

It took an enormous effort not to look at the stranger again as they left the playground. He remained on the bench, but she could feel his eyes following her, along with his amusement, as she latched the gate. She could tell he knew exactly what she was thinking. That didn't mean it wasn't true.

The next day she made Dani go with her to the library, where, as he did too often, he angered the librarian: this time not by playing with the buttons on the elevator or racing up and down the aisles but by sneaking away while Tommy was hunting for a book, setting off a ruckus that was instantly identifiable as a cascade of volumes tumbling from their shelf.

The day after that, a day of buoyant warmth, she had no choice more logical than the playground. Dani found a schoolmate in the sandbox, and they set about digging a pit with the friend's toy tractors. Tommy took from her book bag the one novel she had managed to check out of the library before they were given the boot: *The Return of the Native,* ostentatiously above her grade level. She settled onto the shadiest bench along the iron fence. Dani's friend was with his mother, so she could immerse herself happily in the sure-to-be-tragic scene of Egdon Heath.

"Hello."

The voice came from above and behind her, on the other side of the fence.

The man with the sketch pad.

She frowned and tried to resume reading.

"I brought you something—or, really, it's for your brother."

"We don't want anything from you," she said, without turning around again.

But he was slipping something through the rails of the fence, to her left: a book with a colorful jacket. Attempting to hide her curiosity, she took it. The title was *The Boy Who Was Afraid of Being Afraid.* The author's name was Mort Lear.

"Would you let me come in without calling the cops on me?"

"Why should I?" But she twisted to face him.

"That's my book. I mean, I wrote it."

Tommy turned the book over; opened it. There was no photograph of the author. "How do I know that?"

"My word," he said. "And this." He extended his sketch pad through the fence. Hesitantly, she took it. At first she saw no sense to the gesture. And then she realized that he meant her to compare his sketches with the illustrations in the book.

The illustrations were, she had to admit, graceful and enticingly dark: not goofy or clunky like the condescending art in so many children's books. She turned around and said, "I don't know why you keep pestering me. I'm too old for this book anyway."

"Well, first, Miss Daulair, the book is for your brother, not you. And my 'pestering' is also about your brother, not you. All I want is to draw him for a few days. Here. In the playground. Without your treating me like I'm a hoodlum."

"Why does it have to be my brother?" she said. "Don't you have friends with kids?" She barely held back from saying, *Or maybe you don't have friends.*

"I like the look of your brother," said the man who claimed to be Mort Lear. "Or what I mean is, I like the look of him for a new book I'm writing—and drawing."

"Are you going to try and make him pose? Because good luck with that," said Tommy. "He's not going to do what some stranger tells him. Not even if I tell him."

Why was she cooperating?

"Will you let me come in without blowing the whistle on me?" Mort Lear said in a low voice. He reached through the fence to take back his sketch pad.

"Do what you like," said Tommy. "I don't really care."

When he came around through the gate, he walked up to her and said, "So let me try this again. Clean slate." He held out his hand. "I'd like to introduce myself. My name is Mort Lear, and I live over on Greenwich Avenue and Bank Street, and I like drawing kids because I like making up stories for kids. And I'm lucky enough to have a publisher, even if they don't pay me a whole lot."

Reluctantly, she shook his hand. "Tomasina Daulair."

"Ah. Well, it is *pronounced* the same way."

Dani's friend's mother was watching her now. "Everything cool, Tommy?"

"Sure!" she said.

She handed the sketch pad and the picture book back to Mort Lear, but he wouldn't take the book. "That's for your brother. But you might like it, too. I don't think anybody ever outgrows a good story." He glanced at the book in her lap. "I'm pretty sure Thomas Hardy would agree. Is that your first of his? I'm partial to *Tess*. Dickens is much better, though. Or try *Middlemarch*. That's a masterpiece."

"Look," said Tommy, who had never read another word of Hardy, or a single word of Dickens, though all these names were familiar to her from the classics shelves at the library. "Okay. You can stop trying to make me like you. Draw Dani if you really want to. But only when we're here. We are not going anywhere with you. And I'm not saying anything to him, because believe me, somehow I'll get in trouble."

"That's perfect." And just like that, he opened the sketch pad, took a pencil box from the pocket of his paisley jacket, and started to draw. After a moment, when she hadn't stopped staring at him, he said, "Back to your Victorians, Tomasina Daulair."

As the trees in the playground grew leafier and the sun leaned in closer and jackets were shed, Mort Lear was a frequent (if barely conversational) companion, as close yet indifferent as a shadow. Dani began to notice him, but when he asked his sister, "Who's that man?" she said, "Oh, a friend of my art teacher." This satisfied Dani, whose current obsession was learning to swing as fast as possible, chimpanzee-style, from rung to rung on the overhead bars.

The book Mort Lear had given her, she kept to herself. If she gave it to Dani, their parents would ask where it came from. It was a strange story, about a boy who was so cautious toward the world around him—so fearful of running into things that might scare him—that his parents didn't know what to do. Finally, they arranged for him to spend time with different adults who did jobs that most people would find pretty scary: a beekeeper, a cave explorer, a mountain climber, a helicopter pilot, and a firefighter. Hardly ever were the adults pictured; only the boy. But the captions to the pictures—in which he wore an odd headdress and gathered golden honey (which he then spread on toast); discovered a glowing underwater cavern with beautiful fish; scaled a cliff to visit a family of mountain goats; flew over a city made rosy at sunset; and quelled a forest fire (from which flocks of birds rose in gratitude, spelling their thanks on the sky)—were the words of the wise people who did these jobs every day. Somehow they were always offstage—or tiny figures, way in the distance.

Being brave, said the firefighter, the last of the boy's mentors, *doesn't mean never being afraid. There's no such thing as never being scared. Being brave means knowing your fear, even being friends with your fear. You want it to tell you when to push past it and go on ahead, when to hold its hand and walk side by side, or when you're better off following, walking in its footsteps.* All you could see of the firefighter were the toes of his large rubber boots.

One day, sitting on the bench beside Mort Lear, bored silly with math yet again, Tommy said, "Can I ask you something about the book you gave us?"

"Sure."

"How come you didn't include a soldier?"

Mort Lear had paused in his drawing, but he kept looking at it. He didn't answer. Maybe he didn't know what book she meant.

"The book about the boy who's afraid. I mean, a soldier is somebody who has to do something scarier than anything. Kill people. Maybe even get killed."

"Why do you think about that?" he said.

"Well, like duh, there's a war right now. My dad says he's lucky, being the age he is, or he could have been drafted. He says he would have died of fright before he could even get to the fighting."

Mort Lear seemed to ponder this for so long that Tommy wished she had kept her mouth shut. Then he said, "I'm lucky like your father. I was the wrong age for all the wars in my lifetime. I don't want any children to think about that before they have to. I don't want to make anybody have nightmares."

"My social studies teacher says nobody wants to talk about the war and that's why we're still there when we shouldn't be. Silence is a cop-out. It's just as bad as fear."

"She's right," Mort Lear said quietly.

"He," said Tommy. "He drove an ambulance in Korea. Another war."

Mort Lear went back to drawing. Tommy thought she saw tears in his eyes. Had she made him feel ashamed?

"I liked the pictures in the book. Your drawings are good."

"I treasure that compliment." He smiled at her briefly. "I do."

Suddenly, summer arrived. The last day she and Dani went to the playground before their two-week family vacation (this time on Cape Cod, where Tommy knew they would hop and skip from one place to another, to sample "getaways" for her parents' clients), it occurred to her that she should tell Mort Lear they wouldn't be around for a while. But it happened to be one of the days he didn't show up. At dinner, their mother announced that Tommy would be going to a sleepaway camp in Massachusetts right after their vacation. "You will love it. All art and drama and books. Even books! At a camp!"

"So who'll be with Dani?" asked Tommy.

Her father laughed. "You'll miss that? Spending your precious time with, and I quote, 'the little monster'?"

"Well no. I suppose I won't," she said, feeling cornered.

"We're going to hire a sitter to take Dani to day camp in Central Park," her mother said. "Business is picking up! People are going places! And so are we! Your father and I are going to find us a bigger apartment. Maybe in Brooklyn. How about a room of your own, Miss Virginia Woolf?"

Tommy was walking back from school on Court Street when she first saw the book. For over a year, they had been living in Brooklyn, where they rented a tall, skinny limestone house, and Tommy had found what Dad called her quotidian groove. She liked to stop at the Italian bakery, halfway home, and buy a bag of pignoli cookies. The bookstore, a block closer to home, was another favorite stop, though it meant holding off on eating the cookies, which was awfully hard when the smells of the bakery still lingered in her nostrils, especially if the cookies had just been baked and their warmth had spread through the waxed-paper bag in her hand.

She was already devouring the cookies, her fingers coated with nutty oil, when she stopped in front of the bookshop, brought to an involuntary halt by the display: the same book again and again, stacked up, lined up, fanned open. The little boy on the cover, facing the prospective reader, meeting your gaze directly, was Dani. He wore his most mischievous smile, the one that made Tommy (when she was in charge) worry what on earth he had just done and whether she'd be in trouble because of it. He wore denim overalls and a white T-shirt. His bare feet were dirty. At his side, he held a fistful of paintbrushes, an artist's bouquet.

Above the many copies of the book, a board hung from the ceiling on fishing line. MEET THE AUTHOR! SATURDAY STORY CIRCLE, 10 TO NOON. ALL AGES WELCOME!

Tommy rolled up the top of the cookie bag and stuffed it in her book bag. She wiped her oily fingers on her skirt and walked into the store, where the girl at the counter greeted her by name.

Tommy realized that she was shaking slightly as she reached for one of the copies on the display table.

"For your brother?" said the girl at the counter. "Maybe a little young for him."

"No," said Tommy. "I just—just like the drawing." She wished, for the first time, that she were a stranger here. And couldn't the girl see that the boy on the jacket *was* Tommy's brother? Wouldn't anyone see that?

She carried the book to the back of the store, where there were tiny chairs and tables. She set her book bag on the floor and squished herself down onto one of the kiddie chairs. She heard the bell at the door, grateful the girl would be distracted.

Ivo. The boy was named Ivo. Watching him move from page to page—climbing, reaching, crouching, then running, wrestling with a panther, swinging from branches, sleeping in the grass . . . Tommy felt as if she were being transported back to the playground near their old apartment in Greenwich Village. Here was Dani in a pose he took at the top of the slide—or concentrating on digging a hole—or racing through the sprinkler the first day the park lady turned on the jets.

After closing the book, she sat for several minutes, uncomfortably, at the miniature table. Why did she feel as if she had committed a crime? She hadn't done anything wrong. No—she had helped Mort Lear make this book. Shouldn't she be proud?

But what she felt was the fear of being discovered. Of her parents seeing the book in the window of this or another store and recognizing Dani. Because they would. And then they would wonder. And they would ask.

And what about Dani himself, once he saw his own face on the cover of a book? Or maybe Dani would be pleased.

Tommy went through the next few days waiting for the discovery. She only half absorbed the books she was reading, the history she was supposed to be learning, her lessons at the piano. Her heart would accelerate the minute she heard a parent's key in the front-door lock.

On Saturday, Tommy stayed inside all morning; to even step outside would have been to risk running into Mort Lear, going to or from his time at Story Circle.

As the days and weeks passed, and other books took the place of Dani's book in the shopwindow, Tommy began to feel strangely angry. It wasn't as if she'd gotten away with something; it was as if Mort Lear had gotten away with something.

But all these feelings faded as another summer loomed, the welcome return to the arts camp where Tommy could fully become her obstinate self (the Most Different Girl), away from her father's homegrown folk songs and her brother's burgeoning muscularity, the loudmouth antics of his friends in the room next to hers.

By sophomore year she had an after-school job shelving books at the library, and she started a club she called Plays for Non-Actors, where students who didn't want to be one of the show-offy theater kids could read plays aloud together. She had forgotten all about Mort Lear—until one afternoon, on the subway, she saw a little girl clutching a cloth doll whose features were printed to look like Ivo's. Tommy changed seats to get a closer look. She had the sensation that the doll was looking right at her from across the rackety car. She thought, My brother became a drawing and then a book and now a doll.

The weird thing was, nobody seemed to know except Tommy.

Not long after, she went away to college in Vermont, where she majored in English literature and spent so much time reading novels and poetry and plays that at first she forgot to have much of a social life. Her friends were the students she studied with, most of them girls. At last, in September of her senior year, she let a boy (one who read as much as she did) kiss her. His name was Scott, and his favorite writer was Henry James—which meant, she warned herself, that he wouldn't know much about happy endings. But Scott, like Tommy, had thus far neglected to listen to his hormones, and so—in the age of sex-for-all-and-all-for-sex—they took shelter in their mutual shyness. For two months, they did little more than kiss. They moved beyond their bruised faces to necks, shoulders, arms, even ankles. They kissed in library stacks and common rooms, along wooded paths and in sandwich shops, behind a white clapboard church, beside a Civil War plaque inside a domed memorial, and finally, finally, Tommy let him undress her in his dorm room and do what they had both wanted to do all along. After the first time, they laughed at each other on and off for hours, at how silly yet how sensible they'd been to hold off.

That's when Tommy realized she had to wake up and find something to do after college—as if having sex introduced the idea of intercourse with the wide world itself. "What are you planning to do next?" she asked Scott. "After they kick us out of here."

"Law school," he said. "What about you? Graduate school? I can see you teaching. You're patient that way."

Did Tommy want to teach? She didn't think so. Nor did she see herself as patient; cautious wasn't the same as patient. "Maybe library science?"

Scott shook his head. "Librarians are going high-tech. Have you had a good look at the library here? Those people are glued to their computers all day."

Scott asked her if her parents weren't pressuring her to do something practical. "My dad totally rides my case. He told me literature is fine to wallow in if you're rich."

Tommy told him how her parents prided themselves on never pressuring their children to do anything other than what they loved. She knew that her father's true passion was songwriting, that making music with friends was the work he lived for. She also knew that her parents' business wasn't what it used to be—thanks in part to the computer nerds who were taking over not just the libraries but the so-called travel industry (as if "travel" were a manufactured commodity, churned out on conveyor belts). She could never ask them to help with graduate school.

Scott got into Stanford Law. His father told him that for the summer he had to buckle down and make money, so he went home to Chicago and waited tables at a tourist café near the art museum. "Maybe you could visit, take the train out?" he suggested while she watched him pack, but his tone made it clear that he didn't expect this to happen. Tommy wished she had chosen a Jane Austen scholar for her first boyfriend, but she understood, objectively, that they were still so young. He was leaving her for another place, another way of living: for another chapter in his no-longer-literary life, not for another girl.

Worse than breaking up with Scott was having to move back into her old bedroom in Brooklyn. Dani was working for their parents at the agency (his penalty for a dismal report card), and they didn't have another job for Tommy.

She walked up Court Street to see whether she could work at the bookstore.

What block was the bookstore on? Wasn't it supposed to be just . . . here?

The bookstore had vanished. The space had been divided up into a bank branch with nothing but a pair of ATMs, an overilluminated Thai restaurant, and a cosmetics shop. She walked farther uptown.

The Italian bakery was gone. So was the shop where a father and son had sold fresh mozzarella, twisting and knotting it right before their customers' eyes, as if the cheese were rope.

When her parents came home that night, Tommy expressed her astonishment at how much had changed—and how fast.

Her mother took on a mournful look. "Oh, the gentry wave has hit."

Her father said, "Look who's talking. We were the wedge, you realize that."

"I'm Italian," protested Mom.

"Half," said Dad. "Half Italian, half bohemian. Bohemians are deadly to a neighborhood like this. We are the toe in the door, the canary in the coal mine, the nip in the air." Out came the guitar.

That week, walking the streets just for the sake of staying away from the house, Tommy saw that the ethnic community her parents had chosen for the safety of its Mediterranean coziness (and nosiness) was dissipating. Looking through row-house windows, she saw funky patterned curtains in place of metal blinds; in front yards, the stucco saints were vanishing one by one, along with the lawn chairs where Italian women had smoked or crocheted, gossiping about their husbands, who worked as longshoremen or butchers or hung out too much at the social club on Court (now a Laundromat).

Tommy's father reassured her that she deserved a little vacation after doing so well in school, time to "find her feet." She did the shopping and vacuuming and some of the cooking, but mostly she walked and she read, plunging into long, heavily plotted novels. On random afternoons, she took the F train to Manhattan, getting off at West Fourth to wander the streets in her first neighborhood as well. Everything in the Village was changing, too. There were perfume stores where there had been dry cleaners, video stores in place of musty caverns selling tools and paint or yellowed maps and botanical prints. Her parents had moved the agency to Brooklyn Heights; the rent, not the commute, had driven them out. On Bleecker Street, a wine-tasting bar occupied the storefront where they had started the business twenty years before.

But there were still plenty of bookstores. In them, Tommy found refuge from the heat and consolation from all the unsettling changes; new books might arrive daily, but none would displace Hardy or Eliot or Tolstoy. She tried to summon the nerve to ask for work, but she failed.

She was in the basement of the Strand, leaning against a table looking at a cut-rate art book, a volume filled with glossy reproductions of the Sistine Chapel ceiling, when someone leaned across the table and murmured, "Tomasina Daulair?" Jolted, she raised her eyes to meet those of Mort Lear. He was short-haired, clean shaven, and he wore a pair of owlish tortoiseshell glasses, but she knew him instantly.

"It is you, isn't it?"

"It's me," she said.

"You're all grown up. Now you really are a Miss Daulair. Pardon me; a Ms. Daulair."

Stupidly, all she could do was stare.

"Do you still live in the neighborhood?"

She closed the art book. "No."

"You disappeared on me."

"We moved. I didn't realize . . ." *I was just a child,* she wanted to say, except that it would sound pathetic. "I saw your book. Your drawings of Dani."

"I probably owe you a princely sum."

What did he mean by that?

"That book bought me my apartment," he said. "And things of greater if less definable value."

Still she was mystified. Clearly, he wasn't going to leave her alone—though she didn't want him to leave her alone. How odd it felt to stand nearly eye to eye with him now. They were no closer in age than they had been on the playground, but while she felt eons older than twelve, the changes she could see in him were mostly a matter of altered fashions. If anything, he looked younger, like a photograph brought into better focus. Had he always been so handsome?

"I would like to have met your family, you know—properly."

"The book is beautiful," she said.

He looked at her intently, as if he were judging a contest. "I wonder if you realize . . ." He laughed. "Come with me. I mean, I want to show you something. Here in the store."

So she followed him through the heedlessly book-littered aisles of the basement, past the desk where a pair of sour-smelling employees were slitting open cartons of battered, has-been books, to a part of the store she didn't know: the children's section.

It was clear, from the Siberian location of these overflowing, underlit shelves, that the store did not cater much to children. There would be no Saturday Story Circle here, no tiny tables and chairs encouraging patrons to bring their toddlers. But right away she saw it: the small bookcase dedicated to Mort Lear's books, crowned with a display of Dani's book. She also saw, right away, the two gold medals affixed to its jacket. And here was a copy in Spanish, another in . . . Hebrew? On a shelf below was a gift box containing two cloth dolls: the Dani doll, like the one she had seen on the subway six or seven years ago, and a panther doll. She picked up the box. "Wow."

"I'm practically a franchise," said Mort Lear, "and sometimes I think that your not turning me in to the playground police led to my being a rich man."

"You're rich?" she said, immediately regretting it.

"Yes," he said, in a surprisingly straightforward way. "Well, by normal standards. And fortunate. And, you know, even happy. Which children's authors are not supposed to be. Trust me on that."

They faced each other, Tommy holding the gift box to her chest.

"So what can I do to repay you, Ms. Tomasina Daulair? Name a favor and it's yours. Something more than a triple ice-cream cone."

Before she could stop herself, she said, "Help me find a job?"

Four

She and Franklin sit side by side at Morty's desktop computer, an expensive machine, both brawny and sleek, that he used for e-mail, record keeping, and late-stage design decisions, once his finished drawings and stories came together as books. He used it to tinker with fonts, make color adjustments to page proofs, record additions to his collections, and—Tommy notes the folder labeled *Book Museum*—track loans of his work and his most valuable antique editions. The Cadillac, he called it—or the Commandant, on days he felt resentful toward technology for the ways in which it had shanghaied the making of a book.

Franklin has opened a virtual folder called *NFP DOCS,* which contains pdf files of forms related to obtaining not-for-profit status. Franklin clicks on *Mission Statement,* a one-page draft of a proposal to create a residential and social-services center for homeless boys. . . . *Ideally, we want to repurpose a large (industrial?) building in a high-needs neighborhood. (U of AZ collaboration??) We would engage a local architecture firm to gut and retrofit (etc. etc.). A garden space, preferably enclosed, is essential. . . .*

"Did he write this?" Tommy cannot imagine Morty using the word *retrofit.*

"I gave him some advice," says Franklin. "I thought he could . . . explore it. See what his intentions would entail, practically speaking."

Tommy notices his evasiveness. "You knew more about all this than you are letting on."

Franklin turns in his chair. "Two months ago, he dropped by my office and said he wanted to talk. I'm paraphrasing by a long shot, but he told me he'd decided that if he was going to be remembered for something, put on some kind of Mount Rushmore, he'd rather have it be for 'doing good' than 'being good.' For making things happen, not just making things up. He seemed agitated. It wasn't my job to ask why."

"Morty made lots of things happen. Good things." She needs to think about this before she can say anything more to Franklin. Morty was upset. He was unreasonably upset. But she did not expect him to act on it—not on a scale like this. She says, "Let's get started on these files."

Together they read, Tommy aware of Franklin's citrus cologne, the comforting heat of his body through his pale-green cotton shirt-sleeve; for the moment, she isn't alone in this mess. She never noticed before that Franklin is left-handed—which surprises her, considering that he's eaten with them on and off for five years. For a decade before that, it was Bruce, who bequeathed his boutique firm to Franklin when he retired. It's still small, its clients entirely local—Morty the whale among the minnows (or maybe not, considering the rumored ballooning of wealth behind Orne's hedges). Morty defected from his large, multipartnered big-city firm after having a ten-minute conversation with a total stranger, in the Orne village drugstore, about how to find decent firewood. The stranger was Bruce.

Franklin slides the open file up and aside on the screen, opens two more, one a scanned letter from a child-welfare agency in Phoenix, the other a letter from the director of Eagle Rest, the resort (once rugged, now refined) where Morty and his mother lived when their names were still Frieda and Mordecai Levy. Both letters are dated about a month ago. One pledges counsel and assistance, the other money (though neither writer gives specifics).

"All of this," says Tommy, "is . . . it's just that he told me *nothing.*" In the letter attached to the will, one of the dictates that makes her heart sink is the paragraph that directs her to *auction off my collec-tions and to sell and* widely disperse *my work as necessary with the express intent of funding the Mort Lear Foundation and the social service facility, as described below, that I would like to call Ivo's House (unless some fat-cat do-gooder offers a hefty sum to attach his or her name).*

"I'm sorry."

Franklin is in his late fifties or early sixties. Like Bruce before him, he's been a frequent adviser to Morty. Tommy knows, from joining the two men during the meetings that turned into meals, that Frank-lin has two grown sons, both married. He's been divorced from their mother since the boys were in their teens. Is he attractive? she won-ders as they breathe quietly side by side, taking in the documents and their contents. She has never looked at him like that before; why now? Now that Morty is gone, will she begin to think of herself—or worry that others see her—as a spinster? Does anybody think in those terms anymore?

"I knew this was why he established the new trust," Franklin says. "And, of course, the new will. I told him I thought he should look into it further before putting it down on parchment. But that was Morty: seize an idea first—run with it—then do the research later. I'm sure you know that much."

Tommy thinks of Ivo, heading into the forest without his mother's permission (not that his mother is around to ask). "Do you think . . . he was doing this rationally?"

Franklin hesitates. "Are you asking me if he was in his right mind?"

"I don't suppose you'd answer that."

"Not my job, assessing people's mental fitness." He smiles at Tommy, meeting her eyes over the glint of his reading glasses. "But I had no reason to think he wasn't. I did offer to talk to a law school classmate who helps bankroll safe houses for teens in trouble. He pointed me to the director of a place in Portland. We had a brief conversation, and I passed the woman's number to Morty. That's a kind of mecca for runaways. The railyards . . . There's a whole sub-culture of kids on their own. You can imagine what goes on, what they resort to."

"Oh God," says Tommy. "I don't want to."

"Nobody does, right? So it's heroic when somebody wants to do something about it other than put them in juvy. You have to guess that Morty was thinking about his 'legacy.'"

And, Tommy thinks, about what might have happened to him if his mother hadn't found out what her son was enduring—or hadn't chosen to sacrifice their security to take him far away. Morty's books are filled with boys out in the world on their own, some by choice, others by chance. And when they're not alone in the world, they're often alone in the sanctuary of their imagination.

As for Morty's "legacy," what she won't be telling Franklin about—why bother?—is the tantrum Morty had (and it really was a tantrum, belligerent and shrill) when he found out that the children's wing of the book museum had been reconceived to give as much weight and stature to the work of Stuart Scheinman, a man Morty regarded as a "closeted Nazi" and a "barely literate comic-strip dweeb." This was, no coincidence, not long after Stuart won a MacArthur.

At too many recent book festivals, Tommy saw Morty eye the much longer lines of fans waiting to have a signed Shine. Not that Morty's star had fallen, but Stuart's ascendance looked as steep and sure as the takeoff of a jumbo jet, and he cultivated a physical presence that led critics to call him "one of a kind" or "an off-the-grid visionary" or even "a hip-hop Shakespeare for Generation Tattoo, the last remaining hope for the future of the book." There was also no denying that Shine's characters, though they occupied a narrow range of experience (street smart, tough, rebellious to the core, frequently even homeless), were varied in their ethnicity, earning him praise for, as one reviewer put it, "addressing a refreshingly diverse audience, a pomo-punkster-grunge fantasy rainbow."

"Oh for God's sake, let's all sacrifice a few goats at the shrine of political correctness" was Morty's reaction.

"Stuart didn't write that review," said Tommy.

"But I'm sure he's crowing all over town about it," Morty fumed.

Whenever Shine's name came up, or whenever he and Morty were at the same literary function, Tommy could feel the tension in Morty, as if he were a boy whose girl had been stolen, as if he were literally itching for a fight.

The crowning insult (in Morty's eyes) was when Stuart, at one of those festivals, had bid him farewell with "See you at the next one, pops!" Tommy had no luck persuading Morty that Stu meant it fondly, even ironically; that he was, underneath his blowhard shtick, a well-meaning guy.

"Right. And Hitler loved dogs!" bellowed Morty.

Tommy knew better than to argue with Morty when he worked himself into a humorless lather, but she had never seen him so vitriolic about a fellow author. "I suggest you keep associations like that to yourself," she said. "I mean, not from me, but from . . . you know, friends of yours who might not feel the same way."

"I'm no poker player," he said curtly.

"Yes, but you garden," said Tommy.

"What the hell does that mean?"

Tommy said, "You have faith in the seasons. That what goes around comes around—what's properly planted and tended will always steal the show." She had no idea where this came from, but it seemed to appease Morty.

"Tommy," he said, "will you marry me?"

Morty had begun to issue these mock proposals after Soren died. Tommy didn't find them as endearing as he might have assumed, but she let them go. (She had, at some point, become a master of letting things go.)

Tommy pushes back from the computer. "Want a sandwich, Franklin?"

"In fact, I do," he says heartily.

"What I don't get," she says as they leave the studio, "is how he ever thought I'd be up to this."

Franklin holds open the door to the kitchen. "Not to insult you, but he didn't. His long-term plan was to set it all up for you—with my help—letting you bask in the glow of his goodwill from the grave."

"He told you that?"

"Well, it's what I told him he'd have to do. Or we'd have to do."

Clearly reading her expression, he says, "You know he loved you. Like a daughter."

Franklin can't know, and wouldn't understand, how this wounds her. Was she, after all, as Soren had mocked her, Lear's "little Cordelia"?

"Two nights," says Nick. "Maybe three. I'll put the driver at a B and B in the village, so I have him on call. The place is a trove of—"

"Three nights?" says Silas. "Andrew wants you out there the minute your cummerbund hits the floor on Monday morning. He thinks you're avoiding him. They're working out the kid's schedule, and Andrew wants the two of you to meet."

"Avoiding Andrew? Rubbish. I *do* know what's good for me, Si." Why does Nick go on the defensive like this? Why does he so easily, instantly feel like a child when others question his judgment? Literally, it might be true that he's avoiding Andrew—just putting him off a bit—but to a worthy end! Yet stating his plan out loud does make it sound like a private folly, absurd and self-indulgent.

Nick and Silas sit in a corner booth of the hotel bar, its twilight halogens obscurative enough that Nick, who faces the wall, feels relatively safe from intrepid fans, at least till the two of them go their separate ways for dinner. He's made no concrete plans, and right now he's tempted just to eat in his room, though it makes him feel like a social refugee. Friday night alone in front of the telly? He needs to ring Tomasina from somewhere quiet, somewhere he won't be interrupted. He promised he would ring her as soon as he confirmed dates with his manager. And then there's the e-valanche, the digging out from under the messages that pour through the pipeline every time he clicks on the envelope icon. Sometimes he feels like the Sorcerer's Apprentice, heaving buckets of water against a flood. Most of the e-mails are from his agent in London, who needs answers yesterday on the Stoppard (a dream, but the schedule's pretty impossible) and the Edinburgh *Hamlet* (he could go down like a minor *Titanic* on that one)—and by the way, isn't it beyond high time he employ a personal assistant? (Since the Kendra flame-out, he's felt the need, however irrational, to handle his private life as independently as he possibly can.)

"Look. Here's a plan: I head to L.A. first thing Monday, then make a quick turnaround for a weekend at Lear's. You'll know exactly where to find me."

"And if the wrong person peeks through a hedge, so will the rest of the world."

"It's not like I'm made of bone china," says Nick. "Or like I'm Tom Cruise."

"Lord, let's hope not." Silas glances at his phone, frowns, and pushes it away.

"I'll keep the room here. In case I have to flee."

"I suppose you're a grown-up."

"Some people think so." Nick winks at his manager.

"An incredibly stubborn grown-up."

Evidently not enough of a grown-up, thinks Nick, to employ a manager who wouldn't dare talk to him like that. Or who wouldn't dare answer his buzzing phone—not that he doesn't have other clients to deal with.

Silas gestures that this is a call he has to take and carries his phone away from the booth, into the alcove by the coat check. Nick signals the waiter through the thickening crowd of weekend celebrants. Maybe it really is time for that personal assistant, someone as devoted to Nick as Tomasina Daulair was to Mort Lear.

Tomasina—he's simply started to use her first name, cheeky though it may be—has agreed to let him stay at the house for a couple of nights. Nick persuaded her that to know Mort Lear well enough—now absent the chance to spend a few hours with him in person—and to portray him more than superficially, Nick needs (or would dearly love) to spend two or three days among the man's belongings, eating off his dishes, paging through his books, greeting the day as he had done. He promised to "keep a low profile," to provide for himself, to observe any boundaries she sets.

She seemed skeptical (in point of fact, she looked briefly as if her heart had stopped), but when he described his intensive correspondence with Lear, told her some of the stories they had shared (the innocent ones), she went silent for quite a few long seconds. They were standing in the studio, where she had shown him Lear's collection of Alice in Wonderland novelties (and that rather lasciviously illustrated antique vessel), and finally she said, "I had no idea."

Nick said, "That we connected?"

"That you were writing to each other."

"Well . . . I suppose it just . . . you know, to be honest? It surprised me. I can't claim that we became friends—that would be an exaggeration—but I was devastated when I heard the news. It felt . . . personal. Does that sound ridiculous?"

Again he seemed to have robbed her of words. Much as the silence tempted piercing, he waited.

"I'll think about it, and I'll phone you this evening," she said. "Though you probably won't give me your number, will you?" She smiled slyly.

"You bloody bet I will," he said.

She rang him while he was still in the car returning to the city. "I may be out of my mind," she said, "but this is what Morty would have wanted. And I have to warn you, nobody but you. Same as today. I won't have people tramping through the bushes again. And don't let your director think that I would ever—"

"I am perfectly clear on all that," said Nick. "Crystal clear. Thank you."

Silas returns to the table. "Sorry. Misha. Listen—you're sure about this?"

"Sure as rain and fog," says Nick. "And I'll catch up with Andrew tonight."

"I'll have Linda book your flights. Out Monday, back Thursday?" Silas slides his card into the wallet containing the check.

"Brilliant. Thank you."

"But while you're out there—at Lear's—you'll stay in touch?"

"Goes without saying," says Nick, and once again he feels as if decades have slipped from his age. His mother has given him permission to venture alone, just a few blocks, to buy himself a sweet. A kind son, an attentive son, he offers to buy her one, too. No, she says; she's watching her figure. She denied herself so much—and, in the end, for what?

۶ی

From the moment *Colorquake* won the Caldecott—an event that took place entirely outside Tommy's narrow adolescent consciousness—Mort Lear became a revered and envied figure in the domain of children's books. More than that, however, the sudden prestige of his book (and all the intellectual suppositions flocking around it like crows or gulls, a lot of inconsequential flap and clamor) seemed to empower that entire domain, as if authors who wrote for children had been a small army lying dormant, waiting for their moment to conquer the world's attention.

Well, perhaps that would be an overstatement, but when Tommy started to work for Morty, she sometimes spent her idle time browsing through the file folders (everything stored on paper back then) in which he had saved the numerous clippings, citations, fan letters, and invitations that filled his mailbox daily following the publication of *Colorquake*. That first year, he had been invited to give commencement speeches at half a dozen institutions (accepting none, though later he would learn to tolerate wearing a robe and mortarboard over a suit in the heat of early summer). He had been invited to visit teachers' colleges in Australia and Poland; he had been offered the use of a summer house on Lake Geneva. That was, she sleuthed between the lines, the year of the wealthy boyfriend on Mykonos. She has never seen pictures—surely there were pictures, perhaps torn to shreds in jealousy or rage?—but she knows his name was Panos. The one other souvenir of that liaison is a far less valuable cultural artifact, hanging in the back of the pantry: a facsimile icon of Saint Phanourios (his name printed, in English, on the back). It's a tourist keepsake, but Morty did not like the idea of discarding a saint, no matter how cheap his incarnation. "He's one of those guys you pray to when you've lost stuff—your car keys, your contact lenses, your faith in humanity—and God knows what would happen if you tossed him out or gave him away. You just might lose everything."

Morty's success was the most dangerous kind, he liked to say, because it was intoxicatingly sudden and fierce. "The kind of success that causes spiritual nosebleeds," he said at one dinner party during the Soren years. "The kind that bucks you off and breaks your bones."

But he was old enough to stay on that horse, to breathe at that altitude. He spent the first windfall on his duplex in the Village. He learned how to tell the useful invitations from the frivolous, how to say no cheerfully enough that he would not make enemies but firmly enough to make it clear that he understood the value of time.

When Morty wrote Tommy her first paycheck, which he did in her presence, ripping it from a black ledger he pulled from a desk drawer, she noticed right away the name of a major investment bank embossed on the cover. But in most ways, even if he bought his shirts at Paul Stuart and ate twice a week at Raoul's, he was still the sneaker-shod beatnik artist she'd met when she was twelve, the man to whom she had given a brave if ingenuous scold about the importance of telling children the hard truths they need to know. (He would tease her about that for years.) Once, hanging her coat in his closet, she spotted the paisley jacket. Sun had faded the fabric across the shoulders. He no longer wore it, and one day it simply wasn't there anymore.

It's rare, everyone knows, for an artist of any medium to surf the crest of the wave for very long. Yet across three decades Morty's name never faded in esteem or recognition, though his prominence in book news waxed and waned according to his productivity. For several years after *Colorquake,* he alternated between publishing books all his own and illustrating the words of other authors, as if to spread his light around. He collaborated with a director at the Met, creating sets for Philip Glass's opera *The Juniper Tree.* One Christmas, he designed a suite of department-store windows; the next, a collection of dinnerware for a Japanese ceramics studio.

And then he retreated—from fashionable consciousness, at least—emerging dramatically with the first novel of his trilogy for teenagers, which came out in the midnineties, winning him as much praise and as many awards as *Colorquake* had. Over four years, he produced the second and third novels; all together, *The Inseparables* had sold, in hardcover, more than ten million copies in English alone.

Tommy, who by then had been working with Morty for more than ten years, watched him struggle with his own burgeoning hubris. They would even joke about it. (She, to him, as he entered the kitchen after receiving the biggest royalty check of his career: "Your head still fits through that door?" He, after an invitation to the White House: "Do shrinks shrink egos? Maybe I need one after all.") But Tommy also knew there were certain professional slights that, while hardly personal, wounded him cumulatively—and these were nothing to toy with.

Since the publishing cluster bomb detonated by the Harry Potter series—followed by the high-toned spiritual controversy of *His Dark Materials* and the quasi-feminist siege of *The Hunger Games*—the kind of children's books that succeeded in "crossing over" had risen to establish a ruling class from which Morty and his work were somehow exempt. Morty admired Rowling, Pullman, and Collins—he spoke glowingly about their books on panels at booksellers' conventions and in radio and morning television interviews—but he drew the line at another rising group of artists he saw as impostors: not all graphic storytellers, no, but those he regarded as little more than scribblers of glorified comic books, stories he saw as rife with gratuitous violence and aesthetic anomie. "They're a cancer on literature," he said the week that Shine's second novel (or "novel my royal Jewish ass," as Morty put it) commandeered the first page of the *New York Times Book Review,* earned a gushing notice in *Library Journal* and a minor fanfare in *Time* magazine.

It didn't help that Morty's new book at the time, a spin-off of his trilogy called *Moocho and the Afterlife,* told from the dog's point of view, did not replicate the popularity of its predecessors. Reviewers praised it, but a few hinted that, charming and uplifting as it was, its author might have left well enough alone.

So when, just a few months ago, Meredith Galarza let him know about the "split showcase" she and her colleagues had dreamed up as the heart of the new galleries dedicated to children's books, Morty returned from the city in a rage so profound that he hardly spoke above a whisper when he told the news to Tommy. "'The yin-yang of classic versus cutting edge' is what she now envisions," Morty said.

"And she *breezed* her way through that lunch, chitchatting the notion up as if she couldn't possibly imagine that I might find it benighted, stupid, I mean never mind fucking insulting!"

There was no point in Tommy's pretending she didn't see the insult—or how insulting the change in plans must feel. She asked if he had let the director know his feelings.

"Tommy!" he shouted, startling her. "Do I listen to you? Of course I do! I *held my tongue*. I *smiled through my spaghetti*. I even offered to *pick up the tab*. I thought I would vomit."

"I've never suggested you not stand up for your interests. I only meant—"

"It's a done deal, Tommy. I heard it in her voice, saw it in the way she buttered her goddamn bread—stop me before I call her a gluttonous cow. Oh sorry, did I just do that anyway? The point is, there are plenty of other institutions out there. Her pet museum is not the end-all and be-all, I don't care if Frank Lloyd Wright rises up from the grave and wrests the gilded T square away from that vain metrosexual they've enlisted to build it. On the Gowanus Canal, of all places. Embalmers' Canal is more like it."

"So what are you saying? Are you going to just take back your promise, take your toys and go home?" Tommy regretted the words as soon as she'd said them.

"Do not talk to me like that, ever. Like I'm your child," said Morty. "If I decide to leave my scrawlings to the Playboy Mansion, that is my goddamn prerogative and you will arrange their fucking first-class passage to Holmby Hills."

She lowered her voice. "Morty, your work will outlast Stuart's, if that worries you in the slightest."

"Worries me? *Worries* me?" He laughed angrily. "Tommy, what worries me is whether I might die of a stroke standing next to that graffitied buffoon like I'm his lapdog at whatever circus they expect us to put on when they build their little palace by the cesspool."

"Morty, stop. You need to go back and talk to her. Or one of the trustees. Go over her head. You can't—"

"I can do anything I like," he said. "I can also not do anything I don't like. Maybe what I want is my own museum. Maybe I'll change my will so that this place—this very house—turns into the Museum of Mort Lear when I die. Just think: my very own gift shop, filled with artifacts and mementos of me! Or maybe I'll have a pyramid built on the back lawn and have it all buried around me like King Tut with his mummified posse of catamites and lapdogs."

Before Tommy could think what to say, he rose abruptly from the kitchen table and made for the stairs without bidding her good night. The next day, neither of them mentioned his outburst. Tommy assumed he was embarrassed, that he hoped she would forget he had ever exploded. Apparently she was wrong.

So now this: broken promises, hurt feelings, an Everest of paperwork in two different time zones. So much for her timid, peacekeeping instincts, her make-no-waves advice, for a way of life that won her few friends of her own. This is how you end up a spinster in charge of a refuge for runaway children.

Dear Mr. Lear,

Where to begin? Obviously, perhaps, by thanking you for taking my telephone call and permitting me to poke and prod at your life. I write to you now from my underheated flat, where I am in a period of blessed, blissful solitude between projects—in fact, preparing for what I think of as "yours." Preparing to become Mort Lear, to swim down deep into your story, even your self, as it's been presented to me—but by others, by writers who have never even met you. Which is what I long to do—and am grateful you've agreed to allow when I come to New York in the spring.

It's a rather outlandish livelihood, the one I've lucked into. (To be honest, I've also stubborned into it, survived into it, endured into it; perhaps, in your own endeavors, you've sometimes felt the same way? I am ridiculously far behind you, of course.)

As I told you on the phone, I remember your book Colorquake *from my childhood. (Hardly the only literate or even semiliterate adult who does, I know!) I wasn't an only child, but I might as well have been—my two older half siblings were a pair, close in age, with the same father—and, like you, I never really knew my own father (though the circumstances were different, mine probably being alive somewhere out there today, simply having opted out of fatherhood, at least of me). So the creative boy with the preoccupied, unmarried mother—somewhere unconsciously, I saw Ivo as an alter ego of myself. (Again, I know I was far from the only one who did. But when you're small, you don't think of yourself as part of a collective, a statistical mass, an average anything.) And your* Inseparables *series—I remember the thrill of walking into the bookshop the very day the second volume went on sale, the even greater thrill of carrying it out, wrapped in brown paper I couldn't wait to tear open.*

You receive volumes of flattery, so I will stop the gushing there. But you see, to penetrate that aura of "greatness" surrounding you, the Man as Living Legend, is my challenge—especially because your greatness is so aligned with the innocence, yet also the terrible vulnerability, of being a child. This is the irony the film will portray, and no one, believe me, is more qualified to make it than Andrew Zelinsky. Both you and I are in the hands of a genius (another living legend!).

There are actors who would consider it a violation of pure craft to be in touch like this, but I am not one to squander the chance of meeting the man I will become.

I do want to say, again, vis-à-vis the interview, that I admire you enormously for coming out with such difficult truths about where you come from. This is a story that will move everyone who sees it, and make people talk, and think, and return to your books with a fresh eye. The more I can know of you, your history, the more powerful this project will be. Truly!

I have written far more than enough, and I expect you to respond only if and when you wish.

Yours in admiration,
Nick Greene

Dear Nick Greene,

Your repeated allusions to my "greatness" are a bit excessive, even off-putting. But I will take them as a mark of your genuine enthusiasm for the (yes, I agree, OUTLANDISH) work you have ahead of you, and I thank you. Who wouldn't bask, speechlessly, in the glow of such compliments from a certified star? I intend to become more familiar with your past work, as clearly you are familiar with mine.

I would like to say something, right off the bat, about the article, which came out so long ago (practically in another century) that the thought of its being an inspiration for any new creative venture I find rather Wonderland-esque. To think about that moment in my life is to plunge down a rabbit hole. Different times, different motivations. Not that I had any particular motivation I can remember in making that disclosure when I did.

But you want history? I'll give you history.

I have to disabuse you of the notion that my mother was unmarried. She was married to a man who was twice her age and doomed, before she even met him, by grave illness. His lungs had been burned and scarred by mustard gas in World War I. That part was cut out of the published interview you read, although to me it's the crucial tragedy in my mother's life, the poor choice she made that only spawned others. Damaged men hold an allure for so many women, I have no idea why. I don't mean to sound cold. I loved my mother, and she loved me even more, but here's something sad I concluded a long time ago: she married my father because she felt sorry for him—and probably because she had so few choices in that godforsaken part of the world. Even if she had lived somewhere more populous, remember how many men that war wiped off the face of the earth. She did not love him: she resorted to him. How do I know? Because she displayed no pictures of him after he died, and she spoke of him only when I asked. What little I know about him is what you might call "the facts." And they are few.

Tucson, Arizona, in the early decades of the last century was a backwater in the extreme (or a backdesert? not much water!), peopled by libertarians, prospectors, social outcasts, a whole lotta nogoodniks . . . and, among other technicolor characters, a benevolent heiress-cum-denmother who decided to provide solid occupation for a few dozen severely damaged men who could no longer breathe any air but the warmest and driest. She trained them in wood-work (not personally, I assume) and set them up in a shop. Yes, making furniture! And when they'd made so much furniture that she ran out of rich friends to buy it, and the Depression gutted the hell out of the urban department-store market, she bought it all herself and constructed a sprawling hotel to put it to use. (A fairy tale, right?)

My father, Myron Levy, was one of those damaged men. He made tables and desks and chairs with the best of them. In 1935 he met my mother, a laundress at the hotel. In 1940 I came along: me, Mordecai Levy. Of course, this part you know from that ancient interview over which you and your colleagues have been poring, dissecting and deconstructing. Two years later, the father I never knew—technically, can't remember—expired from terminal suffocation. He lived his entire adult life struggling to breathe. I can hardly bear to think of it. It's the reason I never took up smoking. Not even ganja.

So: my mother. A woman with parents to fall back on would have done so, gone to them with this pink-cheeked little boy, started over however she could. Mom had no parents—or none she'd divulge to me. My grandparents stand behind a curtain that's never been lifted. (Other than saying they were dead, she was so tight-lipped on the subject that even back then I was skeptical.) So she stayed at the inn and by that I mean literally. After my father's death, we moved into an annex, a nearby outbuilding where some of the more itinerant workers lived. It was small but bright. Two rooms. My mother kept it tidy. She messed up a number of things in her life, but never her domicile. I suspect my little shirts and coveralls were pressed to the nines.

Work calls me. I look forward to hearing from you again. Present me with the blanks and I will fill them in. I'm at that stage of life when simply being able to remember this much is a source of comfort. You intersect with me at a propitious time, Mr. Greene.

Yours,
M. L.
P.S. I am an acolyte of e-mail, happy to correspond by that means.

Nick owns a photocopy of his own letter and the posted reply from Lear, handwritten on four sheets of paper the color of sunflower petals. After that, their correspondence slipped into the ether of e-mail—but somehow (he wishes he knew how), Nick turned a key in Mort Lear's psyche. And, to be honest, Lear turned a key in his own. Divided by some forty years, an ocean, and most of a continent, their boyhoods had been remarkably similar, at least in their emotional essence. With their single mothers too busy working—

and Nick's siblings so much older that their lives were almost self-contained—each of them had spent countless hours alone at home, creating and inhabiting other worlds: Nick in books and, later on, plays; Lear in drawing—with and on any materials he could find. (When the maids at the hotel aired vacant rooms between guests, he would sneak in and steal a single sheet of stationery, hoping that no one would notice such a minor theft.) Had either been a sporty lad, there would have been scant if any support from the sidelines. *For you, a cricket bat, for me a Louisville Slugger, right?* wrote Lear. Nick replied, *Well, at school, I did take a whack at squash. A literal whack—my racquet landing on the back of my poor opponent's skull! At which point I was banished to the poncy stage.*

Lear confessed that he envied anyone who had siblings. Nick wrote back that while they practiced all the holiday-card formalities, he had seen his brother and sister only a few times in the years since their mother's death. *My fault entirely,* he explained. *I turned down one too many invitations. For about ten years there, I was terrified that if I stepped away from London—unless it was to step on a flight for New York or L.A.—I'd miss the Fateful Call. I'm still trying to figure out which call that was!*

Lear assured Nick that his best family years were ahead of him: that he'd find a wife, have children, and even reconnect with Nigel and Annabelle. (Nick startled at seeing their names in Lear's e-mail; he hadn't recalled sharing them.) *For obvious reasons, that wasn't an evident path for me,* wrote Lear. *Nowadays, young homosexual men are pairing off with the very intention, from Day One, of furnishing and filling a nursery. I am in awe. I do not wish to stop and wonder if, given the chance, I might have gone that way myself. I suspect not. Certainly not with the men I kept company with. But the "company" was of a rather different nature than the kind that leads to sharing fatherhood.*

Their initial dialogue comprised a cheerful volley of such observations, as if they were engaged in an old-fashioned epistolary courtship, eloquent yet timid and banal, touching by fingertips only. Nick, however, was alert to the proper moment when he might ask Lear to tell him more about the incidents in the garden shed.

Except that he did not have to ask. Nick was still in London, still in a low-key hiatus after convalescing from the cyclone of parties and awards and talk shows and photo shoots and more parties, taking deep, savory drafts of a rather spartan indolence that, if you were lucky, could last a month or more between commitments. He was messing about with the friends he thought of as "civilians" (anything but actors!), reading everything he could find by and about Lear, and contemplating a future role in a new Alan Ayckbourn play while holding fast against accepting the sort of pretty-boy rom-com pirou-ettes that had funded the purchase of his flat. He was also holding fast against the urge to ring Kendra and patch things up. Late nights, alone in the flat, tired of skimming some half-cooked treatment of a Jane Austen remake or a script about space explorers in peril, trying to resist another whiskey, presented him with far too many foolish doubts.

He had also been avoiding e-mail all day. So when he finally broke down (as a desperate alternative to making that foolish groveling phone call), Lear's message came as a rather seismic surprise.

You will receive this in broad English daylight, but I write to you in the godforsaken hours when even owls and foxes are well tucked in. Insomnia is having its way with my aging self. Not that I'm in pain, but the mental gears do not disengage as easily. I am never inclined to draw at this hour—I am spoiled by the daily luxury of working in natural light—and to compose nar-rative of any kind I consider the business of morning. My verbal acumen is the sort of flower that opens wide soon after dawn and begins to droop by noon. (Are these details useful to you? Your interest in my everyday habits could lead me to bore you silly. What I am going to tell you, I think—what I am about to type into this machine and suspect I will send—is, on the other hand, far from silly. I do not yet know how it will feel to "get it down," but the urge to do that is upon me.)

For most of my life, I hewed to the belief that what happened in Tucson would stay in Tucson. And then it became clear to me, whether because of the age we live in or the age I was accruing, that when it comes to the sordid, just about nothing stays where it should. I finessed the story in that magazine interview. The cub reporter they sent out here might have spun the whole sorry thing from me like cotton candy from one of those centrifugal tubs at a county fair . . . but he was shocked (and satiated) by the bit he got. And perhaps I was only flirting with the truth; I wasn't ready, as you youngsters say, to commit.

What am I going on about?! Myself. Ah yes. Again. Is Ivo ME? Note the boy's navel-gazing initial I: aha! Can you believe I never saw that until some forensic bookworm brought it up in the New York Review of Books *or some such rarefied rag? Honest Injun, as my Brooklyn street chums used to say. And is the panther a ped-oh-phial? My answer is that cats were the animals I could draw with the most confidence back then. I could never have managed an anteater or a bison or even a monkey. I drew boys, girls, plants, and cats (and birds and insects and lizards). I employed the menagerie I knew best.*

Well, who doesn't believe in the unconscious and its sly-dog tricks these days?

TELL THE STORY, you are thinking as you peer into your screen. Just tell the bloody story, old man. Thus:

My mother is a laundress at a stately, remote inn, the sort of place called a retreat, where senators and stars of the silver screen meet their mistresses— sent ahead in large, plush-upholstered automobiles, thus allowing them to greet their illicit lovers already posed in swimsuits by the rose-bordered pool or lying in opulent wait on a large dark-wood bed, possibly fashioned by my own father. Discretion is a costly but plentiful commodity here.

My mother is treated kindly, paid decently. But also, she is lonely. She has a girlfriend or two among the other staff, but they go home to husbands—or go out to find one.

The staff is legion. Among those who tend the outdoors, there is a head gardener. Perhaps he is called a groundskeeper. He contemplates the proper irrigation, trains the men who prune and weed and make sure the fountains drain well. He wields a certain power.

He has a wife and two children, but they live in a real home "out there," beyond the walls of the hotel. Let's say his name is Leonard.

I am seven. The war is well over—which makes just about everyone happier, even if it doesn't make them richer. I remember, more than once, men in uniform walking through the gardens of the hotel, how heads turned, nodding with approval or admiration. I think about what I know of my father, the way he died. My mother did have one picture of him in uniform, before he went to his own, earlier war, which she brought from a drawer when I asked. Already he looked miserable. (Of course he was.) His war has been gratefully pushed out of memory by the newer war, the one any simpleton on the street can justify, at least in retrospect.

One thing I know at age seven is that I will grow up to be anything but a man in uniform. In the library of the hotel hang beautiful dark paintings, mostly landscapes and still lifes. (One, which mystifies and spooks me, is of a dead rabbit lying on a stone next to a stalk of wilting roses.) In the hotel's small chapel, there are also dark paintings. There are Madonnas and saints, but there are also flowers and fruits and landscapes with fraught, tempestuous skies. I tell my mother I want to make pictures. She spares me a frugal supply of the cheap buff-colored paper she uses to package the pressed table linens, to protect them from the red dust that drifts invisibly everywhere and settles on everything. (When I bathe after playing outside, the water turns a rusty pink.) Sometimes she gives me a pad of lined paper from the hotel office. For Christmas, she gives me watercolor paints: a box containing six disks of color and two brushes. I can still see it clearly; my fingers remember gripping those spindly shafts.

I begin to paint the cactuses and flowers around the grounds. I try to memorize birds I see in passing, to paint them, too. Leonard, as he makes his rounds in this horticultural paradise, often stops to admire my work. Leonard also takes care of the one cat on the grounds, kept here to ward off mice. It's an elusive creature, that cat, though I try to draw it whenever I find it resting from its predatory labors. For the most part, everyone else ignores me in a benevolent way. Guests smile blandly as they pass me. A woman might touch my head, as if to bless me.

The hottest months, when school is out, are the ones I spend mostly outdoors. My mother makes me wear a hat, but still my skin burns. At night she scolds me, tells me to sit in the shade, rubs white salve over my nose and cheeks and knees. "If this happens again," she warns me, "I'll have to keep you cooped up inside." An empty threat, because she does not have the time to police my comings and goings.

One day Leonard spots me, huddled in the shade of an awning by the pool, *my face probably peeling. He tells me that there's a place I could work in his shed—and there are resting plants that would love to have their portraits drawn. "You understand the value of drawing from life more than most children your age," he says. "I am very impressed." I blush at the flattery, which works wonders.*

I've passed the shed a hundred times but never been inside. It's a large structure on the edge of the property, under a big cottonwood that grows by a trickle of a stream, and it's larger than your average potting shed. The demands of this beautiful garden would be many and complex. Inside, it's dim—though only at first—and cool, a rackety fan moving the air in circles. Dozens of tools— clippers and scythes and machetes and saws with slim but sturdy blades— hang on hooks across a wall. Shelves hold burlap sacks of fertilizers, pesticides, lime, birdseed, and peat moss; cans bleeding dark rust-tainted oils; terra-cotta pots in tall snug stacks. "My kingdom," says Leonard.

Oddly, there's a weary couch against a wall. The cat, caught shirking, jumps off and dashes out the door.

"Sometimes I sneak a nap," Leonard says, then holds a finger to his lips.

A skylight and one side window facing a hedge illuminate the space, along with a few suspended bulbs. Anyone who's been to the movies enough would see the place as sinister. I see it as a laboratory, a library, a place to do as one pleases in privacy and peace. I like the idea that the cat might keep me company here.

"And how about this." Leonard points to a door, opens it, ushers me in. It leads into a smaller room with a workbench and stool, a gooseneck lamp. Leonard uses a hand to sweep sawdust off the rough wood surface. "You can work here."

The room is stuffy and smells of sulfur and dirt, but it's sumptuously quiet. Several potted plants, in varying states of prosperity, languish on a shelf beneath a purple light.

"The convalescent ward," Leonard tells me. "Plants on probation." He's tall, his head nearly brushing the unpainted ceiling. "And now . . . wait, my friend . . . there's this."

He bends down and opens a drawer in the workbench. He pulls out a flat box and slides it open: it's a set of pastels in two dozen colors. In a book, I've seen pictures of ballet dancers by Degas in pastel, and in the schoolroom we have colored chalk, but these are a luxury. CARAN D'ACHE, says the box in a scarlet flourish. I wonder what the word "ache" has to do with the alluring contents, but I don't ask. I do know I ache to use them.

From the magic drawer, he also hands me a tablet of thick, toothy paper, white as powdered lime. "Yours," says Leonard.

And it begins. With no schoolwork to take me away from my pictures, I go to the shed as often as I can. All I tell my mother is that I've found a way to stay out of the sun. This makes her happy. As long as I'm on the hotel grounds, she knows I'll be safe, watched over. And as long as I read—which I do, every night after dinner, while she listens to the radio and presses our own clothes— I am free to do as I like all day long.

Sometimes she'll say she is spoiling me, that if my father were still alive, I'd be learning his craft—or "whatever men teach their sons," she says, sounding sad but also dismissive. I can tell she feels sorry for me.

The hotel stands at the edge of the town, and though there are a few other boys with parents who live on or near the grounds, they prefer athletic pastimes. That summer I'm left to my own devices, and at first I am content. Sometimes I do wonder whether, if my father were alive, I might have brothers and sisters. I wouldn't have to entertain myself. On the other hand, I begin to realize that I like entertaining myself.

Nick scrolled quickly ahead, just to see how long the e-mail would be. Interminable, it seemed. He was knackered and, though he felt ashamed (hadn't he asked for the full-on saga?), impatient. For a children's writer, the man was anything but concise.

And yet it was ominously gripping. Lear wrote about the plants he chose to draw, how he imagined entire landscapes around them, with wild creatures and birds. Once he found a sun-baked lizard on a walkway. It was stiff, brittle as a dead leaf. He carried it carefully to the shed and drew it several times over. He turned its likeness into a dragon, a prickly succulent into a fantastical forest. He found ways to use pencil, chalk, and his Christmas watercolors (nearly gone) along with the velvet pastels, which loved the heat, turning soft and slick in his sweaty hands. He found the right blue-violet mix for shadows, the most convincing blend of ochers and greens for the desert grasses. He began to sign his work, the way artists had signed the paintings inside the hotel, even the weird painting of the dead rabbit.

And one afternoon I am lost in my shadings, speaking silently to the colors, commanding them to do my bidding as another boy might have commanded toy platoons, when I hear the outer door open—not unusual, as Leonard comes and goes with some regularity, mostly ignoring my presence, humming to himself. But the murmurings I hear aren't his alone: his whisperings are mixed up with those of a girl, high-pitched giggling and shushing. At first I tell myself that I'm mistaken, that the rackety fan is the source of these noises. Maybe something's caught in the blades and Leonard will fix it. Or maybe the cat is playing with a mouse.

But no.

I am unsure whether to speak—Leonard greeted me just an hour ago and surely knows I am there—but I wouldn't dare, because the girl's giggling quickly becomes something else: groaning and sighing. I hear the scrape of furniture legs and the wheezing give and take of old upholstery, stiffened springs.

I hold my colored stick above the paper and listen. I know, though I don't want to know, that the deeper groans I'm hearing are Leonard's. I hold extremely still. The sounds might be sounds of pain, but I know that they aren't. I know, by instinct, that this is pleasure I'm hearing, however alien a pleasure it is. I imagine that I am not supposed to know about it, but I do, and that only deepens my alarm and shame.

A silence arrives, followed by quick shallow breathing and, again, giggling, whispering.

I hear Leonard say, his voice a rasp, "You'd better go, baby."

The sound of scraping furniture legs. The outside door opens and closes. I wait for a time I cannot possibly quantify, until I know I am alone in the shed. I pack my pastels into their box. I put it, with my drawings, into the drawer. I go out into the main room, surprised that sun is still streaming through the dusty skylight, the sun stained pink like everything else. I go home and am relieved that my mother isn't there.

Whether because he was too stunned or too cold (the temperature in the flat, on an icy April night, dropping swiftly), Nick set aside the laptop and reached for a jumper slung across a nearby chair. Some noise in the street drew him to the window. For a moment, he wished he had never started this correspondence; would Olivier or Guinness have considered it necessary, or even desirable, to know the flesh-and-blood counterpart to any of their creations? Would Peter O'Toole have longed to get pissed with T. E. Lawrence, soak up tales of his rugged beginnings? Maybe Nick was in over his head. And yet, at the same time, he realized how badly he wanted back in: to work, to public exposure, to what just might be the role of his career.

When he entered his flat after dark, sometimes he was startled at the alien glitter of his trophies lined up on a shelf that fell within a bar of streetlight projected through a window. They caught his attention often by day as well (too often, really), but at night they threatened to come alive, a quartet of eccentrically handicapped friends. Top dog— yet clearly of questionable intelligence—would have to be the opulently body-conscious Oscar, his sidekick the anguished, hollow-eyed BAFTA bloke. Here, too, was Mr. Verdigris from SAG, incapable of speech, caught eternally and nakedly in a moment of sartorial indecision: comedy or tragedy, oh what to wear! Finally, the stalwart G.G., odd man out (because he wasn't a man at all), his domed, columnar silhouette undeniably akin to that robot in *Star Wars*.

Clearly, Nick had too much time on his hands.

He needed to embed himself anew, burrow deep. And *The Inner Lear* would be nothing like *Lawrence of Arabia*. Andrew wasn't interested in the spectacle history could make of a man; the spectacular, to Andrew, lay within the soul. He had said to Nick that what he wanted to make was not so much a film as a kaleidoscope: a prismatic portrait of Lear's childhood, love life, and art, how a great artist's fully recognized existence is a mosaic, its sundry components entirely interdependent. The best actors, said Deirdre, become both engorged and engulfed by a role, containing and carrying it all at once. "A hack impersonates," she said. "A master inhabits."

Nick went to his kitchen and flicked the switch on the electric kettle. He took a mug from the sink and rinsed it, reached for the cannister of tea. He had a feeling that, inhabiting Lear already, he would be awake long beyond the owl and the fox.

Five

Has spring ended before it's even begun? The first Sunday in June and it must be ninety degrees in the park.

Children with white balloons weave among the trees behind Alice and her cohorts; some of the children are dressed like Ivo in *Colorquake*. Adults mill about awkwardly, trying to find places to settle on the wooded slopes that surround the small plaza carved out for the sculpture. Three women confer beside it, holding folders; she recognizes Katelyn. The ceremony is set to start in twenty minutes. Factoring in the probable delay, Merry isn't eager to spend half an hour making tense small talk. She is fairly sure that the news about Lear bolting from his commitment to the museum isn't out yet, but Katelyn is as connected as anyone in their parochial world—and even if everything were humming along the way Merry would have assumed as recently as last month, she finds that working with Katelyn always sets her teeth on edge.

Katelyn is the manager of Tumnus and Friends, the last independent retailer in the city devoted entirely to children's books. Lear almost always staged his first appearances there whenever a new book launched. One has to assume that Katelyn is smart, simply because she's still in business, but she speaks in a helium falsetto that, whenever she's talking to anyone "important," takes on a painfully affected British edge, giving her a voice that calls to mind the innkeeper's wife on *Fawlty Towers*.

Katelyn has masterminded the ceremony (for which Merry should be grateful, under the circumstances). She wants to begin with a reading of *Colorquake* in its entirety—which seems ill judged to Merry, even aside from the soul-parching heat. Several children have already scrambled onto and then quickly off of the statue, scalded by the sun-baked bronze. And who exactly is this gathering for? Not Lear's closest associates and friends, who are invited to the private memorial at the Met—as is Merry, to her simultaneous gratification and chagrin. Perhaps this one is mainly for all the adults who fell in love with Lear's various books at various times in their younger lives and look back on them with a foggy, nostalgic wonder. But then, there are all these children—many merely towed along—and Katelyn doesn't seem to realize that they are not going to sit happily through endless recitations without pictures.

Katelyn has also enlisted a trustee from the New York Public Library, an older woman named Hannah who claims to have known Mort "intimately" yet isn't on the list for the Met.

I am turning into a platinum-grade bitch, thinks Merry as she listens to the two other women going over the program. But who wouldn't, with perspiration trickling down the channel of her spine and slowly soaking the waistband of her linen skirt? She has determined to go with the flow, just follow directions: read what she's told to read, introduce the guest speakers, even lead the singing of "Ivo's Serenade," a song written by a *Sesame Street* composer for an after-school special featuring a Muppet tea party at which Mort was the guest of honor.

"I am strictly against the releasing of the balloons," Katelyn is telling Hannah. "It is dangerous for the birds."

Hannah argues that a few balloons sent nobly aloft will be much more inspiring to the children than they will be hazardous to a bunch of pigeons, which are little more than airborne rats.

"Ivo would not approve," says Katelyn, standing her ground.

"We have fifteen minutes to get our ducks in a row," says Merry. "Speaking of birds."

"And in fact, Ivo is here in person," says Katelyn.

Merry and Hannah stare at her wordlessly.

Katelyn beams. "My assistant found a costume to rent! Can you believe it? Mask and everything. He'll lead the singing, so you don't have to worry about that, Meredith. Cool?"

"Perfectly." Merry glances at the bronze Mad Hatter, said to be a caricature of the publishing tycoon who commissioned the statue in memory of his wife. Suddenly she's thinking, mournfully and covetously, of Mort's Alice collection: the Victorian playing cards, the letter from Dodgson to Rossetti, the shoes allegedly worn by Tenniel's model for the title character, a sewing box that belonged to the actual, inspirational Alice. . . . "Really," says Merry, "I'm here to help out. You just boss me around."

"And I'll do you the same favor at the opening for the new museum!" Katelyn clasps her hands together.

"Excuse me a moment," says Merry. She wants to find Sol, who promised to make an appearance—as did Stu and a few other authors. As she looks around, she notices a middle-aged man pacing at the periphery of the convergence. The small arc of benches facing the statue filled up half an hour ago; newcomers are struggling to find space for their blankets and beach towels in the midst of the grove spreading north from the statue. Some are laying out picnics. (As usual, Katelyn's planning, though well intentioned, is maddeningly impractical.) But the pacing man seems uncomfortable in a different, possibly worrisome way. He is searching, frowning. That creepy mantra *If you see something, say something* drifts through her brain.

Bull by the horns, she thinks, heading toward him. "Are you looking for someone? You're here for the Lear memorial, yes?"

He looks startled. "Yes," he says, "and yes."

"It'll start in a few minutes. Sorry there's so little room to sit."

"Are you running this show?" he asks.

"Helping."

He's quite tall, this broody man, and she has to look up to meet his eyes. After a moment of peering around, scanning the assembly, he says, "Do you know Tommy Daulair?"

Merry sounds hoarse when she speaks. "Do you?"

"She's my sister."

"Your sister!" Of course she must be here. "You're meeting her?"

"No," he says. "Or I don't know. I just figured she'd come, and I'd . . . find her."

"I've met your sister."

They regard each other uncertainly.

"Actually, I'd like to reconnect with her," Merry says. "Do you see her?"

"No, not yet." He sounds impatient. "I didn't think . . ."

Merry hears an electronic screech; the audio technician is testing the mikes. "I have to get ready. Will you stay till after? I, actually"— why does she keep saying *actually,* as if insisting on some suspect reality?—"in fact, I should introduce myself."

He tells her his name is Danilo. They shake hands awkwardly.

"When you find your sister, would you ask her to stick around, too?"

"If I can," he says. "I don't know if she's coming."

"Well, look," says Merry, and she hands him one of her cards. "In case we don't see each other later. Please tell Tomasina I'd love to meet up."

The man's anxiety is obvious and unsettling—but perhaps he really did know Mort, through his sister, and is genuinely mourning. Merry notices that he's probably her age, his thick dark hair subsiding toward the same degree of gray that would overtake her own head if she were to give up the costly dye job.

Now Katelyn is waving at her, both arms beckoning grandly, as if Merry is a plane being guided toward a gate. As she heads for the podium someone has positioned right beside the pond, facing the statue, she spots Sol and Stu, just arriving. Together? She is pondering the unlikelihood of their companionship when she also becomes aware of a tangible atmospheric shift, a sluicing of mercifully cool air through the heat—but it comes with an inrush of clouds, drawn over the blue sky as deftly as a curtain over a window. Thunder mutters in the distance.

"Really?" she says to the sky. Rain was not in the forecast as of this morning.

The guitarist (Katelyn's husband) begins playing something Spanish, heartfelt, verging on flamenco, then downshifts toward Bach, that famous piece about the safely grazing sheep. Even the children settle down, reeling in their balloons as a breeze rises. Each one is etched with Ivo's likeness: Ivo in the forest, with his entourage of butterflies and bugs. The drawing in Merry's bedroom.

"We are here to celebrate the colorful life and the even more colorful work of Mort Lear," Katelyn chirps into the mike. "Does anyone out there love him as passionately as I do? Give a joyful cheer for yes!"

The crowd erupts, a sweet mélange of voices young and old. Even Merry, as damp and cranky as she feels, is moved. She stands between Sol and Stu, off to one side of the podium. Stu is holding a piece of paper—is he scheduled to speak?

"Alice, the White Rabbit, and the Mad Hatter were all great inspirations to Mort, so it's only fitting we invited them to join us," says Katelyn, sweeping an arm toward the statue, "but Mort had many living friends, admirers, and colleagues as well, and they'll have memories to share. First, however, a reading of everyone's favorite, iconic, never-to-be-rivaled storybook, *Colorquake*. And by the way, if you don't own a copy, they'll be for sale later on." After pointing to a table stacked with books, she pulls from her pocket a pair of pink cat's-eye glasses and slips them on. She begins to read not from a book but from a typescript.

"Ivo's mother kept a perfect house, a house among the trees."

Stu steps up next to Katelyn and, a few sentences on, joins her in the reading; they are alternating pages. To Merry's knowledge, Stu hardly knew Mort. (Now she knows why Stu's latest book is for sale on Katelyn's table, along with Lear's greatest hits.) Meanwhile, the wind becomes insistent, tossing and tangling the balloons, pilfering napkins and cups. Many of the adults glance up at the heavens, look at one another for cues, then begin to corral their belongings, ready to flee.

How long the story seems in words alone. Where was Lear's true talent? wonders Merry as the story flows along. Is the persistent popularity of that slim book in the union of language and image?

Or, had it been published three years earlier, or later, would it have been nothing more than a passing entertainment? Did it strike some kind of Cold War, post-Watergate cultural chord? Not that Mort was a literary fluke, another Margaret Mitchell or Harper Lee. Or a coloratura, like Virginia Lee Burton or Margaret Wise Brown, working in a range that was vivid but narrow. No, Mort was a writer of staying power and versatility. (Good Lord, what in the world is she doing, writing wall copy for an exhibit?)

She surveys the audience. There is the brother, standing against a tree, still searching the crowd.

Could Merry even find Tomasina Daulair in such a cacophony of faces? She has encountered the woman three or four times but only in the context of galas and openings where Merry's primary task is to condense and focus all her verve and vigor on anyone who might become a benefactor. She becomes a heat-seeking laser. (Someone ought to invent a pair of party-vision goggles that would reveal not just the richest occupants in a room but the ones most likely to share their wealth.) Sadly, the artists—the people with whom she *wants* to drink and dance and share the festivities—are all beside the point at such events. Their escorts? Less important than the waiters bearing trays of tiny crab cakes. Less important than the crab cakes.

Stu, in his sonorous baritone, reads, *"Everything was just as he left it, but . . . wait . . . where was his panther?"* With his lips nearly touching the microphone, he hisses the last four words, as if he's reading Edgar Allan Poe, as if the final note of Mort's book is one of foreboding, not delight.

Every single person under the roiling sky knows this book so well that hardly a beat of silence passes before they applaud. Stu bows. Katelyn steps to the mike and says, "In case you don't know him, ladies and gentlemen, boys and girls, meet Shine."

Compared with the roar that rises from the audience now, the applause for Mort and his book was anemic. Stu raises his tattooed arms like a football player who's just made a touchdown.

Stu is now Merry's ace in the hole, but she does not join the adulation. What is he doing, hijacking Mort's memorial? She leans over and takes him by the arm, gently pulling him toward the side. ("Beautiful, Stu. Beautiful," she says, feeling just how phony her smile must look. Ambiguously, he answers, "Just giving it up for The Man.")

And now the ruggedly elegant Peter Sís steps to the microphone and tells the story of how he met Mort in the Village, some thirty years ago. His voice is gratifyingly soft, reminiscent, his delicate accent underscoring his role as an elder statesman of sorts. Stu's problem, thinks Merry, is that he wants to turn everything into a rock concert. Well, maybe that's the flow with which she'll have to go from now on. Maybe she should have one of Shine's characters tattooed on her chest, the way his oldest fans have done. She listens to Peter and resolves to write him a note. She's heard rumors that his work is ultimately headed for that greedy archive at UT Austin—which seems to suck up way too many literary estates, relegating them to every sensible person's least favorite part of the country—but rumors are just rumors.

A loud crack of thunder sets off a collective shriek among the children. A significant number of adults leap to their feet and start stuffing things into backpacks and diaper bags.

Katelyn comes over to Merry. "What do we *do?*"

"Didn't you have an indoor alternative?"

"Yes, but it's blocks away," says Katelyn. "It was for if the day was rainy from the start. No one's going to go there now."

Flight is contagious, of course, so more than half the audience is leaving, most of them rushing toward Fifth Avenue.

"It's not actually raining, so let's just soldier on," says Merry.

"But lightning!" Katelyn protests.

"Mort would have enjoyed the drama," Merry says. "And it's not like we're in an open field." (Which, paradoxically, is the sort of setting that ought to have been chosen for a gathering of this size.)

"The trees don't make us any safer, you know."

Ignoring Katelyn, Merry steps to the mike and introduces the next guest, who seems gratifyingly undeterred. Charlotte is the editor who has worked with Mort since Rose died. The first book she edited was volume one of *The Inseparables*. This is the book she's holding now and from which, without preamble, she begins to read.

> *To look back at their beginning, their unity almost from birth, is to marvel at how an arbitrary confluence of geography and timing may determine the course of history, the fate of an entire species: ours, to be exact. And their beginning was as simple as could be.*
>
> *They were neighbors, meeting only because their six parents, almost simultaneously, happened to have chosen this plain but deliciously shady street as the best place to make a life—and because their three mothers, all new to the job, were lonely and desperate for comrades with whom to share the particular raptures and fears of caring for a baby. This is how, looking back from later, they came to be best friends from so long ago that they couldn't even remember the first time they had played together. Was it digging moats in Greta's sandbox . . . bombardiering down Boris's slide? Or maybe they had joined forces when Stinky was the first to get a trike. Stinky's name was Stanley, but nobody called him that. He liked Stinky. He said so even when they moved up to the middle school, when it would have been easy to leave his nickname behind. But he refused, claiming it gave him "panache."*
>
> *"Whatever that is, you can keep it to yourself," said Boris.*
>
> *Stinky was the word nerd.*

Merry wonders how much Charlotte plans to read. She reminds herself that she isn't the one in charge here; perhaps she should have been. She fantasizes briefly about an alternate scenario in which the *Times* obituary included the announcement that Mort Lear had bequeathed his entire literary estate to . . . *Stop*. She glances at Sol. He is whispering something to Stu.

Charlotte is now through the part of the narrative identifying Boris as the science nerd, the trombone player Greta as the music nerd. The first chapter is a swift summary of the protagonists' shared childhood, their uneventful passage toward the sudden crisis that kicks the plot into surreal motion by Chapter Two.

> *"You know what we are? We're a phalanx," said Stinky.*
>
> *Boris asked what a phalanx was. Greta told him that, in their case, it*

meant a chemical union so stable that to threaten any change, to remove a single atom, could lead to the implosion of the cosmos.

"Sort of like the Hadron Collider."

The others looked at him suspiciously.

"Do you guys ever listen?" Boris rolled his eyes. "That tunnel I told you about, the one in Switzerland."

"Precisely," said Stinky. "We are the force they are trying to create in that tunnel."

Charlotte reads the part about how, in high school, they end every day by e-mailing one another their last thoughts, often sitting at their desks in the dark, in their pajamas, their parents and younger siblings long asleep. Does it matter to teenage readers now that the ways they keep in touch have changed so dramatically in just a decade? Secretly, Merry has never loved *The Inseparables*. She understands why the books were and still are iconic, but they're so melancholy, so fatalistic, the humor so chilly. . . .

The year they would all turn sixteen (Greta first, then Stinky, then Boris), one by one, they fell sick. First they were tired, then they had headaches, and then they didn't want to eat. One by one, they were taken to their family doctors by their parents, and all of them, one by one, were told that they had the same rare malignancy.

Boris and Greta did not need Stinky to tell them the meaning of that word.

The three afflicted friends overheard their mothers weeping together, their fathers making lists of specialists and world-class hospitals in other parts of the country. Weary though they were, they went on Stinky's computer—he'd been the first to get his own, just like that trike—and they did their own research.

"We'll be cured together," said Greta.

"Or die together," grumbled Boris.

"Don't get all creepy and morbid," said Stinky. "Remember: we are a phalanx."

"Inseparable," said Greta.

It occurs to Merry that the smaller children in the audience (actually, very few of the smallest ones remain, since their parents would be the most protective) might be extremely disturbed by the beginning of this older book. Ultimately, there would be a bittersweet, mostly happy ending—at least to this book—but not before a great deal of peril, catastrophe, and heroism (the Hadron Collider a crucial factor).

Charlotte sets down the book to tell the audience how surprised she was to find out, after reading this book before it was even published, that Mort was a funny man. She does a rather credible impersonation, and she talks about his love of Lewis Carroll's famous book and how he collected eccentric, silly objects related to Alice and her fellow Wonderlanders. "One day he hoped to illustrate a new edition of *Alice*. It would have been, I know, his crowning achievement."

Just as Charlotte reaches toward the bronze Alice, as if to invite her for a hug, rain falls in a rush, like the breaking of a dam. Even those who have readied umbrellas leap to their feet and dash away in search of better shelter than the trees can offer.

Katelyn and her husband, who clutches his guitar case against his body like a wounded child, rush to the book table, covering it clumsily with a large sheet of plastic.

Only the poor audio guy—scrambling to pack up the microphone and speakers—and Sol, who stands impassively by, under a wide black umbrella, do not run. Nor does Merry, who feels that it's her responsibility to take over. At the very least, she can bring this bloated ceremony to a merciful close. "I'm sorry," she calls out to the few diehards, shouting to be heard over the rain. "Mort must be telling us he's too modest for us to make this big a fuss on his behalf."

Mort, modest? Well, that's amusing.

She is soaked, and her shoes are ruined. Exasperated, angry, she leans over, pulls them off, and tosses them into the pond. Too late, she realizes that she'll never find a cab in this downpour. She turns to ask Sol if he has a car, but he's gone; in the distance, she sees him leaving the park, sharing his umbrella with Stu.

❧

"Turn on your TV. CBS."

Tommy hurries to the den. Remote in one hand, phone in the other, she is looking at a red-carpet promenade, the milling about of a chosen tribe in finery and jewels: the women absurdly gorgeous, the men more diverse in their looks (some of them downright toads).

But in the foreground, here he is, leaning toward a microphone held by a woman's hand. The camera zooms in until, for a moment, his face nearly fills the screen, far larger than life, and then withdraws to include a shapely reporter in a tight pink dress, though her prettiness is nothing to the luster of the women gliding along behind her.

He smiles gamely at the reporter. "I am indeed!" he says forcefully. "And I am over the moon about it—though at the same time I am crushed by the news. It's such a terrible, terrible loss, his death."

"Yes, just last month. Tragic." She nods emphatically and tries to look sad.

"So I feel as if my responsibility to get it precisely right, to do him honor, is all that much more serious now. I owe Mr. Lear the performance of my life. But of course, it's not all me, not by a long shot. Andrew's vision for this film is genius. His mind is like a bonfire."

"A bonfire! Absolutely." The reporter giggles. "But hang on a minute, Nick. We're here tonight to celebrate the stage, to which you are no stranger. So will we be seeing you on the boards again anytime soon?"

"Oh, I'm a homing pigeon," says the actor. "Always return to my roots—my roost? Bad joke there—sorry. But, honestly? Whatever else I'm doing, the theater's where I go to find myself again. Replenish my soul."

"Absolutely! Are you presenting tonight?"

"I am!" He presses a hand to his chest.

"Well, we look forward to that, Nick. And congratulations on all your success this year. You are the man. It is," she says, looking hungrily into the camera, "the Year of Nicholas Greene." And then, in a gesture that would be rude in any other context, she pivots her mike toward the next aggressively good-looking person in line.

"Franklin?" Tommy is still holding the phone to her ear. "Where are we?"

He laughs. "The Tonys. Come on, Tommy."

"I've never watched the Tonys in my life, Franklin. Well, okay, maybe when Morty designed that set. You watch the Tonys?"

"Without fail. I love the theater. It's part of why I sold out, why I like making money. I'm a front-of-the-orchestra snob. You don't like plays?"

"Of course I like plays," says Tommy. "I just don't find these dog-and-pony shows all that interesting. I don't even know who most of these people are."

The televised view is now swooping into a vast theater, toward a stage where the curtains slide open to reveal a ranked platoon of dancers in skintight glitter.

Franklin says, "Did you go this afternoon?"

Tommy is tempted to lie, but she says, "No." There's little point in making excuses—not that she owes excuses to Franklin.

"You know, the longer you hole up, the harder it's going to be." After a pause, in which Tommy realizes (thankfully) that he doesn't expect her to answer, he says, "Do you feel guilty? Don't answer if that's too personal. But you shouldn't. Feel guilty."

"Guilty?"

"Tommy, you know what I mean."

"You mean because I'm getting it all? Except that I'm not, actually."

"No. About being given control."

"I don't have that, either. I mean, come on. Morty's the one exerting control. Wouldn't you agree?"

In the ensuing pause, she can guess that Franklin thinks he's gone too far.

"I didn't mean to snap at you," she says. "If I feel guilty, and maybe I do, right now it's about not showing up for that thing in the park." And for not answering Dani's note, she thinks. "Listen, Franklin. You're keeping me sane. I have no business scolding you."

"Vent all you like, Tommy. I mean it. But you know what? The show is starting. I'm shameless here. Don't tell my other clients I'm a sucker for show tunes."

She thanks him and lets him go. She stands in the middle of the den and focuses on the arabesques and pirouettes of the chorus line, the entrance of the slim, athletic host. His tribe roars with self-satisfied approval.

Oh, tribes. She knows about tribes. Tommy went to at least a dozen awards ceremonies with Morty, before and then after Soren. Of course, they were book awards, not Oscars or Tonys. Some of the authors looked colorful, a handful elegant or eagerly stylish, but when literary stars turn out in their most celebratory attire, more than likely they fall shy of the mark. The tuxedos smell of mothballs; some of the dresses look as if they are past the days of fitting properly. Tommy owns three formal dresses, two black, one flowered, just for such occasions. Her mother bought her the flowered one. Though bald and bruised from treatments, she had taken Tommy shopping, as if Tommy were still a schoolgirl, another September looming. "Just in case you have to attend my funeral, I want you in something festive," said Mom.

She clicks off the TV. She doesn't need to wait for Nicholas Greene's turn onstage. What she needs to do is write Dani. Somehow, she can't bear the thought of speaking to him, not yet.

In his note, Dani included a picture of his baby, Joe—named for their father, a gesture that surprised Tommy when she received the birth announcement in March. She knew she should send a gift, with a note of congratulations. But wouldn't it be duplicitous to acknowledge the birth of her nephew without offering reconciliation? She couldn't bring herself to do that, not yet—not without Morty's say-so. In March, she assumed she had all the time in the world to figure it out.

Their mother's concerns about Dani had proved justifiable. Not that he became a troublemaker, a drifter, or a gutter-bound addict, but the work he did to make money through his thirties was odd-jobbish, nothing with security or benefits. He did carpentry and construction, working projects at which most of his coworkers shared a higher dedication of some sort, sculpture or song. The job he liked best was the stint he served, for several years, as a bicycle messenger, sprinting up- and downtown for financial firms back before e-mail and Skype made such work obsolete. "Closest I've ever come to flying," he said. To Dani, a bike meant freedom.

But it was the freedom-loving Dani who moved back in with their parents when Mom had cancer; who watched over Dad in his loneliness after she died. Dani never wanted to leave the city, never even wanted to see what another city might feel like. He had a series of anti-conformist girlfriends and was happy to live in neighborhoods that were inconvenient to public transportation; he rode his bike everywhere, all seasons, all times of day and night. He liked to brag that he was a prisoner to nobody's schedule but his own—and certainly not to the chronic delays of the subway.

And then, ten years ago, as he was inching up on forty, he met Jane. Jane was a bona fide grown-up, a pediatric speech therapist who happened to ride her bike everywhere, too, mainly because her work took her to a number of doctors' offices, even to patients' homes. They met when Jane stopped after seeing a cabdriver clip Dani's back wheel and drive off without so much as a glance in his mirror.

Tommy was hardly her brother's confidante, but when he mentioned Jane for the first time, Tommy knew he was fishing for advice. They were in touch fairly often back then. It was the beginning of their father's breakdown, the loosening of his grip first on short-term memory, then on everyday logic.

"I told her I was thinking of starting a business."

"Are you?" said Tommy.

"Don't make it sound so unlikely."

"I'm not making it sound like anything. I'm just asking."

"So, a bike shop. In a neighborhood that doesn't have one. There's this guy I met who thinks maybe, with all the crazy upscaling of way-west Chelsea, all that luxury 'greening' of the riverfront—I guess that's the word these days. . . . Gareth thinks we could get a space on Tenth or Eleventh. We'd have to get a loan. Trying to get my head around that. A *loan*. As if, next thing, I might own a station wagon, a lawn mower. . . . Jesus, in the old days Dad would have written a song."

"I love that idea," she said. And despite the passing shadow of their diminished father, Tommy felt a surge of disproportionate relief, as if Dani were her son, not her brother.

Within the month, Tommy had gone into the city for dinner with Dani and Jane. Jane was so unlike Dani's previous girlfriends—so much more, in a way, like Tommy—that their conversation progressed in fits and starts, as if it were a job interview. And maybe, for Tommy, it was. Maybe she felt as if she were inspecting not just a future sister-in-law but a stand-in for their long-lost mother. Maybe Jane was looking for a genetic affirmation of Dani's fitness to become a fellow grown-up—though Tommy could hardly picture him as a husband or father.

The bike shop became a reality. Dani seemed at last to be settled, to have found the perfect urban vocation. Tommy attended the opening, a boisterous gathering of Dani's, Jane's, and Gareth's friends that spilled out onto the far-from-glamorous sidewalk of Eleventh Avenue, adjacent to the West Side Highway crush. The shop was a virtual forest of shiny, tropically colored bicycles hanging from elaborate racks that lined the ceiling. Tommy enjoyed herself, but she stood mostly apart, watching. She knew none of her brother's friends (though had she ever?).

If Tommy hardly heard from Dani once the shop was up and running, she made the no-news-good-news assumption, glad that the only family member she had to worry about was Dad. Once in a while, she spoke to Jane, who told her how hard they were working, both of them. She was paying off her student loans; Dani and his partner were gaining a foothold in a neighborhood whose luxury value seemed to rise by the minute.

But a few years into the venture, something went wrong—not that he told her, no. If he had told her, she might have helped him. That he didn't ask for her help was, she came to realize, far more hurtful than his stealing, or trying to steal, that book.

Merry stands in her dim kitchen, peeling off her sodden clothes while trying to appease poor Linus, left alone far longer than she expected. Through the window, a perfect June twilight deepens toward night, the hour-long tempest forgotten . . . except by those caught in its fury.

"Hold on just a little more, my all-suffering friend."

She is stark naked, barefoot on the cold linoleum, bleary from the glass of wine she had at that bar to wait out the rain (so crowded, thank God, that nobody noticed her unshod state), when she sees the blinking 2 on her wall phone. With a sense of defiant foreboding, she pushes PLAY.

"Hi, Merry."

Oh, Benjamin. When it rains, it pours.

"I was wondering if you'd give me a call. I'm sure you're not dying to speak with me, but maybe there's a way we can be, like, not totally out of touch. I was hoping to tell you some news in person or, okay, at least over the phone. Which these days I guess is the new 'in person.' Anyway. If you could call. Thanks, Merry. Take care."

What, does he think she's an idiot? She knows the news without his telling her. He's getting married again. Or he's dashed right around the game board, express to GO, collected his two hundred dollars without having to pay rent on any of the expensive pastel-colored properties. (How she loved the colors of those little property deeds when she was a girl.) Except that the payout isn't two hundred dollars; it's a baby! Or a baby in progress.

The second voice is Sol's. "Meredith. Sorry about that fiasco at the park. I wanted to catch you at the end, with Stu. He's been conferring with me and a few of the other directors. He has an interesting proposal. Would you give me a call this evening if you can? I'm in meetings all day tomorrow."

This cannot be good. There is no way this can be good. Not that Stu's work isn't vital to Merry's overall mission, but whenever she's with him, she knows she's dealing with one of the most bullish egos ever to intersect with the writing of books for children (or children who think they're adults). Six months ago, Stu snake-charmed half the board simply by setting foot in the tiny conference room—

though she cannot deny that giving him the audience was her own idea. At the time, Merry understood how important his "modern" persona would be to the fiscal interests of the new museum—in crude terms, milking money from the hipster elite—but she also calculated that Sol's conservative distaste for the Shine Phenomenon was a fortunate shield against an aesthetic takeover. If not for Sol, Stu might have had a say in the choice of architect. (He wanted them to hire Bodley Brigand, a dystopian soul mate whose buildings look like glorified coastal surveillance towers from World War II: acres of concrete, long slits for windows, an allegiance to unforgiving angles.) As Merry's mother might say, the man is getting too big for his biker britches.

Wearing no britches whatsoever, she heads to the bedroom and opens her underwear drawer. Linus follows her, whining.

"Sorry, shmoo. I'm getting there."

The day the divorce came through, she ransacked her drawers and closet and discarded every piece of clothing that Benjamin had given her—or that she had bought with him in mind: a garter belt from the days he called her his hot date (a garment that had, perhaps prophetically, already lost its elastic zing), a dozen lace camisoles (in festive Monopoly-board colors), the zipperless red dress that made her feel, every time it dropped over her body, as if she were being washed in silk (and, every time Benjamin took it off, as if she were receiving absolution).

Her wedding gown, preserved in a specially sealed box to keep it from discoloring, lives in her mother's suburban attic. Neither of them mentions it. It will go to charity whenever her mother leaves that house. Merry cannot bear the thought of seeing it again.

Nor does she ever want to return to the South of France, least of all to that tiny timbered inn, surrounded by wanton explosions of yellow broom, where the two of them so blithely assumed they were conceiving the first of their children (the first of at least two, maybe three). They lay in bed till noon one day, sparring over which of the suburban options they would choose, knowing they could never afford to buy a Manhattan apartment large enough for a family.

"Maplewood."

"Oh God, not Jersey. Hastings."

"You are a snob. And Hastings is already too expensive."

"Yonkers."

"Yonkers? Be serious."

"Okay. Forest Hills."

"Have you ever lived on the F train? You might as well move to Moscow."

"Dobbs Ferry."

"At this rate, how about Nova Scotia?"

"Christ, can you tell we live in New York?"

"We can find something in Brooklyn. We are not *that* desperate."

"Let's just drill for oil in the building airshaft."

Their assumptions were so bourgeois, so smug.

None of that matters now, of course. The problem is, Merry never fell out of love with Benjamin—even after they came to dread touching each other, to dread looking at the calendar she kept inside her closet door. At the end, they even, or especially, came to dread the couples counselor. Merry still shuts her eyes when the Lexington Express hurtles through that station.

But dread is not the opposite of love.

Linus barks at the sound of his leash slipping from its hook in the closet. Dogs, thinks Merry, really listen to the world. "I am ready, little man," she says as she finds the loop on his collar. "Here we go."

Outside, Linus pulls hard at the leash, aiming for the gated park, a luxury he takes for granted, as he does his mistress's pure if sometimes negligent love. Merry orders herself not to cry as she unlocks the gate. She releases Linus from his leash, to hell with the rules. Let some enforcer ticket and fine her. She feels a wave of satisfaction, even joy, as she watches the small dog run ahead, pause to glance back, then streak headlong toward the tree that harbors the taunting squirrels.

Six

Andrew has a brand-new wife, and it's hard not to watch her, beyond the colossal picture window, as she glides and flips, glides and flips, bisecting the pool from one end to the other and back again. The pool is coal black, its surface sunstruck obsidian, and the wife's suit is neon yellow (her hair just about the same color, gleefully artificial).

On this side of the window is the long couch on which Andrew and Jake are seated. Jake is the alpha screenwriter. Nick has been around long enough not to get attached. As Deirdre said, writers are the zombies of the business: just when you think a certain chap is riding high, he's dead and buried—but then lurches to life in another project . . . until he's mowed down again, consumed by the next of the writer-zombies. "It's a cycle," she said. "Every writer has his good seasons and his bad. Until he doesn't. And it's almost never a she, by the way. As if I need to point that out."

Nick is on the twin couch, facing Andrew's across an oval sheet of frosted glass the size of a dory, its surface virtually obscured by papers, tablets, phones, laptops, and small Japanese bowls filled with resistible snacks like desiccated soybeans and diminutive rice cakes. Next to Nick sits Hardy, whose exact job is unclear. He's been discussing the animated footage they've already shot (or cyber-engineered, or super-digitized; however it is they make cartoons these days).

Andrew wants Nick to look at the sequences they have so far: Ivo wandering in the jungle, the panther following him, cunningly silent, at a distance. As in the correspondent part of Lear's book, the images are black and white—although furtive twinges of color flash now and then beyond the trees, like distant detonations—as if, Andrew explains, color is trying to force itself back into the world, all on its own. Nick marvels at how well they've captured Lear's way of drawing—yet turned the story so much darker than it is in the book. This film is not one for the nippers.

"The audience will believe that the panther is stalking the boy as prey. This is before we go to live action, the pivotal scene in the shed, with Toby and Sig." Tobias Feld is the boy actor; Siegfried Knutsen plays the gardener.

Nick has been trying just to listen. He had expected to meet Andrew alone, at least to begin with, though he realizes how naïve he was to believe that Andrew has much time to spend with any single person (except the wife—who, being new, probably gets as much of him as anyone possibly can).

"About the shed, we really need to speak," Nick says.

The others turn to him, expectant.

"Because, as I mentioned to you last month, what happened to him—to Lear—as that boy—wasn't what you've imagined. It's . . . more complicated."

"How much more complicated can it get than being sodomized?" says Andrew.

Nick pauses. "I just can't ignore . . . I mean, to have it from the horse's mouth that what people *assume* is the case isn't the spot-on truth . . . I can't ignore that." When no one speaks, he adds, "I don't mean just morally. I mean in terms of getting it right—which I see as my work."

Oh God, how grandiose, even priggish, did that sound?

Andrew stares intently at Nick. The other men watch Andrew. They remind Nick of a pair of spaniels, waiting for their master to don his Wellies, take his gun from the rack. He also notices for the first time that Andrew has an earring, with which he fusses when he isn't talking. He did not have that earring when they met up in London. Privately, Nick believes that getting an earring after age thirty—and Andrew's more than twice that age—is unseemly, but he chalks it up to the influence of the new wife. Call it rejuvenation. She looks barely this side of twenty. As she passes through the living room, quite unself-conscious in nothing more than her scanty fluorescent swimming costume, all three visitors have a clear view of the red rose tattooed across her back, in succulent bloom from her tailbone to the nape of her neck. Their eyes follow her in awestruck unison.

Andrew extends an arm in her direction; she reciprocates. Their pinkies clasp. "Take a break," he says. "Hardy. Jake. Have Flora fix you a juice. The oranges are killer." He nods to Nick, rises, and heads outside, along a walkway sheltered by a tempest of bougainvillea.

Nick can only presume he's to follow.

They enter Andrew's office bungalow. Since Nick was last here—two years ago, the first and only other time he's been here—the photographs on the wall have been rearranged, presumably to erase any history of Sasha, wife number two, who lasted nearly twenty years and mothered three of Andrew's (thus far) five children.

Andrew sits behind his desk and, as if Nick isn't with him, begins scrolling through messages on his tablet. "Never, never, never ending." He sighs. He still cuts the lean, agile figure he did, decades back, as an actor in a spate of highly praised films about moody young men (saboteurs, insurgents, tragic lovers), but in unguarded moments like this, Andrew's age surfaces in the sun-carved lines of his face, the softening of his jaw. Abruptly, he looks up. "So. Your revelation. Let's hear it. But realize that we're on location in three weeks. I'm not counting out rewrite, but these animators are breaking the bank. Used to be done by artists, down from their garrets—honest-to-God classically trained draftsmen. Not that the new artists aren't geniuses, too, but they're computer geeks who expect to be paid what they'd make if they were designing search engines at Google. And listen: Toby's mother has vetted the script so tyrannically that I think she might've missed her calling with the Stasi. So tell me what's up."

Nick sits in the upholstered chair facing the desk. It's the sort of chair in which you sink so far down that your knees rise toward your chest, making you feel inescapably childlike, as if sitting opposite your headmaster, waiting for him to hand out punishment for bad behavior.

"I'll just say it outright," Nick says.

"Only thing we have time for." Andrew's smile is genuine but brief.

"Lear wasn't sodomized by the gardener. The gardener never touched him. He was forced to witness, from a hidden space, the gardener having sex with various women. One was Lear's mother."

Andrew looks directly at Nick, but his face is devoid of emotion. After several seconds have elapsed, he makes an odd sound, like a grunt.

"He heard them more than saw them," Nick says. "He was in a tiny room in the shed where he went to . . . draw pictures."

"You're claiming he was a juvenile voyeur."

"No, no. And I'm not just 'claiming.' I'm telling you what he told me."

"He told you this when?"

"We e-mailed back and forth. I was planning to—but you know that. I was supposed to meet him last week. I was hoping to talk about it in person."

"Why would he tell you all this?"

"I don't know. Which is why I know it's the truth. Who would trade the easier version—the victim, plain and simple—for the stranger one, in which he might have refused, walked out, blown the whistle at the get-go? Theoretically. But the thing is, I understand how he couldn't, how trapped he was. By so many things. I *feel* it."

Andrew suddenly beams and waves; Nick realizes he sees his wife outside the window of the bungalow. Andrew blows a kiss.

"You see," says Nick, "it's like the cat's out of the bag for me. It's worlds different from what I'd imagined."

Andrew eyes the ceiling, where reflections from the rippling surface of the pool cast a zebralike pattern. "I could point out that you're not playing the child."

"I know that, Andrew. But I'm playing that child grown into the man who can't bloody forget what the child went through. It's not as if he'd blocked the memory. He lived with it for half a century. He lived with a mother who knew what he knew."

"The mother knew?"

"God yes! That's what makes it especially frightful. The mother found out that he was behind that wall, though not before she'd been to the shed, with that evil man, more than once. Lear finally couldn't stand it. He made his presence known. Later, he broke down and told."

"You have all this in writing—the e-mails."

Nick groans. "No."

"No? Nick . . ." Andrew frets with his earring, toggling the tiny gold loop between thumb and forefinger. Nick can hardly stand it. He wants to reach out and pull Andrew's hand away from his ear.

"He didn't reveal any of this in the interview."

"The interview is ancient. He clearly wanted to amend it, or why would he have—"

"Look. I don't see how we can change this aspect of the story this late in the game. For so many reasons, some of them probably legal."

"It's not just an 'aspect'!" cries Nick, then lowers his voice. "Andrew, it's the crux of the story as we're telling it."

"I'm not sure I agree with you there."

Andrew's phone buzzes. He pulls it from his pocket. "Flora's serving lunch. We have to wrap up the meeting in half an hour."

"Are you just going to ignore this?"

Andrew sighs, toys with the earring for a long excruciating moment. "Nick, I don't want to. I wish you'd spilled the beans sooner."

"I wanted to talk with him first."

"What Lear might have wanted, whatever his peculiar motives were in making this confession, none of that matters to me. Not to insult you, Nick, but this is my film, not his, not yours—and I am not sure I would have bought the version you're giving me."

"You don't believe him?"

Andrew shakes his head, but he is already out of his chair, aiming for the door. "I mean 'bought' in the literal sense. It's . . . there's something over-the-edge about it. Too kinky. Ambiguous. The studio—"

"Kinky and ambiguous never scared you off before." Nick follows Andrew back onto the trellised walkway.

Andrew pauses and turns around. "Let's talk tonight or tomorrow morning. Right now I have to finish up with Jake and Hardy— but stay for lunch, will you? You'll still have time to go back to your hotel before meeting with Toby and Trish. You'll love Trish—she's just out of ABT. And let's get a couple of images for the bloggers to nosh on, shots of you and Toby while I've got you together. Can't have you going stale. I'm tired of those *Taormina* stills, which is what your growing army of fans get right now whenever they IMDb you— you and, if you'll forgive me, the not so gracefully aging Deedee. I'd rather have them find the surprise of you with the fresh-faced Toby. Oh—and I forgot to say, you were great on Sunday. *That* was the perfect nibble. Thank you for that."

Nick silences himself. For now. Shading his eyes, he looks toward the pool, its inky darkness elegant yet forbidding. At a table sheltered by a wide ivory parasol sit Jake and Hardy, between them Andrew's wife, who has donned a translucent caftan in that same virulent yellow. Her matching hair erupts from her head in blunt, effusive tufts. She touches the two men frequently on their shoulders, arms, and hands, making them laugh freely.

She reminds him of Kendra, those easy public charms. At moments, just isolated moments, he misses Kendra, the way she could weave a kind of warm, protective aura around him, especially in social situations like this one.

"Sir."

He turns, startled, to see a dark-skinned older woman in a flowered dress holding a tray occupied by a single glass of deep red liquid.

"Blood orange," she says. "You must try."

I am in a fairy tale, he thinks, and now I will drink the blood. The sangfroid, he muses as he grasps the icy glass.

Of course you will, Deirdre would say. *And listen up when the wizard speaks, or you just might lose your head.*

How searingly lonely he feels in this instant: how far from home, far from certain, far from any sort of lasting love.

Franklin finally gave in and agreed to a gin and tonic. "Oh, corrupt me."

"I'm bribing you."

"No need, Tommy. Morty's still paying me plenty, even from beyond the grave."

Today they are attending to what Tommy thinks of, with no small dose of irony, as "the easy stuff," beginning with Morty's wish that they auction off his small but precious Dickens library, as well as the Alice ephemera. They've just arranged for representatives from two separate auction houses to show up the following week. This will be the first of the seed money allocated directly to Ivo's House.

"I have no idea what it's worth, any of it," she says. "I'm sure Morty didn't. He collected the things he did like a kid collects stamps."

"I don't think kids collect stamps anymore," says Franklin. "Mine didn't."

"I collected toy harmonicas."

"You're musical?"

"No. My parents were." She thinks of her abandoned piano lessons, Dani's resistance to the guitar.

Dani. Her brother, like so much else, will have to wait.

"I played the sax in high school," says Franklin. "Badly but with hormonal passion. Or desperation. 'Sax gets you sex,' some older punk told me when we were choosing instruments. Talk about false marketing."

"Tell me you still play." Tommy pictures a smaller, bow-tied Franklin playing "Watermelon Man" or "How High the Moon" in an adolescent jazz band.

"Not even in my dreams. Thank God."

Franklin turns back to the statements from Morty's investment funds. "I mentioned the life insurance, yes? Payable to Soren Kelly, in the beginning, but then to you. Five hundred K. On top of this property, of course, which he didn't want you to feel you'd have to sell."

Tommy is growing weary of the figures. She wasn't hired to handle figures, shift beads on an abacus. She was hired to handle art and words and people and travel plans and prize ceremonies; in the end, to keep an aging man company, deflect his fear of death by leaving her bedroom door ajar at night.

"I don't know how I'm going to make all this happen," she says.

"You won't. Not by yourself. We'll get through probate, pay the taxes, sell whatever you decide to sell. We'll find the people to make the rest happen. They can fund-raise their hearts out if Morty underestimated the grandeur of his plans."

"Franklin, you sound like a therapist."

"The best lawyers are therapists. We just charge more."

"I thought you told me that assessing mental fitness wasn't in your job description."

"No diagnosis. Just a lot of constructive listening."

"Which you're awfully good at." Is she flirting with Franklin? How long has it been since Tommy's flirted with anyone?

"Friday the actor's coming," she says after an awkward silence. "Again."

"Greene?"

"I'm letting him stay for the weekend."

Franklin whistles. "A weekend tryst with Nicholas Greene?"

"I'm old enough to be his mother. And you know what? He's very well mannered. Or he's fooled me into thinking so. I suppose the best actors, like the best lawyers, are therapists of a sort as well."

"Do you want me to stop in and check up?"

"I've got you on speed dial now. Speed text."

"Use me as needed." Franklin tips his glass back, draining the last bit of liquid from the ice. He gets up and puts it in the sink.

She might have asked him to stay for dinner, but she is planning on watching the actor's latest movie, the one that raked in the awards. Tommy feels illogically sheepish, as if it's obsequious to "study up" on Nicholas Greene.

She walks Franklin to his car. From behind the wheel, he says, "Maybe I'll stop over anyway. Do a little stargazing. Who gets to meet movie stars here in the Connecticut boonies?"

"Plenty of movie stars live in the Connecticut boonies."

"Must wear camo. Or come out after dark."

After he drives off, Tommy walks toward the studio. She is drawn there, unavoidably, several times a day. She realizes that she hasn't been filling Morty's bird feeders, which stand outside the window that provided the view from his drafting table. At least it's spring; nobody's starving in the snow. She goes back to the shed and takes down the two kinds of seed: thistle for the finches; for the rest, what Morty called aviatrix—short for "avian trail mix." The shed is stunningly hot inside. It smells of terra-cotta and the fancy brand of seaweed compost Morty liked for the gardens. The shelves are dusty, fragments of broken flowerpots strewn on the floor; he refused to hire any professionals. He mowed while Tommy weeded. Together, they planted and pruned.

It strikes her only now as obvious—or is it?—why he never wanted to hire a gardener. To most people, gardeners are nurturers, growers, experts on how to keep the planet photosynthesizing at a healthy clip. Not to Morty.

Will she have the nerve to ask Nicholas Greene about the script? About how they plan to "handle" that material? She's no fool: that's why they optioned the magazine piece. It wasn't for Morty's reminiscences about how he discovered his talent or how he got famous or even, at least not primarily, how he fell in love with a beguiling, opportunistic man like Soren Kelly. However unkindly, Tommy will never really think of Soren as a man. Looking back at 1991, the year Soren made his entrance, Tommy sees it like a spike on an EKG, but at the time it felt like an accrual of crises, unfolding one small drama at a time.

Morty had just won a second Caldecott, for *Rumple Crumple Engine Foot,* in which a small boy, playing on the floor beside his writer-father's desk, pulls discarded wads of typescript out of the wastebasket and holds them up to the light from a window, imagining each one as a different object. The boy crafts an entire story of his own from the balled-up waste of the story his father is failing to write. (The reader sees only the father's feet, on the floor beneath the desk, side by side in wing-tip shoes. Every so often, the top margin of the book exudes brief, child-friendly cursing and noises of adult frustration.)

In the same week, however—almost literally overnight—Morty's mother stopped recognizing him. Her Alzheimer's had been progressing at a dismally steady rate, and Morty had less and less time to get to Brooklyn, where, for several years, he had paid for Frieda to live in the best transitional home he could find near the places she knew. During those years, however, her friends had died or simply stopped visiting, and the places she knew became places she no longer knew. So what was the point, Morty felt, of keeping her there?

That week, he had moved her to a new place, just ten minutes from the Connecticut house. It was a superficially elegant (and breathtakingly expensive) "memory-care haven," with a staff better equipped to care for Frieda, but her Brooklyn doctor had warned Morty that taking her to live somewhere entirely new was risky. It might drive her further into the darkness.

As if to provide an appropriate background to this heartache, too many of Morty's friends and colleagues—Tommy's, too—were dying. To look back on that sinister era feels now, to Tommy, like going to a history museum and gazing into a glass-front display, a sealed-off epoch as remote as the ones portrayed in the dioramas with covered wagons or roaming mastodons. Perhaps that's a disgraceful thought, but barely twenty years after the panic began—the wildfire of fear and pointed hypochondria, the escalating number of phone calls with worsening news, the gridlock of funerals—it petered toward an end. Not an end to the entire epidemic, of course, but an end to its tyranny over their particular world, to the lengthening roster of its victims. Morty had pointed out, grimly, that if you knew your social circles well enough, you could have set up a solid betting pool, a kind of actuarial poker. "You could donate the proceeds to cover the health care of the uninsured, how about that?"

Between spates of touring and their separate day trips to the city, Tommy and Morty had lived an intensely focused life in the two years they had shared the house. One month Tommy's life was

a cram session of readings, parties, school visits, radio interviews, and—back when authors had any cachet—television talk shows. And then, for a season, it became a serial monotony of paperwork, phone calls, gardening, tending to the needs of a geriatric house. The longer stretches were almost monastic, but Tommy didn't see it that way, because the small, hectic periods of travel and fuss, of managing so much attention (both welcome and intrusive), filled her days with more people than she might have met in the entirety of any other viable life.

So it surprised her one day when Morty said, "Do you realize what a pair of sorry introverts we are?" He had just pointed out that a visiting plumber was the first person either of them had spoken with, face-to-face, in nearly a week. "Maybe we should start making jam or cordials. Wear ropes around our waists."

They were bound together as well by their mothers' failing health, though they spoke only rarely about this kindred burden—perhaps because each of them felt inadequate, never attentive enough. Tommy had Dani and her father to cover for her periods of absence and negligence—and, in hindsight, it's clear that Tommy's mother did her best to minimize the trials of her treatment, always insisting that she looked much worse than she felt. As for Morty, he could tell himself that his mother hardly noticed when he came to visit—and surely wouldn't remember once he left.

But at the time, Tommy had no intention, at least in the long term, of giving up on finding a separate life of her own. About children, she wasn't certain, but who didn't want to fall feverishly, lustfully, then lastingly in love? Since Scott, her Jamesian lover in college, she'd had two short liaisons, both disastrous, with men she met while she lived in the city. When they had each let her down, she had been grateful for Morty's company during the day. There were times she could even comfort herself with the certainty that here was a handsome, talented man who knew her well and treated her with kindness, even affection. If Morty had been attracted to women, maybe, despite their age difference, they would have married.

But she and Morty did not talk about love, not the kind of love that involved coupling. For too many people around them, death had eclipsed that kind of love. Because Tommy began working for Morty at almost exactly the same moment when whispers of the rogue disease began to circulate, she assumed that Morty had sworn off passionate connections because they were simply too risky. (In Morty's building on Twelfth Street, a downstairs neighbor was the first man Tommy saw whose skin had broken out in those lurid bruises. She saw him just a few times, trying hard not to stare, before she never saw him again.)

Or perhaps Morty kept his love life secret, partitioned into the hours Tommy went home to her walkup on Avenue A. After all, her two badly chosen boyfriends never set foot in Morty's place. So what if discretion seemed quaint?

And then suddenly, if only for six months or so, she had Dani to look after, to distract her from making further bad choices in men. A few years later, after the month during which she stayed with Morty while he recovered from surgery for a burst appendix, he asked if she'd like to move in full-time. The house felt too big, he claimed. And he needed to have an assistant right there, someone who would know how his studio worked, have physical access to his files—and deal with the ceaseless ringing of the phone.

"Are you threatening to fire me? Or 'lay me off'?" she said, trying to make it sound like a joke.

"Not in a million years would I do that," said Morty. "But look around here. Wouldn't you love to escape the mayhem of the city?"

Was it wrong to flee the political epicenter of the crisis? Though little more than an hour away, their affluent country village felt like a zone of both immunity and ignorance. But in the novelty of the move, she was happy to be unencumbered—she would figure out the mating business later—and she assumed the same was true of Morty. If there was a time she regretted her retreat from the city, it was after her mother's death, which left her father alone and numb. Her guilt receded, just a little, when Dani moved back in with Dad. Tommy knew it was a move of convenience as much as compassion—Dani, back then, in a state of serial disemployment—but still, her weekly visits felt paltry. It grieved her to see how her father's playfulness had died along with his wife. (The last silly song he wrote, during her second round of chemo, was a mock love ballad called "Cancer, Cancer, Necromancer.")

A month or so after the awards ceremony and his mother's acute decline, Morty told Tommy that he had agreed to teach a weeklong seminar at Pratt. He would be staying at a hotel in the city. Tommy couldn't remember any teaching invitations from Pratt, but Morty told her the request had come through a friend of his on the faculty— a favor, really. "I'm filling in for someone who's ill." The way he said the word *ill* discouraged her from asking any other questions. Enough said. Increasingly, daily routines involved folding in tasks for the weakened and dying.

Tommy was also distracted. She had met someone, in the plainest of ways. She had chosen the seat next to his on the commuter train, returning from a visit to her father. After an hour's conversation, before he got off, the man had invited Tommy to join him for dinner at a new French restaurant in Greenwich. Tommy chose an evening when she knew Morty would be visiting his mother; she didn't need his teasing.

The conversation at the restaurant was as easy as it had been on the train, though Tommy did not discuss her living situation. "I work for the author Mort Lear," she said, and even though John had no children, "Wow," he exclaimed right away, "a local celebrity!" Perhaps she should simply invite him over for a drink; maybe it wouldn't seem so odd, that she lived in her employer's house at thirty-one—so long as Morty wasn't around; because if he were, he wouldn't be good at making himself scarce.

John was enchanted by the house and garden. He loved the crowded mosaic of artwork on the living room walls, the shelves bowed beneath too many books, the collection of lumpy clay figures that various children had made for Morty over the past decade, which he displayed on the deep wooden mantel over the fireplace. She made a point of referring to Morty, often, as her boss.

"So you live with your boss?" John said. "That's devotion."

"It's temporary. Just so I can try out living in the country," she said. "Decide if I want to go back to commuting from the city or find something of my own out here."

"Oh, for me there's no choice," said John. "I love my job, but I also love waking up to the birds. I'd commute *two* hours if that's what it took to have both." John was a banker. He was thirty-seven and had been married, briefly, no children, in his twenties. He was bald, with an unlined, almost childlike face, but he was also tall, with expressive hands and a habitual, trustworthy smile. His brown eyes filled with tears when Tommy mentioned losing her mother the previous year.

The second time they saw each other, they went out to dinner at a café across from Orne's village green. When John kissed her good night, in his car, in Morty's driveway, she loved how the kiss felt half polite, half amorous. "How about a movie next time?" he said. "I know it sounds textbook, but I never get to the movies. Does anybody?" He raised his hands in a gesture of endearing wonder.

Tommy knew that if she told Morty about John, Morty would want to meet him—and would judge him as "too conventional." So Morty's week of teaching in the city felt auspicious: a chance for Tommy to begin something—to be *courted,* as her favorite authors would have said—in private.

In hindsight, however suitable her suitor was, however sweet (and really, did she know him long enough to know him at all?), he was probably more a wish than a real possibility: a wish for the mainstream life she had never led, a life made symmetrical by the gravitas of PNL balance sheets and train schedules and, from what John had told her, a clean modern house on a clean plot of grass. Archetypitis, Morty called it, the longing for relationships without nooks and crannies. But what was so bad about that? "The simple life," said Tommy's father, "is woefully underrated."

As it happened, Tommy never had a chance to find out. The Friday of that week—Morty was to return from his teaching stint on Sunday—John proposed that they meet at the train station when he returned from the city. They could drive from there to the Cineplex halfway between their towns. But when they consulted the schedule and, e-mailing back and forth, couldn't agree on any of the nine movies playing, Tommy suggested they rent one. If he drove the extra distance to Orne, she would make dinner for them. Hitchcock, she suggested. "You're on," replied her suitor.

John met her at the video store. Without a bit of fuss or debate, they chose *Vertigo*. She had already made a lasagna. He brought a bottle of Bordeaux and a bakery box containing two red-velvet cupcakes.

They ate the cupcakes while kissing. The DVD never left its case. Tommy loved saying John's plain, old-fashioned name, whispering it, as they lay in her bed, grappling and laughing in the dark of a moonless night. "Blind sex, don't you love it?" said John when their foreheads collided.

They were both asleep when the phone rang. Tommy woke disoriented and tripped on John's leg as she got out of bed. The upstairs phone lived on a table in the middle of the hall, halfway between Morty's bedroom and hers.

"Let it go," John whispered, reaching for her as she switched on the hall light.

Tommy stood in the open door, aware that John was watching her. The only call she would absolutely need to take would be one from her father or Dani. . . . She waited out the ringing, waited out her own voice telling the caller that no one could come to the phone. After the beep, not so much as a pause.

"Tommy, Tommy . . . *Tommy,* are you there? You have to be there. I need you. I messed up. Oh God, I'm a mess."

Morty's voice was strange—a growl at first, rising to a whimper.

"Please answer, Tommy. Please . . . I'm sorry if I—"

She rushed to pick up the receiver.

An hour later, she was driving to the city, glad the roads were empty, glad to find a station that played nothing but jazz, few ads, few words of any kind. By the time she reached the Henry Hudson Parkway, dawn had defined the horizon. To her right, the George Washington Bridge carved its somber geometry into a lavender sky.

Morty was in his hotel room, dressed except for his shoes. Only the bathroom light was on. After answering the door, he collapsed back onto the bed. When Tommy switched on a lamp, she saw him curled in a turbulence of sheets and pillows. The pillows were streaked with blood.

She was speechless with terror. Even caring for him after his surgery, she had not seen him in this much pain. His nose was clearly broken, the visible ear cut and bleeding, and his cheek was bruised from jaw to temple.

She sat on the edge of the bed and rested a hand on one of his calves.

"Just take me home," he said. "No questions."

"I say we go to a hospital."

"They ask questions."

"Morty."

But he refused to let her do anything more than drive him home. She drove without breaking her silence, which tasted like fear, then anger, then disgust. His breathing, through his broken nose, was loud and ugly. He went straight to his bedroom and slept till late afternoon, and when he came downstairs to the kitchen, his left eye was swollen shut. It was Saturday, so Tommy left a message with his doctor's service and took him to an ER in Stamford.

As they drove home in the dark, she said, "You weren't teaching, were you. All this week."

"No."

She sighed. How far should she go? If she had ever needed to think of him as merely her boss, this was the time.

He said, "I went . . . out a few nights."

Morty was never this short on words. She knew his jaw hurt, but that wasn't it. When they got home, she made him scrambled eggs and mashed up an avocado.

She wanted to ask if he was lonely. She now knew, against all previous evasions, that this was true for her. (She also knew she wouldn't hear from John again. Not that she felt like calling him, either, not after what he'd overheard, not after her abrupt, panicky departure.)

"I just wish you had told me what you were doing."

He looked at her coldly for a moment. "Tell you I was going to the city to . . . prowl the streets?"

"Escape, maybe. Lose touch a little. You didn't need to make something up."

He shook his head. "You can't know everything."

"Right," she said. "But I can't be expected to wake up at four a.m. and drive two hours to pick up your pieces from a bar brawl. If that's even what it was."

He stared at his food.

"Morty, I'm not your mother. I'm not your wife. I don't even get to be your lover." She paused. Why had she put it that way? He looked at her then.

"Tommy, I'm sorry. I don't treat you fairly. I . . . keep you here, hold you back from . . ."

"Leading a normal life? That goes without saying. But I'm not your prisoner, either. I'm here because I like it here. Maybe this is as normal as life gets for me."

The look he gave her then was tender. "I think I'm going a little mad."

"I won't disagree."

"And I'm not cured." He shook his head vehemently.

"So what does that mean? That you'll do this again? Because next time, I don't think I can come to the rescue."

He continued to shake his head. "I don't know what it means."

She pulled her chair around the kitchen table to sit beside him. She put her right hand over his left. She felt older than she ever had before—and more fearful than she'd ever felt except beside her mother's hospital bed on her very last day. "Take a break from everything," she said. "You can afford to. Deserve to. Maybe take a trip that has nothing to do with books?"

"I can't do that," he said. "It's not in my nature. Not now."

"Is it in your nature to self-destruct?"

"Tommy, let me be. Just let me . . . go through what I have to go through."

She stood up and moved away from him. "Fine," she said. "I'll do that. Go be yourself. Last I looked, you had no other choices."

Over the next two months, Morty would sometimes pack a small bag and drive into the city. He would tell her how many nights he planned to be gone; it was never more than three. He would return looking exhausted, often gaunt, and sleep late for the next few mornings, working after dinner to appease his conscience. Rose, in a conversation with Tommy concerning foreign rights, made acerbic reference to a city gossip column that noted a "Lear sighting" at a warehouse-turned-nightclub on Rivington Street.

And then one day when he returned, he wasn't alone. Tommy heard the car pull up outside. She stood at the kitchen window, to get a stealthy look at Morty's physical state when he emerged from the car—but the first person to get out, from the passenger side, was a tall blond man. Alert and confident, he turned in a circle to take in his surroundings. Until he spoke, he reminded Tommy of a beautiful long-legged hound, tensed for the start of a hunt or a race.

"Where in the world am I?" he exclaimed. "Did I die and go to heaven? Though wait—that's not the place holding my reservation." His laughter was raucous, almost brutal.

Tommy watched as the young man went around the car and opened Morty's door, pulling him out with both hands joined, as if leading him toward a dance floor.

Andrew wasn't kidding about this child actor's overbearing mother. Toby is a perfectly composed little boy, far older than his years, and if Mum would just leave them alone to collaborate, Nick knows they would get on winningly, forge their destined alliance. But the mother sits in a chair by the door, watching them intently.

The boy is assured and graceful in his movements—his "Ivo dance." What's equally impressive, if benignly spooky, is how closely Toby resembles Nick. He looks more like the grown Nick than photographs taken of Nick when *he* was nine years old.

A rough, herky-jerky cut of the animated jungle scene is projected on one wall of the dance studio. Ivo is moving through the trees, mimicking different animals as he encounters them; behind him, the panther creeps along in quiet pursuit.

The idea is for the animated Ivo to transform gradually into the Toby-Ivo, and then—though this will happen a few scenes later in the film—Toby as the young, traumatized Lear will, in a complex sequence to be filmed on the Arizona set and in a Burbank soundstage, turn into Nick as Lear the young man, the ambitious artist making his way in New York.

Toby and Nick wear identical leggings and cotton vests. They stand barefoot on the studio's padded floor, facing a panoramic mirror in which they can see the projection on the wall behind them. Nick stands behind the boy, his looming shadow.

"What he'll actually wear won't be so revealing," says Toby's mother. "Right?"

"You can take that up with Andrew or Ned," Trish says brightly.

"We need to have a conversation about the scenes in the shed," says Mum.

Nick cringes. Wasn't that exactly what he said an hour ago, to Andrew?

"I'm just working on coordinating their body language, their way of moving through space," says Trish. "That's my job here."

Nick sees her patience thinning. He wonders if Toby, who moves not a muscle during this exchange, is embarrassed. All Nick can see of him is his head of strawberry hair, just shy of Nick's sternum. On the other hand, the boy must be used to this. Likely the mother is a failed performer. She has the semistarved look of a ballerina.

Trish stands behind Nick; he can feel her breasts beneath his shoulder blades. She interlaces her fingers with his and lifts his arms gently till they are parallel to the floor. "Your hands are the butterflies, weightless, your fingers their translucent wings."

He shuts his eyes, briefly, to feel himself inside the drawing that spooked him as a child but to feel it as a brightening, a benediction, the world quenched with rain after a drought. Then, eyes open, he dances as if stitched to the small boy before him: step, spin, bend, on tiptoe, arms raised, face open—

The mother's mobile rings. She answers it.

Nick stops and turns around. "Would you mind taking that outside the room?"

She asks the caller to hang on.

"It'll be short," she says to Nick.

"No," he says. "It will be outside the room. Please."

She stares at him, deciding. Trish and Toby say nothing. "This isn't a shoot. It's a rehearsal. My son doesn't rehearse without me in the room."

"Then turn off your mobile."

She says something inaudible to the caller, ostentatiously turns off the phone, puts it in her pocket. "Fine," she says, settling back in her chair.

They resume, but Nick feels his heart beating too insistently. Was he wrong to give her orders? Trish is holding him by the waist now, steering him this way and that. "Relax," she says softly. "Nick, relax."

He steps away from her and shakes out his limbs.

"It's cool," Toby says to him. "Let's break." The boy puts a hand on Nick's bare arm, and the warmth of it is soothing.

"Thank you," Nick says. "Just a few minutes and I'll be a hundred percent. Must be a spot of jet lag."

They head for a pair of chairs against the opposite wall from the mother.

Next to Nick, leaning over, elbows on his knees, Toby whispers, "She's just protecting me. After she gets to know everybody, it's fine."

Nick holds off from telling Toby that even at this early stage, her interference is counterproductive.

Sure enough, the mother is approaching them. Foolish Nick wonders if she's coming over to apologize. He stands and makes an effort to look friendly. When she's directly in front of him, she says, "We haven't met before, but just so you know, it's in his contract to have me present, so you'll need to get used to it."

Nick says, "He seems to know what he's doing."

"Sure does," she says. She's smiling, but her arms are crossed tightly. "That's why he's here, Nick."

"I'm sorry, your name again?" Nick can see Trish, the look of concern on her face. But she keeps her professional distance.

"Rebecca," says the mother. Pointedly, Nick is sure, she does not extend a hand.

"A pleasure," he says, as if he means it.

"This is going to be massively cool," Toby says.

Nick turns his attention from the overbearing mum to the diplomatic boy.

Toby is smiling up at him, and for a second Nick is looking in a small mirror at his small self. He has a sudden urge to hug Toby, though there is no way Rebecca would tolerate that gesture—and of course it would alarm the boy. He turns toward Toby (which means turning his back on the mum) and says, "It is going to be awesome."

Seven

For other boys, school holidays meant more time spent with family, or at least with your mum, who was usually at home in any case, doing the normal things mums did to keep the household from teetering into pandemonium. But Nick's mum didn't have the luxury of taking off much time except for a few weeks in the summer, when she'd find a way to take them all for a week at a cottage a friend of hers owned on the Solway Firth. Not far into their teens, Nigel and Annabelle grew increasingly resentful of spending this time away from their friends, and it was Nick who humored their mother by playing word games or reading beside her on the shingled beach. He was acutely aware that she deserved a holiday to go the way she wanted it to.

On odd days off from school, or hols when Mum was working and his much older siblings bolted from the flat, Nick was on his own. He didn't mind awfully, because he could go in and out as he pleased, the flat entirely his. He had two mates who lived near the closest park; some afternoons they'd meet up there, kick a ball around, or rove about and spy on various characters. They looked for the suspicious ones, the oddballs and nutters, tried to follow them at a distance, dream up what crimes they might be planning. But more often Nick hung back at home, reading, watching the telly some, playing patience or, absurdly, solo games of chess.

Mum cut short any complaints of boredom. She told Nick that boredom was a luxury, to be seized on—that she would gladly take boredom over her job at the Indian carryout place. "Boredom," she declared, "is a tunnel. Make it take you somewhere."

They lived on the top floor of a building at the closed end of an old mews, a place of damp stone and crumbling mortar, though Mum insisted she found it romantic. ("Your mother fancies you're living in a Pareezian garret," Grandfather scoffed. The stairs were his excuse for meeting them elsewhere.) Despite the altitude, most of the flat's five small rooms were dark, with low ceilings and miserly dormered windows. The exception was Mum's bedroom, at the back, which looked over a low roof across a wide street with buildings grander than theirs. The entries were flanked by fluted columns, and the windows were not only tall but glistened from regular cleaning. On fair days, sun poured into Mum's room during the morning hours, so Nick, when left on his own, liked to sit on her bed with his book or deck of cards. He also discovered that the window offered a slightly elevated view of another interior, the top flat in one of those grander buildings, where sometimes a woman paced to and fro in a dressing gown, talking and gesturing with feeling. He could never spot a companion and began to imagine she might be a madwoman, ranting to herself. Then one day, though she was pacing expressively, same as ever, he saw that she was reading from a book.

He went into the cupboard he shared with Nigel and poked about till he found the heavy binoculars Grandfather had given Nigel for his last birthday (as if Nigel planned to take up birding!).

Crouching low, Nick rested the binoculars on the windowsill and fiddled with the knob adjusting the focus.

The woman was younger than Mum and, from a twelve-year-old's perspective, fairly smashing. Rarely holding still, she passed to and fro across the frame of her own window, but each time, he got a quick glimpse of her wide eyes, carefully shaped brows, and expressive mouth—and, pressing against her robe, a pair of pretty impressive breasts. That day the robe was red, and her hair was captured in a striped towel twisted turban-style.

What *was* the book? Its face flashed upright for fleeting seconds, never long enough for Nick to read the title. (Did it matter? Never mind. He wanted to *know*.)

Whom was she reading to? Or was she so lonely that she needed the sound of her own voice as company? How could anyone so beautiful be desperate for company?

Nick became obsessed with watching for her on the rare occasions he was home alone by day; most nights (when he could nip into Mum's room for a glance), the woman's flat was dark.

He made sure to smooth Mum's bedcover after he finished his spying, since he wasn't really supposed to be in her room when she was out—and then, of course, she would hardly have approved of his spying. And Nigel would have pummeled him for pinching the binoculars.

He worried that he might be turning into a Peeping Tom, though he reassured himself that he wasn't much interested in going about on ladders at night and sneaking through shrubs. This woman was the sole object of his fascination. She was his personal mystery.

She dominated his waking dreams, and at night he thought of her as he lay in the dark trying to shut out Nigel's snoring. In his imaginings, he gave her the name Sheba. She dropped her robe and turban for him—even her book.

Then, to his terror and delight, one autumn afternoon as he was returning home from a maths tutorial, he passed her on the street. He recognized her at once, though she was smartly dressed and her glossy butter-colored hair was plaited to the back of her head. Without hesitating, he turned right round and followed her. Dark was descending, and he could only hope she wouldn't summon a taxi or make for the tube.

Even in slender-heeled shoes, she was a fast walker; in fifteen minutes, Nick was winded—and he realized that he was paying such keen attention to her blue-coated figure, half a block ahead through crisscrossing clumps of strangers, that he had forgotten to keep track of where they were headed—more important, of how he would find his way home.

She turned down a narrow alley and knocked on a door. He stood back, watching from the corner. Almost immediately, the door opened, and he had only a second to hear her greet the unseen doorkeeper, sounding bright and chipper, before the door closed behind her.

Nick waited a minute or two before proceeding cautiously down the alley. The buildings to either side were indifferent, factorylike, the only windows way up high. The door Sheba had entered, the only break in a long expanse of brickwork, was a dull black, unmarked—no handle or knob. How peculiar was that?

Bewildered and lost—now it *was* dark—Nick left the alley to inspect the front of the building: a long row of doors overhung by a lettered marquee. Had he not been so fixated on his quarry, he would have seen straightaway that it was a theater. And as he stood there, inert, dejected, the marquee blazed to life, the letters jutting forward in defiance of the night.

Henrik Ibsen's
HEDDA GABLER
Emmelina Godine   Donal McSwain

Through the glass doors spanning the façade, Nick could see that only the light in the ticket taker's booth was lit, but he could also see someone walking about, rather aimlessly. And then the someone slipped through an inner door, allowing a brief burst of light to escape.

Nick waited for a few minutes; the someone did not emerge. From left to right, he tried the doors. The last one, opposite the ticket window, opened. Inside the dim lobby of the theater, he was alone. No alarms went off, no one yelled. His footsteps silenced by thick carpet, he approached the line of inner doors, these paneled in a velvety fabric, which he knew would lead him into the maw of the theater itself. He pulled at one near the center, expecting it to be locked. It seemed to fly open, much lighter on its hinges than the glass door through which he had entered the building.

The seats in the theater were empty, but there stood Sheba, in the center of the stage, all lights on her. She wore a flowing gray dress, or perhaps it was silver. It shone like polished steel in the spotlights. She was speaking, her words clear as birdsong all the way to the very back. She continued for a sentence or two, then slowed to silence.

She shaded her eyes, peering out over the sea of velvet chairs. "Hello there," she called out, neither friendly nor irritated. "Who's joining us this evening?" She walked forward to the edge of the stage, and then her voice became anxious. "James. Is that you, James?"

He noticed then that she wasn't alone. Half a dozen heads rose and turned from seats quite near the stage. A man in jeans and a loose tartan shirt stood and said, "Come on down, whoever you are." He walked up the aisle directly toward Nick.

Should he run? Not like he'd broken into a bank.

Slowly, Nick started down the aisle. The man, who waited for him, looked puzzled, not cross. "What can we do for you, lad?"

"Watch?" came out of Nick's mouth. "May I watch?"

The man frowned briefly, then laughed. He turned away from Nick and spoke to Sheba. "Lad wants to watch you, Em. Your youngest fan yet, I reckon."

"Come up here," she called out, beckoning.

Though his legs might as well have been fashioned from wood, Nick found his way to the stage; it helped that the way sloped down. He paused a few rows from the stage, but she continued to beckon. "I'm not a vampire," she said. "No fangs or claws." She bared her teeth and held up her hands.

She waited till he stood with his chest against the stage. He found himself looking up at her from a curious angle (he had always seen her, before, from slightly above). "What are you called?" she said.

"Nicholas Greene," he said. "I didn't mean to intrude."

"Well, intrude you did," she said. "But now that you're here, take a seat." Her arms were joined across her lovely chest.

"Yes, ma'am. Thank you," he said, his grandfather's edicts writ large on his determination not to panic.

"All I ask is that you not leave again till we're through with a scene. No slinking out the way you slunk in." She added cheerfully, "That would be discourteous." They stared at each other for a moment before she said, "Go on. Choose a seat. Not front row, if you don't mind. Not my best angle, for one thing."

Nick went back up the aisle, and as he passed the men who were obviously directing the play, he saw them laughing quietly amongst themselves. He wanted to flee, but he knew he would never forgive himself if he did. And to leave would mean confronting the problem of how to find his way home. So he took a seat in the middle of a row halfway back toward the exit.

Other actors came and went across the stage, and the lines were a blur to him at times: not because he couldn't understand them but because he couldn't stop staring at Sheba—at Emmelina, as it turned out; or Em, as the directors called her whenever they interrupted to make their comments.

He stayed till the end, which might have been one or four hours later. There were no clocks within sight, and he didn't like wearing the old-fashioned watch his grandfather had given him. The few times he'd worn it, his schoolmates had called it "the timepiece" in mock codger tones. Their watches had digital faces.

Finally, when it was clear that everyone was packing up and someone began to switch off the stage lights, he stood. But where was he to go, other than out? Then, to his mortified relief, she was standing at the end of his row.

"You planning to pitch a tent here?"

He stayed where he was, staring at her, barely able to utter "No."

"What brought you in, Nicholas Greene? Boys don't randomly sneak into my rehearsals. At least, not boys your age. What *is* your age? Shouldn't you be at home swotting up on literature and computation?" She tapped her slim gold wristwatch.

That she had remembered his entire name shocked him speechless. "Pardon me," she said, "I did not introduce myself. You may call me Ms. Godine." She held out her blue coat. At first he had no idea what this gesture meant. Then, nearly stumbling, he made his way out of the row and held it open for her. As she backed into the coat, he could see the infinitesimal blond hairs on the back of her neck.

She was shorter than she had looked onstage—in heels, only half a head taller than he was.

She turned around and said, while buttoning the coat, "You're intrigued by the theater, is that it? I can't imagine you want to be an actor; seems you don't much like speaking."

The three men were heading up the aisle. "Need a ride, Em?" asked one.

"No, I'll catch a little fresh air," she said. "See our young friend out."

The man hesitated, looking from her to Nick and back again.

"I think I'm safe with this fellow," she said. And, to Nick, "Shall we?"

He realized he had nearly forgotten his satchel and went back into the row.

"Mustn't leave that," she said.

He walked out behind her. They stood together on the pavement; he watched her kiss the men goodbye. Two of the actors he had seen onstage with her came around from the alley and kissed her as well. One of them gave Nick a small wave.

When just the two of them remained, she said, "So. Did you like what you saw? Curtain's up on Friday. Previews, but all the same. Word travels before the critics get their hooks in. An old chestnut like this, you've got to nail it to the wall."

He had no idea what she meant.

"You do talk," she said. "I believe I heard you speak your name, unless I dreamed it."

"Yes," he said. "I did like it, your play. I'm just . . ."

"Surprised at yourself? Don't I know that feeling." She laughed. She took out a pack of cigarettes and lit one. "So listen, Nicholas Greene. I have a hunch you're too young to be out on your own at this hour. I hope you live nearby."

He had a choice. He could say yes and set off in any direction, and God knew where he'd end up. Or he could . . . "Ms. Godine," he said, "I live near you. I believe."

"You *believe* you live near me?" She squinted at him and lifted her chin to release a plume of smoke. But then she smiled. "I am not even going to investigate that allegation. I suppose the thing is for me to ask you to escort me home. Yes?"

She ground her cigarette into the pavement and, without waiting for an answer, extended a hand. He held out an elbow, as his grandfather had shown him.

"Tell me your story, Nicholas. Let me hear that you have a proper voice."

Her hand warming the crook of his elbow even through the sleeve of his jacket, she cajoled him into talking about his family, his wish for a dog, his favorite shows on the telly. She did not ask how he knew where she lived. Once he recognized the neighborhood, he led her to the foot of the mews, where he insisted she leave him off.

"And you'll go straight home from here?" she asked.

He nodded.

"Are you free Saturday evening?"

When he told her that he was, she asked if his mother worked then. "Surely Saturday she has off."

"Yes, Saturdays she's at home with us, at least the evenings," Nick said. Already he felt accustomed to Ms. Godine's forward inquiries.

"Brilliant," she said. "Then come to the theater on Saturday, by half seven, and there will be two tickets at the window in your name, Nicholas. Decent seats, too. Will you bring your mum, and then will you find me after? I'll expect you. I'll leave a note with the tickets."

He hesitated.

"I will be cross if you don't come," she said, and then she backed away with a soldier's salute, pivoted gracefully round on a narrow heel, and turned the corner.

When Nick entered the flat, he found his mother possessed by a grieving rage the likes of which he had never witnessed before. She seized him by the shoulders, sobbing, and asked, her voice a shriek, wherever on earth he had got to. She had sent his siblings out to search the parks and nearby streets.

"Theater," he said. "The theater."

She laughed manically. "Oh dear God, Nick, are you now on drugs?

This too? You cannot do this to me, you have to be truthful, you have to be straight as a bloody arrow, you have to not make my life harder than it already is, you have to—"

"Mum, it's true. I went out, and I . . . got lost, and I went into this theater to ask where I was, and I . . . watched a play. A rehearsal for a play."

"You watched a rehearsal for a play." She took a tea towel from beside the kitchen sink and wiped it harshly across her mottled face.

"Yes. We have tickets. We can go to the play, the real play, on Saturday."

His mother stared at him, her breath still catching from her tears. "You mustn't fool with me. You mustn't."

"It's true," he said. "On Saturday I'll prove it. It's called *Hedda Gabler.*"

The strange thing was, he had no doubts that what he believed had happened had really happened, nor that Ms. Godine would keep her word.

Emmelina Godine gave Nick a paying job for the remainder of her six-month run as Hedda Gabler. After school, he would rush home and do his schoolwork as quickly and efficiently as he could. After an equally rushed dinner, he would walk to the theater and bring Ms. Godine a newspaper, a sleeve of chocolate biscuits, a bottle of lemon crush, and he would make her tea with the electric kettle in her dressing room. It wasn't large or luxurious, but he liked sitting with her in that stuffy, windowless room while she made phone calls or read the news, sometimes aloud. ("Nicholas, what do you know about China? We all need to know about China.") Sometimes she asked him to step into the hall while she took or made a call. She told him from the start that she would mostly ignore him, that he was free to go (or stay) once he had poured her first cup of tea.

The other actors were amused by his presence; now and then he would run an errand for one of them as well. Donal McSwain, who played Ms. Godine's husband in the play, sometimes knocked on her door and asked, "May I borrow your young apprentice?" McSwain was constantly running out of fags. The smoke in the hallways grew thick after an hour or two; Nick's mother didn't smoke, so he wasn't used to it, and at times he felt light-headed. He went home every night with clothes that smelled like a pub. (The smell of cigarettes, even now, makes Nick nostalgic for the bunkerlike comfort of a backstage warren.)

In the spring, Ms. Godine explained to Nick that the production would travel to America; she and her costar would go as well. "I wish I could take you along," she said, "but I have a feeling your mum wouldn't be keen on that idea." As a farewell present, she gave him the big colorful cigar box where she had stashed her hairpins, stray coins, and the pack of fags she was always hiding from Donal McSwain.

She wrote Nick a handful of postcards, and he wrote twice to an address she had given him—short, awkward notes, because what did he really have to tell her? Once she was gone, she seemed as unattainable as she had when she was a figure of mystery behind a window across a street, unaware of his prying eyes. But she had made her mark on Nick.

That year, his life changed in other ways. One night Mum had a beastly row with Grandfather. It was over the phone, and Nick was in his room, studying for exams. Even through the closed door, he heard every word his mother said to her father. It was obvious that Grandfather had suggested Nick should go away to school; he would pay for it, and why in the world should Mum refuse? He hadn't offered this option to Nigel or Annabelle, but for unknown reasons, he had decided that Nick should attend an independent school. Nick knew that whenever money was involved, Grandfather always won the argument, because money had power—the power to buy not just things and services and privileges but, Nick had only recently grasped, time. And sometimes people. Listening to Mum's raised voice, he could tell that Grandfather was calling her selfish, accusing her of holding Nick back.

The row on the phone ended with Mum shouting that the decision would be Nick's. The flat was silent after that. Nick continued to study, but he kept waiting for Mum to knock on the door. She didn't.

Unable to concentrate, he finally gave up and closed his book.

In his gut, he wanted to go. He didn't want to leave Mum, not if it would make her unhappy, but the flat felt emptier than ever when she was at work. Nigel had just pushed off to university up north, and Annabelle was spending all her spare time working in a dress shop (where, as far as Nick could tell, she must be spending half her wages). Nick had a room to himself now, but if boredom was a tunnel, all it did was lead him only deeper into the earth; these days, boredom was more like a mine shaft. He had no knack for sports, and for spare-time reading, he'd begun to borrow plays from the school library—but to simply *read* a play felt a bit tunnelish as well. He imagined that a public school, surely richer than the one nearby that Nigel had attended, would give him a chance to try out the stage for himself. Ms. Godine had told him that the best foundation an actor could have was solid schooling, that he mustn't think of short-changing himself on that.

Mum cried when he told her he would like to accept Grandfather's offer.

"You are all leaving me, all of you," she wailed. "And you are all I have."

Nick had no argument to offer because he feared that what she said might be true. He said, "I won't go far. I'll come home during holidays—every one, I promise. And now you won't have to worry about me. Where I am, things like that."

When she continued to weep, he said, "And when I'm done, I'll stay near. Not like I'm going to desert you."

Through his early twenties, he did his best to honor that promise: he went to university in the city, studying theater at Goldsmiths. For two years, he lived with fellow students, but when Mum moved to a modern flat with a lift and a lower rent, he joined her. It was smaller than the old flat, but there was a room off the kitchen just big enough for a bed and chest of drawers, and Mum wouldn't let him pay her more than a token rent. This spared him wasting half his life on the crap jobs that other scrabbling actors were thankful to land; time was as crucial as talent. Bit parts on the stage and in radio adverts kept him hoping for more while keeping him close to home.

But then he was cast as Valentine in a West End production of *Two Gentlemen of Verona*; after that, he was virtually handed a plum role as an all-suffering frontiersman in a BBC drama to be shot in the wilds of Canada. His mother's cancer was diagnosed two weeks after he crossed the Atlantic. Annabelle took Mum to her appointments and stayed with her on bad nights. Nick felt helpless and callow, especially when the time difference and the shooting schedule conspired to keep him from talking to Mum more than once or twice a week.

By the time the shoot had wrapped, Nick miserably awake and anxious on the three flights he took to reach home, Mum was weak from radiation and waiting for her place in the chemotherapy queue. Nick was desperate to help her, but it was, effectively, too late, in part because she had lost the will to fight the bureaucracy as well as the disease. Annabelle had been similarly depleted.

And then came the offer of a role in a new series about King Arthur and the legends surrounding his knights. The role was Gawain. Arthur was to be played by Sir Gwyn Pugh, who almost never left the realm of theater, where he reliably filled every seat in the house.

"Go back to your work," Annabelle told him. "I'm not saying that out of bitterness. At this point, it's what she wants for you. She'd murder us both, weak as she is, if she learned that you'd turned this down on her account."

His work, this time around, took him to a punishingly cold, rain-drenched forest in Romania. (Why couldn't he snag a role in a drawing-room comedy? Was it something to do with his bony, hungry-looking physique? Perhaps it didn't help that he *had* been properly schooled in swordsmanship and riding.) So he cleared off, obedient, sheepishly relieved, and found himself so consumed by the daily marathon of racing against a straitlaced budget that his mother's illness began to seem as if it must have been a mirage—until, just a few weeks later, Annabelle called again.

As it turned out, he was the one sitting beside their mother when she died in hospital. Annabelle was running errands on her way there, Nigel pulled out of the room by an urgent call from his wife. Nick sometimes wonders if his half sister can't quite forgive him, though Mum was hardly present much herself at the end of her life.

Nick sees his career thus far as a steady progress, marked by only a few truly galvanic moments, bone-jarring cracks of thunder, strokes of fate. Following Emmelina Godine to that theater was one; his arrival at boarding school was another; the most recent had to be the moment, two summers ago, when he came down from his room to the lobby at the San Domenico Palace, in Taormina—addled by travel delays (a missed flight connection in Milan), unsettled by bad airport food (whatever possessed him to buy *prawns?*), and missing Kendra—to collide, almost literally, with his costar, Deirdre Drake.

"Well met, cowboy," she said in her prairie-wide American contralto.

"I'm so happy, so honored, so gobsmacked," he heard himself gushing. They had met once, for a screen test in L.A. to see how Nick partnered, visually, emotionally, with the woman around whom the film would revolve. They had made no small talk, and a literally gut-wrenching brew of superstition and terror had left him both tongue-tied and nauseated beyond the boundaries of the audition itself.

In the hotel lobby, she took him by the arm and, leaning so close to him that he could feel her breath on his ear, said, "If I'm going to be your mother, boyo, we've got our work cut out, don't we?"

She then set off in a resolute direction, compelling him along. "We're having dinner, yes? Let's skip the bar, though I hear it's in some chapel straight from *Il Gattopardo*. If I cannot drink, and alas I cannot, I'll take pasta, pronto. Pasta with some of that lobster imported to these waters as part of the Marshall Plan. Did you know that this is the only part of the world where the lobsters are as good as you'd get in Maine?" She raised her eyebrows; Nick managed to shake his head. "Sicilian food is unique. You get couscous. North African fishes. And the best of the white wines—if you have doctor's permission—are *molto fabuloso*. As for me, no vino means I get to order dessert. Give me tiramisu or semifreddo. The least pretentious sweet they offer at this pop stand." Her soliloquy flowed seamlessly along as she led him among the tables on a stone terrace, its walls enrobed in pink bougainvillea, its vista one of sun-blazed blue water stretching toward . . . was it Libya or Greece? Nick had looked at maps before leaving home, but in the compass-tilting glare of Deirdre's presence—and in her opulently perfumed wake—he hadn't the faintest notion of his place on any map.

"We are unfashionably early," she said—obvious from the empty tables, all set but still awaiting diners, "or, if we prefer, we simply don't give a high hoot what customs everybody else observes."

He was twelve all over again: weak-kneed, swollen-hearted, speechless in the grip of a confused veneration. This wasn't the same quietly coiled actress he had met in front of that camera on the opposite side of the world.

Thank God the maître d' (who finally caught up with them) pointed out a table set for five. Once in their chairs, Deirdre spread her napkin in her lap, leaned over, and said, "One thing. No matter what you hear from these other jokers, do not call me Deedee. I can't stand it, but the name sticks to me like Bazooka to a shoe. Call me by my proper name and you will not be punished." Up went her artfully shaped brows; crikey, what did she mean by that?

Before he had time to wonder further, they were joined by two producers and Sam Schull, the director. Nick said very little, concentrating on the food, the view, and the incredulity of his being here, on the terrace of this ancient monastery tastefully tarted out for the rich, in thrall to a bona fide American movie star (her radiance only burnished by her resilience in the wake of bad behavior). He found himself listening reverently as she talked about another town in Sicily, high on a small steep mountain, the site of an ancient temple to Aphrodite.

"The priestesses spent their days doing priestessy things: ablutions, devotions, sacrifices, prayers. But at night they gave shelter to beached sailors from all points around the Mediterranean. And fucked them, of course. But nobly, in service to the ideals of the love-

and-beauty goddess. The women who live there today are the most gorgeous women in the world. Part Greek, part Moroccan . . . Spanish, Egyptian, Mes-o-po-tamian. You're laughing? Go and see, my friends. No, no, don't be pigs and look it up on your phones." She rolled her eyes, and then, to Nick, she said, "You and I should take a little side trip. Seriously. If these slave drivers give us a day off."

Listening, marveling, eating his swordfish (which tasted intensely of orange and an unexpected spice; cinnamon?), drinking his effervescent wine, he understood that he was *there:* where all aspiring actors long to arrive. He might have been one of those sailors, having disembarked safely from a rough voyage and climbed that peak to the temple. So here he stood, at the threshold. Deirdre might have been the high priestess herself. Nick could easily see her playing Catherine the Great or Cleopatra. In fact, the more he gazed at her—you could tell she was used to being gazed at, comfortable as the object of attention—the more he saw in her a middle-aged Elizabeth Taylor, seducing with her insolence as much as her beauty. The patina of her aging allure, her very nature, reminded Nick (well, metaphorically!) of oxidizing copper.

When his agent had come to him with the script, Nick had been suspicious that it was little more than art-house melodrama—though when he heard Deirdre's name, he knew he'd be an idiot to turn it down. . . . Or would he? Perhaps actors with far shinier names than his had said no for the very same reason. (Might she implode again, as everyone knew she had, five years before, on the set of *Never, Ever Stop?*) In her twenties and thirties, however, she had been aflame with talent, every camera she faced besotted with her hybrid appearance: delicately freckled skin, thick dark hair, and otter-brown eyes. In her prime, a critic had called her "the love child of Max von Sydow and Maria Callas." Nick's complexion, if nothing else, made their on-screen kinship plausible.

"Listen," said Nick's agent, "think of it as Tennessee Williams hijacking *Lost in Translation,* with an assist from Bertolucci and a sideways glance from Hitchcock. You're lucky they'd take a chance on you. But they liked you in that Lonergan play and know you can do spot-on Yank. Just spend an afternoon in some grotty pub with Schull. That's the way he makes up his mind. Has to know you're not a wanker or a New Age hippie ascetic. Do not so much as whisper the words *yoga* or *vegan* or *mindful*."

Nick's character was Francis Wren, a successful American architect who lives in San Francisco with Conrad, the man he plans to marry; together, they hope to have children, settle in a house with a garden, live a conventionally responsible life—the opposite of the life Francis knew as a boy, raised mostly by nannies at the fiery fringe of his wealthy parents' marital hell. But this was all backstory, emerging mostly through minimal flashbacks, concise bits of dialogue. The film opens with a journey: Francis setting forth, on three successive flights, to arrive at last in Sicily, the place his mother chose to exile herself after her bitter divorce from his father—the homeland of her parents, where people speak the language into which she was born.

The only present dialogue in the first ten minutes of the film is a series of brief, routine exchanges between Francis and various airline personnel. But each time he glances through an airplane porthole, over the panoply of surrounding clouds or down toward the fugitive landscape, a memory emerges, each a small home movie: of hearing from his younger mother her plans to move abroad, of making love to Conrad for the very first time . . . of learning, when he tried to ring her on her latest birthday, that his mother's Italian phone was disconnected.

A son's quest for his mother, hardly offbeat. But the story line accelerates when, in Taormina, he discovers that she's been seduced by a much younger man—younger even than Francis—and has sold her small house to live with the handsome scoundrel in a baroque hotel suite, where he keeps her virtually captive while spending her money to live a louche life out on the town. Yet she seems content, benumbed by the easy, coddling life in a grand hotel . . . possibly even drugged.

In the course of trying to bring his mother to her senses, Francis runs a gauntlet of post-Freudian heroic ordeals that (Nick quickly divined as he read the script) would immerse the chosen actor in scene after scene so emotionally rigorous that his performance would either combust into a critical bonfire or take flight like a phoenix. There would be no middle ground. The screenplay might as well have been the libretto for an opera.

On a second, slower read, he focused on "his" scenes as a kind of slide show: the moment, after flying halfway round the world, when he first spies his mother (on a high balcony in the palatial hotel); his stealthy nocturnal pursuit of her scheming lover through the town's medieval alleys; the confrontation, in which the nefarious gigolo turns the tables and tries to seduce the son; the intimate dinner at which Francis tells his mother about Conrad, the love of his life (this tender scene one of falsely reassuring calm, the eye of the storm); the discovery of his mother, unconscious in the tub, her wrists ineptly gashed; the final, devastating row that ends with his chasing her toward a cliff overlooking the sea.

Nick passed the director's pub test, as his agent called it, and then the screen test. They were to begin with the hard work first—the core of the film, the scenes set in Taormina. Later, they would shoot on location in San Francisco, finishing up on a studio set depicting the long, solitary journey Francis takes at the start of the film.

Before arriving in Sicily, Nick spent a fortnight pacing the perimeter of his flat, running his lines entirely alone. (A pouty Kendra was banished for hours on end.) Once he had committed his lines not just to memory but to heart and mind, he began to absorb them. The shock of it was to find himself reinhabiting his own self in the months before he had lost his real-life mother, to collide anew with the eviscerating sense of what was at stake if she could not be saved. Nick was still haunted by the fearful suspicion that surely there must have been a way to force the doctors to care for her more scrupulously—and it dismayed him to think that had she fallen ill just a year or two later, he would have had the income to buy her the kind of prompt, attentive treatment that ordinary citizens could not afford. He seethed whenever he thought of the money Grandfather had spent on his education and left in the trust he inherited the year after she died. It wasn't a fortune, but it might have made a difference. It might well have extended, even saved, Mum's life.

Nick polished his Francis as if he were an oyster perfecting a pearl, as if the role were both enclosed within and wholly separate from himself, solid and concise, luminescent. Like contraband, he packed it in a deep, protected pocket of his soul and carried it with him to Sicily. Because of Deirdre's earlier commitments, the table reads were to be held on location, immediately prior to shooting.

It took him days to grow accustomed to the way his costar slipped in and out of her character as easily as a practiced swimmer slips in and out of a pool. The way her gaze met his, the rhythm of her sentences, even the feel of her skin when they touched, were all distinctly different from one self to the next, one *instant* to the next. Hadn't he had this experience a dozen times before? Not quite. Her performance, he began to realize, was a masterpiece, but a casual masterpiece, and it stood to raise his own, the way a tide buoys up a fragile boat. For Nick, performance was an exertion, the transformation almost muscular; for Deirdre, it appeared to be organic, instinctive. He felt both humbled and grateful.

A lot of their time together involved waiting, the kind that had to be done at the verge of a scene, not hunkered away in a trailer or green-room. They might be sitting on a rococo settee or in a sports car or across from each other at a table on a patio trellised with grapevine. Three days running, for hour upon tedious hour, they waited near the edge of the cliff from which their stunt doubles would leap into the Ionian Sea (loyal son pursuing depraved, grief-stricken mother) while cameramen, electricians, set decorators, and a swarm of technically obsessed foot soldiers negotiated the details, some fussing with cables and meters and lenses, others just idling about and praying to the meteorology gods for the right angle of sun, the right kind of breeze, the right view of the volcano (which had the irksome habit of gathering round it a frumpy shawl of rust-colored haze).

All the while, Deirdre maintained a motherly (though never ma-tronly) persona, issuing volumes of unsolicited yet diverting advice on Nick's career, his love life, even his diet. Pineapple, she told him, was good for the blood, ginger for the libido, nuts for the cerebral cortex. ("Which is to say, amigo, your better judgment. Nuts are essential for comely young men about to be too famous for their own good.")

She carried packets of shelled, unsalted pistachios in her purse, along with wintergreen Altoids and a tin of adhesive plasters printed with cartoon characters. "At this very moment, I have Tweety Bird on my left thigh," she told him one morning. "A nick while shaving. Not *you,* of course. Though I wouldn't have minded you there when I was half my age."

The more time he spent with Deirdre, the more he thought about Emmelina Godine. In the anxious, self-centered, hormonally enervating years that followed his brief time as her "backstage boy," Nick had almost forgotten about her. Recently, he had looked her up on the Internet and dropped a few heartbeats when he discovered that she had only just died: *of a septic infection while traveling with her husband in Nepal.* According to the *Guardian* obit, she had retired from the stage two years after Nick met her, to marry a Scotsman who invested in coffee plantations. She was survived by a son, James—one year older than Nick—whom she had lost in a custody battle with his father, a married film director with whom she'd had a scandalous affair.

On their third interminable day of waiting cliffside beneath a portable awning, clothing and makeup as stifling as divers' neoprene suits in the heat, Nick asked Deirdre if she had ever met Emmelina Godine.

Deirdre groaned, and for an instant Nick thought she must have felt some actual sudden pain: stung by a bee or, God forbid, bitten by a snake. "Oh, Em," she said. "Poor star-crossed Em. Was *her* life ever grist for the mill."

"What do you mean?" asked Nick.

"I met her when she was just clear of that disastrous fling with Gus Whitehall. What a schmuck. Nothing but a backwoods greaseball under all that Armani. Whitehall? More like white trash. So there she was, single, with a two-year-old, and the subject of pure . . . venom in the tabloids. I mean *venom.* All that tiresome home-wrecker crap. We were in a forgettable movie about New York in the Roaring Twenties. And was I ever roaring back then. I probably didn't have much real sympathy for her—how little I knew of what the future

held for me!—but I liked her. Or I felt sorry for her. Not sure I was nice enough then to honestly *like* anybody. . . . After that, she went back to London, hoping to make life as a mother work with a return to the stage. Desdemona, Titania, Electra; dusty classics at the Old Vic. But wherever she went, the harpies nipped at her heels. Along with Whitehall's goon squad of lawyers."

He asked Deirdre if that was why Emmelina had left acting, married a rich expat, fled the country.

Deirdre smirked at him, carving fissures in her makeup. "Now what do *you* think, bear cub? Or hell, what do I know? Maybe she found true love. There comes a point when you'll trade anything for that. But what makes you think of her? You'd have been too young to see her act. And she never made a decent film. None that I know of, at least."

"But I knew her. A little." He felt a tug of remorse as he told Deirdre about his odd apprenticeship. "I was so thoughtless. I let the acquaintance slip away."

"You were a little boy," Deirdre said tartly. "What do little boys know? That's one of the reasons she *chose* you. You would never judge her; wouldn't even know what to judge her *for.* And you were a passing consolation. I hate to think about that boy of hers, how he was probably turned against her. Who knows what became of him? Barbaric, those tug-of-wars." She paused. "Hm. Tugs-of-war? What do you think?"

And as they made their way back to the set, summoned for yet another take (the sun having achieved the precise altitude and angle of radiance desired by the cinematographer), Nick remembered how, when she had spotted him in the back of the theater that very first day, Ms. Godine had briefly mistaken him for somebody else, quite logically for another boy just about his age and stature.

Eight

The house feels both too large and too small—and too dark. Its comforts have begun to chafe, a rough-knit sweater worn against skin. The trees block the circulating air as much as they shade the roof.

The heat and humidity are abruptly oppressive, August in early June. The picket fence at the front of the property has broken out in verdant acne, a mossy flocking that even bleach will not remove. Tommy called the painter they've used in the past, but his number is obsolete. If Morty were still around, he might joke that it's an omen. Did she depend on Morty for humor? Is she wilting for want of laughter?

Once, she would have moved her laptop to the screened porch, found minor relief in its deep breezy shade. But she avoids the porch now because it looks directly onto the slate terrace where Morty fell to his death, where she waited, with his body, for help. She hasn't even bothered to dust the pollen from the tables and chairs, never mind put out the cushions.

After too much vacillation, she made up the sofa bed in the den. Ordinarily, she would give him the guest room on the attic level— a slant-ceilinged loft with old quilts and hooked rugs (and the only air conditioner in the house)—but "ordinarily" does not apply. Tommy dislikes the idea of the actor sleeping above her. Why? It makes no sense; so little does.

I am going a little mad, she thinks. What would the actor say? *A wee bit daft? A tad round the bend?* His voice has seeped its way into her consciousness, from which it wafts up like the teasing scent of an expensive perfume. (She is dogged in particular by the courteous lilt of his request "May I possibly trouble you to show me the drawings of Ivo?" To which she had had to reply that, no, alas, they were temporarily on loan to a museum in the city.)

She shouldn't be preoccupied with Nicholas Greene—he's just a convenient, even ludicrous distraction—but she rationalizes that once his visit is past, she can bear down on the too many tasks she's avoiding: that "temporary loan," to name just one. For the past two nights, she's awakened in what Morty called the netherland of night, sweaty despite her window fan, startled by dreams involving actors whose movies she doesn't even know all that well. . . . During intermission at a play in New York, she searches for the rest room. She goes up one staircase, but no. She hurries back down and enters a dim hallway. It leads her to a door that opens onto a stone terrace in broad daylight. Waiting for her there is Woody Harrelson. He wants to show her a beautiful tattoo on his forearm: it looks like a pirate map, a guide to finding buried treasure. Woody asks her, tenderly, if she has any children. She wonders if he is going to ask her to have children with him. In the dream, she's not too old to consider it.

Last night it was Ben Stiller—not at all the comic, bug-eyed Ben Stiller but a sorrowful version, haunted, soft-spoken. He was in the kitchen while she was making dinner for Morty. He told Tommy that she didn't need to give him any food, but he needed her to help him learn his lines. He was playing Hamlet. Maybe he wasn't up for it after all.

She woke with a fiercely protective feeling toward Ben, as if his career depended on Tommy.

She got out of bed and went to the bathroom, drank a glass of water, and stared for a few minutes out the window, just to stitch herself back into the real world. The outer night was still, trees motionless around the stern silhouette of Morty's studio. Yet when she returned to sleep, she was once again in the kitchen, and Morty was sitting down to dinner. She asked him if he had seen Ben Stiller on his way in. He told her that wasn't possible. Hadn't she read in the paper that Stiller was undergoing pancreatic surgery? In fact, he might have already died. They must check the obituaries the following day.

Again she awoke, and she had to fight the compulsion to go downstairs, turn on her computer, and search for breaking news about Ben Stiller.

In the heavy air of a morning that foretells a blazing afternoon, these absurdist dreams hover, like the musk of an animal that passed the house before dawn.

Lethargy, she thinks. "Whatever you do, do not let me turn lethargic," Morty told her after Soren died. "Mourning is like quicksand."

Well, now she knows.

It is beyond time to answer certain calls. Too late, she also realizes that it was a mistake to put off the "private" memorial at the Metropolitan Museum, allowing the public ceremony in the park to upstage it in the press. Not that she cares about Morty getting publicity—what does publicity matter anymore?—but the *Times* covered the Central Park gathering on Sunday. Tommy was a coward not to go, and had she gone, perhaps the reporter would have spoken to her—instead of Meredith Galarza.

From all the balloons, picnic baskets and conspicuous gaiety, you'd never know it's a funeral you've come to attend, nor does the whimsical setting— Central Park's Alice in Wonderland statue—lend itself readily to mourning. The sky, however, seems clued in on the gravity of the occasion: to the west, dense pewter-colored clouds loom above the San Remo's imperial towers, and distant baritone grumblings hint at an incoming storm.

Mort Lear, regarded by many parents, scholars and artists the world over as the greatest twentieth-century author-illustrator of children's books, died less than two weeks ago, and it is his legacy that easily four hundred people have gathered to celebrate, the joy his words and pictures have given to millions of children in dozens of languages. "Mort's spirit was totally unique, I

mean totally," says Katelyn Biggs, the owner of Tumnus and Friends, a chil-
dren's bookstore in the West Village.

Ms. Biggs is holding a copy of the immortal picture book "Colorquake,"
from which she will read to open the ceremony. Even the most celebrated
authors of children's books can stroll the city incognito, so it's only thanks to
Ms. Biggs that a reporter can discern who's who among those milling about
sculptor José de Creeft's beloved landmark.

Tommy skims the cataloging of Mort's fellow authors who showed
up—a few of them anything but friends, probably there to gloat.
This part, the obligatory gauntlet of so-sorries and what-a-losses, she
is definitely glad she did not have to endure. There will be plenty of
suspect condolences at the official event.

Also in attendance is a clear exception to the rule of authorial anonym-
ity: Stuart Scheinman, better known as the iconoclastic Shine. Mr. Schein-
man would be the first to say he cultivates a high-volume rebel persona, his
body a Maori-like canvas for ornamentation of his own design. Here, too, is
Meredith Galarza, chief curator of the Contemporary Book Museum, whose
planned relocation and expansion are rumored to hinge on a major bequest
from Mort Lear. "We're in negotiations with his estate," she comments.

Mr. Scheinman approaches Ms. Galarza and greets her with a high five.
The two of them look up, simultaneously, when thunder sounds. "Mort, you
can be sure of it," says Mr. Scheinman. "Checking in with us from that honking
big story hour up in the sky." A fully tattooed arm shoots upward in salute. . . .

What hogwash. If Morty was commenting from the heavens, it
would have been in vehement protest of Stuart's presence. Whose
idea was that? Then again, why shouldn't Katelyn want to sell a few
books? What no one knows is that, twice, Morty gave her large infu-
sions of cash when Tumnus was on life support.

Franklin called yesterday to tell Tommy that he's received an
"inquiry" from a lawyer representing the museum. Tommy has found
nothing in any of Morty's correspondence with Meredith to indicate
that he made contractual commitments.

"Even quasi-contractual could land us in court," says Franklin. He isn't sure yet what the museum's lawyer has to say, but Franklin wants to send an assistant over to the studio to go through Morty's file cabinets as well as the computer files.

The one thing she did accomplish was writing Dani a note. She matched his caution, thanking him for being in touch, telling him how beautiful the baby is, saying how much she looks forward to meeting him but how tied up she is in carrying out Lear's complicated wishes (which she was careful not to specify), attending to the details of turning a life into a legacy. She did not mention their falling-out or, on the other hand, suggest a reunion.

All that, too, is hogwash. This past week, Tommy has felt as if she is proving herself, over and over again, to be an emotional coward—to her mind, the worst kind of coward there is.

Is she somehow afraid of Dani, of the bitterness he seemed to exude the last time she saw him? She still does not understand why he withheld so much from her. Would it have been different if he had come right out and told her about the failure of the bike shop? Did he think she'd just issue a bossy-big-sister *I told you so*? He might have asked her to make him a loan to prop up the business—though she wonders if she would have had enough money. (Now she has more than enough. Way more than enough. Honking way more than enough, as that blowhard Shine would say.)

Or maybe, when Dani came out for a weekend last fall, that's what he had in mind, asking for her help. But he never got up the nerve. Instead, he picked fights with her. It started within an hour of his arrival, in the kitchen, as Tommy made dinner for the three of them—though at first his minor taunting was almost pleasant. The little digs he took at her proficiency were part of a role, Fraternal Thorn in the Side, one he seemed to adopt reflexively to mask the awkwardness of two very different siblings reuniting after months apart.

"Remember when I moved in with you?" He was spinning lettuce while Tommy grated ginger. "You couldn't make instant oatmeal back then."

"I wasn't that bad," Tommy said. "By then I was cooking for Morty. I had a few tricks up my sleeve."

"By now you must have a few thousand. Like, how many years have you been his kitchen wench?"

"I like cooking," she said.

"Are you going to tell me it's 'therapeutic'?"

"You know what? Yes. It is. When I'm *alone* in the kitchen." On the stress, she turned and gave Dani a teasing look.

He poured the lettuce from the spinner into a china bowl.

"Do you know how to make dressing?" Tommy asked him.

"Maybe the one thing Mom managed to teach us both." He went to the refrigerator, the cupboard, found his ingredients without speaking. And then, after he'd set them on the counter, he said, "Jane's pregnant."

Tommy set down the grater and turned toward her brother. "Oh God. Oh *Dani*." Even news of an engagement would have been a momentous surprise.

"You sound like I just told you Jane died."

"No! It's wonderful!" She hugged him, although she felt his physical resistance. When she stepped back, she wondered at the look on his face. "It is, isn't it?"

"Why wouldn't it be?" He leaned against the counter, arms crossed, knees locked.

"Dani, don't do the petulant thing, not now. I just somehow thought—"

"That we'd get married first?"

"Well, I suppose if Mom and Dad were alive—"

"Not like you're in a very conventional situation yourself, Toms."

"Dani, I'm thrilled for you. I love Jane. She'll be a terrific mother."

"She will." He sighed. "But you don't even really know her, Tommy. You never come into the city these days, not since we dealt with Dad's stuff. We've seen you like, what, twice in the past year?"

"More than that." Why was he being so hostile? "And Dani, the train runs both ways. You know you can visit here whenever you like. Why didn't you bring her this weekend?"

"I told you. She's putting in extra hours tomorrow. We need to squirrel away as much money as we possibly can. And just so you know, we're planning on making it legal. City hall, roses from the deli. Betrothal on a budget. Things aren't as . . . The point is, we're trying to be adults. Or I am. She already is one."

"She shouldn't exhaust herself, though. I mean, not now."

"Jane's not made of porcelain, Tommy. Pregnancy's hardly an illness."

The conversation went on in this prickly way, Tommy bewildered to find herself on the defensive, until Morty arrived in the kitchen. Morty was in a good mood, his cheer the antidote they needed. Over dinner, he told Dani about a recent appearance he'd made on a children's television show. "They made me sing and dance. Specifically, the polka. I made the mistake of watching it afterward. I look like Burl Ives. Christ. I am officially *old*."

"That you'd even think of Burl Ives makes you old," said Tommy.

She and Dani laughed, remembering the Burl Ives records their father had played for them as small children. "And Pete Seeger." In a flash, Tommy pictured the turntable their father had given them one Christmas, its case of red plastic textured to look like alligator hide.

"And Woody Guthrie." Dani held his soup spoon to his mouth, as if it were a mike, and sang a twangy verse of "This Land Is Your Land."

"I used to thank God Dad never played the banjo," he said after less than a verse earned him jeers.

"You were lucky. Not much music in my childhood." Morty sounded wistful.

"Careful what you wish for," said Dani, at which he and Tommy fell into a competitive hilarity, trying to call up the lyrics of their father's silliest songs.

So by the time they went to bed, Tommy felt as if they'd made it over the rocky start of their fitting together again—not that she could fool herself into thinking they had ever been close.

In the morning, she woke to find that Dani was already up, in the studio with Morty. She let them be. She also decided that she would take Dani out to dinner at the bistro in the village center. Morty could fend for himself.

After lunch, Tommy went outside. It was time to put the garden to bed for the winter. She would do the final pruning, cut back the long-stemmed perennials. Next weekend, Morty would compost the beds and blanket them in salt hay. Dani volunteered to help, but Tommy liked performing this ritual herself.

"Why don't you go inside and build a fire? Call Jane. Or just have a rest," suggested Tommy. "Not long and you won't have much time for that."

"I'm basically useless, aren't I?"

"Why would you know how to divide lilies?" said Tommy. "Or prune out deadwood?"

"Pruning out deadwood sounds pretty straightforward."

Dani was exhausting her.

"Here's a job. Please go make a pot of tea and take it to Morty. He'll like that. There's a box of Lorna Doones in the cupboard over the back fridge. He loves those."

"Lorna Doones?" Dani laughed.

"I know. Retro in the extreme. That's Morty. Well, a part of Morty. The Burl Ives part, but don't tell him I said that."

For the next three hours, except when he passed her, carrying the assigned pot of tea and plate of cookies, Tommy did not see Dani. She took a bath, answered a few e-mails, and then, as darkness fell, the three of them drank feeble gin-and-tonics by a blazing fire.

On the short drive to dinner, Dani's spirits seemed to have lifted. He told her a few of Jane's work stories, the mysteries she solved about the speech afflictions children suffered—and almost always overcame.

But by the end of their meal, he was out of sorts again, critical of everything from the restaurant's bread to the president's policies in Afghanistan.

Maybe she'd been insensitive, talked too much about the trip she and Morty took to Hay-on-Wye the summer before, how ecstatic they were to visit a town where books, tumbling from the shelves of shop after shop, seemed to outnumber the stars in the sky. The musty tang of aging paper and ink pervaded even the streets, like a cologne. "Let's bottle it," Morty had suggested. "Call it . . . how do you say *bookworm* in French? Or Welsh!"

Had it seemed like gloating? Tommy had no idea if Dani and Jane longed to travel (he was right; she hardly knew the mother of her future niece or nephew), but still. Dani had a business to run and probably couldn't be away for even a week.

She was about to ask him about the shop—knowing that she would be opening a valve to his venting—when he said, "Tommy, are you a lifer in this job of yours?"

She shrugged. "I suppose it's my golden cage. But you know, it's rarely boring. And honestly, I don't miss the city all that much."

"Yeah, but whose life are you living out here? Yours or his?"

"I love Morty. And his life—which is definitely his, not mine— is one I . . . enjoy sharing. Not sharing exactly, but . . . living along- side of."

Dani shook his head. "You liked living alongside that relationship he had with that gigolo? That looked excruciating to me."

Tommy was stunned. Her brother had met Soren once, maybe twice. She did remember inviting Dani to come out and stay over- night for one of the many dinner parties Morty and Soren had hosted in their early, happy days. Except that, really, the happiness wore thin even then; it was too dependent on passion—or on dependency itself. The parties gave their partnership a veneer, the reticent house transformed into a bright stage on which they could push back the rockier side of their relationship: the simmering contention and jeal- ousy, the patent inequalities.

"That's the past," said Tommy as the waiter poured the last of the wine into her glass. She waved off his suggestion of another bottle. She poured the contents of her glass into Dani's.

"But you stuck it out. Like for what, ten years?"

"Eight. Morty was on fire then. It was like being in the middle of a book that's too good to put down. Sometimes it felt like Soren was an inspiration, a muse. Despite everything else."

"I still don't get it."

"Get what, Dani?"

"Why you've never wanted to go out and have a family of your own. Or just a circle of friends, Jesus! Mom and Dad were deluded in lots of ways, but you know what? When I think about those Saturday nights with Dad's musician friends all crammed in the living room? Remember how thrilled he was when they found the Brooklyn house and they could entertain in that tiny back garden? Remember his awful beer-making phase? I felt sorry for him, but guess what? The guy knew how to be happy." Dani laughed. "When I think about their social life, I'm kind of impressed. Jane and I are too busy for much time with friends. But we have them. We have friends."

"Well, good for you," said Tommy, feeling suddenly offended. Was he implying she didn't know how to be happy? "I'm not living in a cave. We entertain. We travel. We go to the theater. I like my life tremendously."

"'We'? Doesn't that kind of prove my point?" Dani leaned back in his chair and stared at her.

Tommy saw, for an instant, the hard-nosed little boy who wouldn't leave the playground, who wrought mayhem at the library, her other home.

"Don't judge me," she said, pointedly pulling toward her the folder holding the check, which the waiter had glibly placed before Dani. She stopped herself from saying, *I'm not the one who's always struggling.*

They walked silently to the car.

As she unlocked it, her brother gazed at her over the roof. "Look. I'm sorry. I just—" He sighed loudly. "It's just a difficult time."

"Don't be scared about fatherhood," said Tommy. "And don't jump down my throat about how I know nothing. Not firsthand. But you'll do it well. And one of us needs to pass on those Woody Guthrie genes, right?"

Dani smirked. "You'd have to be assuming they skip generations."

She went to bed that night with a sense of relief; maybe they had worked something out, like a stubborn splinter.

On Sunday morning, she awoke to find that, once again, Dani had been up and already helped himself to coffee and toast. Morty would be sleeping in, so she assumed Dani was out for a walk. He had always needed exercise to keep himself calm. (In all likelihood, had he been a schoolboy now, he would have been diagnosed with ADHD. Morty was constantly fielding questions about "learning challenges" and childhood reading.)

Feeling restless—and because Dani was family—she decided to strip his bed and get a head start on laundry.

His open backpack lay on the blanket chest at the foot of the bed, and when Tommy pulled the covers off the bed, it flipped onto the floor—a corner of the quilt had been trapped beneath it—and spilled. Among the contents, she saw an antique book. She didn't need to pick it up to recognize it. It was Morty's rarest edition of *David Copperfield,* inscribed, with an elaborate sketch, by Dickens's illustrator, Phiz.

For a moment, she stood without moving in the middle of the guest room, the quilt bundled loosely in her arms. The interior of the house was silent. Tree limbs, now bare, nudged the shingles above her head, a subtle creaking and scraping.

Abandoning the tangle of sheets, she carried the book downstairs. She set it, on a clean linen towel, in the center of the kitchen table. She waited, her back against the counter. At first to her dismay, and then to her perverse relief, Morty showed up before Dani. He spotted the book before he'd even had a chance to say good morning.

As usual, he was fully dressed; he wasn't the type of artist who relished the luxury of nightwear worn well into the day, not even on weekends.

He looked from the book to Tommy. "Davy's joining us for a spot of tea?"

"Don't ask."

Morty sat at the table and pulled the book toward him. Gently, he opened its front cover and turned its first few pages. He smiled at the whimsical drawing and fond note for which he had probably paid a small fortune.

"I found it in my brother's bag. Upstairs."

Morty sighed. "You were snooping?" He didn't look up from the book, though he closed it.

"No."

"Where is he?"

"Out somewhere."

"Still a restless boy."

"Morty."

"What do you want me to say? It's easy to see he's in trouble of some kind."

"Trouble?"

"You don't see it?"

"Men act strange when they're about to be fathers."

"Disappointing." Morty sighed again. "But you know, I could just put it away—say nothing. We don't invite him back too soon, but . . . Tommy, I have no energy for this sort of thing. I'm planning on another good day. I'm nailing swans. Those diabolically long necks."

"Nailing swans?" She tried to laugh.

"Tommy, he's your family, not mine."

She didn't know how to react. Was Morty being generous—or washing his hands of Dani? But Tommy was appalled. All over again, Dani was the misbehaving little brother handed off to her. She thought resentfully of the way he had praised their parents' insular life at the restaurant the night before.

"I'll be in the studio," said Morty. Abruptly, without waiting for her to say anything more, he went out the back door. He left the book on the towel.

Tommy felt herself breaking down. She reached for her phone and called her brother's cell. "Where are you?" Her voice shook.

"Walking. In the village. I picked up some doughnuts at that—"

"Please come back now."

"You okay?"

"Just come back now."

When he came into the kitchen, through the back door by which Morty had left, she took the bag from him, roughly, and pointed at the table. "This is the end of my trusting you, Dani."

At first he said nothing. He sat at the table and crossed his arms. "Did you ever? Apparently you went through my stuff."

"I did not."

Whether or not he believed her, she didn't care. She would make him get his things and she would drive him to the station.

"How do you know he didn't loan it to me?"

"Oh, Dani. Come on."

"He used me," Dani said quietly. "And he's used you. For years. He's fucking used you *up*. I wish you could see what your life looks like from the outside."

Tommy couldn't stop herself from crying. "A whole lot better than your life."

"My cue to leave, I guess." He got up and started toward the dining room, the stairs beyond.

She blocked the door. "No. I'll get your stuff. I'll drive you to the station."

"Tommy, listen to me. Someday—"

"No." She hurried out of the room and up the two flights of stairs, nearly stumbling on the steeper flight to the attic. Angrily, she emptied the rest of the backpack onto the floor. Had he stolen anything else? He hadn't.

She heard herself sobbing as she stuffed her brother's scattered clothing into the pack. Forget whatever he'd left in the bathroom.

In the kitchen, she found him standing where she had left him.

He took the backpack. "You know what? I'll walk to the station." He looked sad now, not the least bit belligerent, but Tommy, her emotions shifting between rage and shame, was too confused to speak. Without waiting to see if she would, he left.

Morty didn't come in for lunch that day. At dinner, he suggested they eat in front of a movie. They spoke a total of perhaps five sentences between their tense conversation over the stolen book and their parting for the night. She had no idea whether he was angry at Dani or disappointed in her—or maybe he was caught up in some private creative turmoil. The thing about living with an artist, she knew, was that an artist cannot leave work aside on a desk or in a briefcase. The mind is the desk, the soul or heart the briefcase.

Tommy stayed up later than usual. She answered the past two days' requests for Morty's presence at libraries, schools, and pro-literacy luncheons. All the while, she kept an eye on the tiny symbol in the dock that represented her personal inbox. Nothing. No note from Dani—or from anyone else.

Three weeks later, she drove Morty into the city, to speak at a school assembly. After dropping him off, she decided to drive past Dani's shop. She hadn't been there since the opening party, but she knew its location.

Or did she? Wasn't this the corner? She couldn't find a parking space, but she drove around the block three times. Had it vanished? Back at home, she looked up the number in her address book; when she called it, that robot woman scolded her for trying to reach an unreachable party.

Tie one on. Where the devil does that expression come from? Tie a what on what? A yellow ribbon on an old oak tree? A bell on a goat? An Easter bonnet on a tiger?

But that is what she's gone and done: tied one on. All by herself. *All by her lonesome.* Linus looks concerned. He lies under the kitchen table, flat as a schnitzel, staring up at her dolefully.

Dolefully. Where did that word come from in her soggy brain? What can it mean to be full of dole? To have eaten too much canned pineapple?

Merry chuckles. I am *chuckling,* she thinks, which makes her chuckle even more. "Not to worry, Linus, not to worry," she whispers in response to his heightened alarm. She starts to lean over to pet him but straightens up when she feels herself begin to topple.

She peers inside the refrigerator. She'd better have something to eat. Something to sponge up the entire bottle of Grüner Veltliner she's consumed since talking with Benjamin. But nothing has changed since she last opened the door: not counting a dozen condiments, the buffet spread before her comprises a container of vanilla Greek yogurt, a takeout carton of cold sesame noodles, a slab of shrink-wrapped deli pound cake she wishes she hadn't bought, and, in the bottom drawer, three withering scallions, half a box of cherry tomatoes, and several curls of molted onion skin.

Noodles and tomatoes it is. After that, she will probably be sick anyway.

He is, of course, getting married. He is, of course, having the baby. Ta-da, the package deal!

The worst part wasn't the news; it was the delicate, tender tone he assumed to deliver it. He actually tried to spiral toward it, asking her about the museum, about Lear's death, about Linus; she finally severed the small talk with "Benjamin? Can you please cut to the chase?"

Sigh. Disclosure one. Deep breath. Disclosure two.

"Oh!" Merry exclaimed, as if she could exhale all her self-pity, indignation, and regret in one audible gasp. "A shotgun wedding!"

When he said nothing, she apologized. She said she was glad to hear that he was settling into a new life. She was doing the same, she told him. She had some great leads on apartments in Park Slope (lie number one), she'd joined a book group (lie number two), and she was seeing a guy she'd met at a Bard alumni gathering (whopper of the century; in fact, there was no such *thing* as a Bard alumni gathering).

"Wow, Merry," he said. "That's great news, all of it."

"And the museum is going up on schedule," she said. (True!) "I'm going to be out-of-my-mind busy for the next year. In a good way. No complaints." By then, a membrane of tears covered her entire lower face. She wiped her chin before the tears could fall onto her favorite I-am-both-smart-and-stylish dress, Italian raw silk in what she thought of as Tintoretto blue. She had worn it that day to the board meeting at which the architect and two of his minions had given them a progress report.

"Terrific, Merry. I'm so glad," Benjamin said.

He asked about her mother, though Merry knew he couldn't have cared less. By the end of the conversation, which lasted all of maybe seventeen minutes, they had managed to be more dishonest with each other than they'd been throughout the entire seven years of their marriage.

Merry wept openly and plaintively, no longer bothering to spare her dress from salt stains. After she was done crying, she fed Linus his dinner. Then she went to the fridge and took out the bottle of wine. It was a good one, a Sepp Moser in a gracefully tapered bottle. What was she saving it for?

She did take out a very nice piece of stemware. Not a wedding present but one of a pair of handblown purple glasses she'd bought at a craft fair in Tivoli, back when she was in grad school at Bard. She had been involved with that violinist at the conservatory. Fede, from Rome. She reasoned that it would be easy to see him go back there, that it would be impractical, imprudent, to aim toward marriage with someone else in the arts. No, she would wait till she settled in the city and met a man with a much more solid professional future. Like a lawyer. Like Benjamin, whom she would meet a few years later at a dinner party, not on some Internet dating service. All so sensible.

Oh, where was Fede now? How stupid she'd been—and how cruel. Remembering how she had broken his heart was now doubly painful.

She intended to have a single glass of wine, then go around the corner for dinner at the new Vietnamese place. You could eat pho at the long bar. The bartender was young and genuinely kind. His major disappointments, if any, had yet to exert their battering effect on his sweetness.

But she made the mistake of checking her e-mail.

Sol, whose ominous phone message she had accidentally on purpose failed to answer. He'd been too busy at the presentation to take her aside.

I know you've been occupied with counsel, untangling the Lear mess. It's worth a good frontal assault. Scare tactics. But I am skeptical about the c/b ratio. Lear is, in a way, the old guard. He hasn't made a real splash since that futuristic trilogy. Stuart's proposal of rededicating the core of the collection to 21st-century children's books is growing on me, despite my age. Forward thinking, of which I approve. Let's catch up tomorrow. I'll have Lez call you to schedule a conference call, maybe pull in Stuart too.

Sol, alas, has a point about Lear. In the dozen years after the third *Inseparables* volume was published, he was as prolific as ever, and his books always burned up the lists, but he turned more often toward illustrating glossy books (an anthology of modern poetry; a clever historical showcase for teens called *Lives of the Secular Saints*) and less toward crafting the quirky stories that had made him a star. In brutal terms, he was no longer a maverick. But as much as Merry champions the vanguard, even the avant-garde, she is also a traditionalist; yes, a goddamned romantic. She wants her cake, and she wants her caviar, too.

Now, one soused and very unsensible hour later, she fills a tall glass with water. She takes it, along with her plate of noodles and tomatoes, back into the living room. She turns on the television. She hunts through Netflix for a thriller. "Thrill me," she says aloud to the screen. "I dare you."

She is now talking to the dog *and* the television. What next, the recycling bin? She is nothing if not the classic modern old maid. Well, not exactly a *maid,* in that she's been soundly deflowered.

She has only herself to blame for choosing the specific forks in the road that led to her becoming a living, breathing urban cliché, the kind of woman who finds herself portrayed generically and tragically, every five years or so, in a *New York* magazine soft-sociology cover story. One afternoon, killing time in a Williams-Sonoma (a decent saucepan cost *how* much?), she stopped at a display of boxed cookie cutters under a pink-lettered sign: PLANNING A SHOWER? One set was designed for wedding-themed cookies (bell, bouquet, bride-affixed-to-groom), the other for infant-affirming sweets (teddy bear, pram, onesie). Well, she mused, how about a set designed for a party celebrating initiation into the class of women Merry thought of as BUMPFs: barren upwardly mobile professional females. You could bake a sugar-glazed briefcase, a chocolate-chip stiletto, or how about a shortbread cookie shaped precisely like the bell curve graphing an ovulation cycle?

She's still clicking through row after row of dismal, obscure movie options when the phone rings. She looks at the caller ID. A Manhattan cell number. Oh please not Sol, Sol the cost-benefit czar, Sol the storm cloud approaching her career. No; Sol has a Westchester number.

"Hello?"

"Hey, is this Meredith?"

A man. Maybe she's wished the fictitious suitor into reality.

"Yes."

"It's Danilo Daulair. We met at the Mort Lear thing. Central Park. Last Sunday."

The caretaker's brother.

"You gave me your card," he says.

Merry takes a gulp of water. "Nice to hear from you. I guess you made it home in that deluge. I barely did. Lost my shoes." She tries to laugh.

"Yeah. Well, I was on my bike." He laughs even more awkwardly. "So I know you want to connect with Tommy—with my sister. And I'm thinking maybe I'm going to pay her a visit this weekend. Out in the country."

"Oh." Was she supposed to ask him to put in a good word for her?

"And I thought. Maybe. You'd like to go with me."

"Are you driving?"

"I thought I'd rent one of those Zipcars."

"I have a car," she says. "I can drive. I'm happy to drive."

"Great," he says. "I was thinking Sunday? I have Sunday off."

"Sunday's great," she says. "Sure. I'll call you Sunday morning, that all right? I have to go just now."

She barely makes it to the bathroom. Everything comes up, and when she finally sinks back onto the cold tile floor, laying a cheek against tufted scarlet bath mat, she feels despair and release in equal measure. "Let's not do this again," she says, admonishing the toilet seat above her. Linus comes into the bathroom and regards her anxiously. She sits up and gathers him into her lap.

"Linus," she says, "we are going to pull ourselves together. Yes, we are."

Nine

"Tomasina? Hello?" The voice, irresistibly cheerful, is his and no other. She realizes, too, that she hasn't asked him to call her Tommy—the gesture seemed impossibly assertive, even when he asked that she call him Nick—and now she finds that she likes the sound of her old-fashioned name in his melodic voice, as if he's given her a newly dignified persona.

But here he is, early again.

She is on her knees in the path between the peony beds, weeding. Pivoting clumsily, she stands in time to see him round the corner of the house. "I wasn't expecting you till two."

"I know, forgive me, tell me to bugger off if you like, but I had an idea, since we made such good time, that you'd let me fix you lunch. I rang, but I got no answer, and we were driving in circles—"

"It's fine," she says. Though she doesn't like the sound of that *we*.

They trade meticulous smiles. Yet again, Tommy finds it irritatingly hard to stop staring at him. Today he's wearing a shirt with dainty gray pinstripes, tails loose over white jeans, the same blue sneakers—their jubilant hue balanced by the same tangerine-colored scarf. His sunglasses nest in his artfully untidy hair.

"Let me just introduce you, quickly, to Serge."

"Serge?"

"My driver. He'll push off to that place you recommended, the Chanticleer. It looks just the ticket—we drove by—but I don't want you startled if I need him to show up here." When he sees her expression, he says, "He won't hang about. I just need to have him on call." As if Nick Greene is the host and Tommy the guest, he beckons her toward the front of the house.

Serge, who fills every seam of his black suit, looks more like a bodyguard than a chauffeur, his reflection in the car's spotless hood magnifying his mass. His handshake is declaratively firm. "Pleasure," he says, with so thick an accent that it might well be his only word of English.

Serge removes a leather suitcase and four grocery bags from a trunk large enough to hold several bodies. Tommy recognizes, on the paper bags, the name of a gourmet shop three towns closer to the city.

The two men carry everything toward the kitchen door. Tommy holds it open.

"Thank you!" Nick says to Serge once they've set the groceries on the counter. "For everything. And"—playfully, he points a finger at Tommy—"I mean what I said about lunch. I'll just see Serge off in the proper direction, make sure we have our coordinates set, watches synchronized, all that James Bond rigmarole. . . ."

The screen door bangs shut behind him. She goes to the sink and washes her hands, then looks inside the grocery bags. Why would movie-star food look different?

And then, as she listens to the car depart, it's as if the calendar's flipped backward to exactly nine days ago, almost to the hour, for here they are, again, alone together in her kitchen: Morty's kitchen to Nick Greene, who's already taking in his surroundings with the hungry eye of a genteel burglar—though even in Morty's day, this room was hers.

"So. So!" He is blushing. "First thing is where you'd like me to stash the goods. I brought my own food, but I'm happy to share. And how's a frittata? Red pepper and goat cheese? Do you fancy sun-dried tomatoes? Does asparagus vinaigrette appeal?"

She wants to ask him to slow down; his effusiveness is wearing her out. But the energy is nervous, and his ardent if bumbling attempts to ingratiate himself are touching. She is also having a hard time reconciling the man before her with the man she watched in the movie last night—the deeply disturbing movie.

It hadn't occurred to her he'd bring his own food—or so much of it. "Why don't you put things in the back fridge?" She points to the pantry.

"Super," he says.

She represses a laugh. Why are the English so English? she wonders nonsensically. "I'll just go outside and finish up."

"Excellent. And not to worry—I'll find my way around the pots and pans. Upside of living like a nomad."

In truth, he's been living mostly in and out of hotels the past year or so—hardly tents or caravans—where he's fed by unseen restaurant minions. Last time he was in his own kitchen, there were signs of mice taking over.

As she heads back outside, she realizes that she didn't show him his room. But through the kitchen window, she sees that he is busy enough. She simply has to trust him. He is just an ambitious young man doing his job. He asked to stay for three nights, and when she said yes, she forgot that Sunday is when Franklin's paralegals are showing up to take Morty's business files.

She rakes the weeds and the wilted blooms into a pile, throws them by handfuls into the basket. She hears the house phone ringing and lets it be.

Cooking—simple cooking, nothing fancy—calms Nick. Clever, his sudden idea at the shop of making Tomasina a meal. Two birds with one stone: his unraveling nerves and her completely rightful sense of invasion.

How perfect to be alone in Lear's kitchen. He removes his jacket and muffler and hangs them on an empty peg on the rack by the door. He runs a hand along one sleeve of a plain brown canvas coat that must have been Lear's. The sleeve is frayed at the wrist. It's the one Tomasina put on when she took him to the studio last week.

(He wonders if she freely wore Lear's clothes when he was alive, that sharing of garments a kinship usually claimed by a lover or spouse.) Nick reaches into the pocket: yes, the key. Not that he'd use it without her permission.

Glancing out the window to make sure Tomasina is still occupied, he takes down the coat and puts it on. As the air held within it is displaced, the coat gives up its hoarded aromas: wool, laundry powder, hay. It fits him like a barrel around the middle, but the shoulders sit square on his. Nick stands a bit taller than Lear ever did; in his prime, however, Lear was also slim.

Time to get to work—the easy, immediate work. He replaces the coat on its peg.

Lear's kitchen isn't especially large, which meets with Nick's approval. He's been to parties at posh American homes where a glimpse through the swinging door, as the servants hustle about, reveals a space the size of a small airline hangar, lighting harsh, surfaces cold and metallic. This room has a cottagey atmosphere, colors earthen, the light cast by wall sconces, not by industrial floodlights.

The pots hang from hooks on the ceiling, knives are sheathed in a block by the cooker, tea towels hang on a rack next to the sink. A sensible kitchen. He pauses to touch and admire the rustic ceramic tiles set in the wall behind glass apothecary jars holding flour, sugar, tea bags. The tiles are glazed an iridescent forest green, the odd fellow embossed with a stag or a boar or—ha!—is that a hedgehog? A porcupine? The counter is copper aged to a mottled umber.

Open any of the drawers or cupboards in Mum's kitchen and you'd confront an unpredictable hotchpotch—at least until the end, her last place, where Nick made an effort to sort and organize, discard the chipped tumblers and splintered wooden spoons. If Mum had precious little time to cook, she had even less to establish physical order.

In his London flat, Nick's kitchen is plain, the surfaces wooden, cupboards white. But this is a storybook kitchen—the kitchen, in literal fact, of a storybook writer. Framed on the only bit of exposed wall is a drawing of a bear—no, an etching. The bear looms in an open doorway, stooping a bit, snowflakes swirling around his bulk. In the foreground, seen from behind, a girl with long black hair raises her hands in fright. Penciled beneath is the line *"Have no fear! I will not harm you. I am only cold and would wish to warm my coat beside your hearth."*

Cradling the bowl of eggs and milk in his left arm, whisking with his right, Nick stands before the print and wonders about its origins. It's not Lear's work. Lear illustrated few fairy tales—though there was speculation he was aiming toward a new edition of his beloved *Alice.* One of Andrew's early concepts for the film had been to weave visual references to Alice through the scenes of Lear's life in the city. "Too much, and probably too twee," he finally concluded.

Nick's last conversation with Andrew was better than the one in his office, that awkward meeting with Jake and Hardy, followed by lunch with the pixieish wife (who turned out to be an intellectual property lawyer; imagine that prenup!). California is not a place Nick could ever envision as home. After a few days in L.A., he's homesick for the restorative gloom of January in London, pigeon-colored skies and blustery damp. Kendra loved California, told him he was a snob. She was thrilled when a photo popped up on some gossipy website showing the two of them sharing a kiss at that place with the stars embedded in the pavement. When the notices for *Taormina* began to build, Kendra took out a Google alert on Nick; nearly every day she'd receive at least a crumb of news including his name. She would hold her phone up to Nick, saying something like "You are gaining traction, love." At first he couldn't deny how exciting it was to see himself becoming a Somebody. It was like sitting for a portrait, watching his likeness accrue and intensify as something separate from yet fully dependent on his flesh-and-blood being. But then he grew weary of Kendra's daily crowing at her tiny screen. And after the Oscar, once the actual thing, the shiny, rather steroidal-looking fellow, had sat on his dining table for a month, once the press siege had begun to abate, Nick found himself wondering whether anything *essential* had changed in his life. The answer was no. Not that nonessentials couldn't drive you mad.

He met Andrew on neutral ground this time: lunch at a Brazilian tapas lounge on Sunset, a hipster hangout by night, sleepy by day. Andrew acknowledged that the story line of the trauma in the shed needn't be set in stone, so long as they kept to the same location and sets. He also liked the idea of giving a more pivotal role to Jessica, the actress playing the younger Frieda, Lear's mum. She had just received a run of good press for her leading role in a black-comedy series about a mobster's wife who receives a blood transfusion that gives her the knack of knowing, absolutely, whether someone is lying or telling the truth.

"But how do you think it will affect your character in the later story?" said Andrew. "The New York scenes, the ones with Magda when you realize she's losing touch with reality. Which we'd have to reexamine, too." Magda is the actress playing Lear's mother as her mind begins to falter.

"Spot-on question," Nick answered. "I need to get back east, I really do want that time in Lear's house, his studio."

"A little sleuthing?" Cunning smile.

"I wouldn't call it that. I simply plan to ask everything I can of Tomasina Daulair. Draw her out."

"The caretaker woman."

"Oh, she was—is—more than that."

"Nick, you are such a well-behaved boy." Andrew's voice was kind, but Nick felt belittled.

"Andrew, I'm going to give you the performance of a bloody lifetime," he said. "Don't expect me to 'behave.'"

"Countin' on it. Bankin' on it. Nobody goes to see movies like this otherwise."

At which point they were interrupted by two young women who wanted a selfie with Nick. They were oblivious to Andrew, the far more powerful, talented man. (Perhaps Andrew was relieved at his generational anonymity.) After the women retreated, Andrew said, "Or maybe some people will see it no matter what, pretty boy."

Nick no longer denies it: that he's the object of fantasies, crushes, minor obsessions—and not just by women. His agent alerted him, regrettably, to the website addictedtonick.com. This sort of fandom ("fanzy," Si calls it) comes as a surprise to him, however. Even when he landed his first decent roles, he was gawky more than lean, wan more than fair, a skinny boy-man who could easily play five or eight years younger. Not that he didn't have his followers, his autograph hounds.

What had changed? Was it Taormina, the place as well as the film? Seeing himself in the first dailies had been more unsettling to Nick than the very first time he'd seen himself on-screen. Did he really, all of a sudden, look so much older, or was it the weight of the character? Had he broken through to a deeper level of transformation? Or was it merely the sharpening effect of the strong southern light in all those exterior scenes? Fretting about it isn't wise, because if there is any kind of "magic" to his work, he mustn't question the enchantment. He has little patience (or is it discipline?) to adhere to any method. Acting, when it succeeds, feels to Nick like crossing a membrane or swimming underwater. The passage might be unpredictable, even sudden, but the otherness of where you arrive is real.

Tomasina comes into the kitchen, in her arms an exuberance of peonies. "You're tall. Would you mind grabbing that jar?" She nods toward a high shelf.

It's a jar that looks to have held jam for a giant. He takes it to the sink and puts it under the tap. "Magnificent, those," he says as he watches her trim off excess leaves. "Aren't they everybody's favorite flower?"

"My mother liked sunflowers best," she says as she places the jar on the table.

"And I suppose mine liked heather. There you go. White heather. Supposed to bring luck," he says. "Didn't bring her much."

Tommy thinks, But she had you.

She recalls his speech at the Oscars, the tears; it might be prudent to steer clear of talk about mothers.

Too late. He says, "She worked too hard and she died far too young."

"I'm sorry." Tommy hesitates, then says—what the hell—"My mother died young, too. Or younger than she should have."

"I know," says Nick. "Breast cancer, just like mine. Not a terribly exclusive club, is it? Children orphaned by that disease."

"'Orphaned' is a bit dramatic. I mean, we weren't children anymore," says Tommy. How does he know about her mother? She sees him read her face in a flash.

"I'm sorry. I get obsessive with my research. Turn over more stones than I should. If I weren't an actor, perhaps I'd be a detective. Except that I'm not all that sneaky. And I'm rubbish at keeping secrets." (Bugger, why did he say *that*?)

"Don't worry about it," she says. "I am sorry about your mother. Both our mothers. Here—I'll set the table." She needs a task, a way to reorient herself, yet as she arranges the forks and knives, the napkins, puts the salt and pepper in their customary places, it's all as if in a dream—come to think of it, not unlike those dreams with Ben Stiller and Woody Harrelson. "How long ago? Did you lose her, I mean."

"Five years. I was twenty-nine. Not so young to lose a parent, I know. But maybe since I never had a dad, I felt I was owed twice as long with a mum."

"Makes sense to me."

"Oh blast—" He turns to the stove, grabs a mitt, hastily opens the oven.

The eggs are perfect. Tommy sees the pleasure on his face. He might be ten. Thinking of him as a child, she realizes that she might be just the age his mother was when she died—though of course *she* hasn't been obsessive about her research.

"I saw your movie last night. *Taormina*," she says when they are seated.

"God, talking of mothers. Please say you didn't feel you had to watch it."

"Of course I did. And I see why you won all those prizes. You're amazing. And the actress who plays your mother—"

"Is a miracle. Right? She ought to have taken every trophy in the bloody book."

"But . . . you die. Your character. I wasn't expecting that. I'm not sure I felt it was right. It was too much. Morty used to talk about how too much drama can crack the beams of a plot. Threaten to pull the house down. The story."

Nick is nodding emphatically. "That story's quite baroque. It is. But I came to feel that the idea, the weight of the drama . . ." He's stopped eating for the moment. Tommy watches, fascinated, as he runs both hands along the edge of the table, then grasps it firmly, leaning toward her. "It's the only way the mother can break into reality again, the way she surfaces from the lagoon and looks everywhere for Francis. She knows, before they even find his body, that she's lost him. That it's her bloody fault. And by the time she gets to San Francisco, she is fully inside her senses again. There is no escape, no avoidance. No way to atone, really."

"So her life is over."

"No, no," says Nick. "It's not. When you see her together with Conrad—the boyfriend, the fiancé—you know she sees her son in him. And he sees Francis in her. They mirror each other. And then you find out about the adoption, the child who would have been mine."

"But would you forgive your lover's parent for putting him through all that—leading him to his death? Literally?"

Nick waves his fork in the air. "Remember, Conrad doesn't know half of what went on in Taormina: the horrific bathtub scene, the attempted seduction, the circumstances that led to the jump from the cliff. . . ."

"All the same, it's devastating."

"It is. But what makes it supportable is entirely, absolutely, Deirdre's performance in that last scene. That *wordless* performance, when she's with the child. The camera's on her for nearly five minutes, a *single take,* during which she utters not one bloody syllable. . . . Deirdre taught me a lot about using certain parts of my face as well as the rest of my body. Just watch her *shoulders* in that scene. Genius. I am such a creature of words that I can only aspire to such a performance."

And aspire he must. In a key scene close to the dénouement of *The Inner Lear,* after Soren Kelly's death, Lear revisits the desert hotel where he lived as a child, walks the grounds in search of the gardener's shed, only to find that it no longer exists. The dread he had felt gradually becomes a yearning; he finds himself looking around the property, intently, perhaps frantically. He *needs* to find the shed. Wouldn't its nonexistence, its very erasure, be a blessing? Why does it feel like a heartbreak, a curse? When Nick mentioned the notion of voice-over, Andrew gave him a scolding look. "Voice-overs, unless you're Hitchcock making *Rebecca,* are for directors on training wheels." And so, for several minutes, the camera will track a solitary, speechless Nick.

"What about this movie—the movie about Morty? Will this one be devastating, too?" Her voice is solemn.

"No," he says. "Sad in places, but it ends on a high note. Same as *Colorquake.* The nightmare is over. He is home. And home is—well."

He stops abruptly; is he holding something back? Yet Tommy is grateful for a break in the conversation, a chance to enjoy her food. Nick is a natural cook. The lemon dressing on the asparagus, which Tommy watched him mix with a fork in a juice glass, is perfect. She's afraid to tell him so, however, for fear that the recipe comes from his mother and that she'll open that grab bag of emotion all over again. She thinks of her parents' twin graves, in northwestern Connecticut— the small town where Dad grew up—and once again (again; again; it will never stop) wishes that she were the kind of daughter to make a pilgrimage there. Does Dani ever visit? She doubts he does, but that she doesn't even *know* dismays her.

She refills Nick's water glass from the pitcher he put on the table (one, in fact, that belonged to Tommy's mother). "So tell me what you need from me. I have a lot to do this weekend—I'll be out in the studio a lot of the time—but I want to be available. You have questions, I'm sure."

"Have I *questions?*" Nick leans toward her; would this be his devilish smile? He seems to have quite an arsenal. "But right now, Tomasina, all I need is a room assignment and a loo and a Wi-Fi password, if you don't mind. And I hope you might let me wander about. May I see the upstairs? His bedroom?"

Tommy knows that seeing Morty's room, contemplating and handling his private things, is a logical purpose of the actor's field trip—and as it happens, Morty's room is exactly as he left it (bed neatly made, a habit his mother enforced from early on). The thought of going through Morty's clothing and the books he kept close at hand feels obscene to Tommy, even if it's not a task she would delegate to anyone else.

"Of course."

The texts, expressing a mounting impatience, are from Si. Andrew's on the warpath because Toby Feld's mother is threatening to withdraw him from the picture. Domineering bitch, thinks Nick. But they cannot lose the boy. So Andrew's now wondering, What if Nick phones the mother directly? *Pull out all the stops on your Rule Britannia charm.*

It won't be the first time Nick's been asked to deploy a kind of persuasion to which Americans alone seem epidemically susceptible: the Colin Firth Special, Nick privately calls it (not that he wouldn't kill to share a stage or screen with that man). At least he can be genuine about his desire to work with Toby. The boy is talented and, because of his looks, virtually irreplaceable. The thought of placating that woman, however, sets Nick's teeth on edge.

Sitting on the couch, he assesses the room. It's the room with the main telly, with the bookshelves containing the least personal books: tree-felling tomes of Master Artists, showy references on everything from geography to gardening. There's also a shelf holding at least a hundred DVDs.

On the wall between a pair of windows looking out toward the studio hangs a large framed black-and-white photograph: a winding alley in some medieval-vintage European village. The photographer signed it—nobody Nick's ever heard of, but what does that mean?—with a penciled note: *Let's go, M, shall we?*

A lover? There had to be others, before and even after Soren Kelly.

Soren Kelly was the last major role Andrew cast; the two actors at the top of his original list were superstitious about dying of AIDS on-screen—and the script does get a little grisly. Finally, in one of

those counterintuitive strokes of genius, Andrew landed Jim Krivet, known to most people only for his buffoonish role in that series about the out-of-work solicitors who start a moving company in L.A. In the one reading they've done together, Krivet was a marvel. Extraordinary how, by the end of the reading, the prospect of making love to this other man, if only (only!) on-screen, seemed quite plausible to Nick.

There's no cupboard, but Tomasina set out a rack for his suitcase, and a narrow dressing table stands against the wall beneath the photograph. After putting a jug of those divine peonies on top of the dressing table, she said she would take him upstairs in an hour; she has to make certain calls before the end of the business day.

Nick texts Silas and Andrew that he'll do what's necessary to appease the devil mum, but can it wait till Monday? He then idles through the DVDs: old classics, new (or newish) classics . . . a lot of American comedies, from Ernst Lubitsch and Preston Sturges to John Hughes and Albert Brooks; a boxed set of *Bleak House,* another of the Peter Sellers *Pink Panther* films. (Whose taste is represented here? Probably not just Lear's.) No sci-fi or horror. To the far right on the shelf, he finds a few copies of the PBS documentary on Lear, which Nick has watched three times. He'll watch it again while he's here. He looks around for the remotes.

Another text: *Needs to happen this weekend. Tomorrow if not today. Sorry.*

Andrew himself this time.

Leaving his phone in the den, Nick goes out into the living room. It's not a bright room, but it's lovely and cool, antique chestnut-colored paneling from floor to rafters, ceiling and windows low. Without even straightening his arms, he can easily clasp his hands around one of the coarsely hewn beams. Just beyond the two dozen panes of each window, delicate trees grow close to the house, the sun casting through their fresh foliage a mosaic of watery light.

He walks the perimeter, taking in watercolor landscapes, a small collection of American Indian baskets and pots, and, on the mantel, pots of a rather different spirit: children's lumpen representations of Lear's fictional characters, mostly Ivo and the panther. Then he arrives at the built-in glass-front case of very old books, leather-bound, nearly all of them by or about Charles Dickens. Tomasina opened it when she showed him around last week, pulling out a couple of her favorites. Is he allowed to handle the volumes on his own? The case isn't locked.

If he had the money and the time—and, of course, the inclination and the focus—what would Nick collect? He doesn't have that urge. Nor does he own anything he would consider an heirloom. When Grandfather's house was finally sold, Nick told Nigel and Annabelle to take the lot of it. He was still too heartbroken after Mum's death, too angry at the injustice.

In the front hall, walls are colonized with framed sketches by Lear's fellow illustrators. Several are scribbled with fond, jaunty notes. In one ink drawing, Nick recognizes Lear's house, a moon overhead, a scrum of animals beside a glowing window. Typed across the bottom,

A light in the dark.
Woodland creatures gather close.
Hark: the genius snores!

There is also a beaky caricature of Lear himself; it might have appeared in some literary journal. A platoon of tiny children frolic in his grizzled hair.

Many of the pictures are hung along the large triangle of wall flanking the staircase leading upward. Nick leans over the banister and glances toward the top, where another wall displays yet more pictures, the odd photograph or letter.

Pictures everywhere. Each one a window onto its own whimsical world. Was Lear a romantic? Did he love children or simply see them as his source of bread and butter? As a gay man, he was too old, as he admitted to Nick, to contemplate seriously the possibility of becoming a father. But what if he had?

Nick opens the front door and steps out under the trellised weave of roses, the sharp glossy leaves brimming with spearlike buds, some revealing a wink of crimson. (Rose Red: *that* was the fairy tale with the bear who comes in from the cold.) He walks out a few meters and turns to look back at the house. After browsing the gallery of sketches, so many made in a childlike spirit, the house reminds him of a cottage drawn by Beatrix Potter. Annabelle took the few Beatrix Potter books that Mum had saved all those years; they're Fiona's now.

Nick can't help feeling ashamed that he has let the ties with his siblings fray so badly. Someone might say, *Well, it takes two . . .* , but he knows that now, after all his good fortune, it's entirely up to him if they're to remain connected. When he finishes shooting this film, should he invite Fiona to spend a weekend with him in London? Is she too young for that?

"Leaving so soon?"

Tomasina stands in the open door to the house.

"Oh! Of course not. You won't be rid of me so easily!"

"Your phone's making disgruntled noises in the den."

"Bollocks."

"Do you still want a tour upstairs?"

"I do! And now is perfect—if it's good for you, Tomasina."

He reenters the house. She shuts the door behind him.

They stand awkwardly in the front hall.

"You had a look at all these pictures, I assume."

"Yes. They're brilliant," he says. "I imagine lots of these artists are quite famous."

"In Little Reader Land," she says. "But that is not the world at large."

He sees her repressing a smile. She is thinking that of course he, Nick, is famous in the world at large.

He says, "I think I'd rather be quietly, lastingly famous—I mean, deservedly so—in Little Reader Land than famous for a minute in the world at large."

"I'm very happy with all-around obscurity," she says as she starts up the stairs.

Was that a rebuke? Nick wonders.

At the top, the stairs split into a T, three steps leading left, three right.

"My room's at the end, up there." She points right and heads in that direction, but she stops at a closed door near the entrance to her room. "This is a room we hardly ever used. Barely big enough for a bed. It's mostly full of books now, all Morty's, in unopened boxes. We called it the nursery. As if one day we might have had a child."

Had she been in love with the man, possibly wished they *could* have had a child? Nick resists the fretful urge to make a joke.

She returns toward him, ignoring a set of narrow ladderlike stairs that must end in an attic. She stops at the door beside him. "Morty's bathroom." She opens it briefly, giving a glimpse of a claw-foot tub, a toilet, a sink. Closing it again, she passes Nick and takes the three steps leading up to his left. She opens the final door. "Morty."

The first surprise is that the room is fairly small. The one solid interior wall is covered by a built-in bookcase, flush against it a wooden bed with a plain headboard. The coverlet is powder-blue chenille. Two side tables flank the bed, on each a tall reading lamp and a precariously towering stack of books. On the near stack lie three pairs of reading specs tangled together.

A pine dressing table, a rectangular wood-framed wall mirror, a weary upholstered armchair backed into a corner.

"Mine's the master bedroom, the one with its own bathroom," says Tommy. "He claimed he felt safer in a small room, but I think it was his way of giving me the best room. He would let his studio go to bedlam, especially when he was finishing a book, but this place he kept shipshape. Made his bed every day. Put his clothes away or in the hamper." She points to a wicker basket. "I still haven't done his last laundry."

Nick is quiet, hoping she'll say more. When she doesn't, he says, "It's very, very hard, figuring out what to do with the things that were closest but that nobody has any use for."

"You and I both know about that," she says.

He nods toward the closed door across the room. "His cupboard?"

Now she's tearing up. "Would you mind awfully," he says quickly, "if I just stayed in here on my own? I feel as if I'm subjecting you to torture."

"No, no. I just realized I've hardly set foot in here since . . . I need to crack the windows, pull down the screens. At least that."

"Can I help?"

The windows are stubbornly shut, swollen from disuse and heat, and it's Nick who forces them up from the sill. Tomasina jiggers the screens into place.

"Thank you," she says. "All right. All yours. Look at whatever you like in here. I'll be downstairs. I eat around seven these days. I'm making a big salad. The lettuce in the garden is, as Morty liked to say, legion."

"Lo, the lettuce is legion," Nick declaims in a theatrical baritone.

She laughs. "Anyway, I'm happy to have you join me—or not. Whatever you prefer. Obviously."

Should he say yes? This is all more awkward than he had imagined.

"You can interrogate me then if you like."

"Then yes," he says. "But let me do the washing-up. And I bought plenty of veggies, so please nab anything useful."

She leaves him alone. For a long moment, he simply looks around, takes in the faded, balding kilim (worn clean through to the floor around the legs of the bed), the astonishing crush of books in the bookcase, volumes jammed in willy-nilly, horizontal atop the vertical. But there isn't a single book on the floor, the dressing table, or the chair. Nor is there anything beneath the bed—not even a pair of slippers. There, the kilim's zigzagging pattern is darker: the rug's been here forever.

On the dressing table, a red lacquerware box and yet another pair of reading specs sit on a delicate white runner embroidered with daisies—a keepsake from Lear's mum? Many of the room's appointments seem old-ladyish. Nick reminds himself that the Lear he will become is far younger than the Lear who last slept in this bed, who regarded himself in this looking glass that now reflects Nick in his place.

He can't help it: he opens the box. It contains a cache of chemist vials—medications related to pain and digestion, as best he can tell—along with a few safety pins, spare change, a ticket stub from *The Book of Mormon* (two years old), and a claim slip for shirts from a laundry service.

As quietly as he can, he opens the top drawer: underpants, all white; socks, an array of sober neutrals. A dark velvet jeweler's box holds a set of prim gold studs and cuff links. Slipped in sideways, face to the wall of the drawer, a framed photograph. Pulling it out, Nick guesses before properly seeing the picture that it's Soren. Strong, beguiling, healthy. He puts the picture back and pulls from behind it a wooden cigar box. This time he hesitates.

Enough, he thinks, replacing the box and closing the drawer. Or enough for now, perhaps.

He goes back to the cupboard and opens the door. Ignored for weeks, it must have gathered in the summer's early heat—which radiates into the room, conveying with it a thick, muddled odor of dusty wood, leather, ripe old plimsolls, and a chimeric trace of cologne, a properly masculine scent like coffee or tobacco leaf.

Shirts, trousers, suits, neatly hung; affixed to the inner door, a rack of neckties; on the floor, half a dozen pairs of shoes. Lear was no dandy, but his garments were well kept. The shirts, many still sheathed in polystyrene, are of three varieties: white or pastel cotton, short-sleeve stripes and tartans, thick wintry fleeces and woolens. There is a standard-issue evening jacket, lapels narrow, and suits in olive seersucker and gray wool; khaki trousers (cuffed), a navy blazer. Nothing monogrammed or bearing a logo.

The neckties, however, are a circus in silk. There are regimentals, polka dots, and paisleys, the quotidian fare of businessmen, but scattered robustly among them are ties with scholarly totemic prints of open books, inkwells, quill pens, library shelves—and garishly clever ties depicting characters from cartoons and storybooks: Eeyore, Road Runner, Kermit the Frog, Ferdinand the Bull, Tenniel's big-headed Alice, and those two notorious felines: the toothsome Cheshire Cat and his mischievous compatriot in the striped stovepipe hat. Most striking of all is an indigo tie that portrays Rapunzel. Her small, inscrutable face, leaning from a bright chink of window (her tower itself unseen), must fall just below the knot; luxuriant tresses of golden hair tumble and coil down to rest inside the tie's angular end point. It's an object that merges masculinity with the unbridled feminine.

Nick handles the ties tenderly, without removing them from the rack. To which occasions did Lear wear these fanciful bits of silk? Were they reserved for appearances with children, or might he wear Rapunzel to a posh charity banquet? For a few years, while he was with Soren Kelly, Lear was a conspicuous presence at auctions, luncheons, and staged events aimed at raising funds for nonprofits offering help to people stricken with HIV. But after Soren, he seemed to fall away from those snippets of gossip in the New York papers, the photographic collages on style and society pages documenting all the Most Important Parties (the parties at which Nick is now welcome, often expected). He saw a series of these pictures thanks to Ned, the film's costume designer—who would probably keel over in rapture were he allowed to flip through these ties, this cupboard filled with Lear's real-life wardrobe.

Were his phone not downstairs, Nick would be tempted to snap a quick photo and shoot it to Andrew.

The one shelf above the clothing holds stacks of neatly folded blankets and linens, though a straw panama is wedged in at the left. Nick pulls it down. He smiles. The price tag is still attached to the brim. Good intentions gone south.

Turning his attention to the shoes, Nick sits on the floor. Quite unlike the neckties, they are all practical: a graying pair of plimsolls with cracked rubber soles, two pairs of loafers, suede wing-tips, patent-leather dress shoes, doe-brown walking shoes, and a pair of blinding-white trainers whose unblemished state betrays, again, healthy intentions deferred. But among the shoes, there is nothing whimsical, no purchase made in a fit of delusional modishness. No velvet slippers.

He takes one of the plimsolls and holds it, sole to sole, with one of his own. Lear's feet were smaller than Nick's.

Nick closes his eyes. He must simply sit here for a time, inhaling the subtle effusions of all these neglected garments. A breeze from the open window behind him cools his neck; he hears the whisper of fabric stirred. Since fathers were never a part of his growing up, Nick had no experience of cupboards like this one until he had his own. Even when he was away at school, the boys hung their clothes together in doorless cupboards. In the communal crush, one or two unlaundered shirts and the funk became contagious. When the lot of them dressed up and sat shoulder to shoulder at vespers, a faint barn-like stench rose from the assembly. In school plays, from up onstage, he could smell it, too, the audience filled with boys who were mostly impatient to be elsewhere, bored and itchy in their soon-to-be-outgrown blazers.

He rises to his feet and closes the door to the cupboard.

Brooklyn makes sense. That's where she will be working. Enough with the hysteria; no matter what happens with what she thinks of as the Lear Catastrophe, she is not going to lose her job. But even out here, the prices are insane. What is going *on* with this city? Are the rentals monopolized by Russian mafia princesses going to NYU and Parsons?

She called in sick—which she certainly was—then downed four ibuprofen with a carton of orange juice from the corner market on her way to take Linus for a good, long, penitential walk. After returning to the apartment, she did what she had been putting off: called that real estate broker in Park Slope whose card she had taken at a baby shower for their mutual friend Renee.

The broker took her to a dozen apartments in Prospect Heights, Ditmas Park, and Bensonhurst. "The crème de la crème of my very best deals for people who aren't worried about their school catchment. When you don't have kids, your choices are much wider—and, frankly, of better value. More bang for your buck."

Every single option cost more than her current rent (the one about to be launched to the moon), and not one came with a perk like her key to Gramercy Park—never mind the responsible twelve-year-old girl next door who was practically willing to pay Merry just to spend time with Linus. Okay, she'd been spoiled. Except that right now she feels anything but spoiled. She feels embattled.

After parting ways with the broker (Yes, wasn't Renee's little Cressida the most adorable baby ever?), Merry pulls out her phone and orders an Uber. She needs to remind herself what it's all for, why it's worth staying in this magnificently heartless, ego-crushingly fabulous city.

"Yes, really," she says when the driver, an overly friendly twenty-something, doubts her destination.

"Whoa," he says when they arrive at the building site. "You dumpster diving or something?"

"Do I look like I'm dumpster diving?" she says, barely omitting the *young man* with which her mother would append that question.

He actually leans over backward and looks at her attire. "Yeah, well, no way."

"Could you wait? I'll just be ten minutes."

"No prob."

Because she cannot enter the building site itself (where, reassuringly, workmen are marching around giving orders and operating a lot of manly machinery), Merry asked the driver to drop her at the adjacent site, the one that's destined to become a parking lot. She walks carefully through the broad stretch of industrial flotsam to the edge of the canal. Chain-link fencing prevents casual swimmers or desperate depressives from jumping in—not that the water looks enticing—but a year from now, this plot of wasteland, obscured by pavement, should stand in the shapely shadow of the zero-carbon-footprint palazzo from which she will reign, Lear or no Lear. And Jonas Hecht's design is virtually all glass on the canal side, its top floor just high enough to offer views of New York Harbor.

What if she were to invite Tomasina Daulair to visit the site? Take her for a cozy-groovy girls' lunch in Dumbo (but no: almost overnight, it's turned into Broville Central) or Cobble Hill (much better), then grab an Uber (hopefully not this dweeby upstart) and share a thermos of iced tea while Merry shows her the architect's renderings on her smartphone and explains her own vision. Maybe she can dragoon Hecht into coming along, giving them a hard-hat tour.

Worth a try. She picks up a small stone and tosses it over the fence into the water. She makes a wish: that a few years from now, wherever she's living, she'll feel a lot less ungrateful toward the world.

"Manhattan," she says when she gets back into the car. "Gramercy Park."

"You do the extremes, don't you?" says her driver.

"That is one way to see my life," she says, then makes a show of pulling out her phone and texting, though it's nothing but pretend. The weather is sublime today; maybe she'll take Linus and have dinner at that Park Avenue bistro with the sidewalk tables. Coq au vin, potatoes dauphinoise. Then she will walk Linus over to the West Side, admire the lights of New Jersey casting their confetti on the Hudson, circle back home. Which reminds her that it's high time to visit her mother, who rarely complains about Merry's chronic negligence. Perhaps she should drive out and take Mom to the garden center next weekend. The woman loves to plant shrubs. You'd think she has stock in azaleas.

Merry laughs at the thought of her life as one of extremes. Tame, tame, tame—but there are comforts in that. There's stability in that. Call her a bourgeois fool.

Just as she's begun to feel moderately calm about the weekend, certain that the actor is what he appears to be (as her father might say, *a fine young man, artistic to boot!*), now this: a letter sent to her care of Morty's agent. Angelica included it in yet another batch of correspondence from people not yet aware of Morty's demise. The letter is dated ten days ago, though it feels as if it's caught up with Tommy from decades gone by, as if it's been chasing her down, a messenger from her past, inept but resolute.

Dear Tommy,

I don't know when I last wrote a real personal letter to anyone, but even if you were on Facebook (good for you, resisting that social dominatrix), it wouldn't feel right getting back in touch that way.

As you can guess, I saw your name in one of the many articles I've read about Mort Lear's death. My daughters loved all his books, and so did I. They're among the ones I turn to when I'm feeling nostalgic about my life as a dad. (Keira, Dominique, and Jo are all out of the nest, to my perpetual astonishment.)

I sometimes wonder if you ever forgave me for more or less vanishing, but I'm not so vain as to think you dwelt on what was probably an inevitable parting. Still, I owed you more than an over-the-shoulder wave. To explain, not excuse, I let law school swallow me whole, and when I scrambled out of the whale's gullet, I found myself engaged to a classmate and tackling the treadmill of pursuing partnership in a big firm that handled stuff like mergers and acquisitions. Mortgaged my soul to the devil, I know. My wife, Louise, worked in family law, giving me the lame justification that somehow she could balance our collective karma. (Not that I believe in such things.)

Three children and one college tuition later, I got my comeuppance during the Big Bang. Our firm shriveled from a plum to a prune. I was one of the cruise-line passengers thrown to the sharks. I went back to square minus-one and now I'm teaching high school English. (After leaving the law, I felt like a dog off leash for the first time in years. I even wrote poetry for a while. And I still take too many bad metaphors out for a spin. Professor Matz would be horrified.)

I am happier and poorer, as you'd expect. And I'm still in Chicago, to which I boomeranged right after Stanford. Louise was from Milwaukee, and our families made us a deal we couldn't refuse: down payment on a tiny house in Oak Park.

Here, Tommy sets the letter down and wonders why in the world he is telling her all this, thrusting his life with its bumpy but more-or-less stars-aligned trajectory in her face. Yet back she goes for more.

I'm now in a condo in the city, Louise in the larger house to which we "upsized" in my professional prime. You were right about me: I didn't have much faith in happy endings. I won't blame it on poor Henry James, and I suppose the "divine justice" in my fate is that the restrictive curriculum of my public school system compels me to teach The Turn of the Screw, *year after year. Louise and I split up five years ago, after Jo, our youngest, left for Barnard. Pretty amicable—though I hate that word—for a pair of attorneys. Maybe we gave up too soon—but she's remarried.*

You must think me selfish just to send you my life story like this . . .

As a matter of fact, Tommy has begun to fume, just a little.

. . . but for the past week I've been thinking about you and wondering if it might be a good thing to meet up again the next time I'm in New York. Daughter Jo went straight from Barnard to NYU Law. She's crazy about New York, and I try to visit her at least two or three times a year. A classmate of ours (do you remember Josh Stark?) lets me crash in his guest room. I go to museums and bookstores while Jo fills her head with legislative lore and lard. She assures me she'll put it all to work for the Right Causes. I'm probably jealous.

Would you consider meeting me for lunch the next time I head east? I'll be there next month. Are you still living in the city? I remember your stories about growing up in Greenwich Village back in the hipster days, so I can't imagine you anywhere else. And I'm sure you have a family of your own. (I do read the alumni notes, even though I never write in. I see you never do, either. But we loved it there, didn't we?)

I realize this letter might not even reach you, but if it does, I would enjoy hearing your news, now that I've forced too much of mine on you. Whether we meet again or not, know that my memories of our year together seem sweet from this vantage point, like looking at Planet Earth from the moon. Or maybe I'm just turning into a sentimental fool. My students tease me that I'm incapable of reading Keats aloud without a box of Kleenex at the ready. I'll stop there.

It's not as if Scott has slipped her mind. In one context or another, she probably thinks of him once a week or so. Back when Google was a novelty, a party trick to be practiced again and again (generally late at night, when sleep is elusive and what-ifs loom large), Tommy searched for Scott online. That was before social media, before LinkedIn, and what popped up was the website of his big, muscular law firm. It offered no folksy pictures of the partners, just the sense that they were the sort of people who made the world safe for capitalism. You need not see their faces or know their hobbies to trust in their power.

She reads the letter a second time. The water for the corn has boiled, and she's turned it off. The salad is made. The chicken breasts are in the oven, done. Once Nicholas Greene said he'd like to join her, she felt insecure offering little more than salad.

She should get up from the table, set it, and summon her guest. But Scott's letter leaves her emotionally winded. Why does it make her feel both angry and affectionate toward him? He never did her wrong; they both walked away. Not even away; their paths did not diverge on purpose. And surely "they"—twenty-two-year-old Tommy and Scott—are barely cousins to fifty-five-year-old Tommy and Scott.

"Smells divine in here."

Enter stage left, again, the movie star. She wishes it didn't startle her every time.

"Anything left to do? Always happy to help."

"No, no. Or—set the table? I'm afraid I got distracted. I'll just finish the corn."

"Another of the reasons I love eating in this country," says Nick. "Have you had that Mexican street corn? I had it in L.A. last week. Brilliant."

"Mayonnaise slathered on just about anything makes it brilliant," says Tommy. She tucks Scott's letter in the bedlam drawer and reignites the burner under the water. The ears are already shucked.

"How about candles? I'm a sucker for candles," says Nick.

Tommy points him to a shelf in the pantry.

"I've got to ask you about that extraordinary collection of neckties," he says as he sets the candlesticks on the table. "Did he actually wear the ones with all the various characters? Road Runner? The Cheshire Cat?"

Tommy slips the corn into the water. "They were all presents. He accepted them as if he was thrilled, and then, with me, he pretended to despise them." She smiles, remembering the time he came downstairs wearing the Cheshire Cat. Rose had given it to him, so he claimed that he was wearing it to a certain party only because she would be there. But Tommy saw him preen, just a little, before the front-hall mirror.

"When he was young, when I met him, he dressed like a hippie. Shirts in crazy patterns, jeans self-consciously patched. Back then, that was a kind of conformity. If you lived downtown. But later on, he liked to think of himself as having the plainest, least extravagant taste in clothing. Mostly that was true. But he had his vanities."

"Don't we all."

Is he inviting her to ask about his? The candlelight disorients her, lending their shared meal the aura of a date. She wonders what it would be like to go on a date, essentially a romantic audition, with a man so idolized that you couldn't possibly get a straight view of his self, perhaps not even of his face. There would always be something askew in any attempt to *know* him.

But this is not her problem. "Please. Sit down before it's cold. I'm afraid I may have overdone the chicken."

"Better than underdone." Playfully, he seizes his ear of corn and takes three quick, lunging bites. After setting it back on the plate, he says, "This. Now this is bloody perfection."

Bloody perfection, thinks Tommy. (And it is.) Well, she got one thing right. Perhaps it's a start.

"I'm all yours," she says. "Ask me anything."

He looks up, his eyebrows raised, as if she's said something unexpected. Kernels of corn speckle his chin and lower lip, the butter gleaming in the candlelight.

He wipes his mouth and says solemnly, "I want to ask you about the interview. Mostly, really, about Arizona, what happened there."

She sighs. "You know, he didn't tell me much. I barely knew about it before he decided to tell that story to the world. The first I knew of it was after Soren Kelly died. I think his death sent Morty down a chute, back to—I know this sounds trite, but the death of his innocence. He would roll his eyes if he could hear me."

"It doesn't. Sound trite." The actor's hands are in his lap, and he sits up straight, ignoring his food.

"I have to tell you, he didn't go into the gory details. He just said that he had undergone a . . . sexual humiliation." Tommy suddenly worries for Morty. Nicholas Greene's alertness seems too acute. "Can I ask how graphic it's going to be, the movie?"

"Not," he blurts out. "What I mean is, it's going to be . . . handled indirectly. Aesthetically. Folded in with the book. With *Colorquake*. Andrew's no Quentin Tarantino. What I mean is . . . Look. What I'm asking you is more for me, privately. The script's written. I just wondered if there were things he shared with you that . . . maybe weren't in that magazine. Journalists mess things up, as everyone knows!"

She shakes her head. "I think I'm going to disappoint you. Morty wasn't much of a 'sharer.' He kept a lot to himself."

And a lot he didn't, thinks Nick. Oh Christ.

He cannot even approach the brink of sleep. It isn't the mattress on the foldaway, which is surprisingly decent, and the feral chitchat of the nightlife in the woods is soothing. It's the sense of sleeping under the roof of a house that is more than a house. Wandering through its rooms that afternoon and evening, Nick understood that it is one of those rare homes which appropriate the personae of their owners.

Tomorrow, Tomasina has promised to give him a "tour" of the sketches stored in the flat files, of handmade books, papier-mâché masks, ceramic figures, and other whimsical objects crafted by Lear that very few people have seen. He does want more time in the studio and, childish though it may seem, wonders if he might try out the "napping chair." But this house is the place that feels like it must have held Lear's heart. No wonder he abandoned the city. This was his hive, his burrow, a place where the modest size of all the rooms makes a reassuring kind of sense. Not for Lear a palace or villa or manse but a haven of peace, a daily retreat, the monk's cell, the badger's den.

If only Nick's flat felt like such a refuge—though what can you expect of a place you must repeatedly neglect?

His mobile tells him it isn't even three o'clock. He goes to the water closet tucked behind the stairs. The sink and the shower are fit for a sailboat, which Nick finds amusing, as if the room were borrowed from one of Lear's picture books, a Lilliputian loo. When he washes up, the fragrance of the sandalwood soap makes him feel more awake still.

Latching the door as quietly as he can, he pauses in the dim blue glow leaking through the sidelights of the front door. He considers the stairs. They are carpeted.

She mentioned that she sleeps lightly, but if he leans up and listens closely, he can hear that she has a fan on in her room. Would it be a crime to find out what it's like to lie on Lear's bed in the middle of the night? Before he can change his mind, he ascends, tread to tread, stealthy as a cat (as a panther!). Left, up three more, along the soft runner to Lear's door—miraculously, still ajar.

Once inside the room, he closes but does not latch the door. He climbs onto the bed, transferring his weight from floor to mattress one ounce at a time. Here is where dance training comes in handy: no creakings.

The pillows are soft: feathers, not foam. The ceiling above him is awash in faint leafy shadows, the curtains back, the windows wide open. The air is dead still, but he can smell the adolescent greenery of June, sense how everything alive is burgeoning, not resting, in its reprieve from the blaring sun. Connecticut smells more like Dorset or even a London park than it does like L.A., but still it's entirely new to Nick.

He sits up and gazes around. Wait—there. Down to his left, in the lowest of the bookshelves against which the bed resides, his roving glance snags on a pinpoint of pulsing green light. He leans sideways to feel for it, though he knows what it is: a laptop—kept beside the bed and, he knows as well, within the insomniac's reach.

This would be trespass, but something too tempting crosses his mind. What if his correspondence with Lear—the e-mails he promised to delete and did—are on this computer? Could he at least reassure himself that he is right, read them again?

No doubt the access is locked, password protected.

He crouches beside the bed and delicately extracts the laptop, which is wedged between a stack of books and the shelf above, its cord snaking under the rug. Sitting cross-legged on the floor, he balances the computer on his thighs and flips it open. The image that springs to the screen, background to dozens of neatly ranked azure file folders, is a photograph of Lear's house at the height of autumn, trees ablaze.

He is a cat burglar at his first heist and here is his first jewelry box. The touch pad wakes the little arrow, which, like the intruder's gloved hand, roams covetously over the contents, pausing, hovering, questing for something of particular value. If he had all night, he could take everything, but he must choose. As he guides the cursor to the sound icon at the top of the screen, as he slides it to mute, he has the disembodied sense of watching his own conscience drift out the nearest window into the night.

Celia. Abe. Rosie. Coleman.

Arbitrarily, he chooses Coleman: just a peek. Inside the folder is a line-by-line list of dates.

He closes Coleman, returns him to the jewel box. Scanning the screen more closely, he sees what he's looking for.

NG.

Date by date by date, over just the couple of months they wrote back and forth, here are the e-mails Lear sent him—almost always in the middle of the American night—copied into files. Or did he write them as files and copy them into e-mails?

Does it matter?

He closes the folder and, as he does, spots another one in a remote corner of the screen labeled *Leonard.*

She couldn't stop thinking about Scott, couldn't stop cartwheeling in and out of those memories until she felt dizzy. How was she going to reply to his letter? Well, let it take its place in the long line of other letters she had yet to answer.

So she was wide and painfully awake when she heard Nicholas Greene ascend the stairs. His footsteps were inaudible, but she heard his breathing. So many years of listening for Morty's breathing in the middle of the night—even through the hum of her window fan or the restive grumble of the furnace—have made her unwittingly alert to human otherness in the house she's begun to inhabit alone. She realizes that Nick is the first person to sleep in the house, with her, since Morty died.

She rises onto her elbows, preparing to go out and intercept him, but what kind of a confrontation will that be? She feels herself redden at the thought of saying anything whatsoever to Nicholas Greene under these circumstances: surprising him in the dark hallway, catching him there in whatever it is he wears to sleep (or to sneak around people's houses when he thinks they're sleeping). Forget the thought of his seeing her in the skimpy threadbare nightgown she reserves for the hottest nights.

When she thinks of how loquacious he is, she's surprised at his gift for stealth. Now that he's in Morty's bedroom, Tommy hears nothing.

Her back aches from the tension of her indecisive posture. She lies back down.

What crime would she prevent by apprehending the actor, who is—in whatever unorthodox, meddlesome fashion—simply doing his job? Lying there in the dark, she is astonished at herself for two reasons. She is completely unafraid of this virtual stranger and his sneaky behavior, and she is fed up with this never-ending urge to protect Morty—as if he were a child in one of his own stories. Or no, not at all—because those children always figure out how to take care of themselves. The grown-ups around them are distracted, unreliable, or simply moot. Those children even know how to take care of others. So often, they're in the business of saving the world.

Morty wasn't one of those children. He never had been one of those children, not even when he was a child.

Ten

She was in the kitchen, the three layers of Morty's cake cooled on the counter before her, when she heard their voices rise—Soren's first, as always—and hoped in vain that it wasn't the start of an argument. Or, just as likely, a tantrum.

"It's not a metaphor, honey. It is a *gift*. G. I. F. T. Gift. Do you have to be such an *artist* all the time?" Ten minutes before, not a squall on the horizon, the three of them had been drinking champagne in the living room, toasting Morty's fifty-fifth birthday. Tommy would serve dinner as soon as she finished frosting the cake.

Morty's reply was hard to discern, but she was sure she heard him say, "Rapunzel."

"In case nobody's informed you," Soren said, "Disney now owns all the fairy tales. They've been washed clean of all that archetypy Bettelheim bullshit. They are just stories with ripping good plots, excellent villains, and sexy heroes—like the princes come in three-packs!—and merchandise potential up the fucking wazoo."

Morty answered again, his voice low but insistent, this time entirely unintelligible.

The pitch of Soren's voice approached a whine. "Oh, so it's like, who is the captive maiden and who the wicked witch? Well, if you want to see it like that, then you are no maiden, honey."

The door to the kitchen slammed open, and Morty stalked through the room. He was out the back door before Tommy could even say his name.

Soren was on his heels, but he stopped in the kitchen. He faced Tommy, indignant. "That went well." From his right hand dangled a necktie. He held it out to Tommy. "Isn't it gorgeous? Do you read it as more than a fucking necktie, and may I say, however bitchy it sounds, a damned expensive necktie?"

Tommy did not reach for it—her fingers were slick with icing—but she could make out the fairy-tale image. "I've never seen anything like it," she said truthfully.

"Right. Exactimento," said Soren, as if this gave him the moral high ground. "And what do you give the guy who has everything—or can buy it if he doesn't have it? Something unique. Something whimsical." Soren examined the tie, frowning.

Tommy did think it was stunning, but Soren had to know by now, four years into their never-placid relationship, that Morty would hardly wear such a tie. It would be the equivalent, to Morty, of wearing a Robin Hood hat or a long purple cape. He didn't even like wearing costumes. Halloween was an occasion whose rituals fell to Tommy. (The house of a famous children's book author, even at the end of a long driveway, could not go dark that night.)

Morty's birthday, however, was a holiday he took seriously. He liked the celebration itself to be intimate—no blowout parties, definitely no schemes involving dozens of friends hiding behind the furniture—but he cared about such niceties as cards and gifts, and, like a five-year-old, he relished ordering up three specific meals: usually, eggs, bacon, and French toast for breakfast; for lunch, an avocado BLT, with corn chowder if the local crops still held, and definitely chocolate-chip oatmeal cookies. For dinner, he'd want either lobster with potato salad or roast beef with Yorkshire pudding. "Surprise me with the cake," he always said.

Soren started toward the back door.

"I wouldn't," said Tommy. "He'll come back any minute. He's not going to skip his birthday dinner." She wondered why she ever bothered offering Soren sound advice (not that he ever asked); more and more often, she wished the relationship would simply implode. She would gladly pick up the shrapnel.

"He's being ridiculous," Soren said, fishing for agreement.

Tommy did her best to avoid discussing Morty with Soren, though her pointed restraint did not stop him from trying to win her approval whenever the two men were on the outs.

"You pushed a button. I think you know that."

"You mean the 'I write for children so I get to *be* a child' button?" Soren snapped. "That one?"

I'm not sure who's more of a child was the obvious retort, but she said, "Would you do me a favor and bring in the champagne glasses? And would you light the candles on the dining room table?"

Morty liked formality on his birthday, too: linens, china, the Murano goblets he'd bought on his first European book tour, and the silver flatware he'd stumbled on at a local estate sale, the same pattern his mother had owned—and sold to help pay for their move across the country. He hadn't told Tommy much about that move, but she knew it had been urgent. On the rare occasions he reminisced— usually when questioned by some adult at a public event: *Tell us about* your *childhood!*—he described his neighborhood in Brooklyn; his klatch of bookish friends; the branch librarian who let him stay after she locked up, then walked him safely home; the pleasure he found in turning his favorite stories into plays. *What about the art? Where did you learn to draw?* someone might ask, and Morty would say that while he did like to draw as a small child, he took a break for a few years— until the art teacher in high school brought him "back to the fold." Word for word, Tommy knew these codified memories by heart.

The one time she had asked him outright about his time in Arizona, he sighed and shook his head. "You know, the older I get, the less I remember. When it comes down to it, my life didn't really begin until we got here."

Tommy thought it was amusing that he used *here* to signify a neighborhood of tenements and plain-Jane houses near Brighton Beach as well as an affluent woodsy Connecticut town—as if he hadn't trav-

eled even further to get from one to the other than he had from west
to east.

There was no formal move-in day, no U-Haul truck filled with
furnishings, not even a delivery of steamer trunks or dented cardboard cartons. It happened quickly, Soren's storming of the castle.
The keep—Morty's heart—had been far more vulnerable than she
thought. She kept reminding herself that Morty was in love, for the
first time she had ever witnessed in the nine years she had worked for
him. That had to be good news, didn't it? He started going to the gym
at the Y and lost the paunch he'd acquired since moving away from
the city and its compulsory-fitness culture. Tommy was also pleased
to see Soren badgering him into eating more vegetables.

So she told herself that maybe the cause for all the drama in the
relationship, right from the start, lay in Morty's long dry spell, his
inexperience at the necessary give-and-take of love. Maybe it would
take time to work out the kinks.

When it became clear to her that Soren was living with them, not
just visiting, Tommy proposed to Morty that she transfer her bed and
belongings downstairs, that they move the television into a corner of
the living room—or even upstairs—and make the den her bedroom.
At first, Morty balked. He pointed out that she wouldn't have any
true privacy downstairs, certainly not when they were entertaining.

"Actually," she said, "upstairs is where I have no true privacy." She
gave Morty a look that warned him not to pursue the debate.

The walls of the house were solid—stalwart brick facing out to the
wind, well-plastered lath and horsehair enclosing the oldest rooms
within—but not solid enough to withstand Soren's voice when he
was piqued or angry or, to Tommy's particular dismay, at the height
of sexual arousal. He had once fancied himself an actor, and no one
could deny that he had the knack for both emoting and projecting.

When she met him—on the day he pulled Morty from the car like
a bride—he claimed to be twenty-eight years old. But something in
the set of his less-than-joyful expressions made Tommy suspect he
was ten years older. Even so, he was still a much younger man than

Morty, and if his charm and wit were too often outflanked by his temper, Tommy could see that Morty forgave a great deal in exchange for his lover's youth.

Morty also used Soren's youth as justification for all the parties they began to host. Within six months of the invasion, Tommy had overheard two testy exchanges in which Soren tried to convince Morty to move back into the city—at least rent a studio as an "escape hatch." In this ongoing skirmish, Morty would not retreat.

"You want the city, commute," Morty told Soren. "Or bring the city here. In moderation."

"That's a tall order, honey. The city doesn't come in moderation. It's why God invented the suburbs. For moderate folks."

All at once, nearly every weekend Morty wasn't traveling, there was a dinner party. Most of the guests came out from the city, most of them men, many even younger than Soren. Before the first of these gatherings, a sit-down dinner for sixteen, Morty spoke to Tommy over lunch—a meal Soren rarely shared with them, sometimes because he was still in bed, sometimes because he was fasting to "maintain his figure." (He also spent long days in the city every week or two, claiming that he was still going to open calls. Tommy, however unkindly, didn't believe him.)

"I think Soren envisions some kind of salon," Morty said. He made a weak attempt at laughter.

Tommy pictured a scene from *Sense and Sensibility:* gentlemen callers, cards on silver trays, vigilant matrons in bonnets and bustles.

"People dropping by when they feel like it? Or just during posted hours?" she said sardonically.

"Sometimes I think he forgets that I work for a living."

Or that Morty appeared to be supporting him.

"Parties," said Morty. He said it the way he might have said *surgeries.*

"So much for the life of the introvert. Which you implied made you happy."

"Yes. So much for that." Morty's smile was, as too often now, an apology. "But, Tommy, you won't be lifting a finger. You'll be a guest—no, a host. Of course a host! I found a caterer in town here that all the right people seem to worship. Why not spread the wealth around? What am I saving all this money *for*? And doesn't our dining table have two more leaves? Where are they?"

At least he made Soren climb into the medieval crawl space beneath the house to retrieve them. They were wrapped in dusty tarpaulins and coated with grime. It was a miracle they hadn't warped. Eagerly, Soren volunteered to oil them, along with the table and chairs.

Tommy wasn't about to protest, even if she was filled with dread—and resentment—at the thought of putting on feasts for Soren and, as she envisioned it, some entourage of aspiring fashion models. She might not have to cook, but she would have to make sure the house was presentable.

She attended the first two parties as if she were a live-in guest. To behave like a host seemed absurd, most of all because she hadn't been a part of deciding whom to invite. She showed the caterer around the kitchen, and then she had little choice but to join the true guests on the terrace. Two of them were old friends of Morty's, both authors she had known for years, so she relaxed. It was fine after all. But then, at dinner, she was seated between two extremely young men—barely men—who knew Soren through the acting studio he attended (or had, until he met Morty). There was one other woman at the table—the wife of one of the authors—but when it became clear that most of the guests were drinking with androgen-fueled abandon, Tommy tried to retreat to the kitchen.

The kitchen was filled to capacity. Tommy apologized and turned around.

To slink away to her room seemed churlish and immature (and pointless, since her room now adjoined the living room). She stuck it out until just before midnight, when a joint began to circulate. (Would cigars have been better or worse?) Two hours later, in bed but unable to sleep, she heard the last guests depart.

After that, she often chose the "party days" as a chance to spend a night in Brooklyn with her father and Dani. She stayed in her teen-age bedroom, where nothing had changed: same curtains and quilt, same gooseneck lamp, same stuffed animals slumped like drunks in their dusty chair. If she were to open the desk drawers, she knew she would find her English papers from high school and college—and, dutifully saved by her mother, all the letters Tommy had written home from Vermont.

Dad still picked at his guitar, quietly, absentmindedly, and he liked to play rummy and cribbage. If they attempted Scrabble, he would fall asleep halfway through the game, waiting for his turn. When Tommy asked about his friends, the ones who used to come over on weekends to share their songs, he told her that most of them had left the city long ago. "Your mom and I were the diehards," he said. "We were so proud of our tenacity. Now look."

"Hey, I would have hated the suburbs," she said. "I was proud of you, too."

He said nothing. He was lonely, plain and simple.

And where did she live now? In the suburbs.

Morty seemed relieved at this solution—relieved of guilt. Perhaps he didn't want Tommy to see that in fact, against his original instincts, he had grown to enjoy the ribald gatherings of uninhibited, self-consciously attractive men and women. He admitted that the company often made him feel younger, even pampered, as if the best of city life were being exported to his house expressly for his provincial pleasure. "And it makes Soren happy," he said, as if to remind himself.

One weekend in Brooklyn, after Dad went to bed early and Dani left to join friends at a bar, Tommy decided to go through the books in her room, most of them untouched since before she'd gone to college. Her mother had been a reader and, to keep books from clogging up the small house, made a habit of frequent donations to a local thrift shop, but she had been sentimental about her children's favorite books.

Tommy sat on the floor with a dustcloth and pulled the books from the shelves, wiping them one by one. She smiled when it occurred to her that she now knew a few of these authors whose words and pictures she had imbibed over and over and over again without even thinking of Horton or Ping or the Moominvalley creatures as beings dreamed up by real live people. And then, pushed back between *If I Ran the Zoo* and a spineless copy of *Burt Dow, Deep-Water Man,* Tommy found the small book that Morty had passed to her, through a fence, more than two decades ago, in order to prove that he wasn't a playground pedophile.

It should have brought her a surge of joy—made her eager to take it back home, show it to Morty and ask if he remembered that day— but instead she felt as if a cold salty wave were washing over her head. She paged slowly through the book, further chilled by its story: a child scared of so many things that he feared fear itself.

In other words, he was scared of life. Was she?

How Tommy had once pitied her parents for what she saw as the smallness of their existence, yet by the time they were her age, they had so much that she did not. Most of all, they had each other. They had married late, had children late—and, as a result, seemed to fully feel the pleasure in life that other people were constantly reminding themselves they *ought* to feel.

Was Tommy small-minded, even greedy, to yearn for a change? She sat on the aqua shag amoeba she had chosen as a rug at age thirteen and realized it was time to tell Morty how much she felt she owed him—and how it was time to think about what she owed herself. But there was no reason to be impatient. The kindest thing would be to wait until Morty's mother died. Frieda Lear had folded in on herself by this point, all her appetites shriveled, her attention a void, and though no one wanted to give Morty a firm timeline, her caretakers believed that she was too frail to last more than another year. Tommy would see Morty through whatever rituals he needed to complete, and then she would give him generous notice. He could hardly disagree that it was time for her to move on, could he?

What would she do then? She laughed at the thought of going to work as the assistant to another genius; how about a scientist next time around? One change she decided she would welcome was a return to the city. She imagined herself living in the Village again (though it was probably unaffordable to lowly genius-assistants) or maybe, just for a time, sharing an apartment with Dani in Hell's Kitchen or the increasingly unfashionable Upper East Side. Maybe they could find a responsible student to live with Dad in exchange for room and board.

For a brief heady moment, she imagined a move to San Francisco, her favorite stop on Morty's touring circuit. It was a city with dozens of bookstores, and they both enjoyed lingering there. They were spoiled, of course, chauffeured from Berkeley to Danville, from Laurel Village to Corte Madera, then back to the hotel Morty loved on Russian Hill. On her own, she wouldn't have such privileges—but the weather was humane, the culture more permissive toward daydreamers, gardeners, anyone who believed in the virtue of time to spare. This fantasy lasted as long as it took her to hear her father issue an exclamatory snore on the other side of her bedroom wall. New York was fine, she consoled herself, always holding the possibility of something unexpected.

When she entered Morty's house that Sunday evening, she felt much calmer than she had in months. She greeted Soren with genuine cheer, and she made the three of them a supper of Italian wedding soup and spinach salad. Morty and Soren told her about the latest party. "Do not, repeat *do not*," said Soren, "count the bottles in the recycling bin! And don't ask who went home with *whom*."

Then he told her who, as well as whom.

"Did you visit Frieda today?" she asked Morty after clearing the table.

"Same as ever," he said. "It's agony. For both of us, I suspect. Except for her, it's a permanent state of being."

"I know. I'm sorry."

"It can't be long," he said.

"I suppose not."

"Your father?" he remembered to ask.

"Same as ever," she said. "But he'll go on for a long time, I think. I just wish he knew what to do with himself."

Maybe, she thought, her father would be game to go with her to San Francisco. He would love all the open-air music.

❧

Two years later, Frieda was still alive—if respiration was the defining characteristic of living—and Tommy found herself frosting a three-layer devil's food cake in the kitchen while Morty sulked in his studio and Soren stood in the driveway, smoking and pacing and ranting to someone on his cell phone. Rapunzel's long tresses dangled from the back of a kitchen chair.

Tommy was thirty-five. When she read the alumni notes in her college magazine, she now saw pictures of classmates with children as old as ten. That, it seemed to her, was the one matter of urgency: whether she wanted to be a mother. Never mind that she was nine years younger than her mother had been when Dani was born. One of Morty's friends, another picture-book author he had known when he lived in the city, had decided, on her thirty-ninth birthday, that she was done with looking for Mr. Right and would adopt a child before it was too late. Now she lived in Milwaukee with a baby girl from India. Her breakout book was called *When I'm Big Enough to Be a Mom*.

Out back, through the door left open to the cool September air, she heard the studio door close and, through the window, glimpsed Morty heading toward the driveway, where Soren paced. She tried not to listen. She knew how it would go: Morty would apologize, Soren would shower him with affection, and later that night they would have profligate sex.

At dinner, the earlier outburst no longer in the air, Morty told them about the story he'd begun to tease out in the studio that week, more words than pictures. In fact, he wondered if pictures would be superfluous. At the very least, they would be marginal, perhaps occurring only at the chapter breaks—or not at all. Perhaps, for the first time, no pictures whatsoever.

Having finished his lobster, he placed his elbows to either side of his plate, folded his hands, and rested his chin on his knuckles. He looked content.

"Three children," he said.

"The magic number!" Soren exclaimed (now the cheerleader, having won his apology).

"Lifelong friends. Neighbors in a nice but square, cookie-cutterish town. Yards, swing sets, the whole bourgeois package."

"Orne, *bien sûr.*"

"No, not at all. More middle class, a place where neighbors *like* having neighbors. They're in high school—maybe sixteen—when they are all, simultaneously, diagnosed with cancer."

"What? Oh my God, that is too grim," said Soren. "Who's going to read that? What are you thinking, sweetie?"

"Wait." Morty gave Soren a sharp paternal look. "Their camaraderie gives them strength. They insist on going into treatment together."

After a pause, Soren asked quietly, "What kind of cancer?"

Morty sat back, folded his arms, and shook his head. "Not even sure I'll specify. Doesn't matter. Maybe I won't call it cancer. It's a . . . tale. It's not realistic."

"Sounds *too* realistic if you ask me." Soren's voice was nearly a whisper.

Morty reached over and put a hand on Soren's arm. "Actually, and don't take this personally, I am not asking you. I'm working it out."

Even after four years, Soren had not learned to do nothing but listen, to hold perfectly still, when Morty chose to talk about his work. Tommy remembered that a week before, over breakfast, Morty had commented on an article in the *Times* about the "cancer clusters" on Long Island and in a bleak middle-of-nowhere Massachusetts town.

"So they go through surgery together, and then they are scheduled for radiation together. Their parents take turns driving them to the hospital. In school, they take the same classes, so their days are now completely in sync. They get a dog they share from house to house. . . . They begin to sleep in the same room, rotating families. . . . I don't know the little stuff yet. The home part, the parents—if they'll even register as full, distinct characters—I haven't figured out."

Tommy could have reminded him that parents were always beside the point in his stories, but she said nothing.

Morty looked down at his plate, fiddled with his fork and knife, realigned them.

"There is an atmospheric flash," he said suddenly.

"A what?" said Soren.

"Shh," said Tommy.

After a long pause, Morty said, "They're in their hospital johnnies, in the waiting room in the deepest recesses of the hospital, about to go in for their radiation, when it happens."

Soren looked antsy. He frowned.

Morty sighed. "I have to do some scientific digging here, but you know how radiation units are always sealed with lead? So those inside are also protected from forces on the outside. I'm thinking there is some kind of countereffect whereby our three heroes are empowered against the sinister force causing havoc outside those walls—whatever it is. They venture out and, when they are unable to find their families, go on a quest, to purify the corruption, the toxicity. Or whatever trauma's been inflicted on the world around them. Maybe it's something local, not global. Maybe it's New York they have to rescue."

"But isn't everyone dead after this . . . flash thing? Is it the Chinese?" asked Soren. "It's got to be the Chinese. I've read they have these überhackers who—"

"I don't want to wade into politics. I'm not sure it's terrorism. It might be something cosmic—something that happens on the sun. But hacking . . . that's food for thought. Thanks, Soren."

Another long pause. This time, Soren held his tongue.

"That's all I have right now," said Morty. "But I see them clearly. Two boys and a girl. And the dog, he's a kind of wolfhound mutt. I see him perfectly. Skinny, wirehaired, affectionate but clingy. The kind of dog who jumps up, who begs at the table, who eats the furniture when left alone. A needy mooch of a dog. Maybe that's his name. Mooch. Moocho. They adopt him, together, when they start treatment. The parents can't say no. Or he arrives, he just arrives. On their way to school, he emerges from behind a bush and follows them. Waits for them. There's no saying no to this guy."

Tommy smiled. This was Morty at his best, letting a subplot unwind the way a ball of yarn unspools as it rolls across the floor. So it surprised her that he had reacted badly to Soren's gift earlier that evening. When he felt the spell of a story descending, he became magnanimous, even calm.

"It sounds amazing," said Tommy.

"But creepy," said Soren.

"That's why," said Morty, "it's for older children. Children who aren't really children anymore. Who understand what they're seeing in the news. And in case you don't remember, teenagers have innately dark thoughts they tend to keep to themselves—among themselves. They feast on fictional disasters. There's a kind of comfort to watching the world burn inside a book. A book, like a furnace, can be closed, the fire contained."

"Well, I'd say this calls for more champagne," said Soren, and off he went to retrieve a bottle from the pantry.

Alone with Morty, Tommy said, "Can I ask you something?"

"You will anyway."

"Isn't this *Colorquake* in a different guise? Not that you shouldn't go there again."

"Yes," he said, "and no. But what's different is that I feel like it's time to really write. Let the words matter more than the pictures. Tell a real yarn, with twists and turns. Knots and tangles. With fully complicated characters who speak their minds."

"Can I ask if any of them die?" Immediately, she wished she hadn't been so intrusive, but Morty looked pleased.

"Not in the first book," he said.

"The first book?"

"I think I'm in for the trilogy thing. It's all the rage." He laughed. "Maybe we can buy a house in the South of France. Or on an Italian lake."

"Italian lake gets my vote," said Tommy, though she felt a pang of betrayal. By then, she would be somewhere else. She would be reading his trilogy-volume-one on the subway, going back and forth, like a normal working person, between home and job, separate places with separate concerns.

A month later, Frieda died in her sleep. The call from the center woke them all at seven on a Saturday morning. Tommy made breakfast. Soren went back to bed, saying he'd be more useful later if he could get a few extra hours of sleep.

Morty ate silently, wiping tears off his cheeks every few minutes.

When Tommy joined him, she said, "Don't be upset you weren't with her."

"I'm not. I'm just sad that the old her—I mean the younger her— had to die without . . ."

"Without your getting to say goodbye."

Morty nodded. "I just never really believed . . ."

She waited.

"That I'd never see *that* her, her old self, again. Ever." Almost angrily, he wiped his eyes with a kind of finality. "But that's it. It's done! If I didn't feel so damn guilty, I'd feel free. I should, shouldn't I?"

Tommy put the dishes in the dishwasher. "Do you want me to drive you over?"

"No. I'd rather do this part alone."

"Did you have plans today that need canceling?"

"No. Soren and I were going to drive to New Haven, see the Constable show. That's all. Did you?"

She shook her head. She had planned to start putting the garden to bed. Any night now, there could be a frost. She might as well buy the hay. And then she thought, But wait. She had reached the moment she believed she'd been aiming toward throughout the past two years.

Morty's mother no longer had significant belongings. Her few pieces of jewelry, none of great value, Morty kept in a box that Tommy knew he had stashed in his bureau. He did bring home, that afternoon, a framed photograph: young mother next to school-age son, behind them a nondescript building. He laid this artifact on the kitchen table.

"What happens now?" asked Tommy. Soren had volunteered to go to the grocery store and cook dinner that night.

"An inhumane amount of paperwork. Cremation. Then . . ." He shrugged. "There's no family plot. No favorite body of water where she wants her ashes scattered. I suppose I'll simply have to bring her here."

there, at least living there? She realized that the moment had come, a week early. She told him there was something she needed to tell him.

Instantly, Morty looked scared. "No bad news," he said. "Please."

Tommy laughed nervously. "Well, I can't say for sure if you'll see it as bad or good—not all good—but . . . so I've decided it's time to"— the problem was, she hadn't yet planned her announcement—"time to spread my wings."

"Wings?" he said, frowning. "What?"

"Morty, I don't even want to say out loud how many years I've worked for you. I mean, it's a testament to how much I've loved it. It's been my life. You—your work—"

"What are you saying? Do you need a sabbatical? God knows I've never thought to give you real, decent time off. Paid, of course!"

"No, no, it's not that. I'm the one who's hardly *taken* time off. Because we went on amazing trips that *felt* like vacations—and there were weeks I probably put in ten hours tops."

"Stop talking in the past tense, Tommy." Morty was now sitting up quite straight, and he looked far unhappier than she had expected.

"Morty, don't you think a change would be good for both of us?"

"No!" he exclaimed. "I am not a believer in change for its own sake. And now, Tommy, now is not a good time."

She leaned forward, uncertain what might happen if she reached across the table to touch him. But she did. "What if it's a good time for me?"

Tommy had seen Morty in physical pain, and she had seen him tearful, and she had seen him angry, even petulant and spiteful, but his reaction to her touch was nearly volcanic. He stood up, knocking his chair to the floor, and shouted, "You cannot desert me now! You can't! I can't tell you why, but you can't. Not now."

Tommy was speechless. "Morty," she finally said. "Morty, do you need to think about this? Or can you sit down and—"

"No." He shook his head vehemently.

"No, you don't need to think, or—"

"No." He took a deep, jagged breath, righted the chair, and sat down.

Tommy picked up the photo. "Where was this taken?"

"Brooklyn, I'm not sure where. I must be at least eight or nine."

Tommy put the picture back on the table. The two of them stared at it, as if it might speak for itself.

"What can I do right now?" she asked.

When Morty met her eyes, she could have sworn there was a flash of anxiety, as if he could read her mind. "Just what you always do," he said. "Or please delete that *just*. The everyday miracles you perform."

"Soren's making us dinner," she said, not knowing how to answer his praise.

Morty was still wearing his coat. He stood. "I'm going out to the studio for a couple of hours. I want to write a few notes, make some calls."

Tommy should have returned to the computer; instead, she went to her room. She sat in the armchair and picked up the novel she was reading. But she didn't open it. She looked out the windows, watched the fiery leaves falling from the trees, prodigiously now, in the strong afternoon gusts. At the height of summer, the boughs were so dense with greenery that she could hardly see the sky; now, as they went through their annual molting, the sun's descent became more and more apparent. In January, from this room, brilliant sunsets pressed through the filigree of branches.

She heard Soren drive in, heard him clatter through the back door, cursing as he dropped a grocery bag. Would he call for her to help him? He didn't.

Would Soren take over some of Tommy's habitual tasks, after she left? He did cook on occasion. His repertoire was limited, but he was good enough. He made an excellent pot roast. Certainly Morty would never consider giving Soren responsibility for the complex web of relationships in his work life. Would he? She did not know what Morty really thought of Soren's capabilities, and she wouldn't dream of asking. Soren was a reader—he loved good stories, whether they came in the form of a classic Greek tragedy or a real-life scandal detailed in a *Vanity Fair* feature—and he liked mixing with Morty's writer friends, but . . . Where was she going with this train of thought?

Soren turned on the kitchen radio. He tuned it away from NPR to a station that played classic rock, the songs that everyone knows. In his pleasant, well-trained voice, he sang along. Soren did have his talents, even if he didn't put them to practical use.

Tommy dozed, waking when Soren called out, "Chow's on, kids!" Outside, night had fallen—or late afternoon—and Tommy could see the lights in the studio window. She watched them flick off, one and two and three.

Had she not waited for another month, things might have turned out differently. But even if Morty's eruptions of tearful sorrow seemed to cease after a few days, she wanted to give him a respectful margin of time. Later, she would look back and realize that the change in the air wasn't the residue of grief—or not *that* grief. She did notice that things were somehow different between Morty and Soren, that she no longer heard them fighting, that they planned no parties, that Soren slept later than usual—and that, when he returned from the city, he had nothing to report. He seemed glum, at times even listless—not his usual prickly, prowling self. But weren't these changes all effects of Frieda's death? Even Soren had to feel Morty's loss.

She decided that she would give her notice after Thanksgiving, offer to stay through February if he liked. Thanksgiving was always a crush. Morty reserved all six rooms at the Chanticleer, the one good bed-and-breakfast in the area, and filled them with a varying group of single or child-free friends from the city, those who looked forward to spending the holiday traipsing through dead leaves and drinking spiked cider by a radiant fire in an underheated country house. The past few years, Soren had cajoled everyone into playing charades. To witness this game played by a group of people who, for the most part, spent their lives crafting stories for children was supremely entertaining. Tommy would laugh so hard that she awoke the next morning feeling as if she might have cracked a rib.

A week beforehand, over breakfast, Tommy asked Morty when he wanted to sit down and plan the menu. They liked to change up the side dishes and make one new, adventuresome pie. "I read a recipe for a Sicilian date pie," she suggested. "And of course I'll make the plum."

Morty stared over her shoulder out the window above the sink.

"Earth to Morty." She waved.

He looked at her and smiled briefly.

"I ordered the usual gargantuan turkey," she said.

"Already?"

"The farm was written up on Martha's website last year. If you don't order weeks in advance now, you're in trouble."

He nodded. "The thing is, I've decided we should go low key this year."

"Okay." She waited. "Then we'll freeze a month's worth of soup. I'll learn to make tetrazzini."

"Can you cancel the rooms? I think it's not too late."

"All of them?"

He shrugged.

"Morty?"

"I've been working hard on this book," he said. "I need the holiday to be an actual holiday."

How silly she had been to underestimate the fallout of his losing Frieda. "Of course. But are you saying . . . just the three of us?"

"Invite your dad," he said. "He's missed the last couple of years. Why is that? Let's get him a driver if your brother won't come."

"I'm not sure he's up for it, but I'll see." Tommy hadn't told Morty that the large, loud gatherings were too arduous for her father, that he preferred being home in Brooklyn. Dani always had a girlfriend willing to pitch in, and there was a widow next door who flirted shamelessly, teasing out Dad's dormant self, if just for the day.

"Or you could go in and be there for a change. I'm selfish, wanting you here every year. Soren and I could use a quiet weekend—whether he knows it or not."

"You can't play charades with two people."

Morty laughed; he sounded so weary. "And thank God for that. Christ, do I hate that game. I always end up pulling or twisting something."

"You just can't stand it when you lose."

"Not true, and look who's talking."

How could she tell him that it would be her last Thanksgiving

"Morty, I've never felt as if you thought you owned me, and I know you have good reason to assume I'm here forever, but the thing is—"

"The thing *is*," he interrupted. He stood up abruptly again and went through the swinging door into the rest of the house.

Before she could decide what to do, he came back and sat down again.

"The thing is," he said, "Soren is very ill."

Tommy absorbed this. Soren did not seem "very ill." She tried to capture Morty's eyes, but he wouldn't meet her stare. She could only hope she was wrong when she said, "Are you telling me Soren has AIDS?"

Morty focused on his hands, clasped tightly on the table.

"When, Morty?"

Still he said nothing.

"How long have you known?" Her mind careened down all the predictable alleys at once, but first, all she cared about was whether Morty, too, was sick. This she couldn't bear to ask. "How long?"

"Two weeks," said Morty. "I think he's known, or suspected, for months. I made him get tested. And I am not, *not* supposed to tell anybody. Least of all you."

"Least of all?" said Tommy. She heard herself make a sound that was angry. She was angry. "Morty, I've put up with Soren's attitude, his freeloading, his . . . shit for years now, so forgive me if—"

"Are you leaving because of Soren?"

"No," she said. "But what if I said yes?"

"I don't know. All I know, Tommy, is that I will absolutely collapse if you leave now. I can't be alone with this. I'm a coward, okay, but if you go . . ."

I'll have blood on my hands, she might have said. She wanted to hear what he would say instead. She stared at him, at his pleading expression, and she was shocked at how unmoved she felt.

"You are irreplaceable," he said. "I love you in a way that is totally selfish and totally unfair to you, Tommy, but if you have to leave me, please give me more time. Please just . . ."

"Morty, I love you, too, but I am not irreplaceable."

"Time, money, a house of your own, whatever you need—"

"Morty!" she cried. "Stop it! I have to think. Please let me think."

What she needed, she realized, was someone to talk to. But other than Dani, there was no one she could call on outside the comfortable circle of Morty's life—now, in part, her own.

"You won't be a nurse," he said, "I promise."

"Is he that sick? He seems all right."

"His counts are terrible. He's lost a lot of weight."

Had she failed to notice this? She paid as little attention to Soren as she had to.

"He's been in denial, and obviously I have, too."

"Morty? I don't want to talk about Soren."

"I know."

"I'm so sorry. I really am. I don't want to sound glib, but I've been reading that there's a new class of drugs and that—"

"We can't talk about this."

She should have had a plan in place; that was her mistake. And yet even if she had, would she have turned her back on Morty? A craven thought occurred to her.

If Soren died, there would be no more Soren.

"If I stay," she said, "Soren has to know I know. He has to understand that I *should* know. He's never thought of me as more than your servant, has he?"

"That's not true! Soren is insecure. He's jealous of you."

"Jesus, I said I wouldn't talk about Soren." She stood. "So I have to go think. I have to get away from you and I have to think."

"Go wherever you have to go. Just please—"

"Morty."

"Come back."

"Stop. Please."

It took Tommy nearly a month to confront Morty—to corner him, almost literally, when she took his mail to the studio one afternoon.

He was hunched at the computer, typing. He swiveled around on the stool to take the packet of envelopes. He laid it on the counter, then stood up to stretch. "My idiot back," he muttered, arching to rub the base of his spine.

"You're getting too old to be sitting on a stool all day," said Tommy.

"Old habits keep me superstitious. And disciplined."

"They do not keep you young."

"I'm honing in on sixty, and I'm not going to pretend it's the new forty. Let nobody tell you otherwise; even forty's an age of decay." He sighed.

There followed one of the long pauses that Tommy, until a few weeks earlier, had seen as natural between them. But since learning about Soren's diagnosis, she dreaded some new unhappy bulletin each time their exchanges faltered toward silence.

"Can I ask about you, your health, your . . . status? Morty?"

His hand dropped from his back; he faced her. "Status? My . . . social status? Or are you referring to the fact that I am physically shrinking?"

"Morty, don't fool with me."

"I'm not fooling with you, Tommy."

"You are belittling me. Talk about the elephant in the room. This is the brontosaurus."

"Apatosaurus," Morty said gently.

"Morty, am I going to lose you? Forgive me if I care less about Soren."

"Tommy, I'll be fine."

"Don't patronize me. Were you tested?"

"I'll go get the fucking test, Tommy, but don't push me about it."

"I understand if you're afraid the news might not be good, but even if—"

"Astute of you! Who wouldn't dread the 'news'?"

"So you're just going to assume the worst."

He swept an arm to take in the room. "Where do you think you are, Happy Outlook Headquarters?"

Where *did* she think she was? She glanced at the computer screen, filled with lines of text: words telling a story about three children with cancer. She turned away.

"I'm sorry. I can only face so much drama at once."

"Right," she said. "So just go back to work. Your personal rabbit hole. No wonder you're so crazy for Alice."

He reached to take her arm, hold her in place. "Tommy, I have no significant secrets from you."

"So do it. Please. Get tested."

Three months later, Tommy returned from shopping to find a letter, on Morty's doctor's letterhead, tucked between the toaster and the blender. It told Morty that his second test had affirmed the results of the first: he was free of the virus. Morty had scrawled at the bottom, *Lucky me,* the sarcasm evident to anyone who knew him.

The year following Frieda's death and Soren's diagnosis was a hushed time—Soren often behaved as if he'd been tranquilized (perhaps he was)—and a diligent time. Morty told Tommy to turn down all speaking requests. He worked like a dervish to finish the first novel about the three teenagers whom he called the Inseparables, titling it, simply, *Diagnosis.* Sometimes, after dinner, he would read a chapter out loud to Tommy and Soren. Soren had finally learned to listen, or it looked that way. His silences felt ominous to Tommy; she almost missed his tempestuous outbursts.

For a couple of seasons, Morty insisted on cooking dinner. The parties dwindled to one every two months or so, and they were small— six dinner guests at most. Had she not known why the volume of their domestic life had been turned down again, Tommy would have found the change entirely pleasant.

But because she did know, she had the eerie sensation that they were waiting for something: for Soren—who now took a dozen different pills and tinctures, though Tommy knew this only through emptying the bathroom trash—to turn a corner one way or the other.

She started spending most weekends with her father, whose memory, like old leather, grew less and less supple, increasingly riddled with cracks and fissures. Dani had moved in with his latest girlfriend, out in Astoria, and worked as a bike messenger for a lofty Park Avenue bank.

Diagnosis came out in 1997. It claimed the covers of *Publishers Weekly* and *Library Journal.* The reviews were strewn with stars and superlatives. Suddenly, Tommy had little time for her father, even less to think (or not think) about Soren. Morty agreed to a major tour; Tommy, as usual, went along. Every night, from whatever suite they shared, Morty called home to speak with Soren. Their relationship had become more like that of a father and son, Morty's voice ranging from tender to tendentious. Sometimes, just to escape the unavoidable eavesdropping, Tommy left the suite with a book and read in the lobby or drank a cup of tea at the bar.

Soren complained of being too lonely at the house, and seeking the company of friends was a trial, since venturing in and out of the city on his own exhausted him now. He said he felt strong enough to fly, however, so Morty decided to bring him along to a festival in Aspen. "We'll stay on a few days after and give ourselves a little vacation," Morty promised. He splurged on the largest suite in an old hotel with high ceilings, deep fireplaces, and imperious portraits of cattle barons. A collection of antique western saddles stood in for barstools at one of the hotel's three restaurants.

But tucked away beneath four floors of faux-frontier decor was the sort of well-staffed spa that every expensive hotel in the civilized world was now obliged to provide for its guests. And this was precisely what Morty had in mind—that Soren would enjoy being lathered and massaged and pumiced while he and Tommy talked up the launch of his trilogy and mingled with authors of everything from diet manuals to biographies of presidents and kings.

For two days, Soren was happy—happy enough. He ate well, and the altitude, which gave Tommy a headache unless she drank vast quantities of water, didn't bother him. On the third morning, over another early breakfast, Morty looked up from his eggs and said to Tommy, "Soren's getting cabin fever. He needs to go out and do something. I'm not sure what."

"I think most of the tourists here go on hikes," Tommy said. "Or shop for chaps."

"Hiking is not going to work for Soren. As for the chaps . . ." Morty, clearly envisioning his lover in chaps, briefly held his napkin over his face.

Tommy said quickly, "Then . . ."

"I thought there would be more culture here. Museums. Georgia O'Keeffe. Custer's Last Stand. That sort of thing."

"O'Keeffe is New Mexico. And Soren going out to contemplate Custer's Last Stand? How cruel would . . ." She stopped midsentence.

Morty regarded her steadily, holding his toast midway to his mouth.

"Are you fishing?" she said.

"Fishing?"

"Morty. Come on. You want me to entertain him, don't you."

He sighed. "I don't know. He's neither well nor seriously unwell. I never imagined this. This long . . . limbo we've been in."

Tommy knew what Morty was implying: that after they had learned the news, after he had sat beside Soren in several doctors' offices (consultations about which Tommy had asked very little), Morty assumed Soren would either get better—that the brand-new "cocktails" would give him a second chance at normal life—or die. Instead, he had become a dependent, not just financially but physically, emotionally.

"There's the gondola," said Tommy. "To the top of the mountain."

Morty's response was an unspoken plea, just a look.

"Okay," she said. "You don't really need me with you today. You have two radio interviews, both by phone, and you're signing stock for distributors." She looked at her agenda. "Gold Rush Salon, anytime from noon to three."

"Thank you," said Morty. "We'll try that nice Italian place for dinner. The one you saw on that side street."

"If Soren's up for it. He likes it better when we get room service."

"He doesn't always get what he wants. I think that's pretty obvious."

Was Morty scolding her? But it was true: she often felt toward Soren as one might feel toward a blatantly favored sibling.

So Morty put on the lanyard with his name tag, took Tommy's copy of his schedule (annotated with names he ought to remember but always forgot), and made his way to the far reaches of the hotel, the conference and screening rooms. Tommy returned to their suite and waited for Soren to wake up.

While he showered and dressed, she ordered him breakfast, and while he ate in front of a morning talk show, she answered e-mails.

The base of the mountain was only a few blocks away, and the air was pleasantly warm. They walked slowly, like an elderly couple, looking into shopwindows and making fun of the theatrical cowboy boots and ten-gallon hats, a woman's silk gown embroidered with a large sequined saguaro cactus.

"It looks like a trident phallus. I don't think even Dolly Parton could pull that one off," said Soren. He seemed to be in a good mood; maybe the mountain air had a healing effect.

Tommy bought their tickets, and they sat on a bench beside the platform where the cable car would pick them up. They were the only people waiting. Looking up the daunting slope, Tommy could see two pairs of hikers on foot, following the dirt track beneath the cable line.

She put on her sunglasses and watched the descending glass pod in a quiet trance. Capturing the sunlight in prismlike flashes, it looked like a giant iridescent beetle. When it pulled up beside them, the doors slid open, and six people got off, including two children who started racing down the flight of steps to the street, their parents yelling at them to stop, slow down, wait! Soren was watching them, silent. Tommy repressed the knee-jerk urge to read his mind, to make herself feel guiltier than she already did about wishing she were with Morty, even back in the airless Gold Rush Salon, grinning relentlessly at strangers, coping with the bottomless bureaucracy of Morty's juggernaut success.

No other passengers showed up, and they rode to the top without comment. Tommy wondered if Soren's eyes were closed behind his sunglasses. His head was inclined against a window, as if he were riveted by a single view rather than the widening panorama of the village tucked snug in its luxurious valley below.

When they got off at the top, they had to walk around an impressive stack of long white florist boxes, each tied with a pink ribbon. There must have been fifty. A slender young man in a blazer and tie paced alongside the boxes, talking on a cell phone in an agitated tone. Pinned to his lapel was a gold name plate. Phillip. From his seethingly enunciated dictates, it was obvious that he was a wedding planner and that someone was actually going to get married in this lofty spot, sometime later in the day; also, that someone else had fucked up.

"Where are the vases?" he said, each word a threat. "I need them by noon or it will not be pretty."

Tommy and Soren walked on in the prescribed direction, toward the deck with the promised view, reaching over the mountain range, its summit shrouded with snowdrifts even in June.

Soren spoke for the first time since they had boarded the gondola. "Some people are planning a wedding, some a funeral."

"Soren, you're doing all right. You've got to be positive," said Tommy.

"Sweetheart, I am positive. That's my problem. Do you know there's actually a magazine for us corpses-in-waiting? It's called *Poz*. Sounds like a magazine for dogs and cats, doesn't it? But no. I see it at my doctor's office. He gets that plus *Popular Photography* plus *People*. How alliterative of him, right? And his first name is Peter!"

Tommy laughed.

"But who do you think is actually going to pick up that magazine in a room full of strangers? I mean, we can look around and figure out who's there for the same reason we are—nobody's fooling anybody—but still. I have no desire to look at articles on, what, how to keep my Mediport in tip-top shape? How to minimize estate taxes for my loved ones? How to avoid getting fired for being in a terminal way?"

"You aren't terminal. You can't think like that."

"Tommy, dear Tommy, don't go all Pollyanna on me, please."

"I'm just—"

"Stating the facts. Keeping hope alive! Good for you." He quickened his pace and walked out in front of her, toward the railing with the informational plaques, the you-are-here maps. A father was posing his wife and five children against the vista, getting ready to take a picture.

But then, without so much as a cursory glance at the view, Soren turned toward the restaurant. Tommy couldn't tell if he wanted her to follow. Just inside the door, he held it open and looked back. "I'm getting a hot dog—or whatever excuse for nutrition they serve up here. You want something? Or are you planning to join the jolly McMormons over there?"

They chose an indoor picnic table next to the window on the side of the mountain view.

"Sit," Soren said. He insisted on going up to order the food. He came back with French fries and a paper plate of corn chips under a pool of fluorescent orange cheese.

"Dig in," he said. "Sometimes this is what does the trick for me these days. A carbohydrate orgy. The only kind in which I may indulge at this stage of my life. A shame, considering specimens like our friend Phillip out there, guarding his lilies."

After wiping cheese from his lips, he cringed dramatically and said, "Oops. Wrong company."

Tommy made no comment. She couldn't tell if Soren was trying to amuse her or to pick a fight. She ate a few fries. They had a wooden texture and tasted as if they'd been reheated several times. But her mouth was full when Soren said, "If I weren't sick, if I'd been healthy as a horse these past few years, you'd be gone, wouldn't you." He still wore his sunglasses, so Tommy couldn't see his eyes. "You're taking care of him so he can take care of me."

It took her a blessed moment to chew and swallow the terrible fries. "I thought about leaving," she said. "It had nothing to do with you, one way or the other."

"I don't believe that, but never mind," said Soren. "Anyway, I sort of dare you to stay through what's to come. As Luscious Phillip said about his missing *vahzes,* it will not be pretty."

"Soren . . ."

"Tommy, you can't hide how little you like me. Though why should you?"

Was he actually trying to drive her away—or maybe, if she could stop and think of him more kindly, trying to "liberate" her? Was there a perverse generosity in this confrontation?

"I could say the same of you," she heard herself say.

Soren shook his head. "Not the same. You were there. You had it in for me from the start. You like to pretend you don't run the show. But"—he raised his hands, greasy palms outward—"I am forced to admit that I'm grateful you've stayed."

She could say nothing to this. She could hardly thank him, and it was too late to protest his assertions—and pointless. Soren might be vain, but he wasn't stupid. He wasn't blind. She said the only honest thing she could: "I do not run the show."

He pushed the remainder of the nachos toward her. "Let's agree to disagree on that."

Dutifully, they spent a few minutes admiring the view. And when the gondola arrived at the summit from its latest ascent, they had to wait for two large cardboard cartons to be unloaded by the wedding planner and a lackey.

"The vases, do we think?" said Soren. "And don't tell me it's a good omen."

They rode down in silence, but it felt to Tommy like a peaceable silence. She understood that Soren had been wanting an opportunity to say what he said to her in the restaurant. When they returned to their suite, Soren went into his bedroom, though not before thanking Tommy. She might have left to track down Morty, but she stayed. She called Brooklyn and spoke to her father, who seemed disturbingly unable to comprehend why she was calling from Colorado. She browsed through the *New Yorker* and ate a fancy chocolate bar from the room's array of overpriced temptations.

Soren was still asleep four hours later, when Morty returned to the room.

"I'm starving," Morty said. "Without you there, I forgot to have lunch. Shall we go out now and bring something back? Leave him a note?"

"No," said Tommy. "Just do room service."

Morty bowed. "Your wish is my command."

The return trip to New York was a terror. The small plane to Denver tilted and plunged on the fickle currents of mountain air. The flight crew remained seated, and the only sound inside the cabin was that of passengers vomiting into their air-sickness bags. Tommy sat several rows in front of Morty and Soren. She willed her stomach to behave.

If Morty was invited to Aspen again, she would decline to come along. If she survived this flight.

In Denver, Soren's face looked as pale as raw codfish. They arranged to ride the airport golf cart to their connecting gate. "I don't think I can do this flight," muttered Soren as Tommy and Morty guided him to a seat in the waiting lounge.

"You have to," said Morty. "We are not staying over in Denver. It's too much of a production. Let's get you home. All of us."

Morty made Soren take a sleeping pill after they boarded. Tommy slept, too, worn out by her sustained fear on the earlier flight.

Somehow, as if the extreme turbulence en route to Denver had shaken free his will to live, Soren's health never recovered.

By the end of the summer, the more dependable drugs had begun to lose ground. Tommy and Morty had been home from the tour for a month when Soren went into the hospital overnight for the first time, with an alarmingly fierce nosebleed.

Tommy did not ask questions. Morty offered no explanations.

When Soren came home, it was clear he had turned a corner: the wrong one. He was scared. Tommy began to wake up two or three times a week to Soren's keening hysteria from the upstairs bedroom. Sometimes he wept; other times he cursed Morty, senselessly and often incoherently.

Soren had always refused to talk about his parents, characterizing them as "wicked, wicked people." All Morty knew was that he had grown up somewhere in Illinois, "a place that is so *not* Chicago." One evening when the three of them were sharing dinner in the kitchen, mostly in glum, ruminant silence, Morty startled Tommy by saying to Soren, "I wonder if you might think of being in touch with your family." (Was he afraid to bring this up when they were alone?)

"That would be you," Soren said. "You are my only family, darling."

After a pause, Morty said, "Your parents will always be your parents."

"Right on up to the pearly gates, where they expect to be welcomed with hula dancers and goblets of sacred punch, oh yes. Though you could pull out their fingernails one by one and they'd never acknowledge my existence."

Morty glanced at Tommy.

"They'd want to know you're not well," she tried.

Soren looked at her with an oddly bright expression. "Tommy, dear, my parents are beyond evangelical. They are *evangelissimo*. If they haven't disowned me already, this"—he leaned back to gesture with both hands at his wasted body—"well, this would do the trick. In spades. In every suit, jokers included. And don't get me started on my sisters. They probably have five kids apiece by now, with those cultishly virile husbands of theirs. They married twins, if you can believe it."

Sisters? Had Morty known Soren had sisters?

"Please stop talking about those people," Soren said. "Please. They have nothing to offer me, and I certainly have nothing to offer them beyond shame and righteous hemorrhoids. Which might give me some satisfaction if I had the energy. But I don't." He reached toward Morty and prodded him with a spoon. "Now tell me about those cancerous punks, honey, what trouble they've cooked up today. I know you're on fire out there in your sanctum."

After Morty had helped Soren to bed that night, he came back downstairs. "Do I hire a detective and find them anyway?" he asked Tommy.

"That is not a decision I want to weigh in on," she said. The talk of family, of parents, had only stoked the guilt she felt at not keeping closer tabs on her father. She had called him while Soren was upstairs, but she got his voice mail. Concerned—it wasn't yet eight—she had then called Dani. "Come on, Tommy," he said, without concealing his irritation, "Dad doesn't answer the phone these days once he's watching his TV shows. You know that." But she didn't.

Even fake, cynical cheer soon took too much effort for Soren. His fear of death seemed to rise from within until it was right beneath his translucent skin, as evident as the blood flowing tenaciously through his veins.

On one of the coldest mornings that winter, following a long, wakeful night of listening to Soren scream, "I will not die! I refuse to die! I FUCKING REFUSE!"—his ragings untempered by Morty's oblique murmurings—Tommy answered the ringing phone and, after asking if Morty could return the call, was told that the news this caller had to relay was very important. Was he there?

Reluctantly, she went through the living room and called up, waking Morty. She handed him the phone midway up the staircase and went back to the kitchen to make coffee. A few minutes later, Morty came into the room, barefoot, in his striped flannel robe, sat at the table, and started to cry. "It's too much," he sobbed. "It's too much, too much, too much." *Diagnosis* had won the Newbery Medal.

She gave him coffee and put a hand on his shoulder. She wanted to tell him not to let Soren's illness poison his success. "Go sleep on the couch in the nursery. I'll take his breakfast upstairs," she said.

In a way, after all, she did end up nursing Soren—and, by the end, sharing with Morty the brunt of his terrified abuse. Remarkably, as if his fear fueled his tenacity for life, Soren held on for another year, during which Tommy realized that she and Morty had, effectively, become Soren's parents themselves. But unlike a parent, she did not entertain hope. She knew that he was dying.

The week before he went into the hospital for the last time, he said to her, "Who are you to just walk in here, to stand there like . . . Who *are* you? Huh?" She was changing the sheets while he sat slumped in the armchair Morty had squeezed into a corner of the bedroom as a place of vigil. Morty was in the studio, on a conference call with his editor and agent; Tommy had been downstairs and couldn't ignore the sound of Soren's retching.

At first, she thought he was suffering from one of the disoriented riffs that occurred more and more often as he relied on the strongest narcotics. Though Morty had turned the thermostat unnaturally high, Soren was shivering.

"It's just me, Tommy," she said as she folded back the quilt.

"Oh, just you," he scoffed. "Just you, you, poor little you, the chambermaid who stands to inherit the kingdom."

"Soren, get back into bed."

"You get the prize. You *win*," he said as he followed her orders, still shivering. "Hooray for you! Healthy, fleshy, normal you!"

"Let me take your temperature."

He did as she asked, glaring at her over the thermometer clamped between his desiccated bluish lips. She turned to look out the window at the studio, hoping to catch sight of Morty returning to the house. He hadn't done any real work, any solitary creative work, for over a week. ("For the first time in my life," Morty told her, "bureaucracy is keeping me sane.")

Behind her, she heard Soren say, "And you get Morty. Don't you?"

She turned around. She crossed the room and took the thermometer from his hand. "What is it?" she said coldly.

"It?" He looked puzzled, suspicious.

"Your temperature."

"Does it matter? Does it fucking matter one way or the other? Hot or cold, I'm cooked. Just slice me up and serve me to the guests. Feed the scraps to somebody's dogs." He lay back on the freshly slipcased pillow and closed his eyes. "Thank you," he whispered.

When Morty returned to the house, she told him they had to hire a live-in nurse. They could take the boxes of books out of the nursery.

"Now we know why we named it that," Morty said drily.

The nurse who came was a man, fortuitously solid as a tree trunk, because his arrival coincided with a new symptom in Soren's decline: sudden physical collapses. From downstairs, where she remained as often as she possibly could, Tommy would hear and even feel the concussive impact of Soren's falling out of bed or faltering on the way to the bathroom. The falls increased until they seemed to occur a dozen times a day. She would hear Morty and Stan in gentle concert, trying to calm Soren.

When he fell, the dishes in the kitchen would shudder inside their cupboards, the lights in the chandelier blink.

Skeins of harsh coughing gave way to bitter respites of gasping and weeping. Morty would gallop down the stairs, lunge into the kitchen, cursing and shouting for a bucket, rags, newspapers, sponges; didn't they have more towels somewhere? Didn't they have enough fucking money to buy more towels?

Tommy ran endless loads of laundry. She made broth, measured Pedialyte, bought invalid accessories at a medical-supply store in Stamford. She made thick meaty sandwiches for Nurse Stan, poured tall glasses of milk and iced tea and orange juice. She would do anything, so long as she could remain downstairs.

When Soren began to cough up blood, Morty called 911. As the EMTs carried Soren through the kitchen, he swiveled his head crazily, and Tommy knew he was looking for her. He wore an oxygen mask over his mouth and could say nothing, so she came close enough to let him see her. His eyes were bloodshot but wide open.

What could she say to him? She squeezed one of his forearms through the blanket, shocked at how bony it was. She said, "Good luck. Be strong." Was that cruel? Stan and Morty left with Soren.

It was late afternoon, light fading through the latticework of the surrounding trees. Tommy was in the middle of making squash soup. She finished and cleaned up. She admired the bright yellow satiny surface of the liquid, a false comfort.

She made a salad, a jar of dressing; took a loaf of French bread from the freezer and removed the foil. The ambulance had sped away an hour ago by then. She left everything out on the counter and stovetop, went into her den-bedroom, and turned on the television news. Somewhere the weather was tropically warm, a dog had rescued a toddler who fell off a sailboat. Bill Clinton was still making excuses for his appalling behavior. Snow, mixed with rain, would bedevil the city and several surrounding counties the next day but would likely hold off until after the morning rush.

She vetoed the news and picked up her book. She read two or three pages without absorbing a single syllable. She should call her father, but she told herself she shouldn't tie up the phone until Morty called. If he called.

Some indefinable amount of time later, she was in the kitchen, idling through a book on Mexican vegetarian cooking, when the phone began ringing. She decided to wait for a voice on the machine; she wouldn't pick up for anyone but Morty—yet, as it turned out, she didn't pick up for him, either. He said her name three times, and then nothing. She thought he'd hung up until he said, "Soren won't be coming home. Ever. Don't wait up. I'll get a cab." His voice was deep and subdued, almost cavernous.

She should wait up, never mind what he said—or go to bed and get as much sleep as she could. Instead, she went upstairs for the first time in nearly a week. She switched on a lamp in Morty's bedroom, which had become Soren's alone in the last several weeks. It looked like a crime scene.

She turned off the humidifier, unplugged it, and moved it to the hall. Slowly, she stripped the bed down to the mattress—which, before Stan had suggested the waterproof cover, had already been ruined, its surface a Rorschach of bruiselike stains.

She rolled up the bed linens and pushed them into a black plastic garbage bag. Into another, she swept from the two bedside tables every eyedropper, syringe wrapper, gauze pad, and wrinkled tube of salve, along with dozens of soiled, crumpled tissues. She emptied a plastic carafe of urine into the toilet and put the emptied container in the garbage bag, too. She tied the bags, dragged them downstairs, and took them out the back door. The driveway floodlight flashed on as soon as the door slammed behind her.

She went back to the bedroom and vacuumed the old rug under the bed (it would have to be sent for a cleaning). She mopped the bare wood around it. Next, she attacked the bathroom. Although it was February, she opened every window on the second floor and let the cold night air invade. The furnace cranked up in protest.

She carried the shower stool and the portable commode downstairs and out to the garage. She should wash them with the garden hose, but the outside valves had been shut off till spring.

When she returned to the second floor yet again, she could see her breath. Frost had glazed the bathroom mirror. One by one, she closed and latched the windows. The furnace growled from below.

So it was over. Or, rather, Soren was over. He had carved eight turbulent years out of their lives, the way wind carves a dune, but now he was gone. Tommy also knew that she was there to stay.

Eleven

Nick goes into the kitchen at six, thinking he just might be the first one awake. But on the table is a note from Tomasina: *Working in the studio. Coffee in coffeemaker—just push button. Help yourself to anything. I'll be in for lunch, but please no bother.*

What does she mean? Don't bother her in the studio? Don't bother about her lunch? He supposes that, in general, he *is* a bother around here. He frowns. Does he want coffee? It's the easy option—and easy is what he needs after a scant hour or two of sleep. He pushes the button, then sits at the table to think.

If it weren't Saturday, he'd Skype with his agent in London. It's far too early in California to speak with Andrew.

Oh bother all the not-bothering. Solitude is not his first choice at the moment.

The coffeemaker burbles a few more seconds, then releases the mawkish sigh that signifies it's finished its wearisome task. He attempts to mimic the sound, trying three or four times. The last voice coach he had, for *Taormina,* made him try to imitate a number of nonhuman noises: a kettle whistling, a spigot dripping, a jet passing overhead, the wheeze and roar of a Hoover in the hotel lobby. He thought it silly at the time, but he's picked it up as a habit. The object is to challenge the limited patterns of mobility to which any native language restricts the various working parts of one's mouth. Like the most pathetic schoolboy, Nick cracked a joke or two about the *other* advantages to "limbering up" one's tongue—which the coach (a clever but humorless bloke) ignored.

Maybe he'll go back into his assigned room and figure out the telly, watch the PBS documentary again. He feels as if he needs to re-anchor himself in a more public version of Mort Lear than the one currently clouding his thoughts. He has to think carefully about what he's found. It's just as well that Tomasina is elsewhere. Nick is prone to blurting things out before he's thought them through. That's what made his rupture with Kendra so messy.

Thinking of Kendra leads him nowhere productive. He awoke this morning with, as usual, a painfully belligerent erection. (Talk of pathetic schoolboys!) Confounding his growing mistrust of himself when it comes to romantic entanglement, he's fully aware that his celebrity gives him carte blanche to bonk just about any woman he chooses (well, maybe not *any*), and as a result he feels paralyzed. Every time he passes another magazine rack blaring boldface gossip about Lorna's fertility woes or Jonnie's cock-up with his children's nanny, he pictures himself on those shiny covers instead, cavorting with some starlet on a beach or a red carpet or just holding hands on the street. (Cavorting! Where did that vision emerge from?)

And he thinks of Deirdre's warnings.

He continues to miss Deirdre, which is unsettling. Long about his third or fourth chummy sojourn on a film set, from which he had departed feeling sure that these latest colleagues were his mates forever, he began to understand that each new project resembles the society of some island marooned in the middle of the Pacific Ocean, one of unavoidable intimacies, intensified aversions, and exaggerated (if productive) loyalties. The long bone-breaking hours, the necessary posturings and psychological bartering, even the financial pressures and the consequent impersonal discourtesies, only distort the relationships further. So now he's an old hand at the beginnings and endings of such associations—which is why he's surprised at the sense of loss whenever he thinks of Deirdre.

The wall phone in the kitchen rings, and he almost answers it. It rings only a few times, then stops. Tomasina must be picking up the call in Lear's studio.

He pours himself a second cup of coffee and decides to go outside, soak up some good unambivalent American sun. He heads toward a trio of rosebushes, two of them effusing blooms, one a boisterous yellow, the other precisely the pale pink of a ballerina's satin toe shoe. As he bends to smell them, he hears Tomasina call out, "Good morning!"

She invites him into the studio and asks if he's had something to eat.

"I'm all set," he lies, feeling hungrier for company than for breakfast.

The wooden countertops that outline the studio are covered with stacks of papers and files.

"Facing the music. The legal music," says Tomasina. "Tuneless though it may be."

"The protocols of death are merciless, positively sadistic!" Nick offers, more ardently than he intended.

"You're telling me."

For a beat, it's clear that they are sharing the unspoken fellowship of their parallel losses, their mothers' unjustly early exits. He notices that Tomasina has grown easier around him—and that she's aware of it, too. (*Yes, Silas, I really am still a people!*)

Tommy feels shamefully gratified to see the actor looking less than photogenic this morning, obviously tired after his middle-of-the-night snooping. His hair is flattened and dull on one side, and the skin around his eyes looks puckered and grayish. She's tempted to mention that she heard him last night in Morty's room, but it would only make things awkward all over again.

"Would I be in your way if I loitered a bit and looked at the drawings again, just the ones on those panels in the back?" he says.

"Please. It's lonely, even with my pals on NPR."

A radio show murmurs in the background, a discussion of the American Supreme Court and the decisions it's soon to render on matters both public and private. Nick feels homesick. He hopes to have a week in his flat before shooting starts.

Dozens of Lear's drawings and watercolors are pinned on large, soft panels affixed to a wall hinge. One can "page" through the panels and see fifty years of his evolution as an artist. Nick lingers at some of the illustrations for the charming tale about the fox who accidentally went up in a hot-air balloon and got to see the world beyond his forest: the cities and villages and rivers, the motorways clogged with lorries, the sea reaching toward the horizon. The supple, changing expressions on the fox's face are what make the book so affecting. It's a book of very few words—which occur entirely toward the end of the journey, when a seagull alights on the basket.

As he browses through the drawings, Nick hears Tomasina on a phone call.

"I am not dying to go to Phoenix," she says. "But I know it has to happen soon."

Long silence.

"I really appreciate that, Franklin. I don't care if you think it's your job. But I mean, didn't Morty get how overwhelmed I'd be?"

Shorter silence.

"Delegate, delegate. Yes, I know. Unfamiliar turf. I *was* the delegate. The whole delegation." To whatever this Franklin chap says next, she laughs. "Of all the places we went together, we never once went to Arizona. He never toured there. I'm positive. I barely stopped to think about why. He did have invitations. . . . Why couldn't he just create a new book prize or endow a children's library?"

Nick looks at the framed pictures and documents on the wall, though none of them really holds his interest. (Awards, proclamations, group portraits . . .) He walks over to the locked case containing the Greek vase, an earthen orange painted with black silhouettes of male figures, some interlocked, at first glance wrestlers. Well, wrestlers of a rather particular *kind*. Talk of cavorting!

Tommy hangs up the phone. She watches the actor for a moment. He's examining the vase. Another task she hasn't tackled: appraisal of this ostensibly priceless object. She almost hopes it's a fake. Because even if it's not, what if it's stolen, if the certificate of provenance is forged? Either way, what if it has to be "repatriated" to some temple in Macedonia? Yet another inconceivable task.

"Are you getting what you need?" she asks.

He turns, looking cheerfully startled. "I'm rather in shock. There's so much to absorb. But I would still—later, if you don't mind—like to ask you some things. I don't want to intrude on your work, I want to be respectful. . . ." How can he be respectful and tell her what he knows? Why does he feel he *must*?

"Later is fine. I don't know if you want to have dinner again. We could go into the village."

"Yes to dinner." He pauses. "But no to the village. If you don't mind."

"Oh, of course. You're . . . well."

"It's awful, embarrassing really, that I'd vainly assume anybody would recognize me—or care about it. I'm just not up for that today. The autographs and photos. Because I always want to oblige. And then I have to become . . . my outer self." Which, he sometimes thinks, threatens to become his dominant self.

"I'll make us something easy."

"You won't lift a bloody digit. And now I'll leave you in peace. I probably ought to make some calls of my own." At the door, he turns to say, "Someday, you know, my encroaching like this on your privacy might make a good story."

"Mr. Greene," she says, "I don't have much privacy these days."

"Nick," he says. "Please, please, call me Nick."

"Nick," she says, feeling absurdly special.

Inside the house, he goes to the den to face his phone. Nothing. Nothing! Miracle of blissful miracles.

He opens Lear's laptop, which he smuggled down from the upstairs bedroom—afraid that if he left it behind, it might vanish, along with the proof that, no, he wasn't imagining the famous man's midnight confessions.

But this time he ignores that correspondence and returns to the *Leonard* file. He opens the first of the folders, a letter dated October 10, 1999. The year, he recalls, that Soren died. Is that relevant somehow?

Dear Reginald,

I do remember you and that we played together a few times. I have to say, I'm surprised that your father made the connection. I lived there a very long time ago and then, of course, my mother changed our name when we left. I'm sorry for you and your sister that your father's death has left you with such a difficult situation. A parent's foolish choices should not burden his children beyond the grave.

I imagine those drawings he kept all these years, though I do not know why, are indeed mine. I did sign my art when I was small. I was pretentious that way. They also sound like images I would have drawn. I often drew the plants and animals I saw in the garden at Eagle Rest.

Are they of value? I suspect the answer to that question is a qualified yes. It might depend on the condition they're in. You need not bother to send me photos. From your descriptions, they sound like mine.

How would you sell them? That is trickier. I am sure there is an auction house in Phoenix or even Tucson that will sell them for you. But I think it would be easier if I were to buy them directly from you.

You say you have thirty-two. I am willing to pay you a thousand for each. I assume that is acceptable. Let me know if it is not.

Yours sincerely,
Mort Lear

The next piece of correspondence in the file is a short note, pure business, to a bank agent, requesting a transfer of thirty-two thousand dollars to Reginald's checking account. *This is for a purchase of art,* the note explains.

There are only two more documents in the folder, both letters written by Lear, both dated over a year later, in December 2000.

Reginald:
It's not a good idea to threaten blackmail in print. I have your recent letters in my files. I have a smart, expensive lawyer. (The expensive ones win.)

I am sorry for your troubles, but I believe I was generous with you. I do not ever go to Arizona, so there would be no occasion for our meeting, even if we had a remotely cordial relationship. I have no idea what "stuff" you remember or what kind of photographs your father took. I do not wish to know. If you write me again, you will hear back, but not from me.

Dear Bruce,

I hope Penny and the brood are thriving. Did I promise B.J. an autographed copy of the latest Insep? Either way, I'll have Tommy send one to the house pronto. And please tell Penny her birthday gift of the purple clematis is still blooming up a Shakespearean tempest.

Your time is precious (and don't I ever k$ow it!), so I'll cut to the car chase. I think I'm possibly about to be blackmailed, though I promise you I have committed no crime. Scout's honor. Before you call out the dogs (meanwhile, I can only hope, resisting the urge to alert Page Six), it's something small and sordid, out of my neolithic past. But maybe we could have an actual in-person convo. I estimate fifteen billable minutes max!

Hey, I could kill two birds with one slingshot: I'll bring B.J.'s book along. How's next Wednesday or Thursday? If you're not too busy trimming a tree or throwing the office shindig.

Also make note, for the record, that I have taken a safe-deposit box at the local moneylender, just for the cold storage of an odd batch of papers. I'm not big on these boxes, but it's an "out of sight out of mind" situation. I'm putting the key in my sock drawer. Nothing precious to anyone, really.

In gratitude and haste (I hear the meter ticking!),
Mort

Nick scrutinizes this final item, as if it will solve his moral dilemma. Actually, it's not a dilemma. If he had a principled bone in his body, he would, jolly well *now,* put the key back into the box from which he withdrew it, the one containing a tangle of old-fashioned baubles, costume jewelry from decades long gone, shoved to the back of that sock drawer. But instead, he fiddles with it inside his left-front pocket, twisting it this way and that, like a fetish. He thinks, oddly, of Andrew's earring.

His mobile rings. An actual call, not a text.

As if he's telepathically summoned the man, it's Andrew.

"Nick. Where the devil are you?"

"I'm at Lear's. Si told you that."

"Yes, right. But I've got a situation here. Sandy just called. About Toby Feld's mother. She's prone to tantrums, apparently, but Sandy thinks this one's serious. What the fuck did you say to that woman?"

"All I did was ask her to silence her mobile. We were in rehearsal!" Sandy is the casting director.

Nick listens to silence for a moment. Andrew finally says, "I almost wish I'd gone with the other kid, the one whose mother stays home, where mothers belong."

Nick says nothing.

"You know what I mean," Andrew adds. "In any case, we've decided you shouldn't call her. But can you and I get square on a few things? It's like you've gone rogue on me out there."

"I found them."

"Found what?"

"Lear's e-mails to me. About what went on in that shed."

Andrew sighs loudly. "Nick, you are a dog with a bone."

"I am." Nick's heart is pounding.

Andrew's laugh is all-suffering. "All right then. Send them. Let me have a look."

I can't, Nick thinks. "All right," he says.

"You're out of there when?"

"Monday. I'll be back in the city, then I'm yours."

"Good. If I lose Toby, there'll be hell to pay, but we'll pay it."

"I'm sorry if I—"

"It's not about you, forget it. Gotta run. Hey. We'll houdini our way around it."

That's Andrew, sure of a way out before a crisis has even taken hold. And that is so *not* Nick.

"I am a fucking blighter, a scoundrel," he says to the blank face of the telly.

The bedeviling phone tells him it's barely nine o'clock. He could take a shower, try to calm down, but he's already dressed and experiencing the surge of panicky adrenaline that strikes whenever he feels guilty of even a microscopic misdemeanor. This time it's a capital crime. Or is it?

He has an idea.

He rings Serge, then rummages in his suitcase for one of the half dozen baseball caps Si gave him after the Oscars—gift-wrapped, with a card that read, *For the new, conspicuous you.* This one tells the world he's a fan of the San Francisco Giants. He snatches his shades off the dressing table and goes out to wait in the driveway.

Tommy looks up from her sorting and stacking at the sound of tires on gravel (a surface Morty chose over asphalt for its telltale nature). From a corner window of the studio, she can just see the turnaround by the kitchen door, where Nick Greene is climbing into the Town Car, Serge closing the door behind him.

Is he leaving already? She sees no baggage, but she feels remorseful; has she done something to drive him away? She will not go back to the house just to check if the actor's things are still in the den.

She cannot believe how many, many papers Morty kept: everything from expense receipts gathered on tour (all tallied and packaged by Tommy) to correspondence with his mother's physicians, from bookmarks advertising every bookstore he'd ever set foot in to faded scribbles he made on memo pads in hotel rooms around the world. Some of it is well organized, but much of it isn't. In a single folder she found an orphaned brokerage statement, an illustrated thank-you letter written by a first-grade class in Hartford, a shopping list (in Tommy's handwriting) on which he'd sketched a parade of insects, and the receipt for a Navajo weaving he bought in Santa Fe. Only the dates, all in the spring of 2007, unify these items.

The studio was, of course, Morty's personal kingdom. Tommy expressed no opinions on its tendency toward bedlam and spent very little time here. But the file cabinets devoted to Morty's personal and professional correspondence with editors, agents, educators, academics, and fellow authors—including significant e-mails printed out on paper—were the domain where he wanted Tommy's hand, her imposition of order. They were both well aware that one day these papers would be valuable to archivists and scholars of children's literature, and until recently, Tommy envisioned turning it all over to Meredith Galarza. Now it is Tommy's to do with as she deems fit, so long as she keeps in mind the goal of financing Ivo's House. Franklin has already found a candidate for the directorship. Tommy will have to fly out and meet with the woman.

She stops for a moment just to look at Morty's drafting table, so far untouched. What will become of this space? Did Morty expect her to stay on here, alone, indefinitely? It occurs to her that the Tommy he envisioned as his executor and heir would have been at least ten years older. And she would have been prepared for all this. Or she would have talked him out of it.

"The place we're headed," Nick says, leaning over the front seat, "should be up there, on the left . . . yes! There's a space just . . . Exactly. Brilliant."

As the laconically obedient Serge backs into the parking space, Nick pulls the key from his pocket and reads the name on the manila tag again, as if he might have imagined it: Pequot Trust & Savings. The same words chiseled in granite beneath the pediment of the faux Greek temple across the street.

Oh God, that word: trust! A virtue spiraling swiftly down the drain.

Serge kills the motor and gets out.

"I'll be in there a bit, I think," says Nick as Serge opens his door (a gesture Nick has given up on trying to deter). "You have coins for the meter?"

Serge nods.

Nick sprints across the street and up the steps of the bank. Yes, it's open on Saturday. Till noon. Plenty of time. Before opening the door, he fills his lungs and hums slightly, to steady his voice.

Once inside, he feels a good deal less sure of his mission. He stands in the center of the reassuringly old-fashioned space—marble floor, fluted columns, walls muralized with primitive scenes of bucolic goings-on—until a young woman in a camel-colored suit approaches him and asks if she can be of service.

"Why, yes, thanks so much," he says, instantly removing his hat and shades, as Grandfather taught him, before remembering—as the young woman's recognition lights up her face—that this courtesy is one he's lately been advised to ignore.

But she's a game professional and says calmly, "How may I help you, sir?"

"I have a key to a lockbox I'd like to visit." He hands her the key.

"Come this way," she instructs.

She leads him into a blessedly secluded cubicle, where she takes a ledger from a shelf and opens it on her desk. Once she arrives at the desired page, she looks back and forth, three times, between the key and the tiny number on the page at the tip of her frosted-lavender fingernail.

She looks up at him and, for another long moment, is evidently struggling at what to say. "This box belongs to Mr. Lear," she says. "I know he's recently deceased, and I imagine it falls to his executor to claim the contents of the box. Do you by any chance have . . . a letter, or . . ."

Her expression is one of sheer muddlement—and Nick is confident that the one on his face isn't much different.

"I'm sorry, but I can't let someone visit Mr. Lear's box without proof of claim or permission. And I'm afraid I know you're not Mr. Lear." She blushes profoundly.

"Well, gosh, how obvious is *that*," says Nick. "*I'm* the sorry party here." Crikey, will she call the coppers? Did he sound sarcastic just now?

"I'm sorry," she says again, "but aren't you Nicholas Greene?"

He whispers, "I am, and I'd be so very grateful if you'd keep that to yourself. I am gobsmackingly mortified here, and I'm hoping you can just forget that I ever so much as walked into your establishment."

She whispers back, "No problem. Wow. I am a really big fan."

"Thank you. That's kind of you. I . . . well, I'm just going to go out the way I came."

She's still holding the key. Will she confiscate it? But she passes it back to him. "Okay," she says. "We're cool."

"You are an angel," he says.

She sees him to the door; outside, he dashes across the street to the car. "Bloody, bloody hell, what the bloody hell was I thinking?" he says as Serge opens the door. Nick throws the hat and shades onto the seat and climbs in as quickly as he can.

"I cannot answer that, sir," Serge answers, barely repressing a smile.

Tommy sees the car pull up to the house not twenty minutes after it left. She forces herself to continue making her piles; the actor's errands are none of her business. One constructive thing she has managed to do is to give the heave to dozens of envelopes containing receipts and canceled checks that are twenty, even thirty, years old. "Morty, you pack rat," she's muttering when the door to the studio opens.

Nick Greene stands in the doorway, looking even more unkempt and sounding out of breath.

"I've gone completely round the bloody bend," he says to her, "and I have a ghastly confession to make."

She's unsure what to say. She knows what he's going to confess— his nocturnal snoopfest—but what difference does it make? Or perhaps he's broken something in the house? She wonders if he's been drinking.

"Can you please come into the house with me? Please."

Now Tommy feels unnerved. People say that all actors—all good actors—have to be unhinged to some extent, and suddenly she's not sure that the idea of being alone with him was such a good one. Not that she feels in danger, but she hasn't a single mote of energy to spare for somebody else's mental instability.

Over his shoulder, she sees Serge standing in the driveway beside that grandiose car. Supposing Nicholas Greene wanted to kidnap her? She envisions Serge tying her up, duct-taping her mouth, bundling her trussed-up body in the trunk. (In the presence of an actor, maybe drama is contagious.)

"Please," he says again.

She follows him. In the kitchen, he asks her to sit, to wait for just a minute. He leaves the room but comes back carrying a silver note-book computer.

"You're probably going to give me the boot, but I honestly can't bear this much longer." Sighing heavily, he sits across from her at the table, both hands flat on the computer, as if she might reach over and snatch it. "So," he says, then eyes the ceiling.

"Tomasina"—and here are his famous eyes, focused imploringly on her—"you know that I had a correspondence humming along with Mr. Lear before he died. I can't quite figure out why—or yes, perhaps there was something simpatico about our boyhoods that drew him out, I was hoping to solve that mystery by meeting him—but the thing is, he told me a great deal about . . . Arizona, that gardener, the shed . . . things that weren't quite . . . well, not the same as the story in the film we're making. Or the story people take from that interview."

Tommy waits through a silence. What's the fuss here? Morty was starstruck. His back-and-forth with Nicholas Greene was a platonic fling of sorts. That much she has figured out. She says, "Morty surprised a lot of people, even me, when he said what he did in that interview. It changed how I saw him—I mean, the way he decided to tell the whole world."

"I doubt we'd be making this film if he hadn't! But listen. Because—so last night I went into his bedroom, just to . . . you know, to soak it all in, to inhabit what's left of him there. I couldn't sleep and I thought it might not be so bad if—"

"It's fine, really," says Tommy. "I get it."

"What's not fine"—he pushes the laptop toward her—"is that I spent a good two hours going through his personal files. I wanted to see our e-mails again, because I'd deleted a lot of them, his, which he asked me to do, but then I just had to look at some others that—"

"Wait." Tommy looks at the computer sitting in the center of the table, their four hands extended toward it as if it might be a Ouija board, ready to offer an oracular answer to all their concerns. "Is that Morty's machine?"

"Yes."

"I forgot about that."

She has never looked at this computer. Sometime after Soren's death, she noticed it in Morty's bedroom; she assumed he got it to keep himself occupied through the insomnia particular to mourning. Whenever he started typing at three or four a.m., she would awaken, then drift back to sleep, more reassured than worried. She should have remembered this computer, looked for it, already.

"I want you to look at some of what he wrote to me," says Nick, "if just to corroborate. I'm letting it fuck with my psyche, and I've gone widdershins about the disparity between . . ." He groans. "But there's more." Now he fumbles beneath the table and produces a key attached to a tag, which he slides across the table.

In a guest appearance on a children's television show, Morty talked about making up stories. At one point, he leaned close to the camera and said, "A story is just like a road. It's got to take you somewhere. Somewhere fun, somewhere new! But you don't want the trip to be boring. You don't want to be driving along, flat flat flat, nothing but cornfields on either side for miles. *Iowa,*" he whispered, as if the entire state were a secret, and held up a photo of said agricultural bounty stretching to infinity. "A few cornfields are well and good, but you'll also want some very steep hills . . . Scotland!" Now, a snap-shot of an absurdly vertiginous road somewhere in the Highlands, with a road sign that bore only a large exclamation point. "Throw in cliffs for a little suspense. . . ." Photo of that famous Mediterranean coastal road—the Corniche?—favored by Hitchcock. "And the trip would be dull indeed without some unexpectedly sharp corners."

So Morty would have appreciated this moment, a hairpin turn if ever there was one, worthy of that Scottish road sign. Here sits Tommy, at her own table, looking at a computer holding the private correspondence of a dead man (does death negate privacy?) and an old-fashioned key, while this houseguest (a stranger) keeps glancing at the clock, as if he's got to be somewhere else. Wasn't she supposed to be conducting the show-and-tell this weekend?

Now he says, leaning toward her just the way Morty leaned in to his young viewers in that television show, "I'm going to ask you a mammoth favor that you are free, even completely sane, to refuse. But the bank is open only two more hours between now and Monday, and I'm wondering if we could get at a lockbox there. I promise to explain everything, but I'm desperate to get there before it closes. I know it's not my business, but somehow . . ."

How could he explain to Tomasina that it's happening, the thing he strives for: he's slipping inside Lear's skin. He needs, metabolically, to know as much as he can. He needs this answer.

With one hand on the computer, the other reaching for the key, Tommy says, "You're losing me." The important thing, she tells herself, is to act as if she's in complete control of the situation. Even though she clearly isn't.

Morty, you idiot, you ass, she thinks, but what's the point of scolding a man whose ego's gone up in smoke, whose body is nothing but a mahogany box of ashes sitting on a windowsill in the studio?

Tommy examines the key, reads the tag. "Right here in town." She keeps her checking account there, but Morty's finances are still handled by a big-name city bank with a staff of sleekly suited acolytes in charge of "private wealth management."

"My bet is it contains a stash of his childhood drawings," says Nick.

Tommy sees his determination toward calm, his concern that she thinks he's gone crazy. Which doesn't mean he hasn't.

"You want me to open that box, today."

"I have no earthly right, but—"

"But yes." She looks at the key again. "I'm not even going to ask—yet—where you got this key."

Had Morty sent the actor this key? How does he know what the box contains—and why would it contain drawings? The fact is, Tommy wants to open the box, immediately, as badly as he does.

She knows the posthumous rituals by now. "I'll need a death certificate," she says. "Wait here."

She goes out to the studio to get the paperwork she needs. On impulse, she makes a call.

"Franklin, did you know about a safe-deposit box at Pequot?"

"Nope," he says. "No idea."

"Maybe Bruce did?"

"I wouldn't know. You found a key?"

Tommy hesitates. "Yes."

"But where? We scoured those drawers."

"Never mind. Could you do me a favor and call Bruce in Florida? If that's okay?"

From a file folder, she takes one of the dozen certificates she ordered attesting to Morty's demise, along with the notarized proof of her status as Morty's executor. Everyone on the tiny provincial staff at Pequot knows Tommy, but they'll still need to go through the formalities.

Nick insists that they go with Serge, not in Tommy's car. As she gets in, the sensation of sinking back onto the smooth, supple leather reminds her of so many departures, with Morty, from awards ceremonies and numbingly speech-heavy tributes. Slipping away, into whatever hired car Morty's publisher had arranged, they would revel in the collusive pleasure of escape. "Home, James," Morty would say in a bad pompous British accent, not terribly remote from the way in which Nick says, "Serge, back to that bank, if you please."

Tommy removes the drawings from their cardboard folio and lays them out one by one. She does so slowly, not out of reverence but almost out of repulsion. The markings on these sheets of paper are all that remain of Mort Lear's childhood—they ought to be precious to her; they deserve her tenderness and awe—yet their very existence feels like a reprimand. *You were always to be trusted, but not* that *much.* And to have their existence uncovered by someone who never even met Morty? The more she tries to reason back her anger, the more her fingers fumble with the archival tissue that Morty (surely not the satanic Leonard) placed between the drawings.

She must remind herself what good news these drawings represent, in part because they provide literal illustration to Morty's early years—which otherwise threaten to be summarized as little more than trauma . . . *coming to a cinema near you!*

After she fills the surface of the dining room table, she clears the candlesticks and silver bowls from the sideboard and begins there, dealing them out like cards from a deck. The final three go on chairs. Some are speckled faintly with mildew—collectively, they fill the room with a dank, atticky odor—but most are in decent shape. What surprises her is how many were done on high-quality stock, not the throwaway composition paper on which Morty claimed he made all his juvenile jottings.

Tommy knows she should be unveiling this discovery with Angelica, or even Franklin, not Nicholas Greene, though without the actor's meddling, these pictures, the likes of which no one has seen, might have remained indefinitely hidden, emerging from the lockbox only when that stalwart little bank went out of existence—or Morty's preemptive rental fee ran dry.

She has been stunned into silence since leaving the bank, but Nick, as he hovers and watches, exclaims at practically every image. "The cactuses are fabulous!" "Will you look at this bird—is it meant to be, what, a phoenix?" "Oh these leaves, the rendering is brilliant, how can a child this young capture *sunlight* with crayon? And this cat, the way his tail—"

"Nick, please. I need to be able to think." Did she have to sound so harsh?

He apologizes. He retreats to the edge of the dining room and watches from a distance. Dimly, it occurs to her that there is a child-like fragility to Nick, a Peter Pan aura that might help explain why Morty fell so hard for him. Because that's the truth: Morty had a crush on Nick. Innocent, not precisely sexual . . . or maybe she's naïve.

But Tommy is too preoccupied by the mystery behind this folio of drawings to follow that train of thought. All of them are unmistakably Morty's, only in part because they are signed. *M. Levy 1948*— the *y* trailing into a curlicued flourish. In the lower left of a few, he wrote *Drawn From Life*. But then there are the fantastical pictures: a salamander as dragon, with a tiny knight drawn awkwardly before it, flame blasting from the lizard's mouth. A potted plant becomes a tree filled with fanciful birds.

Nick cannot believe his eyes: Mort Lear was a bloody genius even as a nipper. Nor can he believe that Tomasina Daulair has yet to turn him out for his bad behavior, his prurience—his outright invasion. (With pleasant spite, he imagines how horrified Grandfather would be at his cocked-up manners.)

Tommy walks back and forth, round and around the table, just looking. She shakes her head. "Unbelievable." She puts her hands over her face. "Un fucking believable. I am sorry."

Nick holds his tongue. He's forced himself to pull back, to sit on one of the chairs not serving as an easel. Wait till Andrew hears about this. But then, no, what difference would it make to the script, essentially? Though perhaps the drawings themselves—

"All right," says Tommy. The look she aims at him verges on accusation. "Do you get this? Is there some kind of explanation in those files you opened?"

"You should read the lot of it yourself." He thinks for a moment. "You'll need to read his e-mails to me first. I haven't a clue what you know of what he told me. Then read the files that . . . led me to the key."

He motions toward the kitchen, where Lear's laptop still sits on the table.

She follows him. "Would you make me a cup of tea? Any kind," she says, pointing vaguely to the jar containing the tea bags. "Please. And then just . . ."

"Make myself scarce."

"Sorry. But stick around." When she opens the computer, her face lights up in reflection, though her expression is grim.

Nick heads outside. The afternoon sky has turned sympathetically glum, but the air is still warm, too close. He walks around the back of the studio to the swimming pool. Petals blown from the surrounding fruit trees lie on the taut blue cover, as if snow has fallen in June.

Nick unlatches the wooden gate and enters the enclosure. He sits on a skeletal chaise whose cushions must be stored in the cabana behind the diving board. Tomasina told him that Morty had the pool put in "just because." Because, Nick inferred, that's what people do after they earn a certain amount of lucre and are expected to entertain their friends accordingly. He thinks of Andrew's ebony pool, his canary-haired wife doing her knifelike laps. Was she part of that compulsory entertainment?

A week ago he was on fire about this project: nervy with anticipation, yes, but as Deirdre would have put it, "all cylinders ablaze."

He pulls his phone from his pocket. Oh God, how can the list of numbers be so bloody long when he often feels as if he can barely count his true friends on one hand? Though, of course, so many of these "contacts," as the mobile calls them, were transient, never intended for keeping long-term. He must learn how to delete them. No doubt Deirdre would know.

Here she is, twice over: the mobile she had while they were in Sicily and the one she had in the States, when they were hot on the trail of those prizes, ricochet-rabbiting about on that shameless campaign—the campaign that paid off for him.

Wherever she is, the worst she can do is not answer.

"Hello?"

"Deirdre? It's Nick. Greene."

A pause, a spasm of laughter. "*Bear* cub, is that really you?"

"Deirdre, I wish you'd stop calling me that. I'm actually not so young."

"Old enough to know better, is that what you mean? But fresh— you are still fresh, my friend. Don't try to deny it."

"Oh bugger, call me what you like. I'm glad to hear your voice. Where are you?"

"Beside a pool in Palos Verdes. Where I'm staying on the current payroll. And being a very good girl, I might add. Drinking extra-virgin Arnold Palmers and iced feng shui. Pretending I like yoga. Down, dog, down!" More of her consoling laughter.

"Fancy that. I'm by a pool in Connecticut! A dormant pool. No party here. Just me. What's doing, what's the project?" His knee is vibrating. He's sixteen again, juicing up the courage to ask Veronica— what was her surname?—to that dance. Godawful, as it turned out, both the dance and the girl.

"It's a tom-com. Excellent money for solid mediocrity."

"What's a tom-com?"

"Bear cub. Really. Think *Risky Business.* Or, well, I suppose *Splash.* Except the Toms are a good deal older now. Cruise in this case."

"You're in a Tom Cruise movie? Brilliant."

"I'm his mom. I'm a tom-com mom!"

"But you're not old enough to be his mother."

"In Hollywood years I am plenty old to be his mother. According to retroactive Hollywood math, you could easily become a mother at eight. I think . . . I even hope! . . . that I'm consigned to another decade of moms. If I'm lucky. Then grandmoms if I hit the jackpot. Dowager queens! Better than oblivion. Which is not where you are headed, cowboy. Although I see you're in mild danger of typecasting. Another creative homosexual American? I'd go for a Glaswegian meth-head next time around. Or a womanizing con man. You need a palate cleanser."

"Looks like I'm on for a new Alan Ayckbourn. The West End. I think I'm homesick."

"Is that why you're calling? Haven't you acquired a new squeeze by now?"

"Deirdre, you scared me off."

"Off? Honey, I have no idea what you mean."

"Your cautionary tales."

"I was doing my high-horse thing, was I? Lord, but I can be tiresome."

"No, no! You tell it straight, like just about nobody ever does, and it's a massive relief, Deirdre. You are a sage."

On the other end of the line, he hears what sounds like the crunching of ice cubes, then a tide of passing voices. Deirdre isn't alone.

"I'm interrupting your life," he says.

"Interrupting my life? Please. I've been interrupting my own life as long as I've been living it. You are giving me a taste of continuity. Talk to me, in your beautiful swishy-swanky accent, for as long as you like. I'm just heading indoors so I can hear you better. I mean it. You didn't call to shoot the breeze. Hang on."

He waits till she says, "I'm all yours, cub."

He tells her about his back-and-forths with Mort Lear before the man died, how it matters to Nick, somehow it really does, that the story in the film be true to the story that he's sure is the right one, however subtle the differences might seem to most.

"Hardly 'subtle,'" she says. "I'm with you on the departure from truth. Though honestly, all these oh-so-serious, self-satisfied bio-pics depart from truth. People go to movies to part ways with truth. Wouldn't you say?"

Nick is now pacing ovals around the pool, slaloming round the furniture as he listens.

"Bear cub, I have an appointment for a massage with a young man even more fetching than you are, and I'm about to be running late."

"Sorry, Deirdre, I've hoovered up your time—"

"Nick," she says, "you have no idea how much it means to me you called. You're a gem, do you know that? But here's a parting bit of advice, because advice is all I have to give: This is Andrew. As in the Holy See. Next in line to the Almighty. Not that Andrew doesn't care what his actors think; far from it. That's part of what makes him so great. He's an actor, too. Remember? But what he wants, in the end, is what he gets. Have your say, let him listen—because he will—then follow orders."

Nick hears her speaking quickly to someone else, her voice muffled.

"My driver's here. Revving the engine politely. Call again, will you?"

"I will," says Nick, and before he can thank her, she's off.

He takes another two circuits around the pool before his mobile buzzes.

A text from Silas, with a link to TakeItFromSeptimus.com, a tar pit of celebrity gossip that makes the hair rise on Nick's spine even when he isn't the subject of the moment. Si's text reads, *Good job, 007! At client matinee till 5 but will call and stage extraction if necessary.*

Clicking on the link yields—well, of course it bloody does—an amateur photo of Nick standing in the bank that morning, holding his cap and specs by his side, talking to the camel-clad cashier. (The evil thing about mobiles is that they take pictures without a click or a flash. Hundreds of people can snap away while you scratch your bottom or stare slack-jawed into the distance like a doddering basset hound, and you are none the wiser.)

Cheerio, now here's a curio: What in the world could our Favorite Dishy Brit be doing in the hinterlands of Connecticut? A pastoral fling? A yen for hugging trees? Oh, but wait! Rely on Septimus to connect the dots. Because the second film role our FDB has poached from all the properly (or improperly) gay, properly American actors who might have nabbed it is that of none other than the King of Kid Lit, Mort Lear, who sadly up and died while doing a bit of home repair back in May. Where did Lear live? Orne, Connecticut. Where was this picture taken? Ladies of a certain sylvan town, straighten your Spanx and be on the lookout!

Were the pool uncovered, Nick might just toss his phone in the deep end. He starts back toward the house, but suddenly he's paralyzed. What if the media marauders are on their way? (Or maybe they don't bloody care. Surely they're all in the city, stalking the hundreds of stars who walk those streets every day.) He rings Serge and asks him to come back again. "What I need is this," says Nick. "Would you just, please, possibly, park at the road, keep an eye out for unwanted visitors?"

What is the definition of *unbearable*? To Tommy, it's this e-mail from Morty to the actor, written back in March. She can read only a few sentences at a time before she has to look up at something, anything, in the kitchen: the tiles they picked together on their tour of the Moravian Tile Works, the glass jars Morty saw in a shop on the first trip she made with him to England, the oven mitts she bought from last year's Crate & Barrel after-Christmas catalog sale. Those things are bearable—or are they?

After they are gone, I tell myself the woman's voice, her laugh, could not have been my mother's. My mother works all day. I know she gets breaks—

sometimes that summer I have lunch with her—but why, of all places, would she come to Leonard's shed? It wasn't her, I'm sure, though I feel strange in her company that night. I go to bed early.

The second time, a few days later, I try to block my ears when the talk between them turns to something else. I cannot draw, of course, while my hands are held to my ears. And they do not block the loudest noises Leonard and the woman make together. It is in fact the "together noises," as I think of them, that are the most upsetting.

The third time, I stand up and I edge sideways to a place where I can look furtively, just a knife-edge glance, and yes, that is my mother's hair, my mother's profile, though I have never before seen my mother's bare chest. The flowered blouse on the floor is my mother's. I know it because it's her favorite.

I hunch back into my cubbyhole and do not know whether I hope they saw me or not. After Leonard leaves, after I leave, I stay away from home as long as I can, past sunset, till the moment I know my mother will panic. She is unhappy when I return; dinner is cold. I am not hungry, I tell her, and I go to bed with my book, pretending it's so suspenseful that I cannot wait to dive back into its pages.

The next morning I say I do not feel well. I stay in my room all day. Maybe the next day, too.

But I go back, I can't help it—it's my closest-to-perfect place—and when I slip into the shed, I find new materials awaiting me on my makeshift desk. The cat is curled up on the couch. Leonard isn't there and stays away all day. Maybe I am imagining these things. My mother has told me, more than once, that she worries my imagination will be my undoing. Maybe my drawings carry me away to some hallucinatory zone (though I do not know about "hallucinations" at that age; all I know are fantasies and dreams).

The next time—is it a day or two or three later?—I cover my ears, put my head on my drawing, and I am weeping silently. The drawing is ruined. I remember it: an attempt to draw a hawk against a cloudy sky.

I force myself to go home at the usual time. Over dinner, I tell my mother that I am drawing in Leonard's shed. I tell her about the materials he gives me, about my little desk. Perhaps my voice is shaking.

She stares at me, as still as can be. She asks when I am there, how long I have been going. I don't think I'm capable of answering her. All I remember *is her erupting rage (which I do not understand is fear and shame), her tell-ing me she never gave me permission to be in that shed, to take such gifts from strangers. (Doesn't she remember that she told me we could trust all the people who work for the hotel?)*

I cannot say anything. I think I will never say anything again. She sends me to my room, and I hear her go out. Later I hear her crying. The next day she forbids me to leave our apartment.

I never go to the shed again. My mother packs our things, she says we are going east for a new and better life, though she is not acting like someone who has much hope. The next day, we are staying in a hotel somewhere else, noth-ing like Eagle Rest. I am to stay in the room while she goes out, doing errands she does not disclose. A week later we are gone. She hardly speaks to me on the long trip, she stares out windows at the changing landscape. She wears sun-glasses to hide her swollen eyes. I know I am to blame, I am the culprit. I know the life we're headed for cannot be better, and it's all my fault.

Should I wonder about my lifelong relations with women, because of what happened? And never, you can be sure that never, did my mother speak of what she knew I heard or saw. Once she had secure work, once she made friends with a few of our neighbors in Brooklyn, she began to look me in the eye again, to act as if we were just a mother and son making our way in a difficult world. But I was never fooled into thinking that she had forgotten—though maybe she thought I could have forgotten. Years and years later, when I was finally certain that she had lost all touch with memory, the kite string connecting her to memory snatched from her hand by the wind, I felt horribly, horribly relieved.

But women—especially women who flirt with me, and they do (they still do!)—are capable of filling me with fear. . . .

What about *me?!* Tommy is shrieking inside as she reads this melo-dramatic, self-pitying account. Or why didn't Morty ever seek out a therapist, if he felt this tortured?

She looks up again and laughs. Maybe he did have a therapist. Turns out he had a mental footlocker stuffed with secrets, a bank box stuffed with hidden drawings, why not a clandestine shrink?

She thinks of the time she found the guts to confront him about whether he, too, might be HIV positive. He had won her faith, yet again, when he said, *I have no significant secrets from you.*

So what makes a secret "significant"? she wonders now, having shut the laptop in a stew of embarrassment and fury. The computer's battery charge is down to a sliver of red; she'll have to ask Nick what he did with the cord.

Where is he? She stands and looks out the window over the sink. No sign of him. Is he snooping again, now in the studio? Christ, what else is there to find? Is there some law of physics stating that the larger the life lived, the more surprises there will be to discover once that life comes to an end? And was Morty's life large—or, despite his fame and endless supply of frequent-flier miles, surreptitiously small?

Wheels on the gravel; no doubt the bodyguard has been summoned for another errand.

Tommy walks through the door into the rest of the house. What now? She has no stomach for sorting more papers. She goes upstairs and into Morty's room. Dusty sunbeams illuminate the bed. The day is accelerating; it must be two or three o'clock by now. She's had nothing to eat since that piece of toast at five-thirty. Maybe she just needs food to lift her spirits.

She has the sudden urge to open and empty the bureau drawers, pull up the rug in search of loose floorboards, trapdoors. She can't help thinking of *Mimi's Masterpiece,* one of Morty's earliest picture books, in which a family of mice who live beneath the floor of an artist's studio tease scraps of paper and broken pencil points down through the cracks between the boards, making their own fanciful art—which looks completely different from the work of the artist above.

All she does, however, is continue to stand at the foot of the bed.

She is so clenched up that she gasps when she hears a voice calling her name from downstairs. A man, but not Nick, not even the enigmatic Serge. Franklin?

"Tommy? Are you here? Toms?"

She goes to the top of the stairs. "Dani?"

"We tried to call you from the road, but I got the voice mail."

We? Can no one arrive at this house without an escort? But of course he'd bring Jane . . . and Joe. She'll finally meet her nephew. She is struck by a wave of shame. How petty is she not to have made the effort—

She and Dani converge in the living room. Immediately, he puts his arms around her. Her face fits just under his chin; it's the same sensation, physically, as being embraced by their father, Dani the same wiry kind of tall.

"I know," he says. "I should've asked if I could come. I'm sorry, but you haven't—"

"And Jane's here, too?"

"No. I came out with someone else, who offered me a ride and who's been trying to get ahold of you, too. It's like you've disappeared off the face of the planet, Toms. I've been worried."

"Didn't you get the note I sent you?"

"No." He looks defensive. "We moved, you know. We couldn't keep our old place after . . ."

He still can't seem to tell her. "After the shop closed," she said. "Oh, Dani, I don't get why you didn't tell me about that. I found out after you were here in the fall."

They stand a foot apart now, Tommy aware of how defensive they both look. "I meant to," he says. "And then, I don't know. This place isn't good for me. It's always pissed me off. Like I'm the pauper and he's the king. Except . . . fuck. Never mind."

Tommy remembers that he isn't alone. She glances through the kitchen but sees no one coming in. Dani reads her mind.

"Okay, so this might piss *you* off," he says, "and I really didn't get the full story till we were halfway here, but the person who drove me is Merry Galarza. She's outside. She didn't want to come in until I told you. She'll drive right back to the city if you want, but she's desperate to talk with you."

"I'm about to have a nervous breakdown." Tommy sits on the nearest couch.

"I can tell her to go. I can go with her."

"Don't be silly, Dani."

He smiles, flinching. "I wonder how often you've said that to me."

"Can you just let me think for a moment? A lot is going on right now." She sees her brother look around, as if a troupe of acrobats might emerge from a closet, as if she's referring to a physical commotion of some sort. She doesn't need him to ask about the drawings.

"Dani, go tell her she can stay. Did you have lunch? I have no idea what time it is, but I need to eat. And if I put food together, I stand a chance of calming down."

Merry loiters in the driveway by her car, feeling as foolish as she is. When was she last here—four, five years ago? Mort gave her the grand tour. She thought it was such a privilege. How naïve, how vain, was that?

The two hours she just spent in the car with Dani Daulair felt, at once, like a shaming and a liberation. Her fraying nerves turned her, as usual, into a profligate chatterbox. Before they even hit the Sawmill Parkway, she was well into her narrative of betrayal. "It's like that will of his was a suicide note," she found herself saying. "A final fuck-you before tumbling on purpose off that roof. I know that's a bitchy, selfish thing to say. But if I don't vent before we get there, I'll end up cooking my goose. Or shooting myself in the foot. Pick your cliché. I'm it."

Merry pulled herself up short. This righteous soliloquy had begun to sound uncomfortably comfortable to her, playing itself out in her head so regularly now that she could practically set it to music. "Listen to me. Wow. I'm sorry. You're just trying to see your sister and I'm . . ."

"I have a beef with him, too," Dani said sharply. "It's stupid."

"Stupid?"

"Stale, I guess."

Merry might talk too much, but she knew when to shut up and listen.

"Forget it," he said.

"Please," she said. "Tell me."

"I'm Ivo."

Merry waited for more. What was he talking about? "Ivo, Mort's Ivo."

"I was the model."

She glanced quickly at him. He was looking ahead, no real expression. She tried to guess at his age, do the math. No one thought of Lear as an artist who used live models. In endless interviews, he spoke about his pictures, along with his stories, as emerging from deep within, words and images drawn up from a well in a bucket, brought into the light.

She thought, surprisingly, of Lear's reverence for all the history and lore surrounding Charles Dodgson's inspirational Alice Liddell.

"You modeled for Mort?"

"Except I didn't know it. And I know I shouldn't care. Not like I deserve something in return, but I've always felt . . ." Dani sighed. "It's so stupid."

"It sounds too important to be stupid," said Merry, although she was confused. How was the sister involved in all this?

Carefully, coaxingly, she got him to tell her the whole story.

"But what the hell does he owe me, really?" Dani said at the end.

"I think the problem," said Merry, "the thing that makes us angry, even if we don't have the right, is that we know he didn't feel like he owed anything to anyone."

She realizes she's been standing in the driveway for nearly ten minutes. But she swore she wouldn't enter the house until Dani—or his sister—emerged to invite her in. At least she can wait in the shade. She wanders across the grass to stand beneath a tree by the studio. Too curious to resist the temptation, she presses herself between a pair of shrubs and peers through one of the windows. Papers and files are lying about everywhere; it looks like a burglar's been through. Somebody's already packing things up. "What?" she mutters aloud. Isn't it far too soon to take such drastic measures? Where is everything headed?

She steps back, careful not to snap any branches, and when she pivots, she nearly collides with a strange man, except that—

"Yikes," she says. "Hello." She knows him, though he's clearly out of context.

"Yes, hello," he says tersely. His smile is more like a grimace.

"We know each other, I know we do." Merry extends her hand.

"I'm afraid not."

"But . . ." Merry brushes pine needles off her skirt. She now wishes she had worn jeans. Her skirt and blouse make her look like the kiss-ass she's desperate not to be—though who would she be fooling?

"Nick," he says, holding out his hand just as she's withdrawn hers. "I didn't mean to startle you."

She realizes she's peering at him, as if he's not in focus.

"Nicholas Greene," he says.

"Oh . . . oh Christ—oh *sorry*—I mean, of course you are. God, I'm an idiot." And then the picture does come into focus. "You're playing Mort. In the movie. Oh my God."

"Yes," he says. "And you're not . . . some skulduggerish gal reporter, chasing me into the woods, Diana the Media Huntress."

"No," says Merry. "I don't think so, at least."

What is he talking about? And does anybody really talk like that? And why is he roaming around outdoors, by himself? (Well, what is *she* doing?) "No," she says again. "I'm just a jilted museum curator, here to beg for alms."

Now she's the one talking like that: blather is contagious. "Right. My name." She introduces herself. They shake hands again, too forcefully.

"All square then!" he says. "Should we go in? Are you here to see Tomasina?"

"Yes. Or I hope so. Wow, that was a lot of talk to figure out next to nothing."

All Tomasina can do is tell her to leave. She's endured worse.

Tommy opens the door before they reach it. "I'm thinking lunch," she says, looking straight at Merry. "I'm putting on canned soup and I'm making a salad, and I think I'm opening a bottle of wine." The actor slips past her while she speaks.

"I know I owe you a call," she says, grasping Merry's outstretched hand. "Only now I guess I don't. Come in."

When Tommy closes the door behind her, she sees beyond Merry that Dani is staring, openly astonished, at Nick.

"Everybody, will you please just sit for a minute?"

Like children in a game of musical chairs, Tommy's three guests immediately reach for the nearest chair, pull it out from the table, and sit—even her brother.

"Well," says Tommy. "Something in my life goes according to plan."

Nobody laughs. Nick's phone buzzes from one of his pockets. The others stare at him. He holds his hands aloft. "Not answering." He then reaches inside, pulls out the phone, and disarms it.

"You're not my hostages," says Tommy. "I'm just not sure how to . . ." She turns to Dani, perhaps because he's the one person over whom she has an established authority, however dated, and says, "I wish you had called," as kindly as she can.

They are all silent now, as if chastised. For a few beats, Tommy feels calm—until something catches her eye in the oblique view she has through the doorway to the dining room, the windows beyond. She leaves the kitchen, to get a better view. When she returns, she glares at Nick.

"Did you invite a photographer here? Please tell me you didn't do that."

Twelve

The cancer, too swiftly, wheedled its way into her bones, her spine first of all.

He was in Bucharest when Annabelle rang, hardly able to speak through her sobbing. "All for bloody *nothing*, the slash and burn. Now it's too fucking late for the chemo."

Nick had just returned to his hotel room and wrapped himself in the cheap duvet, exhausted and chilled from hours of shooting outdoors in the morning mist and afternoon rains, sore from horseback riding in ersatz medieval armor, sick of soggy sandwiches by day and meaty, cabbagey stews by night. (It felt as if, even off set, the meals were meant to evoke Arthurian England.) He did not want this news, but he craved a reason to catch a break.

The director gave Nick a three-day leave; they would shoot around him.

"Don't you dare get up," he called into Mum's flat as he let himself in with his key. He threw his bag and his mac on the floor just inside the door, nearly tripping as he made his way to her bedroom.

She was sitting up on the bed, dressed in jeans and a thick jumper, a book laid aside on the coverlet.

He sat next to her, carefully; Annabelle had described how merciless the pain could be, how cunningly unpredictable, how hard it was for her to sleep.

"Will it hurt if I hug you?" he asked.

"Hug me, sweetie," she said. "Hug me no matter what."

He pulled himself up against the headboard, so they sat side by side. He slipped an arm around her shoulder and leaned in. She smelled medicinal. He willed away tears. (How much harder, he couldn't help noticing, it was for him to hold them back than, if required, to summon them.)

"I saw you in the magazine," Mum said.

"Oh, that frothy bit about my show."

"I love the thought of you as Sir Gawain. My noble knight."

"It's pretty daft, really. I mean the whole plot. I don't know how long it'll last."

"Be optimistic, Nicky. I didn't impress that on you, any of you, I see that now."

He wanted to give her the same advice, but it would be insulting. She had asked the doctor not to soft-pedal anything.

He picked up the book. "Iris Murdoch."

"Plot like a maze. Keeps me occupied."

"You have visitors, don't you?"

"Your sister's here too much. I couldn't stay here without her, so I let her come. Selfish, I know. Weekends, your brother takes over."

"High time you were selfish, Mum."

"If only because there's not much of it," she said quietly.

"Of what?" he said, realizing in an instant what a dolt he was.

"Time, sweetie."

She quickly changed the subject to Nigel, how well he was doing, though his advancement at work might mean moving to Scotland. In fact, she said, Nigel had taken over paying her rent—at which Nick felt a surge of envy. He could pitch in, now that he had regular work (if only for a few more weeks).

In the middle of a sentence, she stopped cold, blanched. She looked as if she were holding her breath.

"Mum?"

She closed her eyes.

"Can I get you something?" He tried to take hold of her hand, but she'd clenched it tight, an impregnable fist.

When the pain passed, she told him that it felt as if some invisible assailant were striking her spine with a bat. The blows came without warning. If she took the powerful drug her doctor had prescribed, the pain dimmed to an intermittent ache, but then all of her dimmed, all her senses, her memory, her balance, her consciousness (even certainty) of being alive.

What could Nick say? That he admired her grace, her courage, her kindness to three children who had probably as good as scuppered her prospects of a considered life? And the time had long passed, he knew, when he might have asked her more about his father, something he had blithely expected he would do in some distant future they were clearly never to share. Nick knew the man's name, and he knew that, last Mum had known, the blighter lived somewhere in Northern Ireland. ("Probably has a wife and kids there. Now *she's* a woman I wouldn't trade places with.")

"Are you peckish? Can I go out and fetch us the best carryout in London?" he asked, helpless.

"You know, I am," she said, deliberately brightening. "But no curry. Anything but curry. I went off that for life a good while ago."

"Then I'll be back. Stay right here with Iris." He patted the book.

Even this errand was a matter of his needs over hers. He was desperate to be out in the fickle city air—in the mean wind and temperamental skies of April—not because it would clear his head but because it would allow him somewhere to cry. He walked several blocks in a locomotive rush, wiping his face again and again with the sleeve of his mac, till he reached a small, motley park. He turned on his mobile and called Annabelle to reassure her that he had arrived, that she could take off the next two days.

"I'm pregnant," she told him, just like that.

"Annaboo," he said. "Oh Annie." He found himself crying again, his sister joining in.

"I don't know whether to tell her. I'm barely three months along."

"You have to."

"She'll refuse to let me care for her. What then? Not like Nige can take time off."

Nick was about to say that *he* would refuse to let her care for Mum, but what could he offer—to quit his show and move home, just as he'd found work to sink his teeth into, even if it was second tier?

"It'll give her something to live for," said Nick.

"You haven't talked to her doctors," Annabelle said coldly.

"But it's good news, Annie."

He heard his sister sigh. "Well, it is. For us. Michael's on the moon."

"Congratulations. How could I forget that bit? Congratulations."

She promised to let him know what she decided to do.

He brought back to his mother's flat an Italian lunch, aubergine and chicken dishes baked with tomato and cheese. He'd asked the girl to leave out the garlic. Mum ate a few bites and seemed endlessly grateful. Nick had a glass of the red plonk he found at the back of a cupboard.

Annabelle had told him that if everything went well, Mum would sleep for much of the afternoon (though seldom so well at night). That first afternoon, Nick muted his mobile and slept as well, curled up, prawnlike, on the narrow bed in the spare room off the kitchen, wearing the same clothes he'd put on before dawn in Bucharest.

He was awakened by the sound of running water, the consciousness of a sun much lower in the sky. At least the clouds had cleared.

Mum was leaning against the sink, filling the kettle. From behind, she looked even more alarmingly tiny than she had on her bed. She had always been small—in healthier times, compact and trim, nimble on her feet. More than once, she had told Nick that he was lucky to have inherited two of the three traits that drew her to his father: the man's stature and his striking complexion. "The third, his gift for opportunistic flattery, that one I hope he kept to himself."

"Mum, let me do that," he said in the kitchen.

He startled her, of course, and it distressed him to see her catch herself with one hand, nearly dropping the kettle onto the dishes in the sink. Recovering her balance, she turned. "I'm done for if I can't do a thing for myself, Nicky. But thank you." She set the kettle on the counter and let him take over. She sat in the sole chair beside the café table in the corner.

Rummaging, he found a tin of shortbread biscuits.

"Have as many as you like," she said. "None for me."

"Calories, Mum. According to Annie, the doctor said we're to stuff you like a Christmas goose with calories."

"I have clotted cream with my porridge. How's that?"

While waiting for the water to boil, he struggled for something to say that wasn't about her cancer. He reached for a story about his work on the set in Romania.

His mother saved him the trouble. "Your sister's pregnant."

"Mum? Did she tell you that?" Had he been so dead to the world that he failed to wake at the sound of a ringing phone? What kind of useless carer was he?

Mum shook her head. "Anybody can see. Or any woman who's been through it three times. I hope she plans to let me in on the news. Before it's too late."

Should he pretend he didn't know? The plaintive look on his mother's face reminded him, suddenly, sadly, of the look she often wore when her three children returned home from a posh lunch out with Grandfather.

"I shouldn't say this," Nick said, "but I'm glad Grandfather's gone. I'm glad he's not around to see you like this, and I don't mean because I think it would break his heart or any of that rubbish."

"Oh, Nick."

The kettle began to hint at a whistle. Nick turned to put things together on a tray. "Let's go in the other room, shall we?" He watched to see if Mum needed his help, but she stood and walked through on her own.

After they were settled, she looked at Nick in that lingering way only mothers are permitted to look at their grown sons. He thought she was about to tell him how well he'd turned out, how proud she was of him, that he seemed on a good path; he had heard such homilies from her before, and though he was always embarrassed by them, they had a surprisingly powerful effect. Sometimes he felt as if they literally inoculated him against the kind of crumping surrender that even made sense in his world (that sometimes saved a bloke from squandering a whole life on dreams).

"Nicholas, I don't want to hear you run down your grandfather. He gave you so much."

"But not you. And by withholding from you, he withheld from me—from us, Nige and Annie, too."

"They'd agree with you, I'm sure. But they don't say so."

"Is saying the truth more of a sin than knowing it and keeping mum?"

She looked miserably tired all of a sudden. Why was he arguing, needling her? The emotions stirred up were mostly his.

"I don't know," she said. "But the more you succeed in what you've chosen to do, the more I worry you'll be . . . Americanized. Do you know what I mean?"

"I don't." He did his best to look receptive. As much as he loved her, Mum hadn't a clue what his work entailed, what distortions and deceptions—nor what abasements and fawnings. Perhaps he *had* inherited his father's knack for opportunistic flattery.

"What I mean is, keep the right parts of yourself to yourself. Contain yourself when it's tempting to let too much out. Don't go and . . ." She closed her eyes.

"Mum, we don't need to talk about this. Let's not."

"No," she said. "I'm glad we are. I'm trying to say that the values of your grandparents, if I'd paid closer attention and had more respect, would have served me better. Keeping more of myself to myself. Well. I guess it's true that you grow more conservative as you age." She started to laugh, but her laughter subsided toward coughing.

Nick put down his teacup and stood.

She held up a hand and whispered, "I am fine."

The phone rang; Nick answered it in the kitchen. He turned on the tap to screen his words, and he whispered, "Tell her your news. She already knows it. No, not from me. What do you take me for?"

Then he turned off the tap and called out, "It's Annie. I'll bring her in there."

He handed the phone to his mother and took the tea tray into the kitchen. He could hear the delight in her voice. He might have liked to sit close to her while she seemed so joyful—whatever her flaws and follies, Mum knew how to be genuinely *happy* for her children—but he left the two women alone and went to the loo. He washed the air-travel grime from his face and neck, and he checked to see if he reeked: crikey. After a quick rinse with the flannel, he went into his room to find a clean shirt.

When he came out, he noticed through the nearest window that dusk had fallen. The flat was silent. In the dim living room, he could just make out Mum, sitting where he'd left her, the phone in her lap. Nick turned on a lamp and said her name.

"I'm here, Nick. I'm fine. Don't worry so much. You young people worry more than we did. Do you know, your sister was holding out on me because she wanted to 'make it through' the first few months, in case she lost the baby? As if pregnancy's a foot race. She says it's customary, among her friends, to keep it a secret till then. So you're compelled to be not just knackered and queasy but fearful." Mum shook her head, but she was smiling.

"So you were right."

Her smile tightened. "You knew, Nick."

He sat beside her. "Caught."

"From reel to creel," she said.

"A bounder of a flounder."

"Which makes you my supper." She leaned over, opening her mouth as if to take a bite, then kissed him on the cheek—all of it the routine they'd had years ago when any of them, as children, told an innocent fib.

"So you know, too, that they're in touch with their father."

Nick took this in, tempted to fib again. But he said, "I didn't."

Mum was silent for a moment. "I suppose it'll take some time to sort it all out, whatever relationship they want to have. It's good for Annie, with the baby. Babies make for easy reconciliations." She considered this. "Well, sometimes."

"How long?" He tried to sound casual.

"Six months or so."

"Did you . . . ?"

"Nick," she scolded. "I have no desire. He was around long enough that I can't forgive how short a time it was. Your father, on the other hand, never came close to a promise of sticking around. Him I might forgive—never trust, mind you."

"Mum, you're wise despite yourself."

"Sheer survival does that. To a degree."

The word *survival* hung between them, a dark flag held high.

"Now look," she said. "You've come to care for me, and all you've done is wear me out. So help me to bed, will you?" She spoke from her throat, tightly, in a way that conveyed the onset of pain.

"Won't you take something?" he asked.

"Let's get to the bedroom and see, shall we?"

He stayed with her through the next day and night and another day, of which he spent an absurd amount of time cajoling her to eat. He bought Cadbury bars at the news shop, toffee biscuits and trifle from a posh new confectioner down the street. He made macaroni swimming in butter, eggs with cheese, toad-in-the-hole—the food she'd made for her children when they were out of sorts. Most of it she hardly touched. She did drink the orange squash he squeezed by hand, even after his palms cramped up.

He succeeded in holding back from asking anything more about his siblings' dad. He was less successful at convincing himself not to mind their keeping that news to themselves.

A scant month later, he was back, rushing to the airport the very minute the director released him, the first season wrapped. (And his instincts were right: *Men of the Table* would run for only the one season, though what a boon it was for Nick.) Mum was in hospital by then. By happenstance, only Nick was in her room the morning when the cancer, or the soul-stealing opiates, brought her heart to an unexpectedly sudden halt.

Late that afternoon, all the urgent formalities divided and done, the three siblings shared a meal, neither lunch nor dinner, at an empty curry house. When they parted ways, Annabelle and Nigel in a taxi, Nick alone on foot, it occurred to him that he was now the only orphan. His siblings had gained a father, as if to exchange one parent for another. He went to Mum's flat, abandoned for days, and opened all six of its windows. He fell asleep on her bed, lulled by the incessant surf of traffic in the streets below.

Thirteen

The kitchen looks, as it did on the odd occasion when Soren offered to cook for friends, like an epicurean war zone: spattered saucepans and stockpots colonizing the stove; plates, bowls, and glasses well outnumbering the people present; several dish towels cast aside, an oven mitt and a wooden spoon marooned in the pantry—and five empty or almost empty wine bottles scattered hither and yon. Strangely, Tommy doesn't care (possibly because of the wine).

All three of her guests insisted on "helping." Patching together leftovers from the fridge, greens and early peas from the garden, the canned soups Morty had insisted they stock for "blackouts and bombing raids," the small chicken she'd bought to roast for dinner, the expensive cheeses and two layer cakes Nick had picked up on his way to Orne, they found themselves with an accidental surfeit of food. Nick christened it a "petit bourgeois bouffe."

She and Dani are the only ones left in the kitchen. Merry is poring (or swooning) over the drawings still laid out in the dining room— more important to put away, Tommy reminds herself, than any of these wayward dishes. Nick excused himself first of all, and she's guessing he is holed up in the den, on the phone with one of his minions. Tommy is both tired of him and enthralled by him—tired of his somersaultingly effortful courtesies (though they do feel genuine), enthralled by his attention and his enthusiasm (which also feel authentic). The inescapably mournful look on his face during any talk of family makes her wonder how much there is to envy about the life he leads. And yet, she thinks—now that she and Dani are alone, with no more excuses to avoid their reunion—the actor is easier to be with than her own brother. Dani has finally confessed, though it's no surprise, how much he's resented Mort Lear for decades. He is convinced there would be no Ivo without the boy that Dani was. And without Ivo, there would be, he's certain, no Mort Lear Empire, no estate in the country, no movie, no ridiculous, petty tug-of-war over reams of paper (which Merry seems to have filled him in on, no bias spared).

"And," he says, "no sister enslaved to his greatness. Yes, I know this all reeks of self-pity, and I'm just like a kid who thinks the world should be fair, but fuck it, sometimes the world can be fair. Sometimes people are fair. Do you know what I mean, Tommy?"

"Dani, we've had way too much to drink."

"So what? I speak the truth, and I will not regret any of what I am saying tomorrow, even if I do have a splitting headache. I am sick of being pathetic."

"You are not pathetic."

"Oh, fuck you, Tommy. You of all people know I am. For a nanosecond there, I had a respectable business, but I chose to share it with a guy who turned out to be an embezzler. An embezzler and an addict. Our loan payments went straight into his veins. Great judge of character, that's me."

Tommy wants a respite from conversation of any kind—is it too early to go to bed?—but this confrontation has been sitting off the horizon, like a freighter of a storm cloud, for years, though she has refused to look in that direction.

"Did he ever, ever acknowledge any kind of, even, gratitude for the stroke of fortune I was?" asks Dani. "Can I just ask that?"

Tommy wonders how much truth to tell. "If Morty felt he owed anybody, I think he saw Ivo as my gift to him."

"Yours?"

"I'm the one who let him draw you. I was your . . . watcher, I guess. Gatekeeper. Guardian. Whatever. But this is a pointless topic!" Once more, she takes in the chaos of her kitchen. As Dani would say, fuck it. "I should tell you, Dani, that I'm the one who couldn't forgive you, or thought I couldn't, for what happened last fall. When you were here. Morty would have let it go."

"Of course he would. That only proves he felt guilty. But I was an asshole. I'm sorry. I was desperate. More proof of pathetic. Look at me calling somebody else an embezzler, a thief."

"I don't think you'd have gone through with it—trying to sell the book. Which I don't think you could've done, by the way."

"Stupid as well as desperate."

"Dani! Listen! We both know you got the short end. With Mom and Dad—"

"They loved me; what do you mean?"

"Yes, but they worried about you from the start. In that self-fulfilling-prophecy kind of way. They loved you with all these warnings attached, about all the things you would and wouldn't be if you did or didn't do this or that. Behave. Do well in school. Practice your guitar. Stay away from the wrong crowd. They made your life look like an obstacle course. At least that's how I see it. Now; looking back."

Dani rotates his empty tumbler, tilts it sideways to watch a drop of red wine roll around the bottom. "I thought they were liberal. Loose. For parents. They let us be us."

"That's not really true, Dani. I think what they wanted was for us to be them. Whether they knew it or not."

"That's ludicrous, Toms."

It strikes Tommy that Dani must be thinking a great deal about their parents—because now he is one.

"You're a *father*," she says, and she means it in wonder. This is the first time they've seen each other since Joe was born. Dani is leaner, and he does look older.

He returns her stare, defiantly. "I hope I know that."

"Do you have some crazy notion," she says, "that when Mom and Dad had me, their lives were all pulled together?"

"No. But they were younger than we are."

"They didn't figure out how to support themselves till after I was born, even though they were in their thirties. They had to support themselves *because* I was born. They were still trying to make a life of performing, that bohemian coffeehouse life. Hand to mouth and proud of it. If Mom had believed in a god, it would have been Joan Baez. Boy did I ever tie them down."

"What difference does all this make?"

"You're getting there, is what I'm saying."

"Thanks for the condescension."

"Stop it, Dani. Stop protecting yourself with bitterness. I don't think you'd be with Jane, or have Joe, if you meant it."

The silence settles for long enough that Tommy hears a slow drip from the kitchen spigot, its faint repetitive plink on something metallic.

"Earlier," she says, "I was going to say that you got the short end from Morty, too. He was always kind to you—do you remember how much he enjoyed it when I brought you over to Twelfth Street, back when you were living with me half the time? He liked seeing you do your homework at his kitchen table. You remember when he showed you the drawings. When he told you about Ivo. He didn't have to, and I didn't ask him to. I wouldn't have dared. It was a burst of conscience . . . and then he didn't know where to take it. Whatever favor I might have imagined I did for him, he paid me back ten times over by making that job up for me out of thin air."

"I didn't know that."

"No one does. But then it turned out he needed someone. And there I was. He became grateful, and then he became dependent. No one likes being dependent. Not for so long anyway."

"Tell me about it," says Dani. "I owe way too much to Jane. She's kept her cool through all the shit. She's probably going to have to support us, if I can't get a job better than the one I have."

"What job?" she says.

"I'm a porter. Fancy word for janitor at a big-ass apartment building. I mop the halls. I do the garbage. How did I know about Lear dying? Tying up the newspapers, putting them out on the curb. I can't believe Jane hasn't left me."

"She won't do that. I know you think I don't know her, and I don't, not the way I should, but I can see this: she made room for you. Happily."

Dani is hunched over, looking at the surface of the table, his glass shoved aside.

"Like I have to make for Joe. I mean, want to."

"You already have."

Dani rises and walks to the sink. "Jesus, what a mess."

"Don't touch it. And don't think you're going back to the city tonight. Not unless I put the two of you on a train." She looks at her watch. On a Saturday, the last train into the city leaves in less than an hour.

"I can't stay."

"Yes, you can. Call Jane. She'll be fine. Merry probably wants to stay. I don't think I can tear her away from those drawings."

For once, Dani doesn't argue. "I told her about Ivo. Merry, I mean. That book . . . it's like a mythic thing to her—so she was kind of blown away, I think."

Before sharing the long, boozy meal with Merry—and, before that, the brief drama with Serge, the policeman, and the stalkers in search of the famous actor—Tommy would have been distressed to hear this. It would have been something Merry "had" on her; because without ever having discussed it, neither Morty nor Tommy had told anyone how they met. Or Tommy hadn't. And why would anyone ask? She was his employee; surely she'd answered an ad.

Now she wonders why. Interviewers must have asked Morty about the origin of that alluring boy—so different from the others that came before—yet by the time Tommy worked for him, he was beyond the first thunderclap of fame, the early acclaim for *Color-quake* itself. What was Morty's trademark line? *Ivo is the archetypal boy all grown men wish they had been . . . and wish they could be still.* But Ivo wasn't an archetype, not physically. He was, at his inception, a very particular boy.

Dani turns around. "But what's the big deal, right? It's not as if it *ought* to have made a difference to my life, right?"

"Practically, no."

"You know, I think about Joe and that book. What it will be like for me when he comes to it. In preschool, wherever."

"I wouldn't blame you for banning it."

"You know what's so weird?"

He smiles at her with an unaccustomed tenderness.

"The building where I work? It's right near that playground. I walk past it, and it's like looking in some kind of distorted mirror, only backward. . . . Wow. I really am wrecked," he says, sitting down.

"Call Jane," says Tommy. "I'll make up the guest room. Or wait." Where will she put Merry? "I'm going to put you in Morty's room," she says to Dani. "I'll give you sheets. Really—call Jane now. I am going upstairs, and I'll be back."

She hands him the kitchen phone. "Better connection out here than your cell. I'm going to watch you punch in the number."

In the dining room, Merry is bent down so close to the table that tendrils of her dark hair rest on one of the drawings.

She stands up quickly when she hears Tomasina enter. The last thing she needs is to annoy the woman who controls the fate of this unburied treasure—which, in Merry's state of inebriated overwhelm and geographic dislocation, feels like her very *own* fate.

"Will you please, will you please tell me where in the world they came from, I mean why a *bank* box, why wouldn't he have *shared* them? For God's sake. Not that I understand the man. Not anymore. I should want to rip these up."

"Merry, I don't know the whole story, but listen. You're staying here tonight. Nobody's driving, not even me. I could call a cab, but I don't know if you'd make the last train. There's a guest room upstairs."

"Thank you," says Merry, surprised by the emotion in her voice. "God, thank you. And could you please . . . could you promise that tomorrow we can *discuss* these drawings? Please."

Tomasina reassures her that they can—probably just to get rid of Merry, and why not?—and then says something about towels.

Merry follows her up to the second floor and another flight of stairs, this one dauntingly steep. "Yikes," she says, and she takes off her heels. Tomorrow, she is going to be mortified. And her head is going to feel like a kettledrum in a Russian symphony.

When they reach the attic room, Tomasina asks, "Should I lend you something to sleep in?"

"No, God no," says Merry. "Terrible things happen in fairy tales when you lend somebody your pj's. Enchantments and such. You sleep for a hundred years."

"Until the prince shows up."

"Can't rely on princes these days. They don't make princes like they used to."

"I'll leave the stair light on," Tommy says. As she retreats—careful to rely on the handrail herself—she wonders why she was so afraid to speak to this woman. She likes Merry, and she feels sad that Morty turned on her.

Merry sits on the bed. Except for the AC (and thank God for that), the room does make her feel as if she's tumbled into a fairy tale. The furnishings are old and dainty—egad, there's even a spinning wheel in one corner!—and the textiles are intricately colorful, kaleidoscopic with pattern . . . or maybe it's her mind that's gone kaleidoscopic. According to the brass clock on the bureau, it's nine o'clock. Is that all? She goes over to the clock and holds it up to her ear, to see if it's working. It hums like a bee.

Linus! She fumbles for her phone, in the pocket of her jacket. She texts the girl next door, who texts back instantly to say it would be awesome to keep him overnight. Maybe she should give Linus to the girl. . . . What a traitorous notion!

Her purse is still in the kitchen. She sighs. Never mind. She will lie down for a few minutes, and then she will go downstairs, use the bathroom, and retrieve her bag. She could use the bottle of water she packed, and she'll have her comb, so that in the morning, when she has to show her face again, at least her head will not resemble a vulture's nest.

Tommy returns to the kitchen. Glancing toward the den, she sees a seam of light along the bottom of the door. She stops to listen: nothing. Perhaps he's fallen asleep with the light on. There's no reason to feel she must outlast her so-called guest; what is the point when he's made himself so outrageously at home? But she smiles at the singular mayhem Nicholas Greene has brought to her life. The coming week will be a trial by fire, or perhaps by ice (an element more appropriate to legal matters).

Dani is washing dishes.

"I asked you not to," she says.

"Just want to do my share. Need to. Start the atonement before the guilt slams me tomorrow morning."

"Well, that's your share then. Done." She reaches around him and turns off the water. "How about a cup of tea? Something."

"Sure." He reaches for the kettle and clears a burner to put it on. She gets out the mugs and the tea bags.

"I was remembering that time I came out here when you had that big party."

"Which one?"

He laughs. "The only one I ever came to. One was enough. It was Soren's birthday. I'm sorry, but he was insufferable. I don't even know why I was invited. I shouldn't have said yes."

There had been half a dozen birthday parties for Soren. Like Morty, he liked it when friends remembered the occasion. Unlike Morty, he wanted everyone there.

"It was early on," says Dani. "He wasn't sick. Or maybe I just didn't know if he was. You were pretty tight-lipped about all that."

"I don't think Morty was ever totally comfortable with those blowouts," Tommy says. "I think he was just happy they made Soren happy."

Dani looks at her for a moment, squinting. "He's got to be a saint to you, no matter what, doesn't he? Like one of your hats was excuser-in-chief."

Today, she can't really argue with that, even if she bristles at the accusation.

"So at that party," says Dani, "I got to the point where I gave up struggling to make conversation—though I met a couple of cool people, I will say that. But I ended up mostly watching. Kind of spying on people right to their face. People didn't care. They were too drunk or too high, a lot of them. Not like I was Mr. Sobriety.

"So some dude, a guy you could tell was totally in awe of being around this Great Man, smoking this Great Man's pot, bingeing on cake with the Great Man's forks touching his teeth, I watched him hovering for an opportunity to approach His Greatness. And he sidles up, and he gushes—and of course apologizes for his gushing, like people always do—and says he's a portrait painter. I remember that because it was this little pop-up surprise, this hipster-looking dude doing something so . . . classic, stodgy. It made me sort of notice him more."

Tommy has no idea who this young artist might have been; she still has no fix on exactly which of the too-many parties Dani is describing.

"And the kid asks the Great Man about his drawing. He says something like 'Gosh, I just cannot *believe* how amazing you are at rendering, Mr. Lear. I mean there's like *nothing* you can't draw like a pro!'" Dani quotes the artist in a Tiny Tim falsetto.

"You are cruel," says Tommy.

"Okay, okay. The guy was just being a fan. Which is cool. But then he goes on to name some specific books, Lear's books. I hadn't even heard of a couple, and he asked if Lear used models, if he went out and sketched landscapes or did any kind of picture research at libraries, that kind of thing. So Lear goes, 'I haven't drawn from life since I was a child. I did so much drawing in school that I grew my own picture library here.'" Dani taps his forehead. "The kid was blown away by this, right? And I thought, You fucking liar. Like you can't even give credit to the world around you for posing the way you want it to?"

The water is ready. Tommy was about to pour it into their mugs, but she is mesmerized by her brother, by his emotion.

"Dani, that was just the easy answer. And you know, by then, he did most of the drawing automatically, from memory, from the experience in his hand. Sometimes he'd ask me to get him a book on horses or city architecture or he'd go out into the garden and sketch one of his favorite trees again, but he did carry a whole virtual suitcase, a warehouse of images inside his head by the time he died."

Dani throws his hands in the air. "There you go again!"

"There I go where?"

"Oh come on, Tommy. You're like a human moat."

She pours hot water into the mugs now, speaking to her brother while her back is nearly turned. "Dani, you're obsessed with this imaginary debt, as if you were some kind of . . . primitive from New Guinea who thinks a camera steals your soul, or like you had a magic lamp and Morty released the genie and took it home for himself."

"Yeah, well, he kind of did. Because"—Dani waits till she hands him his tea, so he can look her in the eye—"because you know what I realize? He stole you."

Like a miniature riptide, messages flow steadily, ominously, into the in-box when he turns on the phone—too many from Silas. But floating in the current is an e-mail from Deirdre, a welcome bit of driftwood. The subject line reads *I AM A NINNY.*

I cannot believe I cut you short just to run off for a massage. Your voice was far more therapeutic than any rubdown could ever be, even from Mr. Hunkadelic. And I was touched you'd turn to me about anything more than how to fold a cocktail napkin or pry the last olive out of the jar. I forgot to say two things. 1. Erice! At least pretend we have a standing date, someday, for that mother-son field trip we never got to take, thanks to Sam's draconian call sheets. He should've stayed on to run Italy itself. They'd be a superpower! 2. I think it's time you think about making a nest. I don't mean get married, and I don't mean buy a penthouse. (Do not ever buy a penthouse. Photographers have learned how to dangle from choppers.) It looks like I scared you off L-O-V-E when we spent all that crazy time together on that fucking cliff. So what do I mean? Maybe I mean toss an anchor overboard. You sound so *at *sea*. You are a smart boy. Smart MAN. You get my drift. (All this nautical metaphoring. OK! Basta!) Please call me any time you like. ANYTIME. In general, all the wrong people do. Good luck with your Andrew masterpiece. Because it will be. Count on it, bear cub. xoxD*

L-O-V-E. On the list of perks for which people envy and, in truth, despise lucky buggers like Nick, wouldn't that come first, ahead of mansions and yachts and grateful haberdashers and first-class travel with free-flowing Dom Perignon? The logical conclusion being that when you're beautiful and talented and loved by all, you will be loved by "any." *Anyone* will say yes; *anyone* will marry you, have your children, be yours to gaze at every morning, never leave your side. And conversely, if, like Deirdre, you suddenly disappoint the masses, then doesn't all that love simply vaporize, the way treasure won through deceit or larceny crumbles to rubble in a fairy tale? Or maybe love turns black and white, like Ivo's world in *Colorquake*.

It stuns him, the story about Tomasina's brother. Why wasn't it in that tome about Lear? Merry was the one who told him, in the dining room, after they left the kitchen to look, really look, at that miraculous trove of drawings.

Merry gave him the best laugh of this entire, farcical day when she shouted, after the four of them had returned from the front garden (where they had rushed from the house to witness Serge tackling the two lurkers with the cameras), "Oh my God you really *are* a fucking movie star!" Tomasina and her brother gazed at Merry as if she were a madwoman, but her shameless delight, her exuberance at the obvious, gave Nick a surge of joy, as if she had released him from some invisible truss.

"I suppose I am!" said Nick, as the two trespassers fled toward the road.

One of them actually had the nerve to ring the police, claiming that his shoulder had been sprained by a "thug." Thank heaven Tomasina knew the copper who showed up. The bloke had no sympathy for a pair of nosy wankers shoving their mugs against other people's windows. And it wasn't as if Serge had cracked somebody's skull. A bit of knocking about, message delivered. Tomasina said she couldn't wait to see the police log in the weekly paper.

After that, the meal they scrummed up became a rowdy affair—or maybe it's simply been a dog's age since Nick has felt so relaxed in the company of people he's only just met. They talked about the drawings first, though no bloody way would Nick have blurted out what he knows about where they came from. Tomasina gave him a severe look—a mild insult, but fair enough—when Merry said, "Did he keep them under a mattress or what?" They exhausted a wide and rather loopy range of speculations as to why Lear would have concealed the artifacts of the shadowy childhood he had so deliberately shared with the world.

Talk of children led to talk of Dani's new baby, which led them to talk of fathers. Nick's heart plummeted; this was precisely the sort of share-all he wanted to avoid, on this topic practically more than any other (except, perhaps, his anything-but-rosy love life). There was a wistful go-round about how sad it was that Dani and Tomasina's dad had missed meeting his grandson, his namesake, by just a couple of years.

"My dad was around for *too* long," said Merry. "He should've left my mother after she broke the news that one kid was plenty. That would be me." She toasted herself. "Dad wanted the big Catholic brood. He never said so—not to me—but he always looked too long at the families on the beach where that jolly kind of pandemonium reigns. The parents who have kids to create their own self-contained society."

"What an odd concept," said Nick.

"Oh, but it's a true phenomenon. At least in this country. Maybe not in England. I suppose if you have a lot of kids in England, it's to ensure the *lineage,*" she teased. "No lineage in my mongrel genes."

"Your mum," said Nick, "she was Catholic, too?"

"Oh no," said Merry. "She was a smart college girl who threw her lot in with the wrong guy far too soon. I've seen smart women throw their lot in with the wrong guy because they figure it's about to be too *late,* the sands of the hourglass are dwindling fast, but Mom simply fell for Dad's Latin charm. Even she admits it. The Ricardo

Montalbán factor, she says. And to give him credit, he thought her braininess was sexy. Or so he liked to say."

"Latin?" said Dani.

"Spanish. A wine importer. She met him while buying champagne at a liquor store for a pal's wedding shower. Adios, terra firma."

"But maybe she wanted 'just one' so she could work," said Tomasina.

"Or because you were perfect and quite enough," said Nick.

Merry shook her head. "The problem was, Mom studied art history in college. She needed graduate school to do what she had in mind."

"Don't tell me," said Dani, "she wanted to work in a museum."

"I'm afraid," Merry said, "that I kind of co-opted the life she had dreamed for herself. Except, in my case, no kid. But you know what? She doesn't mind it. She likes it when she can visit the city and we do the Old Masters tour. She loves the Frick."

"The Frick's brilliant," said Nick. Safe subject, art museums. "It must be everybody's favorite, don't you figure?" Disagreeable as it was to recall, Kendra was the one who first took him to the Frick, back when they were in the shimmery phase and everything they did together took on a sacred glow.

Tomasina laughed. "You said that yesterday, about peonies."

Was that only yesterday? Though he'd slept barely two hours the night before, he was wide awake as they sat in the kitchen, consuming a bewildering range of foodstuffs.

"My mother," said Merry, "gets weepy every time she sees that painting of Saint Francis. It's magnificent, obviously, but you know, I think she sees in it her lost opportunity to convert for my dad, be the good Catholic wife. Not that she'd say so."

"Which picture is that?" asked Nick.

"The huge Bellini." She pushed back her chair, stood, and struck a beatific pose, arms spread, palms out, eyes toward the ceiling. "The painting is a whole cosmos unto itself, every single leaf and flower and cloud a tiny masterpiece. Like the painter is pointing everywhere at once, telling you, *God created* this *and* this *and, dude, can you believe it, even* this!" She looked at Tomasina. "Do you remember the donkey?'

"I do. Morty *loved* that donkey."

"Now that you mention it," said Merry, "I have a feeling he's the one who brought it to my attention. Though we never saw it together."

Nick's focus shifted to Dani, who looked back and forth between the women not as if they were daft and snockered but with a cheerful, boyish wonder.

From fathers and art and donkeys, the conversation meandered to living in the city versus living in the country, to the difficulty of making a decent living in any creative or independent enterprise.

"Unless you're a *film stah*," Merry said in a dime-store British accent, smiling at Nick.

"I did have my decade of cadging and scrimping." He tried not to sound defensive.

"A whole decade," said Merry. "Poor you! So tell me this, star man. What was the craziest, most jackassed thing you ever did to get ahead?"

Nick stared at her for a moment. Not a single interviewer, over the months of campaigning for *Taormina*, had ever asked him a question like that. Along that circuit, there was an implicit code of courtesy, a no-fly zone. Even Deirdre's history of toppling off the wagon was clearly taboo.

"That's easy," he said. "Decide to spend the weekend here."

The others laughed, and someone uncorked another bottle of wine.

Then it started: the questions about his favorite roles, the perks he gets, the attention from strangers. He didn't mind their curiosity, though he was grateful nobody asked if he has a girlfriend. When they asked him about the Oscars (and he told them how tediously regimented the whole affair turns out to be), he was almost surprised that Merry didn't come up with something like "Whatever happened to that blonde on your arm, the one in that spectacular purple gown?" How well he remembered that gown, the complex fuss required to get it off Kendra's body after four hours of manic celebration.

Merry, he suspects, is a woman who works so hard at what she loves that she has forgotten to attend to other passions. But what does he know? And who is he to take a pitying stance toward someone who hasn't figured that bit out?

After reading Deirdre's note, he sets the phone aside to take off his shoes. Then he sits on the couch and, bracing himself, opens the first message from Si.

News from Andrew: Toby Feld may be off the project.

His second: *The kid is out of the picture. This is not good. Nobody blaming you, btw.*

Which means that surely somebody is.

He skips over other, less important senders en route to Si's next missive, sent an hour after the second: *See this, from Andrew.*

Forwarded is a message from the almighty pontiff: *Losing the boy was fortuitous. The animation will carry those scenes.*

"Fortuitous?" he hears himself utter. That's it?

Baffled, he opens Si's fourth and final communication: *Call me, would you please?*

Nick becomes aware of how stuffy the room is; all at once, he's unbearably hot. He also has tears in his eyes. Well, this sort of tension is the payback for stepping out of the stream for several hours.

He manages to wrench open both windows beside the chest of drawers. The third seems stuck fast. He yanks off his shirt, almost angrily.

This is absurd. He worked with the boy for a few hours, posed for a handful of pictures. Yet at the news that Toby's out, and then that there may be no replacement, he feels a creeping sort of . . . what, loneliness? As if Toby was a genuine ally. As if Nick failed to protect him.

He pulls the cushions off the couch, hauls out the bed frame. He retrieves the feather pillows from the chair on which he threw them that morning. He sits on the edge of the mattress, takes a deep breath, rings Si.

"There you are. I wondered if we'd lost you." Si's voice is kind, bemused.

"What's going on?" says Nick. "Enlighten me?"

"So Andrew had been thinking, before the snarl-up with Toby and his mother—God help that boy, never mind his career, of course what am I saying, he's *nine*. . . . Anyway, it turns out Andrew's been talking to the graphic team about dropping the live action with the boy, going with Sig on green screen, so that Lear himself is just Ivo, just the boy in the illustrations, during those scenes. This would bring you in sooner, take advantage of how young you can look. Use your voice for the boy as well."

"Did Andrew talk about my . . . our conversation?"

"What conversation?"

Nick hesitates. "Not to worry." Andrew has moved on, beyond Toby, beyond Lear's confessions. "Does this mean delays in the schedule?"

"No. In fact, Andrew wants you back in L.A. now, before Phoenix. He wants you back in the studio, with Sig this time. And Trish. Your decks are clear the next week or two, right?"

"I'd miss going home."

"Could you?"

I am a boat without a mooring, Nick thinks, though how maudlin is that? He must be channeling Deirdre's message: *Toss an anchor overboard.* "I could."

"Beautiful. I'll let him know."

"Si?"

"Nick."

"I'm going to bed now."

"It's nine-thirty. Keeping country hours?"

"I know what time it is, Si."

"I'll let you go."

"Please."

Nick lays the phone on the mattress beside him. He stares at it, as if it's a novel object, something he just found. In that small box reside just about all his relationships. A halfhearted breeze from the window brushes his back. He looks around and notices a portable fan beneath the spindly chair on which he tossed his shirt; somehow this reminds him of Mort Lear's laptop. He looks around anxiously before he remembers giving it over to Tomasina. So much for forwarding those e-mails—though Andrew's had enough of his natterings by now. Happenstance will keep him honest.

Just as he finds a place to plug in the fan, he hears the door open behind him.

"Oh God *sorry!* I thought you were the loo!"

"I've borne a number of insults in my life," says Nick, "but that's original."

Merry starts to retreat, but she hesitates.

"You're not made of glitter after all," she says.

Nick looks down briefly. He folds his arms across his bare chest. "Alas, just flesh and blood, skin and bone."

Still she stands there, in her skirt and blouse, bare-legged, her boisterous hair sprung free from the pins that tamed it earlier on.

"May I come in?" she asks in a girlish voice.

"Whyever not?" Nick means this sarcastically, but in fact, though he's knackered, he's not eager to be alone with his madly colliding thoughts and concerns.

She looks around for a place to sit. His clothes and two scripts occupy the only chairs. All of a sudden, she hikes up her skirt and sits on the floor, cross-legged. It's a funny, boyish act, as if they're mates settling in for a catch-up on football or who's snogging whom.

"I want to ask you something," she says, "while I have the nerve."

Oh God, what now? But he likes her, this blurty, broad-tempered woman. Charming, the way she's modest yet unbridled all at once.

Though he does not encourage her to go on, she says, "So this movie you're making. The one about Mort. I was thinking, because we hope to open the museum by the end of next year, the fall if we're lucky . . . and isn't that maybe when your movie might come out? Probably that's an insane question. But what if maybe, if I could coordinate with your producers, and you, you too, we could build a thing—listen to me, Jesus!—build a *special event* around the movie and have you talk about . . . you know. The movie. Being Lear. Inside him. Understanding him."

Nick sighs. "I'm not at all sure I understand him. Less and less,

I fear. . . . But I'd love to see your museum, and I could speak with Andrew, my director, about . . ."

Is she beginning to cry? Nick stares at her for a moment, puzzled. "Merry?"

"The truth is," she says, "I for one will *never* understand him. That man broke my heart and I owe him fucking nothing." She wipes her eyes with both hands. "I am so angry at him, most of all because I fell in love with him. Which is the stupidest thing of all. And seeing these crazy beautiful drawings he did when he was just an innocent little boy—it's sort of wrecking me. Because I want them. I feel like I would kill just to . . . Oh Christ."

"I'm so sorry," says Nick, the only thing to say.

"I am *such a fool.*" She is struggling to get to her feet. She makes it onto one foot and a knee, but her skirt is not cooperating.

Nick rises quickly and crosses the room to steady her before she keels over.

She grasps his bare arms with her hands.

"Oh God," she says as she stands back, straightening her skirt, "why are you so easy to talk to? Does everybody use you this way? I honestly didn't mean to barge in."

You must not fucking fall down, Merry instructs her woozy self. *Leave the room.*

But all she can manage is to brace herself against this man—who is almost shockingly slight in build. (Christ, she could knock him over!) She is looking straight at his freckled throat, the faint V where the sun has traced what must be the line of an open-throated shirt, such civilized attire. She can see the shadowed hollows behind his collarbones. As she regains her balance, he says, "Here. Just sit for a minute. You're wobbly."

She lets him lead her to the couch—except that it's a bed.

They sit at opposite corners of the opened mattress. When she looks at him, this time at his face, she senses that he shares her mirth. Not that he's laughing at her; more like he's—but there's no way he could be thinking what she's thinking. No earthly way.

She begins to laugh, quietly. "I'm having this insane fantasy that I'm going to . . ."

But Nick *is* thinking what she's thinking, and he knows it. He could tell himself how unwise it is, an impulse he should resist, but there's something exquisite in the way she now inclines her head toward her lap, her hair obscuring her face like some lush Edwardian hat. "This is silly," he hears her say to herself.

"You don't quite see it, do you?" Nick says. "How rather lovely you are. Strike the *rather.*" She *is* lovely. Or he is lonely. Good God, does it matter?

"You are mercifully soused, and so am I," she says, looking up and turning toward him.

"I'm not sure I bloody care." Now he's the one who's laughing, which gets her laughing again, and then he's actually leaning rather confoundedly far over in order to touch her irrepressible, irresistible hair and then pull it aside in order to kiss her.

She stops laughing. Her eyes shine, still teary, but she says, "If you don't, then I most certainly do not."

Sleep is a high shelf, just beyond reach, but for now Tommy doesn't mind. She lies in the dark listening to the sounds in Morty's room. Last night it was Nicholas Greene's sleuthing; tonight it's the muffled murmur of Dani talking on the phone to, she's certain, Jane. He laughs occasionally, is silent for brief spells. He is doing most of the talking, and from what she can tell, it's calm talk, idle talk, just-be-with-me talk. Tommy imagines he's trying to tell her about the day. Were Tommy telling someone, she would not know where to begin.

She has taken four aspirins and set her alarm for five o'clock to be certain she's the first one awake. Wondering if there will be further intruders, she also made sure to lock the doors and downstairs windows. Lieutenant Keane told her he'd keep an eye out. (Serge volunteered to stay, but Nick sent him back to the Chanticleer.)

She hopes everyone will leave first thing tomorrow—though now she recalls that Nick is staying till Monday. Well, fine, let him pursue his Goldilocks routine, so long as she doesn't have to entertain him. She has far too much to do, which she's known for days; only now she's ready to do it. She is almost so antsy to get on with it that she would go back downstairs and begin her lists, send Franklin an e-mail, tell him she wants a second, independent legal opinion on the liberties she can and cannot take with Morty's will—though who, really, would show up to contest her actions?

Amusing, the notion of her gaining any sense of control, harnessing this octopus Morty has left in her charge. Except that the tentacled creature to be tamed is Morty. It's Morty's beautiful, complicated, secretive, shadowy, selfish life—or the story his life will become. And now it's hers. Or does she, at least for the moment, share it with Nicholas Greene—like an unruly foster child thrust into their care by authorities unseen? She might as well have thrown off her clothes and jumped into bed with the actor, because it's as if they've engaged in an act of rough yet mutual intimacy—as if, through Morty, they will know each other better than they ever meant to.

Is this always what it's like at the end of any richly consequential life? Do the heirs always uncover inconvenient, even inconceivable, secrets? Is there always a shoe box of letters at the back of a closet, a cache of forbidden images deep in a drawer, a code to a lockbox the decedent didn't have time or mind to throw in a nearby river? These are not things people talk about freely—except perhaps in dense, thick, full-fathom-five biographies.

And yes, those inquiries have begun to trickle in through Angelica. But when it comes time to choose the worthiest supplicant, the knight permitted passage across the moat (Dani nailed it there), Tommy will no longer be the warden at the drawbridge. What she knows tonight—maybe the only thing she knows—is that the life Morty left to her, his, will not become hers. If he wants his artistic legacy *widely dispersed,* so be it. Though now that she has spent a few hours with Merry, she feels both callow and guilty. Merry loved Morty, that much is clear. Typical Morty, he met her halfway—and then he stepped back.

She could lie awake till dawn simply contemplating how much more, and how much less, she suddenly knows about the man from whom she had allowed herself to become, unwittingly, inseparable. How could it have taken her so long to wonder why, of those three heroic but deeply unfortunate children, Morty had killed off the girl?

Fourteen

I saw the police log. Paparazzi in Orne, world watch out!"

"The idiots in our yard were hardly worthy of such a glamorous word."

Tommy unlocks the studio; Franklin follows her in. Most of the surfaces are startlingly clear, the counters fully exposed for the first time since the day the final coat of varnish dried, their once-perfect finish now splattered with ink stains, nicked by blades, and graffitied with notes and reminders. The drafting table and workboards are equally bare, except for a scattering of tacks. All the boxes of documents from the file cabinets are now at Franklin's office, being parsed and pored over by a gang of freelance paralegals. Only the contents of the flat files and the bookcases remain undisturbed, awaiting whatever future Tommy determines they will have.

And the mahogany box on the sill. Tommy wonders if Franklin has guessed what it contains. She hasn't moved it yet, ostensibly because she has no idea what to do with Morty's so-called cremains—though there is a certain petty pleasure in thinking of the box as Morty himself, relegated to the role of mute, immobile witness to all the dismantling. *Be so very careful what you wish for,* she tells the box, silently, again.

Franklin runs an idle hand along a row of multiple identical books,

all by Morty. He kept his own books shelved by the dozen, in chrono-
logical order, beginning with the tiny, charming *Thank You, Thea. Stop
It, Seth. And Yes, Yolanda, PLEASE!*, ending with *Lear on Lear (Apologies to the King),* an exhibition catalog including an essay that was
sketched out by Morty and polished by Tommy.

"I think last weekend might go down as the most insane forty-
eight hours of my life, and that's nothing trivial," Tommy says. "The
last few nights, I've been sleeping nearly nine hours. I feel like I've
been drugged."

"The actor left on Monday?"

"Actually, he left Sunday. He left just after Dani and Merry. I was
almost sorry. You know what? He's sweet."

"Give him time."

Tommy never did get to interrogate Nicholas Greene about the
movie, the details of its narrative. She had meant to ask if he would
let her look over the script, which she had seen him toss on a chair in
the den the day he arrived. How much she agonized about that only
a few days ago; now, how little she cares.

"So." Franklin's back is to the picture window, its postcard view
of the house and the bright sky surrounding him; Tommy can't read
his expression. Yesterday she spent two hours with him in his office,
explaining what she hopes they can accomplish together—and how
she hopes to free herself, within a year if she can.

Now she claps her hands, just to break the portentous silence.
"Let's do this thing, shall we? I called the alarm company ten minutes
ago. And remind me to text them the code right after."

Franklin lifts the case off its shelf, high over Morty's main desk.
He places it in the center of the empty conference table where, after
a dry run with Tommy, Morty always presented a new book to his
agent, editor, and art director.

She produces the futuristic key and the card bearing the combi-
nation. The numbers on the tumbler are small, and her eyesight is
growing miserly. She borrows Franklin's reading glasses to unlock the
plexiglass box. Franklin removes the vessel. Once it's sitting in the
open, they both exhale audibly, a mixture of awe and relief—as if

it might have slumped into a pile of shards once released from its prison.

"Who gave it to him?" asks Franklin. "I still can't believe it was a gift."

"Before my time," says Tommy. "Sometimes I forget I haven't always been with Morty. I missed all the fuss when *Colorquake* came out. It must have included a lovestruck shipping tycoon. Or a cunning art thief. I asked him once, when he decided to have it alarmed."

"What did he say?"

"Something dismissive, like 'A profligate scoundrel. Another life. You wouldn't want to know.'" Tommy hears herself mimicking Morty as she's done for decades, even to his face. She imagines she'll be quoting him, reaching for the gruff voice of his last years, for the rest of her life. It's the voice he left her with.

Franklin peers into the narrow mouth of the vase. The body of the vessel is nearly a globe, eight or ten inches across at the middle, its neck a shallow collar. Using three fingers like pincers, he draws out a sheet of paper folded several times. As Tommy expected, though only based on Morty's say-so, here is the certificate of provenance, printed on letterhead from a gallery with addresses in Athens and Mykonos.

Tommy texts the designated code to the alarm company, then picks up the paper. She's reading the English translation typed below the original Greek when she looks up to see Franklin still peering into the vase.

He teases out a small envelope, the size that fits a personal check or a mannerly thank-you note. He hands it to Tommy, but he's still looking inside the vase. "Huh."

A second envelope emerges, a third.

All are addressed to Morty, here in Orne, all postmarked Tucson. The handwriting looks pained and skews downhill. The return address is a post-office box.

Tommy sets them aside and tells Franklin she'll look at them later. "I doubt they have anything to do with the pot."

Franklin looks at her skeptically but shrugs. "All yours."

The auctioneer is due in an hour. He will look at this object, first and foremost, but also at the Alice collection, a few pieces of early American furniture in the house, and then, because it suddenly occurred to Tommy (how obvious) that a market would emerge for Mortabilia, too, the whimsical necktie collection. She has Nicholas Greene to thank for bringing it to her attention.

Tomorrow, when only Tommy will be here—God, so she hopes—the broker will come. Tommy doesn't want Franklin to know, not yet, that she's thinking of selling the house, not that she can do it until the estate clears probate. He assumes she regards it as her home for the near future, if not indefinitely. A glance out the back of the studio toward the useless, accusatory pool reminds her that she regards it as neither.

Nick wakes to the repugnant sensation of his cheek mashed flat and numb against the cold, sticky window. He peels his face away from the plexi and rubs the nerve endings back to life. The landscape below is flat and obstinately brown, divided into rectangular plots like a counterpane made of worn-out tweeds. He's flown this route so many times by now that even without the tracking map on the seatback in front of him, he could place a hefty wager on their being two and a quarter hours short of L.A. The fellow beside him (well scrubbed, thank heaven; the state in which some people travel is hygienically hazardous!) leans close to his computer, mesmerized by muted gunplay in some film—more likely a television show. These days, films seem almost parenthetical.

"I envy you," the man says to Nick without taking his eyes off the screen. "You can actually sleep on a plane."

"Occupational necessity," he says, and then, "Oh God, did I snore?"

The man laughs, pulls out an earbud, and looks directly at Nick. "Wouldn't know. But can I ask you something?"

Nick smiles politely. "Quarters are too close for me to say no."

"Are you somebody important?"

"Hardly, mate."

"Three of the flight attendants joined forces to watch you for a few minutes while you were out. I gave them the evil eye and they backed off."

"I'm one of those people who's cursed to look like somebody else," Nick says. "Like your Uncle Mick or a bloke from the office."

The man gives him a smirk of disbelief. "You don't look like anybody I know."

Hoping to deflect attention from his face, Nick asks what the man is watching. It's a series Nick's heard of but hasn't seen. He lets his neighbor tell him all about why he can't afford to miss it. "And I'd watch anything with Derek Unwin. Even though I've read he's one of those creepy Scientologists." The man glances at the frozen image on his screen. He points to another actor, who looks like he's about to shoot Derek Unwin square in the face. "And *he's* supposedly bisexual. Jesus, you could not pay me to do what these guys do, I don't care if they can get any babe they want—or, I guess, any guy. No judgment, of course. To each his own."

"I hear you," says Nick. "Well, go right on back to it. I'll be sure to give the show a once-over when I'm home." If he's ever home again.

Nick now rates an airline escort whenever he boards a flight. Deliberately businesslike, the attendant sees him directly down the Jetway into first class, where he settles in a window seat close to, but never at, the front. Ironically, this special treatment makes him feel more conspicuous than ever, so he does not remove his shades or cap till the last passenger's on, then spends a few minutes pretending to be fascinated by the goings-on out the window, the hustling of baggage and forklifting of beverage-cart supplies. Invariably, however, someone will pass his row and stop to tell him they admire his work. In general, he doesn't mind, but today he's keen to give it a miss. He's grateful for a seatmate with tastes too masculine to have seen so much as a trailer for poncy *Taormina* or tune his telly to the networks recycling British fare.

Nick turns down the offer of a mimosa from a flight attendant who sees he's awake. He looks back out the window. In his seat pocket is a copy of the third book in Lear's *Inseparables* trilogy, *Remission*. He set it aside in the penultimate chapter, the one where Greta dies after absorbing all the fallout of the optic wave. She lies in her berth in the abandoned schooner that's served as a home for the three heroes and their dog since the first in a series of global and familial calamities, back in the initial book. Stinky and Boris are with her to the end, Moocho curled beside her.

Did Nick actually endure the cruel sorrows of this story when he was a teenager? This time around, he finds himself too sad to read further. Maybe he won't. Who in the world—with a heart—would kill off the *girl*? Is he some antediluvian sexist to think this a moral crime? Wouldn't you reasonably expect the girl to head off into the sunset with one of the boys who love her, requiring the sacrifice of the other, luckless lad? But Lear pulls the rug from under *that* reader. Maybe that's the point. Maybe, in the end, the one who makes the ultimate sacrifice is the most powerful one. Is there a perversely feminist message here?

The attendant is back. "Tomato juice? Coconut water?" She knows who he is—he can tell from the daft glint in her eyes—but her job forbids her from fawning.

"I am perfectly satisfied, thank you," he says, perhaps too curtly.

He should be relieved, not despondent. The last conversation with Merry, on his mobile in his hotel room last night, was a godsend. He'd had to drink two glasses of Malbec to dig up the courage to ring her.

"Beautiful man," she said, "you have nothing to worry about. From me, that is."

"It's not as if I think you'll be ringing the tabloids—"

"Don't insult me!" she said, but she sounded playful. "I'm talking about emotions, not publicity. I seduced you, pure and simple."

That wasn't accurate, and both of them knew it, but why should he object?

"I'm rather proud of myself," she added. "You're a feather in my cap. An ostrich plume. Hot pink with a dusting of glitter."

"Merry, you gave me a most unconventional night, which I needed rather badly." He felt desperate to be chivalrous (as if!) without lying or leading her astray.

"Everything is just fine between us," she said. "Though I still do hope we can strike a deal about the movie. If I blew *that* chance, I'll never forgive myself."

"You have my word. Or no, just yes, absolutely. I promise."

"So I'll see you again, Mr. Greene, and I vow discretion."

"I am grateful."

"Well, I shouldn't say this, but me, too. I'll say goodbye first, since that's the way to do things here, isn't it?"

"Merry."

"No, let me have the last word. A perfectly cheerful *goodbye.*"

And, however awkwardly, that was that.

What, of Lear, has he carried away with him as he makes his way west to begin the work in earnest? The feeling of sitting in that cupboard, contemplating the shoes, the hems of the jackets, the orphaned shirts, is the one that seems most vivid to him now. So oddly codgerish, the clothing ranked above him; what did any of it have to do with the character he would play? Is the stodgier version of Lear, the one he glimpsed inside that house, a kind of shell the man grew as he aged through various indignities and sorrows—or is it the core of the man that was revealed, unsheathed, by all those same ordeals?

Nick doesn't know the man he will play any better now than he did two weeks ago. Yet perhaps that leaves the way clearer; maybe the task at hand is one of invention more than translation. There is no escaping the fundamental loneliness of it, either.

Merry sobbed, but not entirely out of unhappiness, not even mostly, when she hung up her phone last night. Maybe *she* deserved the Oscar.

The sensation in her chest was both a seizing tightness and a blooming warmth, the feeling of having done something courageous, even if it wasn't wise.

Linus, who seemed to be acclimating to her tsunamic emotions of late, merely glanced at her from his favorite spot on the couch. He pretended to be watching Julianne Moore lose her grip on reality. Why had Merry opted for such a distressing movie, a movie about a woman on an irreversibly downward spiral? She turned it off. Linus gave her a brief look of annoyance. He jumped down from the couch and settled on the floor at the opposite side of the room.

Was it her imagination, or had Linus grown a bit haughty? (She almost felt as if she'd been unfaithful to her dog. Now *that* was a desperate state in which to be.)

But tonight he is once again her devoted companion, curled up at Merry's feet as she drafts a fantasy proposal for a special fundraiser combining an early screening of the Mort Lear movie with the unveiling of those fabulous rogue drawings from the bank box. Tommy says she certainly has control over when and where they will have their debut viewing; where they will end up, she's not so sure. It never hurts to prepare yourself for the best as well as the worst. But Merry is determined to mount an end run on Sol's sudden alliance with Stu. She mustn't alienate them, she must charm them. And wait until Enrico learns about the drawings. He is certainly the best man to doctor their minor afflictions; he'll want them as badly as she does.

Meredith Galarza fucked Nicholas Greene. This improbable yet accurate statement has been running riot through her head the past four days, like one of those LED headlines urgently chasing its tail in the middle of Times Square.

It held no promise of a future—how beyond obvious was that!— but it was fun. No, it was rapturous, at least in memory . . . which is the place where it has come to permanent rest. There was a fumbling tenderness to it, a lot of muffled laughter amid the fireworks. Since she's the girl, to say it spun no longings or attachment wouldn't be true, not for her. All kneecaps, elbows, and a rack of ribs, Nick wasn't the most comfortable lover—but he was passionate, and Christ almighty, was he ever *diligent*.

Merry feels both less and more lonely than she did before—and, of course, she longs to tell somebody other than Linus, who isn't impressed enough. Or maybe Linus adores her so much that he sees her as perfectly worthy of Sexiest Man Alive Number 7, according to the most recent list in *People*. (Maybe she can work her way up that list? Just think: she won't have to stoop to, as 7 might put it, boffing 8 or 9.)

She needs to de-obsess. And she needs to keep up the conversation with Tommy Daulair, who suddenly returns her every e-mail. By some stroke of fortune or accidental charm, not only did Merry get Nick Greene into the sack, but she got the loyal guardian of the duplicitous Mort Lear's estate to use the word *compromise*. "It will only happen after a lot of legal shoptalk, a lot of ifs," Tommy said as they parted on Sunday, "but I would like to see Ivo in New York, which is where he came from in the first place. As Dani told you."

Merry is forbidden, for the moment, to say anything to Sol or the other directors, but right now they are so head over heels with their flashy architect in his plush velveteen trousers and his exotically shaped eyewear that the contents of the museum itself are of less concern, even with Stu threatening a takeover. To be fair, Jonas Hecht was Merry's top choice. Her only objection to the man is that he doesn't seem capable of eye contact with women over the age of thirty. (Maybe glasses as expensive as the ones he wears render them invisible.)

"Linus," she says, "if only he *knew* how hot I secretly am."

Linus utters a noncommittal bark.

Merry's heart lunges at the sound of the phone. But of course the call is not from Number 7.

It's the real estate broker in Brooklyn. That she's calling after hours is probably good news, but it means Merry must shift gears from fantasy back to reality, from reaching for the stars (hey, sometimes they reach back) to settling for less. Surely she can find an affordable place to live where she can learn to feel she belongs.

As the broker lists the allegedly rare, definitely underpriced virtues of a condo she *must* drop everything to see *pronto*, Merry walks through her soon-to-be-former home until she is sitting on the end of her bed. Linus jumps up beside her.

When she disconnects from the call, she looks at the picture on the shelf and says, "Well, boy, new chapter." It's time to take her borrowed Ivo back to the museum, whether that's where he belongs or not.

Tommy's list grew incrementally shorter today. With a child's sense of satisfaction at earning praise for chores completed, she checks off these items:

Appraisals (Franklin)
Finalize memorial service (Angelica)
Talk to Tucson (Juanita)
Call Scott

After Sunday's memorial at the Met, where she will deliver a succinct introduction to eulogies by eight of Morty's closest friends and colleagues (none of them truly "close," but Tommy would be the last to dispute their delusions), she will stay overnight at a hotel and meet her old flame for breakfast near Washington Square. Scott will be in the city, visiting the daughter.

But she cannot think about Scott just yet.

She sits at the kitchen table, which seems to have become her command post. She realized today that, except for satellite trips to the studio, usually with Franklin, she lives between kitchen and bedroom, as if she's regressed to the days of her tiny apartment on Avenue A. Good practice for the future. The near future, she hopes.

Loose papers and folders fan out haphazardly from where she sits, but her focus is on the laptop Nicholas Greene unearthed in Morty's bedroom, open to the bewildering contents of the folder titled *Leonard*—and on the three letters Franklin pulled from the Greek vase.

What would she have made of these letters had Nick never shown her Morty's side of the correspondence? Would she simply have thrown them away?

The first of the letters from Tucson is dated September 23, 1999. It's written on a piece of workaday lined paper, which seems to keep the writer's unruly penmanship from yielding to the sloping habit shown in the address on the envelope:

Dear Mr. Lear,

I will go right to my point and then introduce myself although I think you will remember me. Are you the grownup Mordecai Levy who lived at Eagle Rest about 50 yrs ago? My father died resently, but about 5 yrs ago he figured out the famous author "Mort Lear" was you. He was exited and told me and my sister. He said he always knew you were a "tallented" kid. He kept "drawings" of yours that you did when you were little. That's when he was the gardener at Eagle Rest tho he left that job a long time ago. I would call them "nature drawings"—flowers and birds. Some are signed "Mord. Levy" and I guess this is how he knows you changed your name. Of course I remember you my own self, how we used to play our "games" the times you came home with dad. Do you remember the fort we made? Do you remember that one game we made up, I don't think you would forget it.

Anyway, our dad died resently as I said. He left us nothing really except his detts. It's sad to say but he wasn't a good father to us and caused us a lot of misery when we were little and then more resently when we had to take care of him because he lost his apartment. He was good at losing stuff, but he did not lose the "drawings" done by you. He said he always knew you would be famous. So he told me to sell them after he died because they might be worth a lot of money. I don't know how we are supposed to do that and wondered if you could tell me.

For a famous person, you are easy to find on the web, you know.

I hope you will answer. I remember you pretty well and think you will remember me too. Maybe not my sister, who was a baby in those days. I'll bet you come to Arizona sometimes and I would like to see you if you do. Do you?

Yours truly,
Reg

The second letter isn't dated, but the postmark is June of 2000, eight months after the bank transfer Morty made to pay for the drawings.

Mr. Lear:

I guess you figure it was all about money. The money helps, it's not nothing. But you go silent? I asked if you come out this way, you don't even answer.

It's all about the pictures I tell you I have and now you have. Which now I wonder if you paid their "true" value (figuring you of all people would know!) My father was messed up but he wasn't a bad man. He said you and your mom "disapeared" and it was a shock to people at the hotel. He thought you were our friend. People wondered if your mother was "running away" from something like a crime, dad didn't believe that.

I figure you won't answer this now that you got the pictures. You're famous now and don't have to pay attention to losers like me. I get it. But I remember "stuff" you might not. Just so you know.

Yours truly,
Reg

Again, the handwriting is arduously legible, as if each letter was traced, but with the writer's ill-accustomed hand. The third and last letter, undated and less legible, is written on a piece of blank, unlined paper.

You cannot just be rid of poeple, "Mr. Lear." People have feelings. They get hurt and then mad. Dad had some photos, you know, I found them after he died. I would never share them, but I've got them. Just so you know. I think they include somebody you know. I was nieve to think we could be friends. Well, OK, you're a "busy" guy. Famous people are always busy, aren't they. I'm curious. What comes first, Mr. Too Important, being busy or being famous? "Chicken and the egg" right? If you're so busy, maybe I could visit you there. My sister says we should leave you alone. She thinks you gave us plenty of money for your pictures. But she's nieve too is my guess.

Yours "Truly"
Reg

Reading back and forth between the computer and the paper letters, Tommy feels more sad than appalled. The jocularity in the note from Morty to Bruce, Franklin's predecessor, feels offensive when juxtaposed against the cold, impersonal tone Morty used with the creepy but probably harmless Reg.

"Morty, you owe me," she says as she drags the entire folder labeled *Leonard* (not, she notices, *Reginald*) to the computer's virtual trash can. She does the same with the folder containing Morty's correspondence with Nicholas Greene. Let the actor do what he likes with his own computer files, but for at least a few more days and weeks, Tommy will be completely if not unquestioningly loyal to her boss. That's how she thinks of him now, the way she thought of him at the very beginning: as her boss.

She is stiff from too much sitting, too much hunching over computer screens and balance sheets and price lists. She closes the laptop.

It's dark, even moonless, but she needs the air. Tommy takes the flashlight from beside the door.

She was twenty-nine when Morty bought the house. She remembers how impatient he was, as soon as he closed on the purchase, to drive her out from the city and show her.

"I'm going to walk you around the outside of the property first, just the way the broker did," he said. "The house is going to be great when I'm done with it, but this is about the landscape. I think I've always wanted a house in the woods. I just didn't know it. And wait till you see the funny little club house I'm turning into my studio. But the trees are the kind that take years, centuries, to grow. Money can't buy you a maple tree that was planted before the Civil War."

She follows the same journey now, the flashlight alerting her to the roots that meander searchingly away from the hornbeams, sycamores, oaks, and birches. The south side of the property is a long, sumptuous hedge of old white lilac bushes. Tommy and Morty took a pruning class together at the garden center, the spring after she moved in. Morty was confident that they could maintain these and the hundreds of other shrubs and small trees on their own; for the most part, they did. At the end of the lilacs, where the property line turns back toward the house, stands Tommy's favorite tree, the Stewartia. It's an understory tree, lorded over yet also mothered by a magnificent copper beech on the adjoining property. The flashlight confirms that its tiny camellialike blossoms will open soon; she'll see them one more time.

Not long after Tommy moved in, a new neighbor to that side contemplated taking down the beech. If Tommy hadn't seen the tree surgeon's truck pull in next door, they might not have known until it was too late. When she told Morty the news—"He was there to give them his bid; if they take it, the job happens tomorrow"—he dropped his work. That evening he delivered (to the neighbors they had yet to meet) a broadside titled "Humble Petition for Clemency From the Celestial Society of Arboreal Samaritans and Busybody Citizen Tree Huggers." It was covered with inked sketches of various trees and the "signatures" of individuals with names like Elmira Dutch, Leif E. Japonicus, Sumac Limbly, and Gnarleigh Spurgess Knott IV. They invented the names together, at the kitchen table, breathless with laughter. Morty tied it into a scroll with a green ribbon and delivered it with a bottle of champagne nested in a basket of fir fronds.

Here the tree still stands. Were it human, cognizant of how Morty saved its life, it would probably beg to deliver a eulogy at Sunday's gathering—and Tommy would have to say yes, since Morty trusted trees far more than he did people. "You know what a tree can and cannot give you," he said in one interview. "It's very straightforward that way. And I am not talking about that cruel Silverstein book, one of the only children's books I've ever thought ought to be banned."

The next swatch of the property was, when Tommy first saw it, a small meadow. It is now filled with the fruit trees they planted together. And looming over the return route toward the house are the biggest trees: two maples, an oak, and a colossal willow whose trailing fronds murmur like a waterfall whenever a wind kicks up. Out front, halfway between the house and the road, stands a katsura, the kind of tree that begs for a swing—or for a child to climb brazenly high into its boughs. In his books, Morty gave these trees a second life in which he fulfilled such anthropomorphic wishes.

But Tommy curtails her loop at the foot of the granddaddy maple, the one that imposes itself over the back of the house, the one whose branch Morty was trying to dislodge from the roof when he fell.

She shines the beam of the flashlight straight up. To her surprise, she can still see the raw, pale lozenge of inner tree where the limb broke off. Has it really been less than a month?

When she left the house that morning, Morty had just come downstairs, an hour later than usual. He blamed the champagne they had shared the night before. Tommy poured him a cup of coffee, then told him she wanted to get to the copy shop when it opened. "I'm going to be hogging the machines, as usual," she said. Angelica had asked to see the first of the finished full-color drawings for *Love Beneath a Watermelon Moon,* Morty's first original picture book in a couple of years. Most of it was still in early sketch form, and he had yet to finalize the text.

"Let's splurge on a color copier," said Morty. "One of our own."

"You mean, could I research color copiers and find out which one's the best and the most consumer-friendly—maybe the most eco-friendly too—and talk to the customer reps, and do all the footwork and phonework so *you* can splurge on it, right?"

"Tommy, you are so clever," he said, beaming. "I do not deserve you."

"No comment," she said, and she left him alone with his coffee.

As she drove off, she acknowledged yet again how tiresome the ritual was: her doing whatever task was required; his lavishing her with praise; his saying he didn't deserve her (or couldn't function without her). She, according to script, would agree. But if it was irritating, it was effortless, like the redundant avowals of ordinary love passed back and forth between spouses. She knew she would never leave this job, because at some point it had simply become a life, and who would opt to leave a life?

Exactly two weeks ago today, she waited for Nicholas Greene's first visit with such fearful, protective anxiety. The peonies were on the cusp of blooming; already, they are done. The short, fierce heat wave hastened their end.

She returns to the house, puts the flashlight in its place beside the kitchen door. She is about to go upstairs when she remembers something. Leaning over the table, she reopens the laptop. She clicks on the trash can, finds the menu she wants, clicks again.

Are you sure you want to permanently erase the items in the Trash? You cannot undo this action.

Erase, she instructs whatever invisible gnome runs the transfer station inside the computer. Morty told her they were called homunculi, the little people one likes to imagine inside the television set, the washing machine, the dashboard of the car—all the appliances that seem to have a mind of their own.

Morty was the clever one. That was no secret. But was it because of his cleverness that Tommy rarely minded his demands? It was invigorating to be indispensable to a man like Morty; at times it was a source of pride—even vanity. But equally vain was her notion that to meet his expectations would permit her to know him inside and out; to know, as the filmmakers believe they do, the inner Lear.

Does it matter that mysteries remain? Don't they always?

Fifteen

It's a school day, and the sprinklers are dry, but the playground is far more crowded than she expected, riotous with children and adults savoring with equal joy the lingering aftertaste of summer. She stops short just inside the gate, unsure which way to go, how to navigate the sea of toddlers, unsteady on their feet, careening around and then into one another, shrieking with glee. Two small boys are taking turns filling bright plastic buckets with water from the drinking fountain, then dousing each other. They are almost polite in this ritual; one fills while the other waits—and then they squeal and run.

Is he here yet? He might not even show up.

A stroller bumps into her calves from behind. "Excuse me, but this isn't the place to stand," an exasperated nanny tells her.

And then she sees a waving figure rise from a shaded bench beside the sandbox, beyond the dormant sprinklers and a trio of knee-high picnic tables. Though unidentifiable from here, the figure is definitely waving at Tommy. And, as usual, he arrived early.

No matter how many times she passes it, the playground will always look smaller than her memory insists, but now that she stands inside for the first time in ages, it feels weirdly vast. She cannot recall ever having been here with so many other children. She has overheard people complaining that too many families are staying in the city rather than moving out, that the schools cannot handle the enrollment, and that the sidewalks everywhere, even in the business districts, are gridlocked with baby carriages, scooters, and roving assemblies of teens. (Tommy has noticed, with amusement and alarm, how the teenagers seem to enjoy walking heedlessly backward while engaged in conversation or, alone, dancing to the music wired straight into their ears.) Her apartment overlooks the entrance to a private school, but it's a sublet, just a temporary foothold; she's too grateful to mind the shrill commotion that interrupts her concentration two or three times a day.

"I had no idea this place would be such a circus," Tommy says when she finally reaches him. She doesn't know if she should hug him; he doesn't offer the gesture. He sits down and pats the bench beside him.

"Oh, I like a good circus," he says. "And your directions were flawless." He removes his sunglasses but not the cap. Is he really a Yankees fan? Well, of course not.

A thin, studious-looking girl sits on his opposite side. She wears a flowered sundress and white, unscuffed sandals. She holds a book in her lap.

"May I present my niece, Fiona," he says. "Fiona, Ms. Daulair."

"Tommy. I'm just Tommy," she says, shaking the girl's hand.

"Are you going to talk?" Fiona says to her uncle.

"We are—but then I'll take you to the shops to meet your mum. Do you want to queue up for the swings?"

Fiona nods and hands her book to Nick. She heads toward the swings with an air of dignified purpose. (How is it that so many British children look like adults-in-training?)

"Thanks for being my cover." Tommy points at the sign declaring that only adults accompanied by children are permitted inside the playground.

"For you, Tomasina, anything." He smiles steadily at her, as if expecting something.

As she feared, Tommy has forgotten how to feel comfortable in this man's company. Once again, especially since the night of the screening, where she watched him navigate an avenue of frenzied photographers—"Nick!" "Nick!" "Look left, Nick!"—he is the actor, the star. (And what is she, now? No longer Morty's proxy or protector, she sometimes feels the way one does in dreams of being naked in public. The uniform was invisible, but it was hers.)

Knowing how painfully predictable it sounds, she says, "First, I just have to say, it really, really was amazing. And I cried so hard at the end."

"Thank you. If you mean it, really mean it, that matters to me more than a thousand critics' praise."

"And that's what you're getting. I went online—"

"Except for the sniping about pedophilia given 'cartoon treatment.'"

"That was absurd. That was one review."

"And there will be others. Of all stripes." He looks over at the swings to check on his niece. Suddenly he smiles up at the trees. "But here! It was here? The place of origin, the ground zero of *Colorquake.* Here?"

"I met Morty there." She points to a spot farther down the long line of benches on which they're seated, where a mother is nursing a baby beneath a tentlike blouse. "Though I'm sure they've replaced the benches. And we never had a sandbox this grand—or slides made out of this space-age rubbery stuff. We had an iron jungle gym, metal swings, a seesaw. Seesaws are a thing of the past. They're considered too dangerous now."

"How old were you then?" asks Nick.

"Twelve," she tells him.

She hears a small intake of breath, as if she's just given him a coveted password or made a confession. "Twelve?" he says. "Oh, twelve."

"A painful age," she says.

"Yes," he says. "But rather an extraordinary age. A crossroads."

Tommy isn't sure how to answer. Other than her meeting Morty—something she might no longer recall if she had never met him again—the few things she remembers from seventh grade are uniformly difficult to think about. She was trying so hard to forge a deliberate identity; in retrospect, her efforts did little more than isolate her from others. She wanted to be like no one else, and as a result, almost no one else found her easy to befriend.

They scan the playground in unison. Nick has replaced his sunglasses.

The movie opened on a blank field of white. Following a significant silence, there were sounds of scuffling, of objects being shifted on a table, and then, startling the audience by revealing the scale of the white field, a vast hand entered and filled the screen. The hand, freckled, knuckles darkened by ink, picked up a thick pencil and began to sketch, at first lightly, tentatively . . . then gradually committing itself to firm, true lines. It began to draw a boy's general form, then limbs, then face and hair. To draw Ivo.

The movie did not show or even suggest a model for Ivo; he emerged from that field of white like a traveler arriving from out of a dense fog. (Later that night, while undressing, Tommy would think of what Morty called the Mother Story: a stranger comes to town. "Goes all the way back to Eden. There's Adam, living his bucolic life. Enter Eve. Boy oh boy.")

Ivo was, in a way, the true star of the movie, at times upstaging the flesh-and-blood Nicholas Greene. Whether Nick had shared the story about the playground with his colleagues, Tommy isn't sure. She only knows how shocked she was to hear from him last month: a casual e-mail in which he wondered if, while he was in New York for the East Coast previews (and had she received her invitation?), she might find time to show him the place where she had met Lear. Why now? she had wondered. What would it contribute to work long finished?

"You know," he says, "I also wanted to see you because I never said a proper goodbye last year, thanked you the way I meant to . . . after that rather lunatic weekend. I behaved badly and then fled like a refugee. Your letting me in . . . your not giving me the boot when I . . ." He sighs loudly. "You were ridiculously gracious."

"You wrote me a very nice note. That was plenty," she says. It's true, however, that he left Orne with a haste that puzzled, even wounded,

Tommy. She had to assume that he was dodging the meddlesome fans who had literally come crashing through a hedge. (Two reporters from regional newspapers called Tommy that week to ask about the actor's visit.)

Now he's just looking at her—or she presumes he is. She wishes she could see his eyes.

"I know it's vanity, and pathetic of me to ask, but what do you think he'd have thought of the film? I mean *really* thought of it?"

For the past day and a half, Tommy has thought almost constantly about the movie—she knows she needs to see it again, alone, without the hoopla, without the fear that others might be watching her as she watches the screen—yet she hasn't thought much, at least not yet, about how Morty might have reacted. What Tommy doubts she will ever tell anyone is how stunned she was to witness how remote, almost irrelevant, she was to the story. Oh, she was there—played by one of those dime-a-dozen bland blond beauties, Hollywood's moths-to-the-flame—but her few lines were pallid, servantlike. She was almost always in the background, no more significant to the veerings of the plot than the absurdly funky furnishings with which the art director had filled the fictional house. (Someone had decided that real artists do not favor classic New England antiques.)

This—her virtual erasure from Morty's life on-screen—hurt her so deeply that she is not even sure she could put it into words. How silly and false she was to pretend that she genuinely hoped the screenwriter and director would demote her, push her to the sidelines. Equally shameful is the way in which this slight makes her feel as resentful toward Morty as she does toward the faceless creators of the movie. It's not his fault that Tommy was inconvenient to the story, once it was reduced to its thematic essence. Perhaps, it comes to her as she sits in this park, that is exactly how Dani felt in all the years after finding out how much he once mattered to Morty's story—yet ultimately didn't.

So what would Morty have thought? Only now does she stop to contemplate this question head-on. Remembering the way he behaved the night before he died, she has to imagine that vanity would have overruled any objections to the inaccuracies (some blatant), that he would have basked in the literal glow of the screen, its spotlight on his sufferings, his genius, and his perseverance more significant than the integrity or verisimilitude of the figure standing in that column of powerful radiance. How silly, yet again, that Tommy was the one who had worried about what such radiance might reveal as well as distort.

"Am I making you sad?" Nick says when she doesn't speak at once. "Forget my asking; it's nothing but my ego whining here."

"No, you should ask," Tommy says, perhaps harshly. She gazes around at the dozen or more children in the sandbox, all busy excavating worlds within their control.

"I know," she says to Nick, "that he would have been in raptures about the animation—I think I forgot to breathe when Ivo was being stalked by the panther—and the music . . . well, you know how beautiful it was. I'm still hearing passages in my head. Was that an oboe where . . ."

His smile seems to have tensed. None of this is what he wants to hear.

"But you," Tommy interrupts herself, "you would have made him feel—I mean your performance, which was just incredible, as everyone's saying—would have made him feel . . ." What can she say that she will mean, that isn't trivial? And then it comes to her. "Vindicated."

Nick leans away from her, against the bench. He glances at the swings, back at Tommy. "Vindicated?"

"You know—I think you of all people *do* know—that he felt wronged in so many ways. But at the same time, he knew he had no right to feel wronged. That all his good fortune was like one big admonition never to complain, never to admit feeling as alone as he did. He was trapped between solitude and celebrity."

She thinks of all the big parties thrown by and for Soren. In the movie, the art director gave them the fantastical, Dionysian feel of Fellini or Cocteau (one of them was even a costume party, which Morty would never have condoned), when, in reality, they felt more like gatherings of extremely privileged people trying on mildly bad behavior for fun—and eating too many deviled eggs. But the movie was art, glorying without excuse in its simplifications and necessary lies as a means to a particular, pointed truth. (Soren's movie demise—at the house, in a bedroom far larger than the one in which the actual Soren had slept, with a weeping Morty sketching his lover's face in death—had a revisionist nobility that might have gratified Morty; perhaps he would have come to regard it as gospel. Not that the two of them ever discussed Soren's physical death, that final night at the hospital.)

Morty, of all people, would have embraced all the fancification—especially because, at the end of the story told in the movie, Mort Lear is a figure whose ordeals have brought him not merely survival but wisdom, generosity, and joy. In the final scene, after his solitary scattering of Soren's ashes from a crumbling pier on the Hudson River (more wholesale invention), Nick-as-Morty returns home by taxi, train, and on foot, through falling leaves—Soren's fictional death occurring in the autumn, not a callow, colorless winter—to spy Ivo lurking in wait, high in the branches of a vast, vibrant tree, a twin to the granddaddy maple. Morty watches Ivo (no matter how supple, always a drawing, never a true boy) clamber down the trunk and then follows the phantom boy into his studio. He watches as Ivo brings to life—and to exquisite, almost supernatural color—all the figures, human and animal, depicted in the monochromatic sketches and drawings pinned on easels, stacked on tables, framed on walls—among them the boy from *Rumple Crumple Engine Foot;* the fox in the balloon; the inseparable, not-quite-invincible trio of Boris, Stinky, and Greta. Even the clay figures made by Morty's youngest fans come to life.

Nick gazes at Tommy, silently, through his dark lenses. Tommy remembers him as someone who talked almost relentlessly; has she offended him? She says, "Do you know what? I think seeing you become him, the Morty of years ago, when he was so much younger, I think it would have made him feel less alone—like bumping into a lost twin. I didn't even realize until after he died how essentially lonely he was."

"Thank you," Nick says after a moment. "Really, quite truly, thank you."

Another awkward silence settles in—especially difficult because it's hemmed in by so much ambient din and hectic, carefree play. Tommy reaches for the book that lies facedown in Nick's lap. "What's she reading, Fiona?"

"Oh, she's ripping her way rather precociously through Andersen's fairy tales. Broody, depressing stuff, if you ask me. Hans Christian didn't much *like* little girls, I suspect. I'm not even sure he liked *people*. Sometimes I think she's only pretending to read it. That, or she'll be growing some very thick skin!"

The jacket depicts an elaborately stylized, Rossetti-esque portrait of the Little Mermaid. *Nothing more tedious than a modern artist putting on Old Master airs:* Morty's sharp, often barbed observations still braid themselves into her own.

Tommy returns the book. "She's how old?"

"Barely six, if you can believe it."

"She's just falling in love with tragedy. A little early, but then she'll get it out of her system earlier, too."

As if having guessed she's under discussion, Fiona deftly halts her swing, gets off, beckons to the next child in line, and strides toward them. She sits next to Nick. "What time are we meeting Mum?"

"Half one," Nick says, sliding an arm around her shoulders. "Can you hold out a trice more?"

She nods and repossesses her book.

"I suppose," says Tommy, "you must be working on another movie by now." How, she wonders, will they bring this meeting to an end? Has she kept him too long?

"Oh no. I mean, eventually, yes; taxes must be paid! But for now, I'm all about the stage. All about sticking close to home—once I'm done with this tour. And talking of tragedy, I am all about comedy this go-round! I'm a rapscallion playboy whose ex-lovers collaborate on a surprise party for his fortieth. Pure farce. But genius. The play, I mean. At one point, I cross the stage—well, I enter and career about for a minute—*on my hands*. We'll see if I'm fit enough to do that night after night! My character's description includes 'nimble as a flea.' Did I ever fool those producers."

Fiona, overhearing, looks up from her fairy tale. "You can walk on your hands?"

"Oh, Fee, wait'll you see your old uncle. Except I've a hunch your mum's not going to let you see this play. Things get a little randy." He turns back to Tommy. "Best thing is, I wake up every day in my own damn bed. The mice are finally clearing off."

Tommy wonders if he wakes alone or with a lover. She feels a twinge of envious longing, though she's not sure if it's for someone to wake up with or for Nick's wide horizons. He's at that age when the most fortunate people cannot possibly appreciate how young they still are.

Fiona now merely fidgets with her book, opening and closing its cover.

"I think we'd best be clearing off ourselves," says Nick. He lays a hand on Tommy's knee—the hand that portrayed Morty's at the outset of the film. "Thank you."

Two women sitting in the sandbox with their children are peering repeatedly at him, turning their heads to and fro like birds.

"But!" he says as he stands and takes Fiona's hand. "I'll see you at the museum thing, right? I have to rush off after the screening, but I'll search you out before." He smiles winningly. She's sorry to be confronting a double reflection of her own face where she'd rather be looking into those indelible eyes.

"Yes. I'm taking Dani and his wife."

"Your brother," Nick says, probably uncertain.

"I'm off to have lunch with him now."

"You're so different, the two of you. Well, as siblings often are."

He begins to walk toward the gate, and Tommy tries to stay beside him. But they have to choose separate detours to avoid collision with oblivious children, small construction vehicles, and a zigzagging tri-cyclist. Tommy barely dodges a soccer ball kicked forcefully through the air by a boy who's really too old to be here. She shoots him a warning look. "Hey!" The boy startles. She retrieves the ball from under a bench and carries it over, hands it back. "Not a good idea," she says as gently as she can.

She catches up with Nick at the gate. He holds it open.

"I want you to know," he says once they're out on the sidewalk, "that it wouldn't have been the same at all, I wouldn't have been the Mort Lear I was, without your being so open to me. I wanted to tell you in person, Ms. Daulair."

"Mr. Greene," she says, "can you please stop thanking me?"

"I can, but I probably won't." He shakes her hand.

She laughs at the formality. If only to bring an end to the awkwardness, she raises her arm at the sight of an available taxi. "You want this one?" she asks.

"All yours," he says.

She meant to take the subway, but on a day like this one, October masquerading as August, it's hard to go underground and leave the sky behind. If she had time, she wouldn't mind the long walk. Speeding north, she passes the little bistro where she met Scott for breakfast the day of their reunion. Before moving into the city last fall, she had forgotten that's what it feels like to live here, how the streetscape itself is a horizontal stratification of memory, landmark by landmark, as meticulously contoured and detailed as a topographical map.

Just to hear Scott's voice for the first time had made her feel winded, as if, with a single blow, the words had been knocked out of her throat. So they had not lingered on the phone, merely deciding on where to meet for breakfast. In person, it was the opposite, words tumbling from Tommy, almost haphazardly, until it became clear that the space of a breakfast was far too small to contain the stories she had to tell. Scott had stories, too, but his letter had outlined his own modest saga.

They walked for hours. At one point, they crossed Central Park from west to east, which they did by keeping an eye on their orientation to the sun. Neither of them knew the paths, which seemed deliberately confusing, as if designed to foil your sense of direction, not deviously but mercifully, as if the park were urging you, *Listen! Life is not a mission. Get lost a little, will you?*

Telling Scott where she had been and what she had done all those years felt like the breaking of a spell. And to see him for the first time since college—his skin loosened, his forehead broader, his thinning brown hair brindled with gray—was to look at all those years in the flesh. (Hadn't he been taller, too?)

Had she offered up her story in a letter, or an e-mail, matching his, she wonders if it would have felt the same. Maybe she would have felt less embarrassed. She could tell, from his careful questions, that the choices she had made since college surprised him. By the end of that long afternoon, it was a relief to know that both of them were glad to be in touch, but it was also obvious that their attraction, the virginal chemistry they had shared, would always be a thing of the past. They parted knowing that they would see each other again, but Tommy sensed she wasn't the only one to recognize that the unspoken question bringing them back together had met with an answer that disappointed them yet could not be altered.

Since then, they have seen each other whenever Scott comes to town, and Tommy has met the law-student daughter; Scott has met Dani. They feel most comfortable when they share each other with family or friends. One of those friends is Merry. And now, because of Merry, Scott comes east more often.

Tommy opens the window to enjoy the passing rush of air, then sits back and closes her eyes. Enough of the landmarks. She reaches into her shoulder bag just to feel the costly softness of Nicholas Greene's orange cashmere scarf. She can't pretend she forgot to return it. She had a feeling she wouldn't.

Nick squeezes Fiona's hand and gives her his full attention. "Miss Fiona," he says, "do you know what I spied, just down that side street, before we arrived here?" He points across the avenue.

She looks up at him in her frightfully serious way.

"A pâtisserie," he says, drawing out the syllables. "Posh cakes of every kind. *Gâteaux*, as a matter of fact."

She brightens dramatically. "But we haven't had lunch."

"What I'm suggesting is pastries *for* lunch. Uncle's prerogative."

If she doesn't know the meaning of that word (she probably does!), she's not going to risk probing.

Inside the pastry shop, he leans down beside her and rolls the savory French words around in his mind as he surveys the options, each identified in affectionate calligraphy on a miniature porcelain signpost. *Mille-feuille, macaron, madeleine, dacquoise. Crème caramel, Reine de Saba, tarte Tatin, financier.*

"Let's each choose two," he says, "and smuggle a fifth for your ma."

He takes in Fiona's covetous wonder, her roving glance reflected in the glass beside his. Feeling hungry, greedy, and childish all at once, he wants to choose everything here, yet these emotions make him dreadfully homesick, too. He cannot wait to complete the appointed tasks of the week—and to get through the necessary mortification of seeing Meredith Galarza, though she's been nothing but completely professional in her e-mails—and then to get on that plane and return to what he hopes will be a stretch of time governed and shaped by the newly precious monotonies of hard work, home cooking, pints at the dim, familiar pub. Can he return to a life like that? Yes, he bloody can.

He is pleased that the clever lad he met on that visit to his old school has accepted an offer to be his backstage boy a few evenings a week—and the mum given her permission. (Her trust in Nick, and her pride in her son, gave him a mournful flash of the afternoon spent in the L.A. studio with Toby Feld and his Gorgon of a mother.) A note in the play's program will dedicate Nick's performance to Emmelina Godine, *whom I first saw on this very stage when I was just an ignorant sprog.*

He thinks of Tommy's remark about Lear: *trapped between solitude and celebrity.* He pictures a bright sandbar dividing a river. Like Lear, he knows he mustn't ever complain. Last week, when he moaned to Silas that sometimes he feels a bit like a chess piece, Si's retort was that Nick should remember he has the privileges of a knight, whether or not he ever becomes a king. Somewhat ironically, the role of Lear, however, is not the role that will lead to Nick's coronation. He can't say his heart wasn't in it: every fiber of his being was subsumed by the project, by Andrew's vertiginously high standards, and Nick lost half a stone by the time they wrapped in New York. Yet Andrew's decision, after contemplating Nick's insistence on some kind of fidelity to the facts as he knew them, was to let the balance tip toward the fanciful, so that the darkest passages of Lear's childhood were rendered by the animators, Nick and Sig and Jim all but enslaved to Ivo's charisma (and to that dervishy cat). In the end, you could almost say it was Ivo's film, not Nick's. Already, though the film has yet to go into wide release, Nick is seeing new editions of *Colorquake* proliferate in bookshop windows and even airport kiosks hawking protein bars, neck pillows, and noise-abating earphones.

If characters brought to life by crayons and brushwork could win awards, Ivo would hoover up the statuettes next spring. It was comical how, once Nick saw the finished film, he had a fiercely schizophrenic feeling toward Ivo. The boy—a being of pen and ink, not flesh and blood—seemed indeed to have stolen the limelight from all the live, human actors around him. It was hard not to see "him" as cheeky and insubordinate. Yet Nick also felt a tender possessiveness toward him, a sense of triumph and ownership, as if, through becoming Lear, Nick became Ivo—and, in turn, Ivo became Nick, became the twelve-year-old boy whose idle hours in a cramped flat led to his spying on a beautiful woman, then following her through the streets of London, and then, thanks to her kindness (or her longing for a lost son; did it matter?), finding the place where he belonged, a place that welcomed his fatherless, unsettled self, his longing to try on other lives.

His twin alliance with Ivo and Mordecai, Morty's earliest self, also compelled him to buy that trove of childhood drawings, though he did not want to own them. He wanted to send them to a home where they would be cherished. He owes Si, yet again, for making that happen.

He thinks of the final scene in the film, which ends in the place meant to emulate Lear's Connecticut home. And suddenly, reminded of Tomasina, Nick feels ashamed of himself. Just now, in the playground, did he ask her a single thing about herself, her life? Hungry to get as close to Lear's approval as he could, he hadn't. He had treated her, again, as if she were little more than a conduit, the bearer of a legacy whose luster Nick yearned to share. He pictured her living alone in that tranquil house with its fine old furnishings, tending her flowers and fruit trees. *Lo, the lettuce is legion.* How selfish he could be. He won't have time to make up for it at the museum; he must remember to write her a proper letter after he returns home, tell her how much her trust has meant to him.

Fiona is asking the man behind the counter about a brick of dense, glossy chocolate, probably a mousse cake. (What are the little purple things on top? Candied violets, the man tells her.) Nick marvels repeatedly at her earnest independence, and yet, strangely, it worries him.

He leans down one more time to finalize his own decision. He does love that mocha ganache filling the *genoise du jour* (imagine: a different sponge each day!). As he sees his face and Fiona's reflected side by side again, it's obvious: the worry over her independence is all about him. If he were the star of a book by Mort Lear, it would be called *The Boy Who Was Afraid of Ending Up Famous but Alone.*

Some girl, Deirdre wrote in a recent e-mail, replying to his mawkish natterings about a matchup gone awry, *will drink up your sweet sentimentality like a good old-fashioned bottle of Lambrusco. Any minute now, bear cub. Just you wait. Be sure to let me know I told you so.*

Deirdre herself has up and married again—her investment adviser, of all people. Along with the rest of the world, including the trash-trolling tabloids, Nick learned about it only after the fact. He has almost talked himself out of feeling wounded that she didn't confide in him—and out of feeling boorishly jealous. After he wrote her a bona fide pen-on-paper note of congratulations, she replied in an e-mail, *Steve is a fine upstanding Jewish intellectual: I wish his brain were contagious. What he sees in me, the gods only know (oh those giveth-and-taketh gods!). I love how he doesn't give a hoot about booze: might as well be mashed turnips. If anyone can keep me in my traces, he will. Books are his drug of choice. That is a direct quote!* Not a word about romantic love, but where did romance fit, as a destination, in a life with a road map as twisty as Deirdre's? Romance is a superhighway, an autobahn strewn heedlessly with breakdowns and wrecks.

There is a girl Nick plans to ask out when he returns to London, when he has a moment to catch his breath. In a queer way, she reminds him of Meredith Galarza: her humor blunt; her gestures wide; her laughter uninhibited, verging on brash. He has to be careful, however, because she is a friend of Annabelle's, and he's only just making headway with his siblings. The friend is earning an advanced degree in agricultural economics and has a passion for seed banking. Seed banking! Nick loves how literally down-to-earth it sounds.

And economics, the sense and sensibility of earning and spending, is something he could use in his life just now, having virtually emptied the till—his paycheck for the film—on that costly donation. But it seemed the just and fateful thing. And fate is a master to whom he owes a king's ransom at this particular moment.

"Box them all up, if you please," he says, a bit too loudly, to the man behind the pastry counter. "What do you say, Fiona, the red ribbon?"

She nods and says (so solemnly!), "Yes, we like the red. Thank you."

She keeps returning to the long wide hallway that leads into Ivo's Room, just so she can walk back and forth, yet again, along the cases displaying the drawings that she knows will attract the most attention. All the galleries on this floor, painted and primped and (in the nick of time) ready to go, are filled with the most glorious illustrations, objects, and books in her favorite realm of the museum's collection, but this hallway, painted a soaring blue, is her pride and joy. It matches the sky at the end of *Colorquake,* the sky once its color is fully restored. All thirty-two drawings—two parades of sixteen, one to either side of the hall—lie flat, pinned to runners of chocolate-colored acid-free linen. They are lit indirectly, the temperature in the cases constant.

At times, she is amused by the absurdity. Ranging from frustrated scrawlings to scrupulous renderings, ingenuous yet grandiose, they are just the drawings of a child, under ordinary circumstances to be praised by a parent, then tossed aside or clamped to the fridge (perhaps with feeble intentions to have them framed). Mordecai Levy was no more important than any other child on the planet when he made them, but the next half century turned him into an adult whose reputation, as if through some cunning trick of physics, could reach back in time to claim these sheets of paper as objects of esteem and value. Why Mort kept them hidden away is a mystery, or so Tommy says. For the moment, Merry doesn't care. Let some snoopy biographer tackle that one. (One such individual has already written her an earnest letter asking for permission to interview her and study her "Lear archive." Oh, all those letters. All that ultimately hollow flirtation.)

Sol came by this morning for a final inspection. The look of admiration in his eyes as he strolled through the galleries devoted to children's literature, a look he finally extended to Merry herself, was more gratifying than she might have guessed. She knows the museum is beautiful. Delphic prophet that she is (or that Sol claimed she was, however seamy his motives that particular night), she knows that by next month, when the final touches go on the educational center and they open the little café in the "skyroom," the cultural eggheads will have declared it a *sculptural triumph,* a *new urban landmark,* a *work of fanciful genius* (she loves dreaming up the clichéd epithets)—she knows all this as certainly as she's known anything in recent years—yet it seems she can never quite shake off the instinctive relief she feels when a male authority gives her the sign of professional approval. *And that's our work,* her new therapist would say.

She also knows that the speed of construction—a four-story building completed in less than two years, as promised—came at a rather scandalous price: perhaps not just in overtime wages but in barrels of Ritalin, rumored to be the architect's stimulant of choice. A few exterior eyesores remain (the strips of "lawn" flanking the pathway to the entrance are dirt with a greenish stubble; the steel railings on the roof-deck overlooking the canal have yet to be installed), but the board did not want to delay the opening until the weather turned unpleasant. Who would venture down from Carl Schurz Park to the banks of the Gowanus in a November sleet storm?

At her new desk—a long, slick blond surface made from sustainable bamboo—she tackles the increasingly challenging job of keeping her head above e-mail. This must be what it felt like at Cape Canaveral when NASA still sent rockets into space.

She scans the senders. Skip, skip, delete, flag for later, skip . . .

Shine Man.

The subject line reads *F # # #.*

Thanks to his genius grant, Stu has been in Antarctica for the past few months, "drawing the soul of apocalyptic winter." Like a fretful mother, Merry wrote him last week that she did not like how close his planned return was to the museum's opening. Everything else has fallen into place so well—especially the uncanny timing of the movie's release—that she ought to have known the gods had a mischievous surprise in store: a broken-down helicopter, the very one that would have delivered Stu to a ship, which would have delivered him to a small plane, then a large plane, returning him to New York with less than twenty-four hours to spare. There is simply no way he will be here by tomorrow night.

She takes a deep breath. Dozens of other celebrity authors will be here, though none of them rock stars like Shine. Well then, a movie star will have to do.

This thought directs her to the e-mail from Alpha Zed Productions. The subject line reads *Guest List: Final.* Her heart is a hammer. She knows Nicholas Greene is coming because it was part of the agreement she made with Zelinsky's studio, but what she's been left wondering (and the magazines at the grocery checkout have been no help whatsoever) is whether he might bring someone. Someone female.

The list comprises five names, each identified in parentheses:

Joy Navarro (producer)
Jacob Steichen (screenwriter)
Nicholas Greene (actor)
Jim Krivet (actor)
Gully Iverson (computer graphics expert)

After opening remarks—oh God, right this *minute* Merry should be on the phone finding a replacement for Stu—guests will be invited to the museum's amphitheater to view twenty minutes of clips from *The Inner Lear* and to ask questions of the actors and other panelists.

As of two months ago, all the drawings from *Colorquake* belong to the museum—as do drawings from a handful of earlier picture books. Tommy divided Morty's published artwork and manuscripts into three lots, each donated to a different museum, but the earliest drawings, the ones from the safe-deposit box, she put up for sale as a single block, to be auctioned online. Funds from the purchase would add to the seed money for the boys' home in Tucson.

Not since her longing for a baby had Merry wanted anything as badly as she wanted that collection of drawings. Thinking that surely the directors would agree that the purchase was essential, she arranged to make her case at the spring meeting. But when she stood before them, projecting the images, relaying the mystery of their concealment, she saw Sol quietly shaking his head. "You do realize," he said after the awkward pause following her overly breathless (and overly confident) presentation, "that we've squeezed all the blood we can from our core donors, just to meet the surplus costs of construction. I know you believe Lear is the linchpin of your collection, but I think we need to say no." Merry felt as if he had slapped her. She managed to admit, without arguing, that perhaps they shouldn't put all their eggs in one basket. She let herself cry in the cab she took home, but when she got there, she resisted drowning her mortification in drink. She took Linus for a long walk in Prospect Park, her consolation prize for moving to a smaller apartment (which did feature lustrous old floors, a working fireplace, and a boy downstairs who loved dogs).

Nonetheless, Merry intended to watch the auction online, even if she couldn't bid. And then, alarmingly, the auction was canceled. An anonymous party had offered a preemptive sum. Oh God, would the drawings go to Japan or Saudi Arabia, never to be seen again? That night, Merry hardly slept. The next day, at the museum, a courier delivered a letter to Merry from the auction house. The contents of the letter led to the ruination of her brand-new yellow suede pumps when she knocked a coffee cup off her desk. The drawings would come to her after all.

When she asked Sol if he could use his corporate-shenanigans know-how to unmask the anonymous donor, he gave her a disapproving look. "Gift horses," he said, "do not like root canals." And then, to her relief, he winked—a grandfatherly wink.

Merry is ashamed that one of the reasons she didn't invite Scott to the opening is that she is worried about how she'll behave around Nicholas Greene. It's true, as she told Scott, that she will be all business and no fun, with less than zero time for friends—least of all a new "boyfriend" with whom she has yet to devise a two-city balancing act. And she can't get too optimistic by flaunting him in front of her associates. Most important, however, she cannot risk even the minor breakdown she just might have the minute Nick walks in the door (or out).

There are so many questions she wishes she could ask Nick, all out-of-bounds. She can step forward after the screening and fawn over his performance; that's the limit. In fact, her job demands that she aim a question or two at the animation expert and the producer. How in the world did they bring *Colorquake* to life? Tell us about the science behind the magic!

But what she will be thinking about is another kind of magic: how, that one long night in that hot room on that miserly fold-out couch, his body felt so slick and silken, yet so angular and sharp (sweat pooling in the hollow at the base of his throat); how ticklish he was; how much they laughed. Several solitary months later, when she and Scott first went to bed together, the inevitable comparisons that flashed through Merry's mind—the readjusting, the surprises, the awkwardly different pleasures—were not with Benjamin, the man she had slept with for years (in the end with more purpose than passion) but with Nick.

Pay attention, she tells herself. Stop pining like a groupie.

Resisting the urge to tell him *I told you so,* she types a mollifying reply to Stu. As it's going out, up springs a message from Scott, asking her how the countdown is going, whether she's remembering to eat, whether she's able to sleep. She will phone him when she gets

home, even if it's not till midnight. He's usually up that late grad-
ing papers or tests, and he's kind about letting her vent when she's
anxious.

She kicks off her shoes and massages her toes. She eyes the much
more demanding stilettos, on a shelf, that she will put on, like Cin-
derella, before the circus begins. Already, her dress for tomorrow
night hangs on the hook behind her door.

In stocking feet, she wanders back into the gallery space, unable
to stay away from Mort's work—and from Mort. He is eminently
present, in the form of a five-foot-square photograph, his face many
times larger than life. Beneath it is a quote from the PBS documentary: *No, I do not qualify as a storyteller. A storyteller is a raconteur, a
Homeric bard, a performer. I can't even tell a decent joke. I think of myself
as a storymaker—a builder, a mason. Every choice my characters make is a
brick, every relationship a layer of mortar. The pictures I draw? Windows
and doors. If, when I'm all done, the lights go on and the roof doesn't leak, I'm
in luck. I'm home.*

Merry took the photograph. A few years ago, she put together a
group show for which she asked five author-illustrators to choose
a bygone role model. (Cleverly, perhaps too cleverly, Mort chose
Edward Lear.) In the photo, he is looking directly at Merry, smiling
that confiding smile, the one that always made her feel as if, in some
parallel life, they would certainly be lovers. She turns away from his
gaze before she can let it take her down.

"No, you don't," she says quietly, firmly. "Oh no you don't." She
returns to her office, reminding herself that everything she's made
here, this sublime oasis of books and art and stories suffused with
the wonder particular to children, she has made (she, too, is a *maker*)
despite Mort and his intentions. Even if there is no genuine consolation for his betrayal, she has won.

She promised to buy sandwiches on the way. Only now, almost there,
does she remember. The past few months, she has been so preoccupied with reading up on the legal ins and outs of artistic estates,
Franklin feeding her one article or case study after another, that it's

the everyday details, the easy ones, she tends to forget. Next week they will look for an office to rent: something small, but they agree it's got to have a good view. Probably, also, an expensive couch, probably from Milan. Aesthetics will matter to the clients they hope to attract. Until their enterprise takes off—the starship, Dani calls it—Franklin will commute between the city and his practice in Stamford. Tommy will visit galleries and publishers and theaters, advertising their counsel.

The road that cuts north into the park is inexplicably closed, and the driver turns east. Knowing that this will mean an expensive, byzantine detour, Tommy asks him to drop her at the Plaza.

She loves this entrance to the park. The path dips down into a horseshoe cleft containing a pond, then traces the contour of the water's reedy edge. Maybe it reminds her a little of Orne, its woodsy trails and pocket ponds, though she hasn't had a moment of remorse since selling the house—or not about giving up the house itself. To empty the studio was the only task that gave her pause. Removing the last vestiges of Morty's working presence felt like a far greater act of treason than taking the furniture out of the house. The buyer is an architect who plans to make her office in this space. Tommy envisions the surfaces monopolized by computers, scanners, and printers—after the woman has scrubbed away all the ink stains, absentminded notations (phone numbers penciled by Morty on doorframes), and the ubiquitous scorings, like ski tracks in snow, left by X-Acto knives. Or she'll simply gut the space, pry loose the counters, discard the fixtures, replace the drafty casement windows.

A friend of Morty's who works at the Met advised Tommy to sell the Greek vase to a museum in Athens whose curator had access to private money. *Fine,* Tommy said, and the friend made it happen. The money (an astonishing sum) went toward the growing fund for Ivo's House. *Perfect,* Tommy said. *Wow, yes!* she exclaimed when the auction house relayed the generous bid for the Arizona drawings, taking them off the block. She likes it now when the answers she gives are affirmative and plain. Sometimes she wills them to overrule the more complicated, querulous answers that would normally come to mind

(*But what if . . . Aren't you worried that . . . I'm not sure it's exactly ethical to . . .*).

Morty's correspondence and sketchbooks went to the library at Tempe, the university eager to claim him as an "indigenous son." After the auction of his Dickensiana and Wonderlandia, his ordinary books went, in dozens of shopping bags and cartons, to the Orne Public Library, which held a special sale to fund a new roof. As Franklin put it, Morty's estate scored major community goodwill and a big fat tax deduction.

But it is the gushing stream of royalties—more like a waterfall, a Niagara of revenue—that, on top of Morty's ample savings, will continue to fund the home he chose as the mark he wanted to leave on the world. And, as he expected, his gesture drew in other benefactors. Tommy can see herself attending the opening of Ivo's House, but beyond that, and beyond her gratitude for the sale of the Orne property, her dedicated inheritance, she will have stepped away from all things Mort Lear.

Despite his self-assurance, Morty underestimated what he was worth—literally and yet, Tommy thinks, perhaps on a human scale as well. Only after his memorial service, seeing all the tears, hearing all the memories, did Tommy remember how many younger writers and artists he had nurtured decades before. If he had withdrawn from those relationships, for that he could be forgiven. Maybe Shine wasn't the only talented young Turk who stirred in Morty the complex anguish of envy. Had he recognized in it the longing toward an earlier life of his own?

When all was said and done (and signed and notarized and taxed), it turned out that his stubborn, contrarian wishes could be fulfilled without selling off too much of his prime work. If he had wanted to see his own deification as an all-or-nothing proposition (he was Rembrandt or he was no one!), he hadn't left instructions tyrannical enough to see it through. Nor had he anticipated that Tommy would defy him—within the letter of the law. Did *widely disperse* mean divide a hundred ways or send to a few carefully chosen, mutually distant points on the map?

She follows the path that bends through the zoo. Even here,

Morty once held court, when he was asked to join a tongue-in-cheek advisory panel convened by *New York* magazine to offer suggestions on how to cure Gus, the resident polar bear briefly renowned for his neurotically obsessive swimming. The magazine had drafted an executive from Steiff, the company famous for its stuffed toys; a woman who designed organic baby footwear under the label Bearpaws; and a wrestler nicknamed Kodiak. To round it out, Morty's editor was asked to enlist a children's illustrator. After Tommy passed the phone to Morty, she heard him say to Rose, "I don't even draw bears. Have you noticed?"

But Soren insisted he accept. "It's all about the cute factor. And you are nothing if not cute." And wouldn't it make a great excuse to book a room at the Pierre, overlooking the zoo, for the night or two after Morty's media moment? Soren was still healthy then, still eager to scheme as much time in the city as Morty would tolerate.

So Soren went along in Tommy's place, saying he could handle the logistics. It wasn't a disaster—even Morty admitted that the piece in the magazine was charming—but when he returned home, he said to Tommy, "You would never have permitted those idiots to lock us up in the putrid penguin house for nearly an hour. Where was Soren? Barneys. Lunch at the frigging Stanhope."

When she passes under the archway with the clock, she sees that she is going to be late by nearly half an hour. She should have taken the subway. One rule of city physics she's learning all over again: the farther away your destination, the more likely it is that the subway will get you there faster.

Dani came to her, over the winter, to tell her about his idea. He might be able to get a grant from the park conservancy, but he needed a loan. His credit had been "cooked," as he put it, by his first business partner's devotion to drugs. He showed her his idea for the kiosk design, the estimate from the friend who had designed the racks for the shop. *Of course,* Tommy said, keeping her answers simple. Franklin helped him go through the licensing process and draw up contracts for two employees. *I'm so grateful,* she told Franklin, who let himself be taken out for dinner.

The kiosk is an electric tropical-butterfly blue, an umbrellalike contraption holding bicycles, large and small, suspended in rows above the ground. On top of the whirligig structure, a bright orange sign reads KICKSTAND, in smaller letters *Rent—Buy—Lessons.* From across the pond, it looks as if a tiny spacecraft has landed off to the left of the Wonderland statue. The first time Tommy saw it, she imagined the *Times* headline: "Alice Abducted by Aliens." The *Post*: "From Rabbit Hole to Black Hole."

As she hurries along the rim of the pond, she sees three parent-child couples waiting for their turn, circling the kiosk, inspecting the colorful choices. But the young man helping them isn't Dani. He's too short.

Has she made a mistake? Today's not the day or, worse, she's supposed to be downtown in that park on the Hudson, at the other Kickstand.

But no—there he is, sitting on the edge of the bronze mushroom, backed by Alice and her cohorts, face tilted up to the sun. Tommy stands immediately in front of him, nearly touching his knees, before he opens his eyes. "Hello," he says, smiling, unstartled. "Hello there, Sis."

"Sorry I'm late."

Dani extends one leg to prod Tommy's hip with the toe of a sneaker. "But you come with a feast . . . yes?" He eyes her bag.

"I forgot the sandwiches. I'm sorry. Maybe a hot dog?"

"Do I have a choice?"

"Sorry."

"I get the bigger half," he says.

"Dani, I'll buy you your own. Two of your own. With a pretzel. A Dove bar. Have you lost weight?"

"More like two or three years of my life." He slides off the mushroom. She waits while he speaks with the boy in the blue apron. Still stirred by the anxious thrill of her rendezvous with Nick, she isn't in the mood for meeting anyone new.

She lets her brother lead the way. Around the first bend in the path he chooses, they see a cart. While Tommy negotiates food, Dani checks his phone. "Jane says hi."

"Hi to Jane."

"Joe is giving her a workout. Did you know a bookcase can double as a ladder?" He puts his phone away to take his food. "Visions of backyards dance in our heads."

They sit on a bench beside the path.

Dani eats quickly, licking mustard from his fingers. Tommy eats slowly; she has yet to finish her single hot dog when he's already done with two.

"Man, did that hit the spot," he says.

She listens to him talk about Joe's latest words and physical feats, Joe's new sitter, Jane's job at the clinic. The only complaint they have about their new neighborhood is that it lacks a good playground or decent grocery store. He wakes from dreams featuring the joyful discovery of lawns and ponds where, in real urban life, acres of deserted railyards await purchase by some deep-pockets developer.

"Are you saying you're headed to Connecticut now that I'm back here?"

"God, no. But now I *get* Connecticut. Conformicut. Predictable, right? Change of subject required. . . . So Franklin. *Franklin.* How is Fraaaanklin?"

"Franklin and I are partners. We are business partners."

"He's a good catch. For an old maid like you."

"That isn't funny."

"Come on, Toms. Loosen up."

"Or it is, but not always. Not today."

"What's up today?"

"Nothing. The Indian-summer blues."

"Please don't start making up a song. Please."

"Oh God. Last week, dealing with more paperwork, ⎍ the one he wrote when they were audited. 'Tasmania, ⎍

"Stop right there. What's scary is that I remember ⎍ those songs. So do not get me started." Dani stands ⎍ in my truck? I have to go downtown. I'll drop you ⎍

"Sure."

Heading back east, they walk without speak⎍ the avenue.

"Dani, can I ask you something?"

"If I say no, will that stop you?"

They wait at a crosswalk. "Dani, do you ever think of visiting Mom and Dad? Where they're buried?"

"I don't know."

"What do you mean? You don't know if you ever think of it?"

The light changes; it offers up that newfangled countdown for crossing. Modern life, at least in the city, seems designed to minimize suspense.

For an instant, Tommy has the impulse to reach for her brother's hand. He spares her this embarrassment by stepping off the curb ahead of her. Glancing back, he answers, "No, smart-ass. What I mean is that I feel like I should, but I don't know what I'd do when I got there. Lay down flowers? Sit on the grass and contemplate their lives? Like that? They didn't bring us up to believe they'd be hovering around in some kind of limbo, waiting for us to join them."

"Let's just go. Sometime."

"Time is what I don't have much of these days. Which is okay!" he exclaims joyfully. "I am not complaining. I am done with complaining." He sees her look. "Well, for now. So I'm not saying no, but it's not happening tomorrow. But sure. Let's do it sometime. Just us."

"That's all I wondered."

As they walk north, the broad Fifth Avenue sidewalk takes them past awning after awning, designed to keep the sun and snow off the rich tenants' heads. Uniformed doormen idle attentively at their posts; it's funny to imagine these men, many of them portly or older, one of them armed, as effective guards against any sort of intrusion assault.

She can't help remembering Dani's stinging remark that she had n Lear's "human moat." But unlike these doormen, Tommy shared life of the man she stood guard for. She was a companion.

much in her life is still so unfamiliar that sometimes she mis- fear or uncertainty for regret. Not that she can pretend she has grets.

took the buyer for a final walk-through of the house in ber, just before Christmas. All the furniture was gone, but

across the wooden floors, dark, well-defined imprints remained of every bookcase and rug; every picture had left its mark on the walls. Had Tommy not spent so much time and care finding the right new place for each and every thing out in the wider world, she might have seen their phantom shapes as a collective scold.

She watched the woman's eyes scan the empty rooms with a triumphant hunger, the child's rapacious *Mine, all mine.* Even this did not give Tommy pause. But when they climbed to the second floor and the architect's gaze (and it *was* an architect's gaze) traveled in an arc, once, twice, and more from end to end of the long hallway, Tommy knew that she ought to have let the broker she used for the contract act as the buyer's escort on this final inspection. They stood where the telephone table once lived, at the single window lighting this in-between space. Its view is the one Tommy faced on countless occasions while receiving momentous news of one kind or another: news of another award, of an illness or a death, of an elite invitation; even, from her father, a song or two. As Tommy took in that view for the last time, the woman said, "I am totally going to respect the bones of this great old house, but I was thinking that up here—"

"Wait," Tommy said, her heart in a minor panic. "You know, I think let's leave it there. I'm glad you love the house the way we—the way I did. But the changes you make are . . . they're yours."

The woman looked puzzled; Tommy's expression was probably unkind. "Really, I'm glad you're the one who's moving in," she said. They lingered in the hall for a few seconds and then, in awkward silence, went downstairs. Only after driving away, as she merged onto the parkway pointing toward the city, did it occur to Tommy that perhaps the woman's passion was a ruse; perhaps she would hollow out and "upgrade" the house till it was unrecognizably symmetrical and spacious, and then she would sell it for twice the price.

Tommy nearly drove onto the shoulder when another thought struck her: the woman could probably sell off the back half of the property; there is enough land for a second house, a "buildable lot," as the broker put it. To imagine the orchard leveled is painful enough, but what's worse, the orchard is where, after much agonizing, she laid

Morty to rest, burying the box of his ashes side by side with the box containing his mother's. Tommy asked Franklin to be her witness; she had already dug the hole. "Is this cruel or weird?" she asked him.

"Maybe weird," he said. "Probably illegal. But Morty was pathological about not expressing his final wishes—about the fate of his body. I asked him, obviously. He was sure that making that decision would hasten his end."

Late at night, she can tunnel herself into a state of thinking that all her actions in the past year have been aimed, unconsciously, at punishing Morty. Franklin assures her that the choices she's made have been fundamentally faithful to Morty's desires. But she cannot ignore that *fundamentally,* even granting that hair-splitting modifiers are a lawyer's stock in trade.

More than once, Soren has appeared in her dreams. He doesn't speak; all he has to do is level at her his most disdainful look and she is suffused with guilt. Never Morty; always Soren. As if he's a proxy for Morty—for Morty's darker, less reasonable side. Waking recently from one of these visitations, she found herself reliving the evening on which Morty received the call from Soren's father. It hadn't been hard, once Soren was no longer there to object, for Morty to use his social security number to unearth Soren's hometown, his parents' address and telephone number. After much vacillation—was there a "proper" way to tell parents their child has died?—he decided to write them a letter with the sad news. Soren's father called a few days later.

Tommy left the kitchen after handing Morty the phone, but she went no farther than the living room. So she knew that Morty hardly spoke, uttering only a few monosyllabic responses to the man on the other end of the line, and that it lasted no more than five minutes.

Morty came into the living room and stared at her, his expression blank. "That was brutal."

He sat at the opposite end of the couch and addressed the fireplace. "He thanked me for seeing their son out of this world, but they fear for his soul in the next one. They will pray for him, and so will their congregation—and they hope I will, too! Christ. Then that son of a bitch asked if I needed money for 'burial expenses.' I said I'd had his son cremated, and then came this . . . black pit of silence. So I asked if they wanted me to send . . ." Tommy watched Morty struggle not to break. She just waited. " 'No, thank you,' he said. That's all he said, that S.O.B. *No, thank you.* Jesus. Soren wasn't exaggerating. For once." That's when Morty cried, finally really cried. And Tommy did no more than put a hand on his knee as they sat near each other on the couch. She was, in that moment, no more effectual than one of these overweight, brass-buttoned doormen, a functionary.

Hadn't Tommy been, essentially, as coldhearted toward Soren as that father was? It didn't matter what she had done, how much she had "helped" while he was dying. If she had been so irreplaceably devoted to Morty, she ought to have been loving to Soren, especially at the end. Did she need to believe that she was the only one who loved Morty enough to deserve his love in return?

But that's the netherland of night distorting what she knows by day, which is that she is back in the middle of life, the roiling, muddled middle, and it's hers. *Mine, all mine.* She is grateful to Morty for leaving her all that he did, and she will think of him every day from now on, that much is certain, but none of what she embodies or owns or watches over is his anymore. Not even his secrets.

Six months ago, when she flew to Arizona to meet with the woman who would oversee the creation of Ivo's House, Tommy carried with her, in a pocket of her purse, Reginald's street address. After lunch and a long afternoon with Juanita and her colleagues—including the contractor who would convert an old rope factory into a rec center and bunkhouse, the social worker who would design the programs, even the grad student from Tempe hired to write grant proposals—Tommy climbed into her rental car and punched the address into the GPS. It was her third and final day in this unfamiliar city, and still it surprised her that a place could be so warm yet fall beneath the blanket of such a dark night so early in the evening. And the Christmas decorations—poinsettias and pine wreaths against the dusty pink adobe walls—still made her laugh.

So the sky was a vivid striation of coral and cobalt when she pulled up across from the ranch house. A compact mouse-colored car was parked in the driveway. Enough light remained that she could see how the stucco hide of the house was cracking and crumbling, the ground out front little more than bare dirt. Blunt-roofed and low, this house and its nearly identical neighbors all looked as if they were struggling against an unseen force from above, a great invisible hand attempting to bully them down into their arid, colorless yards.

Through several windows along the street, lights were coming on. Tommy saw Christmas trees, no different from those she would see through the windows of Orne or Manhattan.

The tree in Reginald's house was aglow. If someone comes into that room, she told herself, I will go up to the door.

She stared so hard that her eyes began to water. Lights strung along the eaves of two other houses blinked on as she waited. Five minutes went by, and then someone—was it a man or a woman?—entered the front room. His or her back to the window, the person stopped to face the tree for a moment, perhaps admiring its ritual glitter.

Tommy got as far as opening her door. But what was the point of this meeting? Was there anything she needed to know? And what good could possibly come of it? She did not have to reread those letters to know that she would be reopening a wound for the man who might or might not be the person standing in front of that tree. She did not need to learn one more unpleasant thing about the life Morty had buried for so long and then, seemingly on impulse, revealed in such a public way. But now she knows why he did: because the time had come to take control of that past, to write and illustrate the story as he wanted it to appear before the world—because if he didn't, someone else might. Morty was always one step ahead of the people around him, even when they didn't know it. He was never going to be duped again, not by fate, not by family, not by lovers or friends or caretakers. Was there anyone he ever really trusted?

At Seventy-ninth Street, Dani cocks his head to the right. "We're thisaway," he says, using his dad voice, and now he's the one to reach back for her hand, whether he means to or not. Tommy takes it as they veer east. After crossing Madison, they stop, in unison.

It's impossible to miss, the poster framed behind glass on the wall of the bus shelter: Nicholas Greene's profile sharp against a cerulean sky, his bronzed hair swept back, tangling with the vines and foliage and fanciful flowers of Morty's imaginary jungle, which looms mysteriously, alluringly, behind him. Out of the trees, straight toward the viewer, bounds Ivo, as if he's escaping the confines of the actor's brain, about to burst through the glass and career down the street toward the park. The poster is so large that Ivo is nearly the size of an actual boy.

Tommy saw a smaller version of this poster at the screening, but to see it like this, out in the bustling world, in broad daylight, comes as a shock. The reflections on its glass face—passing taxis, a jogger with a dog, the splintered dazzle of sunlight—create the illusion of movement, the possibility that art will burst out into life. She isn't sure if Dani has seen it anywhere. She is reminded of the day, long ago, when she was returning home from school and first saw *Colorquake,* copy after copy filling the bookstore window.

"Look," Dani says. "It's your other boyfriend."

"Right," says Tommy. "Not even in my dreams."

"And me, there's me. Famous all over again." Before Tommy has time to deflect whatever bitter remark might come next, he says, "Secretly famous. Which is the best kind of famous, believe me." Releasing her hand, he launches into a series of Ivo-inspired leaps. Half a block away, he halts and pivots to face her. "Hey, slowpoke. I don't have all the time in the world. Do you?"

"I do not." Tommy's left hand burrows into her bag, just to touch the actor's delicious scarf. Then she turns away from the poster and catches up with her brother. The sun is so high overhead that their hastening figures cast but the shortest of shadows.

Acknowledgments

I begin, as always, by wondering what I would ever do without Gail Hochman and Deb Garrison. They have steered me through the publication of every book I've written so far and cheered me on through all the months and years between. The generous and insightful Marianne Merola, Michiko Clark, Altie Karper, Maria Massey, and Kristen Bearse have been loyal allies, too. And this time around, I am equally indebted to David Ebershoff, an essential reader—wise and kind and funny—at the stage when I felt as if I could no longer see straight.

Thank you to the members of the Stonington Village Improvement Association, who take such tender loving care of the James Merrill House and welcome writers to live and work in its uniquely inspiring rooms. I wrote a hundred pages of this novel during the exquisite October I spent there as a solo resident. I don't believe in ghosts, but I am nonetheless grateful to the poet and his companion, David Jackson, whose passions and idiosyncratic tastes linger among the furnishings and books in that colorful sanctuary.

Thank you also, yet again, to Will Conroy, whose history of the Arizona Inn sparked a key subplot of this novel—with apologies for any shadows my wholly fictional characters may cast on that glorious refuge and the integrity of its staff.

So many friends give me encouragement, advice, and the occasional necessary scold each time I wrestle with a new story. Dear

Kate Howe, Mark Danielewski, Loraine Despres, Carleton Eastlake, Tobin Anderson, Laura Mathews, Charlie Clark, Gregory Maguire, Barney Karpfinger, Mary Stuart Masterson, Jeremy Greenberg, Cheryl Tan, Wilson Kidde, Maria Mileaf, Elene Catrakilis, and Patty Woo: In different ways, each of you enriched this book. At home, where the love of my family is the oxygen of my working life, I thank Dennis for, among countless other things, catching my clam-sauce gaffe. I thank Alec and Oliver (and Lucy White!) for making me pay far too much attention to the Oscars—or, rather, to the actors and films they elevate.

Gayle Grader, you too. You gave me the best mantra any writer (or anybody at all) could wish for: Amaze yourself.

In June 1989, Paul McLeod, a newspaper publisher and recent widower, travels to Greece, where he falls for a young American artist and reflects on the complicated truth about his marriage. Six years later, again in June, Paul's death draws his three grown sons and their families back to their ancestral home. Fenno, the eldest, a wry, introspective gay man, narrates the events of this unforeseen reunion. Far from his straitlaced expatriate life as a bookseller in Greenwich Village, Fenno is stunned by a series of revelations that threaten his carefully crafted defenses. Four years thereafter, in yet another June, a chance meeting on the Long Island shore brings Fenno together with Fern Olitsky, the artist who once captivated his father. Now pregnant, Fern must weigh her guilt about the past against her wishes for the future and decide what family means to her. In prose rich with compassion and wit, *Three Junes* paints a haunting portrait of love's redemptive powers.

Fiction

ALSO AVAILABLE
I See You Everywhere
The Whole World Over

ANCHOR BOOKS
Available wherever books are sold.
www.anchorbooks.com